DIANA L. PAXSON

author of <u>The Wolf and the Raven</u> and
<u>The Dragons of the Rhine</u>

THE
LORD OF HORSES

U.S.$5.99
CAN.$7.99

"THE TALE OF SIGFRID AND BRUNAHILD
LEAPS TO LIFE IN
DIANA PAXSON'S MASTERLY RETELLING."
Stephen R. Lawhead,
bestselling author of The Pendragon Cycle

EAN

ISBN 0-380-76528-4

9 780380 765287

50599>

Avon Books are available at special quantity discounts for bulk purchases for sales promotions, premiums, fund raising or educational use. Special books, or book excerpts, can also be created to fit specific needs.

For details write or telephone the office of the Director of Special Markets, Avon Books, Dept. FP, 1350 Avenue of the Americas, New York, New York 10019, 1-800-238-0658.

DIANA L. PAXSON

THE
LORD OF HORSES

AVON BOOKS • NEW YORK

VISIT OUR WEBSITE AT
http://AvonBooks.com

THE LORD OF HORSES is an original publication of Avon Books. This work is a novel. Any similarity to actual persons or events is purely coincidental.

AVON BOOKS
A division of
The Hearst Corporation
1350 Avenue of the Americas
New York, New York 10019

Copyright © 1996 by Diana L. Paxson
Cover art by Donato
Published by arrangement with the author
Library of Congress Catalog Card Number: 95-36060
ISBN: 0-380-76528-4

First AvoNova Printing: January 1997
First Morrow/AvoNova Hardcover Printing: March 1996

AVONOVA TRADEMARK REG. U.S. PAT. OFF. AND IN OTHER COUNTRIES, MARCA REGISTRADA, HECHO EN USA.

Printed in the U.S.A.

RA 10 9 8 7 6 5 4 3 2 1

To Niklas,
brother-in-spirit,
who knows why Gudrun went north
and how she rides

Acknowledgments

In writing, one finds oneself indebted in many directions for help both spiritual and temporal.

In the realm of the factual, I would like to thank those who helped me in working out how the adder could cause the death of Gundohar, especially Tanith Tyrr, Lady of the Beasts, and Dr. Harry Green of the Museum of Vertebrate Zoology at the University of California.

In the other direction, I am grateful to all those who enjoyed the first volume of this trilogy and waited so eagerly for the rest of it. But above all, I must thank Freya Aswynn, Kveldulf Gundarsson, and Raudhild for moral support and validation—

And the Wanderer, who walks among us still. . . .

Erratum: in *The Wolf and the Raven*, first volume of this trilogy, we missed correcting the name of the last rune in the Futhark. Drop the final "z" and spell it *OTHALA*.

Foreword

The trilogy, as commonly practiced today, consists of a lively first book, a climactic conclusion, and a middle which links them. As I have worked my way through the writing of *Wodan's Children*, it has become clear that in this case, the second book, *The Dragons of the Rhine*, is not a link, but the center of the story, the tragedy to which the events in the first book were leading, and with which the survivors must come to terms in the third. But what then is left for this third book, with Sigfrid and Brunahild both ashes on their pyre?

Wodan, whom some might say betrayed them, walks ever more openly among men, still seeking a child who can hear him. Gundohar and Hagano, Sigfrid's murderers, must make their lives justify that deed. And Gudrun, his grieving widow, must choose between hatred and love. The catalyst for all their reactions is Attila, who begins now to take his place as a major power in his world, and Aetius, the last great general of Rome.

For the bards of the Middle Ages, all the tale of Sigfrid and Brunahild was only a prequel to this final, fatal encounter between the khan of the Huns and the Burgund kings, which takes place not in the mists of legend, but in the cold light of history. When it is accomplished, we may say, with the poet of the *Nibelungenlied*—

This story ends here:
Such was
The Nibelungs'
Last Stand.

Contents

You are not
what you believe.
Primal wisdom marches
to its downfall,
your knowledge depends
upon my wishes.
Tell me what Wotan wills.

Richard Wagner: *Siegfried*

Characters
& Places

CAPITALS = major characters
( ) = a personage who died before the beginning of story
* = historical character
[ ] = form of name in later sources

CHARACTERS

Gods and Spirits:

Andvari, an earth elemental who, in the shape of a pike, guarded the Niblung treasure
Donar [Thor], the thunderer, god of storms and strength
disir, idisi, female ancestral spirits who guard the family line
Erda, Holy Earth [Earth Mother], Earth personified as a goddess

Fricca [Frigg], the weaver of fate, wife of Wodan

The Frowe, Froja [Freyja], dis of the Vanir, goddess of love and fertility

Heide, goddess of witchcraft

Hella, queen of the Underworld

Huld [Holda], a German goddess associated with spinning

Norns, nornir—the fates

WODAN [Odin], lord of the Aesir, worldwalker, god of wordcraft and warcraft and magic, also called High One, Old Man, War Father, Victory Father, Lord of the Slain, the One-Eyed, Grim (Hidden One), etc., sometimes appears in human form

Romans:

*FLAVIUS AETIUS, Magister Militiae of Gallia, later Magister Utriusque Militum, supreme commander in the western empire

*Bonifatius, general in North Africa, favorite of the empress

*Carpileon, son of Aetius, for a time hostage with the Huns

*Felix, Magister etc., Patrician, Galla Placidia's compromise choice for supreme commander

*Galla Placidia, sister of Honorius and mother of and regent for Valentinian

*Honoria, sister of Valentinian

*Honorius, Emperor of the West, 395–423

Junius Desiderius, a magistrate of Borbetomagus

Kustubaira [Costbera, Costa], a Roman noblewoman married to Hagano

*Litorius, second-in-command to Aetius

*Plinthas, envoy from Theodosius to the Huns

Father Priscus, Roman Catholic priest

Father Severian, Father Vidulf—Arian priests

*Theodosius II, Emperor of the East, 408–450

*Valentinian III, Emperor of the West, 425–455

Folk of the Burgund lands:

The Burgundians, an East Germanic tribe living in the area between the Neckar, the Main, and the Rhine and from Mainz to south of Worms and the surrounding lands.

(*Gipicho [Gjuki], father of Gundohar)
(GRIMAHILD, Gundohar's mother)
*GUNDOHAR [Gunther], king of the Burgunds
*GODOMAR [Guthorm] (Godo), his oldest brother
*GISLAHAR [Giselher], his youngest brother
HAGANO [Hagen], his half brother
Lords and Chieftains:
   Ostrofrid, lawspeaker (sinista)
   Heribard, a counselor
   Ordwini, Dragobald's son [Ortwin of Metz]
   Dancward [Dankwart]
   Garo [Margrave Gere]
   Sindald [Sindold]
   Unald [Hunold]
   Laidrad
   Deorberht, son of Folco
Gundohar's household:
Andulf, a fosterling with bardic aspirations
Wolcgar [Volker], a warrior and bard
GUDRUN [Gutrune, Kriemhild], Gundohar's sister
SUNNILDA [Swanhild], her daughter by Sigfrid
Bala, an Iazyge slave girl
Ecgward [Eckwart], a Burgund, commander of Gudrun's guard
Locris, a Thracian freedwoman
Udo, Gudrun's servant in the forest
Ursula and Adalfrida, maidens attending Gudrun

xviii   *Characters & Places*

Other Germanic Figures West of the Rhine:

(*Adaulf [Adolphus], brother of Alaric, briefly king of Visigoths and married to Galla Placidia)

Agilo, the reaper

(*Airmanareik [Ermanaric], third-century king of the Goths, defeated by the invading Huns)

(*Alaric, king of the Visigoths)

(*Arius, fourth-century bishop whose teachings were condemned as heresy)

*Gaiseric, king of the Vandals in North Africa

GALAMVARA [Glaumvor], daughter of Theoderid, later married to Gundohar

Gundrada, a cousin of Gundohar, married to Valobald, nephew of King Theoderid

*GUNDIOK, her son

(*Hermundurus [Arminius], first-century leader of Cherusci and Hermunduri against the Romans)

Hildigund, daughter of Hairarik, a Frankish king, wife to Waldhari

Huld, a wisewoman of the Walkyriun (Walada = her magical name), former mentor of Brunahild, nurse to Asliud

Ostbert and Melewida, farmers in the Charcoal Burners' Forest

(SIGFRID Fafnarsbane, son of Sigmund the Wolsung)

*Theoderid, king of the Visigoths of Tolosa

Valobald, a nephew of Theoderid, married to Gundrada

Waldhari [Waltharius], son of Albharius, nephew of Theoderid

(*Wallia, king of the Vandals)

Huns and Germanic allies:

Anagai, king of the Utigur

*Ardaric, king of the Gepids

Asliud [Aslaug], Brunahild's daughter by Sigfrid, raised by Heimar

*ATTILA, son of Mundzuk, khan of the Western Huns

(*Balimber, son of Uldin, Hun chieftain who defeated Airmanareik)

Berik [Berichus], a Goth, one of Attila's chieftains

Bertriud, Bladarda's older daughter

*Bladarda, son of Mundzuk, khan of the Eastern Huns

(BRUNAHILD, Bladarda's younger daughter, formerly Gundohar's queen)

*Edikon, a Hun noble, Attila's advisor

*Ellak, Denzigich, his sons by Ereka

*EREKA [Ari-qan, Helche], Attila's first queen

*Eslas, one of Ruga's officials

*Eskam [As-qam], chief shaman to Attila

*Eskota [Skutta], brother of Onegesh

Heimar [Heimir], a Marcoman, Bertriud's husband and foster father of Brunahild

*Kuridak [Kuridachus], king of the Akatiri

Kursik, one of Attila's lochagoi and counselors

*Mamai and Atakam, Hun princes killed by Attila

*Mundzuk, father of Attila, brother of Oktar and Ruga

*Oktar, khan of the Western Huns

*Onegesh [Onegesius], an up-and-coming warrior

*Ruga, khan of the Eastern Huns, later khan of khans

RUDEGAR, a Marcoman chieftain, one of Attila's lochagoi

Godelinda, his wife

Diedelinda, his daughter

*Thiudimir, Walamir's brother (later father of Theodoric the Great)

Herrad, Walamir's wife

Tuldik, Attila's messenger

(*Ulfilas, fourth-century bishop who converted the Ostrogoths to Arian Christianity and translated the Bible into Gothic)

*Walamir [Valamir], king of the Greuthungi (Ostrogoths)

*Wideric [Videric], son of Berimud, Amaling heir of Air-

manareik, who left the Huns to take refuge with the Visigoths of Tolosa
*Eudaric, his son
*Widimir [Vidimir], Walamir's second brother

PLACES

Waters:

Albis—Elbe
Amisia—the Ems
Danu, Danuvius—the Danube
Hierasus—the Prut
Liger—the Loire
Marus—the Morava
Moenus—the Main
Mosella—the Moselle
Nicer—the Neckar
Rhenus—the Rhine
Sequana—the Seine
Tanais—the Don
Tyras—the Danaster
Viadua—the Oder
Visurgis—the Weser
Wistla—the Vistula
Pagus—the Po

Mountains and Forests:

Charcoal Burners' Forest—Odenwald
the Haemus—Balkans
Holy Hill—Heidelberg
Forest of Vosegus—the Vosges
Harwadha, or Carpatus—the Carpathians
Mirkwood—Bohemian Forest
Rhipaean mountains—the Caucasus

Towns:

Aquincum—Pest (Budapest)
Arelas—Arles
Argentoratum—Strasburg
Attila's Town—O-Buda (Budapest)
Augusta Treverorum, Treveri—Trier
Batava—Passau
Borbetomagus—Worms
Castra Raetica—Regensberg
Colonia Agrippina—Köln/Cologne
Constantia—Roman fortress on the Danube across from
  Margus
Constantinople, Mundberg—Istanbul
Divodurum—Metz
Lentia—Linz
Naissus—Nis, in Yugoslavia
Margus—near Dubravica, east of Belgrade
Mediolanum—Milan
Narbo—Narbonne
Novidunum—Isaccea, in Northern Dobrogea
Ravenna (Classis)—Ravenna
Roma—Rome
Singidunum—Belgrade
Sirmium—Mitrovica or Sabac on the Save, Yugoslavia
Ulpia Traiana—Xanten
Vindobona—Vienna
Walhall—Hall of the Slain, Wodan's hold in Asgard

Geographical divisions:

Aquitanica—southern France, Aquitaine
Asgard—home of the gods
Belgica Prima—eastern France
Belgica Secunda—approximately the Low Countries

Dacia—southern Yugoslavia

Gallia—northern half of France

Germania Prima—lands just west of the Rhine, Koblenz to Basel

Germania Secunda—lands just west of the Rhine, North Sea to Koblenz

Hispania—Spain

Midgard, Middle Earth—the world of men

Noricum—lands south of Danube, Austria

Pannonia—hilly country south of the Danube from Vindobona to Sirmium (Austria, northern Yugoslavia)

Raetia—western half of the Danubian plain and Switzerland

Scythia—term used to designate Hun lands, including Pannonia and Dacia

Ostrogoth territory (Greuthungi)—Hunnish Pannonia

Gepid lands—area around Sirmium and Moesia

Langobard lands—southern Moravia

Family Tree ⚲

(*Italics* indicate an assumed or invented character; an * indicates a character mentioned by history. The others live in legend.)

THE NIFLUNGAR

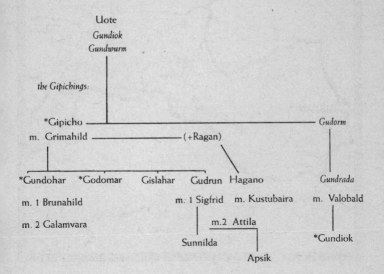

Uote
Gundiok
Gundwurm

the Gipichings:

Gipicho ———————————————————— *Gudorm*
m. Grimahild ————————— (+*Ragan*)

Gundohar   *Godomar*   Gislahar   Gudrun   Hagano   *Gundrada*

m. 1 Brunahild   m. 1 Sigfrid   m. Kustubaira   m. Valobald

m. 2 Galamvara   m.2 Attila

                              Sunnilda

                                   Apsik

Gundiok

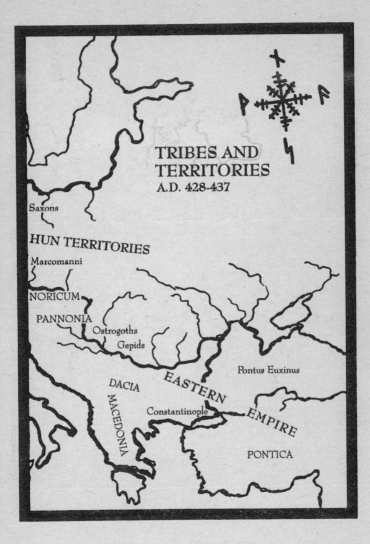

TRIBES AND
TERRITORIES
A.D. 428-437

Saxons

HUN TERRITORIES

Marcomanni

NORICUM

PANNONIA

Ostrogoths

Gepids

EASTERN

Pontus Euxinus

DACIA

MACEDONIA

Constantinople

EMPIRE

PONTICA

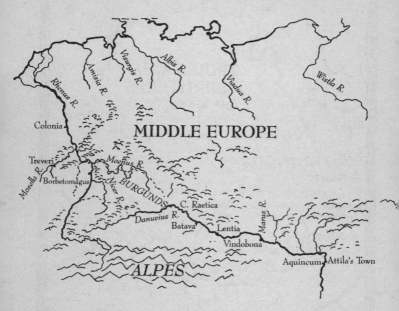

Prologue ☩ Wolf Age

The winds of war blow from the steppes above the Sea of Maeotis to the Western Sea, fluttering fallen banners, bending bloodied grass. Warriors are on the move, Hun horsemen and Roman legionaries and foot soldiers from half a hundred Germanic tribes, calling upon the Lord of the Slain for victory. In the shape of terror their minds have chosen Wodan comes to them, for he *is* mind, and where the armies go we follow—Greed and Hunger, wandering in wolf form across the battlefields.

Long ago we ranged only the forests, servants of life through death, cleansing the world of that which was outworn. But men are much more efficient predators. The Romans fed us well as they marched across their world, leaving behind them peaceful deserts. Then came the Germanic tribes, whole peoples fleeing famine and worsening weather in their lumbering wagons. They rolled over the walls of the Empire in wave after wave, and the Romans fought them and enslaved them and recruited them into their armies.

Four centuries after the birth of the one they call the Prince of Peace, the Christian emperors feed us as well as their pagan predecessors. Flavius Aetius, the Master of Gallia, has gorged us on blood of Goths and Vandals, but the Huns he hires to help him are the most efficient of all, scouring the earth on their swift ponies. The Romans call them the Scourge of God. . . .

1

The Burgunds did well enough for us on their trek south and westward from their home by the northern sea. Since they crossed the Rhenus they have done better, fighting for the Romans or against them. But they were unwise to strike down Sigfrid, for he was a wolf himself, and he was their luck in battle. A woman's pain and men's fear were the forces that felled him, for the season was evil, and the Burgunds believed they could propitiate the gods with an offering. And so the King of the Wood died instead of the King of Men, and his blood fed the ground.

Greed for Andvari's hoard was the other reason for the killing—the golden treasure once offered to the Goddess and guarded by a spirit beneath a waterfall, stolen as a shape-shifter's weregild and kept thereafter by Fafnar the berserker in dragon form. But in the end Sigfrid killed him, set on by Ragan, who was Fafnar's brother, and took the rune rod and the Lady's neck ring and the rest of the gold. The ring he gave to Brunahild, and then, after he had betrayed her, to his wife Gudrun. The rod he left alone.

Hagano, who was Ragan's son by the Burgund queen, desires their magic. Gudrun inherited them, but she does not understand their power.

The Huns press now against the Burgund borders, and Brunahild, who sealed their alliance, is burned on Sigfrid's pyre. We watch and wait, wondering which will be the first to fall upon the other. Sigfrid is dead and the Age of Heroes is ended. The Burgunds have cut their last tie to the world of legend from which they came and must fight for survival in the new one—the world of history. In this new world, what shape will men's minds make for Wodan to wear?

The Christians talk of the four Horsemen who will come at the world's ending, but each time war sweeps through a land, a world ends. When humans fight, the wolves are the only victors.

Ragnarok is now.

Chapter 1 ✤ The Harvest Bride

Charcoal Burners' Forest
Harvest Moon, A.D. 429

The wolf scent, Sigfrid's scent, lay heavy on the darkness.... Gudrun sighed in content, her fingers tightening in the soft fur, and slid more deeply into sleep.

For a time without measure she lay curled beneath the covers with Sigfrid beside her, their bed a fortress that shut out the world. Then an owl hooted outside. She stirred; unusual to hear that call in the Roman town. And there was something else, a breath of cool air as a door opened, the whisper of stealthy footsteps.... Gudrun tensed, but Sigfrid had a wolf's fine-tuned senses. Surely he would wake if there was anything wrong.

"Some took forest fish ... some sliced wolf flesh ..." Half-sung, words whispered through the air. A drunken giggle followed. "To blend the brew, the Gundwurm's spell!"

Then steel hissed through the air, its impact shook the great bed and Sigfrid convulsed beside her. Gudrun rolled away as he reared up with a cry that echoed through all the worlds. He grabbed his sword from the wall and flung it toward the door. There was a scream. Sigfrid fell back and Gudrun recoiled as hot blood gushed over her.

Torches flared in the doorway. She saw her brothers Hagano and Gundohar the king. Gislahar sprawled on the floor with Sigfrid's sword in his back. His own blade was still planted in Sigfrid's breast. She cried out, trying to stop the gushing blood with her hands. There was red everywhere.

"No use," whispered Sigfrid, his skin growing waxen. "No one can

3

ward off wyrd. Don't weep—you still have your brothers—but the day will come when they wished they had me to guard their backs. . . . They'd have found me harder to kill than any wild beast . . . if I had got on my feet with a weapon . . . in my . . . hand!" He tried to draw another breath and choked, bright blood staining his lips, convulsed once more, and fell back again.

"Sigfrid!" she shrieked his name, tasting blood as she kissed him. But her only answer was Brunahild's laugh. . . .

Gudrun clawed free from her blankets, tears hot on her cheeks and that dreadful laughter still echoing in her ears. Where were the torches? She blinked, focusing on the red coal that glowed like an eye from the ashes of the hearth. In the darkness, nothing else was waking. No blood . . . no brothers . . . no Sigfrid. . . .

The old grief ached in her throat. It had been another nightmare. In the year and a half since Sigfrid's murder she had dreamed a dozen versions of his dying. In her waking grief she told herself she could have warned him if she had been there. But even in her dreams she could not save him, not even this time, when she had heard the murderer coming through the door.

Gudrun rubbed at her stinging eyes and sat up in the box bed. The air had the cool hush of the hour just before dawn. Carefully, so as not to wake Sunnilda, who was sprawled beside her with the trusting abandon of the very young, she eased out from beneath the covers, unhooked her shawl from the bedpost, and padded across the packed earth floor. Banked coals glowed faintly from the long hearth, and a line of light edged the central door.

Pulling the shawl around her, she slipped outside. The sky was growing pale behind the beech trees, an early-waking bird began to practice its morning song. Shivering, for the air was chill, Gudrun picked up the bucket and followed the path to the spring, bending to splash her face and drink from the living water before filling it and starting back again.

Of such simple tasks she had made a bulwark against her grief, each step, each act, reconnecting, if not reconciling, her to a world from which Sigfrid was gone. For a summer, a winter, and a summer again she had lived in her mother's house in the forest with only an old manservant and her little daughter for company. The work required for survival here seemed unending. She rose with the dawn and sought her bed at dusk, too exhausted by her labors to grieve— except in her dreams.

But today would be a little different. Self-sufficient as they were, still there were some things for which they were dependent on their neighbors. Old Ostbert and his wife, Melewida, knew who she was, but respected her desire for privacy. She had taken the precaution of calling herself Grimahild, as if she had been named after the old queen. None of the other farm-folk seemed to suspect that the silent young woman living in the forest had once been the radiant princess of the Niflungar. From Ostbertheim she had her milk goat; it was to them that she traded the fine woolen thread she had learned to spin in a royal hall for butter and cheese and meat to feed her child. And as a good neighbor, she had promised to lend a hand with the harvest.

When she came back to the yard old Udo's snores had changed to the rheumy cough with which he greeted the morning. Gudrun pulled open the door in the side of the longhouse to let the light in. The house was built in the old way, with the hearth and the box beds in one half and space for winter stabling and storage at the other. A steeply thatched roof sloped down to a few feet above the ground, leaving space to stack firewood under the overhang next to the whitewashed daub and wattle wall. It was a snug dwelling so long as it was kept in repair. People rarely came this way, and as for the wild beasts, Gudrun feared them less than she did men.

Sigfrid had been a creature of the forest; sometimes she fancied she sensed his spirit roaming here still. What better place to raise his child?

"Mama, is it time to go yet? I'm ready, Mama—see?"

Sunnilda danced through the doorway, her tunic on backward and the snarls braided into her hair, and Gudrun repressed a smile.

"Wouldn't you like to wash your face first, my piglet?" She set down the bucket and reached for her daughter, feeling, as always, a delight in her solid sweetness that was almost pain. "And perhaps"—she hugged her hard and set her down again—"we might just turn your tunic around, and do something about your hair?"

Sunnilda grimaced, but allowed her mother to fuss over her while Udo, dour and uncommunicative as he always was before noon, picked up the pail and carried it into the cookshed. With the storehouse, the weaving house, a pen for the milk goat, and a fenced garden, the clearing was an island of order in a leafy green sea.

By the time the little girl's flaxen hair was braided to Gudrun's satisfaction, the cookfire was going and the water had begun to boil. Udo went to milk the goat while Gudrun measured out oats for porridge. She stood stirring while Sunnilda mounted her stick-horse and began to gallop about the yard. Perhaps she should tie up those flying braids with ribbons, Gudrun thought, watching her. Sunnilda's gown was homespun, but brightened with embroidery at the neck and hem. Gudrun still lavished an attention on her daughter's appearance which she no longer gave her own. Her corn-colored hair would do well enough braided and pinned beneath a kerchief, and for reaping she should wear her oldest sleeveless tunica, its linen faded from the original blue to the color of heat haze in a summer sky.

The porridge was bubbling. Gudrun ladled out portions into scrubbed wooden bowls and called to Sunnilda, poured warm goat's milk into the pitcher, and set out a basket of berries. Food . . . labor . . . the sweetness of her child . . . let night terrors be forgotten; all she needed was here.

* * *

By the time they reached Ostbert's farmstead, the other harvesters, who had been at work since the dawning, were halfway across the nearer field. Gudrun took a deep breath, unused to the broader vision of the open lands after her months in the forest. Behind her the trees were a mass of shadowed green, dappled by the first amber scattering of early-turning leaves. Before her, farmland stretched away toward the river in a patchwork of textured gold, the silken shimmer of uncut grain against the rough-stubbled straw of the harvested fields. The sun was hot on her back, but from time to time the wind brought a cool breath from the Rhenus to stir her hair. To south and north the sky was pale with summer haze, but in the west, clouds were building above the hills beyond the river, blinding white billows shaded with lavender and blue.

Gudrun relinquished Sunnilda to the care of the old woman who was watching all the children and was issued a skein of bast ropes by the Master of the Harvest.

"Grimahild, it is good you are here. Fall in behind old Agilo there"—he pointed to a man who was lagging behind the others—"and work quickly. There are clouds in the west, and it may be we will have to race the storm." Gudrun nodded. A well-stacked shock would shed rain for months, but the grain must be dry or mold could set in before they got it to the threshing floor.

The reapers, most of them men of the farm or thralls loaned up and down the river during harvesttime, moved in a spaced line across the field, reaching with left foot advanced to grasp a handful of stalks and using the short sickle to chop with the right hand, tossing the sheaf behind them as the other foot came forward. Bending and turning, reaching and twisting, their line undulated slowly across the cornfield, its progress echoed by the more angular movements of the women, bobbing as they gathered up each sheaf, bound it with a quick twist, and moved on. The grey hares scattered before them, startled from their forms by the approaching blades, and the ground-nesting birds flew up, lamenting their lost homes. The skilled workmen whose task it was to build up the stacks came last, layering the sheaves heads downward so as to resist the rain.

Singly, their movements seemed random, but for a moment Gudrun saw them as a whole, advancing with a rhythm that had its own grace, like the flight of wild birds or the purposeful circlings of bees. Then she moved into position behind the old man and became part of the pattern, and awareness narrowed to the next sheaf, the next knot, the next few feet of the field.

It was backbreaking labor. Just as well, she thought as she paused for a moment to wipe the perspiration from her eyes, that she had been told to follow the oldest of the reapers. Compared to the other women, Gudrun was woefully awkward. She had not been brought up to this labor. Her mother had been ready to offer up her children for the good of the tribe, but surely she had never expected them to sacrifice themselves quite like this.

After her first spurt of enthusiasm, she worked slowly, stopping sometimes, when the ache across her lower spine became excruciating, to straighten and release the strain. No one was forcing her to continue, but she was a healthy young woman. If she gave up, the others would wonder, and more than her comfort she valued her hard-won anonymity. And so, though she and old Agilo lagged behind the others, Gudrun worked on.

She was regretting she had ever agreed to join in the harvesting long before the sun began to sink in the sky. But she refused to give up after they finished the first field. By the time they were through the second plot, pain had become a part of her, and she followed the others without complaint, almost without thinking, to the third. The clouds were massing now above the river, darkening as they thickened. Sunlight shafted between them and glowed with a deepening gold in the haze of fine dust that hung above the field, giving everything the soft splendor of an old fresco from the Roman days.

The blades of the sickles flickered like sword steel across a battlefield in a bard's tale. Indeed, Gudrun thought numbly, this must be what it was like in battle, when a man went beyond pain or fear, aware only of the need to endure to the end. But who, she wondered, was their enemy?

She was vaguely aware when some of the other reapers reached the end of the field and turned to watch them, laughing. Agilo was pushing himself now, wheezing as he slashed at the grain. She hoped he would not burst his heart with the labor. For most of the day she had seen little of the man but his skinny shanks, but when they had paused for water the old fellow had seemed a pleasant, if somewhat slow-witted, soul, with a gap-toothed grin and a face weathered like an old fence post by the years. His haste was not going to get them finished any faster, thought Gudrun in exasperation, for in his hurry he was scattering the stalks, and it took her longer to gather and bind them.

And then there was only one other pair besides herself and Agilo still working. The other harvesters surrounded them, yelling as if it was a race, and Gudrun glared at them. The other reaper finished his row and the spectators fell abruptly silent. Agilo's movements slowed as if he had finally realized that hurry was hopeless. The last stalks of wheat stood in the stubble like a king's house-guard protecting their master. Gudrun gathered up all those that still lay on the ground and straightened, rubbing her back, waiting for Agilo to finish the job.

Carefully, almost ceremonially, the old man gathered the stalks into his hand and, with a sharp jerk, drew the curve of the sickle through. There was a long sigh from the watchers, or was it the soul of the harvest? With a little bow, he held the handful out to her, and Gudrun, entering into the spirit of the thing, bound it with three precise twists and stepped back, saluting with the grace she had learned in her father's hall.

In the next moment everyone was cheering. Women surrounded her; Gudrun felt her braids come tumbling down her back as her kerchief was snatched away. Two of the children came dancing up, holding a wreath of grain heads wound with ribbons and late summer flowers. The oldest of the women settled it on her head before she could protest.

"The Harvest Bride!" they shouted, "Grimahild is the Harvest Bride!"

"The Old Man!" came a cry from the men. "Here's the Old Man of the Harvest to be her husband!"

The last sheaf had been set upright in the middle of the field; blue cornflowers now adorned its binding. The reapers began to cavort around it.

"Wod . . . Wod . . . Wod . . ." The dancers halted, lifting caps and waving kerchiefs, and, singing, stretched their hands to the sky.

> *"By heaven's great one all is known,*
> *From his high seat all is shown*
> *Full crocks and shocks hath he*
> *That grow so splendidly,*
> *he is not born nor was e'er old,*
> *Wod, Wod, Wod!"*

Then they bowed down before the spirit bound in the grain.

A shudder shook Gudrun. She wanted to tear off the crown, but the women had her by the arms and were hustling her toward the sheaf. In the tumult, the squawk of dismay that was all her parched throat could manage could not be heard. The men dragged old Agilo forward. He had known what was coming, thought Gudrun; it was why he had hurried so, at the last. But now, as they took more ropes and bound the sheaf to his chest and his arms to his sides, he seemed to accept his fate.

A coil went around the captive's neck; another wound his waist and thighs, leaving only his legs free. Someone jammed a straw hat down over his head, decorated like her crown with cornflowers and yellow asters, so that all she could see of his face was one rheumy eye.

"Old Man! Old Man!" the reapers chanted, "We have . . . the Old Man!"

Agilo jerked and swayed, sagging back into his captors' arms, and his eyes rolled upward. The golden air had grown heavy . . . Gudrun shook her head, dizzied. A memory came to her of bonfires and a mountaintop, the Frowe's ring heavy on her neck as the people danced for rain.

She understood now—it was a goddess whose bright shadow was pressing down upon her. She bit her lip, fighting it, wavering on an invisible threshold, aware simultaneously of herself, Gudrun, with a grimy face and her old gown sweat-stuck to her skin, and another personality, radiant, golden, that surged up from the soil on which she stood to enfold her.

It was the duty of a Royal Woman to give herself for the people, in this way or in whatever other was required. But Gudrun had put all that behind her. She had not consented to this, she had come only to do her duty as a neighbor, to help get in the grain.

"*This is the duty of all who eat of the harvest . . .*" came a voice within her. "*For you the grain is cut down; you must be willing to give your blood or your spirit in return. . . .*"

In the distance thunder muttered. A damp wind sent the chaff whirling and passed on. Agilo groaned and went rigid in the arms of the men who held him. For a moment he was still, then he took a deep breath and let it out in a long, satisfied sigh. Eyeing one another nervously, his captors let him go. He stood upright now as a man in his prime, the ropes around him decorations rather than bonds, and when he turned to face her, Gudrun saw beneath the hat brim a glittering eye that observed her own confusion with sardonic amusement.

"I am the Old Man . . ." Eyes widened as his deep laughter echoed the thunder. They had called the god—Gudrun wondered why they were surprised he had come. He looked around the circle and went on. "You have caught me fairly. And I see you have brought me a bride. . . ."

No—thought Gudrun as they pushed her toward him. *I don't want another husband. I don't want*—she looked into that single eye and thought began to fail.

"You are the Lady of the Harvest—" His deep voice vibrated in her bones. Gudrun felt the Presence around her intensify at the words. "As my bride I claim you. Be gracious to your people, Lady, and I will be Wishfather, and give them joy."

"Why?" Gudrun whispered. "Why do you want me?"

"You are the body as I am the spirit. How shall the world survive if we are not united?" His voice was pitched for her ears alone. "Have you forgotten? You are the Lady of the Burgunds, the holy queen."

She could not tell if he were speaking to her or to the goddess who overshadowed her. The Lady rejoiced in his words, but the mortal Gudrun heard them and was afraid.

Still clapping and singing, the harvesters began to form up into a line. Gudrun and her companion were swept into the motion as they started off across the fields. Agilo had moved with painful deliberation; the man beside her strode across the stubbled ground as if he owned it, laughing, and the crows that had been gleaning among the stubble flapped out of his path.

The old villa stood on a rise, its walls glowing pink, its roof tiles even redder in the light that shone beneath the clouds. Thatched farm buildings made a square below it, surrounding an ancient oak tree. Long trestle tables laden with food had been set up beneath its spreading branches. Ostbert, who had taken care to be far from the fields when the reapers finished lest he be taken and bound to the sheaf himself, was waiting, his wife by his side. She blinked in surprise when she saw Gudrun with the wreath of flowers on her hair.

As they came through the gate one of the lads darted forward with a bucket in his hands and splashed water liberally over all in the procession, but especially the Old Man.

> *"Rain, rain fall on the corn,*
> *Good seed in the ground, good grain in the barn!"*

Gudrun twitched as the cool drops touched her skin, feeling the Presence that had overwhelmed her lifting. *Come back* . . . she called the goddess silently, but sensed only an echo of amusement that gradually faded, leaving her alone with the god. Even without looking she could feel him beside her, as if she stood near a fire.

While the harvesters had been reaping, Melewida and her women had been cooking. The long tables groaned with round cheeses and sausages, joints of beef and mutton that had been all day a-roasting, shredded meats baked with onions and carrots in pastry, turnip and cabbage, apples and berries preserved with honey, and loaves of bread made from wheat and rye and barley in every shape and size. They prepared a plate for the Old Man, freeing his arms so that he could eat and drink—mostly, it seemed, the latter. He favored the strongest mead, and Gudrun watched with reluctant admiration as horn after horn went down. The reapers were doing the feast full justice, wolfing down the food as if they were afraid they might not finish before those clouds in the west developed into a storm. Already the light was dimming and the air had begun to cool.

"Drink, my bride—" He turned, offering her the horn. Gudrun took it, and gasped as the strong stuff went down. He laughed as she shook her head and offered it back to him. "Be glad that it is only mead"—his gaze grew somber—"and not blood I offer you."

"I want neither—" she said softly, half-rising from the bench.

He shook his head. "Those who do not choose my joy will find the other. It is up to you."

"Please—" Gudrun whispered, "leave me alone."

"Life will not leave you alone," he began, but Ostbert, eyeing him watchfully, was offering another jug of mead. As he held out the horn, Melewida took Gudrun's arm and helped her to rise from the bench.

"I am sorry you were caught up in their games," she said as they moved away.

Gudrun took a deep breath. "It does not matter. I was the slowest at the work. I deserved it, and they handled me more gently than they did poor Agilo."

Over her shoulder she saw him sag, the mead-horn dropping from his hand. Ostbert caught him and motioned to another man, who upended a pitcher of water over his head. Agilo came up sputtering, pushing back the wreath to glare around him, and it was clear that now he was seeing with two eyes.

."It was not right for you to be laboring with them, Lady," said Melewida severely. "If I had seen you arrive, I would have found nobler work for you to do. But who knows, perhaps this will bring you good fortune. They say that an unmarried girl who is crowned as bride at one harvest will have a mortal husband of her own before the next."

Gudrun stiffened. "Not this time. I had a husband," she said in a harsh whisper. "And I have no wish for another!"

Lightning blinked across the river and men glanced upward with narrowed eyes. Gudrun saw one of the crows— no it was larger, a raven—sitting in the old oak tree. It cocked its head to one side, eyeing her with the same sardonic humor she had seen in the Old Man's eye. *"Enjoy yourself now,"* it seemed to say, *"I am not done with you!"*

She turned resolutely away. *Soon,* she thought, *I will take my daughter home, and I will not leave the safety of my forest again.* Above, thunder boomed, bringing with it a rush of wind and the first spatterings of rain.

"What if Gudrun refuses the marriage?" asked Gundohar.

Hagano turned back to his brother, letting the water he had dipped up spill from his hand. They had left Borbetomagus that morning for the house in the Charcoal Burners' forest where Gudrun was living. The harvest was over. In the forest, autumn was beginning to burnish the leaves, but the days were still warm, and they had stopped to rest their horses at a spring that welled from beneath the knotted roots of an ash tree.

"She has nursed her grief for Sigfrid long enough," he replied. "We can no longer afford her that luxury."

Gundohar took an awkward step forward on his bad leg, hitching the fine crimson wool of his mantle out of the way. "Do you suppose our sister cares? I do not think you understand how much she loved him."

"I understand—" Hagano said grimly. A little breeze stirred in the branches and an ash leaf, transmuted by autumn's chill to gold, came drifting down. *Just so, the gold cups and arm rings from Andvari's hoard shone on Sigfrid's funeral pyre . . .* he thought, watching it settle to the surface of the pool. The rest of the gold was safe in the old legionary treasury at Borbetomagus. Except for the rod and the ring.

"But it does not matter. Her first duty is to her kin." His own life had been shaped, one might even say distorted, by that duty, and he was only half kin to the Niflungar. Why should Gudrun escape those bonds?

"Our mother would have said so," said Gundohar, pushing a lock of lank fair hair back from his high brow. "Mother would have sacrificed anything, and anyone, for the safety of the Burgunds or the glory of the Niflungar."

Something rustled nearby. The king took a quick step backward, shuddering, as a piece of the ground began to move, the zigzag sides and mottled back of an adder dislimning from the tangle of fallen sticks and dead leaves. Hagano laughed.

"Why do you fear the serpent? You are the lord of the Gundwurm!"

"I would rather have been a bard . . ." said Gundohar softly. "But our mother made me into a king. She would have made our sister a sorceress, but though Gudrun seems so gentle, she can be as stubborn as stone."

"She is living in our mother's old hideaway," answered Hagano. "I think she is more like Grimahild than she knows. It does not matter. Without this alliance, the Burgund clans east of the Rhenus will be overrun by the Huns. With her consent or without, she will be Attila's bride." He turned back to the water.

"We killed her first husband! Haven't we done enough to her?" asked Gundohar. "They say Bladarda has another daughter, called Oddrun. Perhaps they would give her to me." The Burgund king set his hand on his half brother's shoulder.

For a moment Hagano saw their faces twinned in the water—Gundohar's narrow, with a beaked nose like some great bird, Hagano's own frame broadened and features blunted by the blood of his earthfolk father, a leather patch hiding the ruin of the eye he had lost to Waldhari's sword. There was little, except perhaps for the shape of their mouths and the line of the jaw, to mark them as kin. Even Hagano's hair had darkened with the years, while the king's was still faded fair.

"Do you think she will grow any happier, hiding in the shadows and brooding on her wrongs?" asked Hagano. "It is not only for the sake of the Hun alliance that I want to send her eastward. Here, she is a danger to us all."

"She is only a woman; how much can she do?" Gundohar straightened and turned away. "But Attila has agreed to take her, so I suppose we must keep the bargain."

Brunahild was only a woman, and she still haunts you. I can see it in your eyes.... thought Hagano with an inner chill, but he did not say so aloud. Once more he bent to the spring. Fallen leaves had stained the water the color of old blood. It spilled over the lip of the pool and trickled across the stony watercourse toward the Rhenus. He blinked, for a moment seeing Sigfrid's blood flowing away with the stream. Gundohar's bitter queen had shown him how Sigfrid could be killed, but his own hand had struck the blow.

It was necessary, but it was also my choice—why do I try to shift the blame?

A murmuring breeze fluttered the remaining leaves in the treetops. As Hagano cupped his hand to dip up water sunlight flared between the branches and the surface blazed. Suddenly all he could see was an Eye, gazing up from the depths as if his own lost orb had fallen there. Then wind shivered the surface of the water and the reflection shattered. If a reflection was what it had been. Hagano closed his remaining eye, but the afterimage remained, glowing in his darkness.

"Shall I blame You, then? You did not stop me!" he addressed the god silently. *"What more do You want of me?"*

There was no answer, but as Hagano rose to go back to the horses, it seemed to him that the Eye in the water had looked back at him with a sorrow even deeper than his own.

The sun had dipped a handbreadth further toward the western mountains when the brothers came out from beneath the beech trees into the clearing. Gundohar eyed it curiously; he had long known that his mother had a place in the woods where she brewed spells, but he had never seen it. It was Hagano, who had shared their mother's secrets, who had guided them here. After Grimahild died the place had been left to the weather, but now new thatching patched the roof and new whitewash shone on the walls. Hens pecked peaceably at the neatly raked earth of the dooryard. Only a child's stick-horse leaning against the woodpile disturbed the order.

In another moment the rider's fair head poked from the doorway. Gundohar winced as golden eyes—wolf-eyes—met his own. Sigfrid's daughter was already showing promise of unusual beauty. What tragedies would *this* child cause when she was grown? Then the child disappeared and they heard her calling to her mother. He slid off of his mount and Hagano reined in behind him.

"Gudrun—" The words died in his throat as his sister ducked beneath the eaves and straightened, facing him. She looked thinner—no, she looked like a warrior in hard training, he thought, and felt an old pain reawaken as he remembered Brunahild's feral beauty in the days when she had been one of the Walkyriun. What had Gudrun's life been like, living here like an outcast with only the one old manservant and her child? At least she seemed healthy. Her golden hair shone pale as wheatstraw and her milky skin was browned and freckled like a plover's egg after a summer in the sun.

"My lord _bendinos_—" She gave him the title of the high king, eyeing him warily.

"A cold greeting for your brothers," said Hagano behind him, and Gudrun's gaze kindled.

"Sigfrid was your brother," she answered him. Gundohar sighed. He had been right. She had not forgiven them.

"In name. But blood binds better than words." Hagano's voice deepened.

"And kin is less than kind!" she retorted.

"Less than kind indeed," said Gundohar, attempting to regain control of the encounter. "You bring us no guest cup or bench to sit on. Even if we were not the children of one mother, you would owe us at least that much hospitality."

Her gaze came back to him and a little of the anger left. She turned to speak to the child, then waited in silence, arms folded beneath her breasts, while Sunnilda brought out a pitcher of ale and a drinking horn and the old thrall dragged a bench into the shade of the birch tree.

"Behold—" she gestured mockingly when it was done. "Be seated and refresh yourselves. And then, perhaps, you will tell me to what I owe the honor of your presence here."

Hagano grunted with what might have been laughter and slid to the ground, then led his mount and the king's to the grass at the edge of the clearing and tied them where they could graze.

"Yes, you may pet the horses, if you are gentle and do not make noise," said Gundohar, seeing how Sunnilda watched them. The little girl flashed him a sudden, blinding smile, then trotted across the yard.

"It is honor that has brought us here," said Gundohar when he was seated and had taken a ceremonial drink from the horn. "Or at least I will hope you think it so. We have found a noble lord to be your husband."

Color flamed suddenly in Gudrun's face.

"You gave me a husband already, or have you forgotten?" she hissed through clenched teeth. "You gave me the noblest warrior who walked the world. And then you killed him. Does this new victim know how you treat your brothers-in-law?"

Hagano leaned against the oak tree, arms crossed, and smiled grimly. "Even against us, this one can protect himself. It is Attila himself who wants you, Gudrun."

She stared at him, then her eyes narrowed again as she began to understand. "Brunahild's uncle . . ." she breathed. "You need the Hun alliance." Suddenly she laughed. "That is another thing you should have considered when you killed Sigfrid. You should have known Brunahild would contrive her own punishment! Is he asking for weregild? Am I the price that will save you from his vengeance for a crime from which I suffered even more than he, or is it a simple matter of business?"

"It is a matter of lives, Gudrun. . . ." the king said heavily. "It is to save the clans still living in our old homeland that we ask this of you. The Huns are pushing westward, and we can hardly feed our folk from the lands we now hold. We cannot afford to lose any territory."

"Push westward then. Gain new territories from Gallia."

"No good, at least not for now," said Hagano. "We tried it this summer, but the Roman lands are too strongly defended."

Gudrun shrugged. "Well, you have come to the wrong market if you are looking for sympathy. Everyone dies, some die sooner, that is all . . ."

"If I had only myself to consider, I would pour out my own blood to appease you, sister, but while the Burgunds need me, it is my duty to live."

Gudrun's eyes glittered. "Brother, I think you speak prophecy. Remember that saying when you come to your own death day, for be sure that I shall. . . ." In the silence they could hear the wind in the treetops; a few golden leaves came drifting down.

"No man can ward off wyrd," Gundohar said tiredly, and wondered why the color drained from Gudrun's skin, leaving it for a moment corpse-pale.

"My husband was the flower of the world's warriors. I was the wife of Sigfrid Fafnarsbane, how can you think I would wed with Attila or any other man?"

"It would be better than living alone in the forest, surely—" Gundohar began.

"You murdered my happiness"—her voice shook—"but here I am as content as I will ever be. If you have any kindness for me, leave me alone."

"Look at it this way, sister," Hagano cut in. "If you go to Attila, you will not have to pretend affection for your husband's murderers. The khan will not expect you to love him."

Gudrun glared at him, and he laughed.

Gundohar shook his head and levered himself up from the bench, allowing for the extra moment it took the tight muscles of his bad leg to adjust to the new position. In the old days his lameness might have cost him the kingship. He did not know whether to be glad or sorry the old custom no longer prevailed. He was clumsy on foot but he could still fight mounted. In the two years since Waldhari had wounded him he had grown accustomed to the inconvenience. And the pain. Sometimes it was even a welcome distraction from other, less visible, agonies.

He looked at his sister's set face and shook his head. He had wept for Sigfrid, too. He was sorry for her grief, but it could not be allowed to matter. One simply went on.

He limped over to the horses. Hagano gave him a leg up and he gathered his reins.

"The khan expects you before the first snowfall. Willing or unwilling, you will go. Make your preparations, sister— you have until the envoys arrive."

Chapter 2 ⚲ Rivers

Borbetomagus, the Danuvius
Hunter's Moon, A.D. 429

The city of the Gundwurm encompassed the old Roman town of Borbetomagus like a dragon coiled upon treasure, some of it decaying, some of it still splendid, all of it guarded with a passion all the fiercer because it had not, in the beginning, been the Burgunds' own. The silver waters of the Rhenus that flowed past the town were a more ancient serpent, rolling northward on a relentless course that had not faltered since the mountains of Middle Earth were fashioned out of Orgelmir's body by the holy gods. From above a high porch of the basilica which was now the *hendinos'* hall, the Burgund's dragon banner stretched and twisted in the wind.

Gundohar stood beneath it with his chieftains, watching the glitter on the road beside the river grow into the figures of men and horses as the lords of the Huns drew near. They came in full festival array, the gear of the riders as usual outshone by the trappings of the beasts they rode. Men were clad in lapped tunics of Byzantine silk lined with fur, with golden tags to their lacings and brooches in their fur caps, but horse harness shone and jingled with golden plaques and pendants. They might be far from the steppes, but they were still, above all, cavalry, and their ruler was the Lord of Horses.

He was trying not to think about the last time he had met with Hun lords to arrange a marriage; striving to keep prisoned, in that deep part of his soul to which he had consigned them, his dreams of happiness with Brunahild. Despite his mother's teachings, he had been foolish enough to hope for happiness in a royal marriage and to seek it for himself and for his sister. Gudrun had found joy in her mating, and he—to the depths of his soul—had endured sorrow, and both his marriage and hers had ended in disaster. Gundohar would allow neither of them to make such a mistake again.

To remind himself of the difference, he had dressed in the style of the Romans, in a dalmatic of deep blue richly ornamented with segmentae and clavulae of brocade worked with gold. There was a certain irony in rigging himself out as a Christian king in order to give his sister to a man who had never made any pretense at adopting Christianity, but perhaps the outfit would impress the Huns.

"By Donar's bones, they've sent Thiudimir with the embassy!" exclaimed Ordwini, shading his eyes with his hand and peering downward as the riders slowed to pass through the arched gateway. He had grown somewhat stout in the past few years, but most of it was muscle still. "That's an honor, if you will."

"I'm sure Thiudimir thinks so," said Hagano, leaning against the wall.

Ecgward looked from one to another. Now Gundohar could see that there were several taller horses among the Hun ponies, ridden by big men with fair moustaches.

"He's Walamir's brother, the Goth-king's heir," Gundohar explained. "The Amalings are a proud race—"

"So are the Niflungar," Hagano put in softly.

"And they are grown all the more haughty," the king continued, frowning at his brother, "because no matter how honorable the place they hold in the Hunnish councils, they have not forgotten that they are still in service to the khans. Be careful what you say to him. They say he can be dangerous when he thinks he has been insulted."

Ecgward nodded. "I can keep my temper, but he had

better watch his own manners with the Lady Gudrun." He stood proudly, his flaxen hair feathered by the breeze, not quite able to hide the longing in his eyes.

Ah, poor soul, thought the king, understanding, *you are in love with her, and she will never even look at you.* If he had known, he would not have assigned the man to command his sister's escort, but Ecgward had volunteered.

"The older man who rides with him is Rudegar, one of the khan's most trusted counselors," added Hagano. "Thiudimir may think more of himself, but Attila thinks more of Rudegar. I expect that it is he who is actually leading the embassy."

"Well, if they are so proud," Ordwini said, turning, "we had better get ourselves down the stairs to meet them. . . ." Gundohar smiled at him gratefully.

"I won't greet them." Gudrun crossed her arms and glared at her youngest brother. When Gundohar had brought Brunahild home to Borbetomagus, the Hun princess had called herself a prisoner. Gudrun was beginning to share her feelings. Her brother Godomar and the escort that had brought her here had been polite, but unyielding. There were, if not at the door of her bedchamber, guards at the entry to the old Roman commander's palace, and at the gates in the city walls, who would no doubt stop her with equal courtesy if she tried to leave.

"They will be drinking half the night, haggling over the treaty," said Gislahar, deliberately misunderstanding. "I'm sure they won't be ready to meet you until tomorrow."

She stared at him, and the anger went out of her. This was not the boy's fault—he was a warrior now, taller than she was, with a soft blond beard shading the pure line of his jaw, but she still thought of him as the baby of the family. He had been too young to swear the oath of brotherhood with Sigfrid, and too innocent to be involved in the plot to murder him. For a moment she shut her eyes. The memory in which it was Gislahar who crept through the darkness to stab Sigfrid in his bed had been a nightmare, and nothing more.

"Tell them—" she began, then shook her head. "No, there is no way to make you understand." Her footsteps rang on the tiled floor as she moved to the window and stared out across the courtyard. Like her spirit, it was in shadow. Torchlight streamed out from the door of the feasting hall, paled by the fires the setting sun had lit in the western sky.

"I understand better than you know," he said with a painful dignity. "I loved Sigfrid, too. But I also understand the need of our people."

"To save the people—how tired of that need I am! Sigfrid was sacrificed to it, and now I am the victim. Don't you ever wish, brother, that you could just once seek happiness for yourself alone?"

He shook his head, his grey eyes luminous in the lamplight. "I was the afterthought, the extra son. I heard our mother say once that when I was conceived she thought it only her woman's courses failing, and by the time she realized she was carrying it was too late to abort the child. To be of some use to our people would be an honor to me."

Gudrun's fingers clenched suddenly in the soft wool of her tunica. "Do not think it—the needs of the Niflungar will eat you, Gislahar. You could go anywhere, carve out your own place in the world. Get out while you can!" That was what Sigfrid had meant to do, her own anguish reminded her, with Brunahild by his side. And she herself had been the bait to trap him here.

"Take your own advice, sister," he said, laughing. "Don't you see? Attila has other wives and is often away on campaign; he will not require much from you. But he has promised you a noble household. You will have wealth and power, sister, such as can never be yours here even with Sigfrid's hoard. If you go to Attila, you will be free!"

To go to a new husband, whom she could never love . . . but in a new land, she thought, where she would not fancy she was about to see Sigfrid in every shadow. And a new people, who would not call her Lady of the Burgunds and require her to give them something she no longer had. Perhaps she should not blame the people, but their god. Perhaps in the country of the Huns she could escape him, too. It was certain, in any case, that the house in the forest was for her a refuge no longer.

Men's laughter boomed inside the king's feasting hall. From the rooftree, as if in echo, she heard a raven's cry.

"All hail to the Lady of the Burgunds! Give greeting to Gudrun daughter of Gipicho as she comes into the hall!" Wolcgar the Bard's harmonious tenor cut through the babble, and like receding floodwaters, silence spread down the long tables to the dais beneath the frescoed wall.

Hagano realized that he had tensed when he let out his breath again, but every other man there was staring in arrested stillness. Gudrun, having agreed to meet with the Hunnish envoys at last, was doing her best to impress them.

She moved down the aisle between the feasting tables as if to music, the folds of her mantle whispering along the floor behind her. It was made of violet silk, not the tyrannous Imperial shade, but a soft, luminous hue like the blush on a grape, the dalmatic beneath it so dark a purple it seemed black. Her golden hair had been braided and pinned into a coronet around her head, its gold gleaming beneath a sheer veil of lilac silk like the sun behind a cloud. Against that somber magnificence blazed ornaments of amethyst and pearl set in gold.

The gear had been well chosen, thought Hagano with reluctant appreciation. White would have shown how her skin had suffered in the forest, but against these dusky purples Gudrun's complexion had the pallor of old ivory. Above the barbaric mass of her jeweled collar, her features seemed delicate, her wrists slender in their heavy bracelets, her frame barely strong enough to support the weight of the mantle with its edging of brocade and pearls. The pale silks which two girls who attended her were wearing somehow made them look florid while serving as a foil to the dark elegance of their lady's gown.

Indeed, almost everyone in the hall appeared overdressed beside her. Except, perhaps, for Hagano himself, who was wearing a single arm ring over his customary tunic of plain black wool.

Silently he applauded as she reached the king and her gliding walk became a smooth obeisance. He saw Gundohar's eyes widen nervously as his sister straightened, eyes downcast as an image of womanly modesty. Where was the witchwife who had cursed them in the forest? For the first time, Hagano began to wonder if they were doing the right thing.

"Sister, here are the Hun lords who have journeyed so far to meet you." Gundohar remembered he was supposed to introduce the envoys. "I present to you Rudegar, a great chieftain among the Marcomanni, and Kursik of the Acatiri Huns, and from the Greuthungi Goths, Prince Thiudimir."

"I am honored—" Once more Gudrun inclined her head with that unnerving docility.

"Lady, the honor is ours!" exclaimed Thiudimir enthusiastically. "And if you will return with us to wed with the khan, it will be greater still!"

"As you know, I had a husband," Gudrun said softly, "and I would prefer to remain loyal to his memory. But as you have come so far, you deserve that I should listen to what you have to say. . . ."

Gundohar blinked, then collected himself and led her to one of the carved chairs on the dais. When the Romans ruled, the hall had been the basilica of Jupiter. In the fading frescoes of the apse his image could still be seen, enthroned in godhome with his house-guard around him. In the years between the departure of the Roman commander and the Burgunds' arrival the plaster had suffered. Parts of the god's face were missing, so that it appeared he had only one eye.

Rudegar was listing the honors Attila had offered to entice his prospective bride.

"Now that Oktar is dead, Attila is second only to Ruga among the Huns. Over all their western lands he has authority, while his brother rules in the lands near the Euxine Sea. In addition to the people and warriors you bring, you will have your own servants—your guards, your maidens, everything, and fine dwellings in each of the principal towns where the khan rules. Attila will visit you, but you will not be expected to manage his household."

Not be allowed to, is more like it, thought Hagano, remembering his years as a hostage with the Huns. Though the khan had sometimes entertained Roman visitors at the houses of his wives, his real household was the gaggle of officers and servants who traveled with him wherever he might go. Since they had moved into the lands of Europe the Hun tribesmen might have abandoned some of their roving ways, but their rulers were still nomads.

"The income from six districts he has set aside for your support."

"That is generous," said Gudrun. She looked from Rudegar to her brothers. "And what will the Burgunds gain?"

"We stay back of your eastern borders," Kursik replied. "Find other lands."

Hagano nodded. That was the crucial point. Two years earlier, the Eastern Empire in an access of efficiency unparalleled in recent years had managed to push the Huns of lower Dacia back across the Danuvius—not their military forces, but families with homes and grazing lands, who had loved the broad Danu plain as a reflection of their ancient homeland. Those people had to be resettled somewhere, and westward into the Burgund lands had been the obvious way to go.

"I am flattered that you think me beautiful," said Gudrun, "but I find it hard to believe that my person would be sufficient compensation for such a loss."

"Oh, well, there's the men and the money—" Thiudimir

began. His words trailed off as Rudegar looked at him.

"We will send warriors to ride with Attila when he asks it," said Gundohar.

"And you will pay—" Gudrun echoed.

She is wondering where we will find the gold, thought Hagano. *She is thinking of Sigfrid's treasure.* Gundohar had been insistent that the gold was Gudrun's and must be kept for her, but if they paid the Huns from their own treasury, Fafnar's hoard would be their only security. It was safe now in the old Legionary treasury. *And if we must spend it to save the people, I will do it*, he thought then, *and when it is done, Gundohar will accept the necessity.* As he had done before, when Sigfrid's life was the price that must be paid.

But Gudrun still held the neck ring and the rune rod that had been the heart of the hoard. The gold was wealth, but their magic made wealth. Hagano could not help but think that if he had the chance to study them, they might be worth more than the gold.

"But this is an alliance, not a marriage, you are negotiating," said Gudrun. "What Attila wants is not me, but gold and warriors. Why not take them and let me mourn alone?"

"Now that I have seen you, I am not so sure he wants only your warriors," said Rudegar, smiling down at her. "And why should you waste such beauty? My khan is a great man who will rule all the Huns some day, and it is no disgrace to take him as your second husband."

"When I was Sigfrid's wife, I need fear no one—" she said in a low voice, and Hagano heard the unspoken,—*except my brothers* . . . "It is a hard thing to journey to a strange country where I will know nobody, and no one cares for me. . . ."

"That is not true," answered Rudegar. "All who see you will love you, lady. And as for myself, I will swear to you my loyalty and that of all my kin."

Gudrun looked up at him with a peculiar smile, her eyes, picking up the color of her mantle, as lucently amethyst as her jewels. "Truly? Would you take oath that whatever anyone does to me, you will be the first to avenge my wrong?"

"Lady, even that I am ready to do," said Rudegar, and Hagano felt a chill, though it was warm in the hall.

Gudrun sighed and looked around her. "And this is the advice and the desire of all of you, that I take the prince of the Huns as my husband?"

Ordwini and Unald nodded, and Godomar, who had always wanted to see the Huns fight and hoped to lead the Burgund allies when Attila's summons came, grinned.

"No one has asked me, and indeed I must protest it—" the voice of Father Priscus cut through the general babble of approval. "She is a Christian woman, and she should not be given to an unbaptized man."

"Oh, you need not fear she will not be able to practice her faith," said Thiudimir earnestly. "There are many Christians among my people. Even the holy scriptures are translated into the Gothic tongue."

"By an Arian!" the Catholic priest said sourly, and Father Severian, the Arian, grinned. Though Gipicho's children had been baptized as Catholics, most of the Burgunds had been christened by priests who followed the teachings of Arius. The chaplains of the two sects had for twenty years served in uneasy alliance, pretending they did not know that most of the people followed their new faiths sporadically, if at all.

"My first husband was the flower of the world's warriors, and he was never a Christian man," Gudrun said sweetly. "I will not judge a man by the name of his god, but by the deeds he does in that god's name. . . ."

"Then you honor Attila," grinned Kursik, "for his deeds are mighty beyond mortals'!"

And unless he invokes the spirit that dwells in his sword, thought Hagano, *he is not acting in the name of any god at all.*

Gudrun rose to her feet. "My friends, I will let your will guide me, and accept this marriage. Lord Rudegar"—she turned to him with a touching grace—"I confide myself to your honor."

"Wealth and power you will have from Attila," he replied, "and my oath will bind me to your service. Even if you had only two men of your own to follow you, you need not fear." He took her hand.

"Truly," she said quietly, "I begin to think so." But as she turned, her gaze went first to Gundohar, and then to Hagano, a distant, considering look he did not understand.

She has no need to fear, but what of us? Hagano felt once more that strange chill. But all the Burgunds were cheering. If this marriage was a mistake, there was nothing he could do to stop it now.

From that moment it seemed to Gudrun as if she had fallen into the river and were being whirled swiftly downstream. She must go to her new home well provided with clothing and ornaments and household gear. Gudrun had no doubt that her new husband would be well supplied with the latest in horse trappings and weapons, but none of the warriors who had been sent to woo her had much to say in household arrangements. And so she addressed herself to gathering bed linens and dinnerware. Attila was marrying a Burgund princess and would expect her to act like one. The rough arrangements of her forest dwelling must be left behind her. Whatever her feelings regarding her brothers, she was determined to do credit to the folk from whom she came.

The night before they were to set out, Hagano came to her rooms.

"What are you doing here?" Gudrun knew her voice was too sharp, but she could not help bristling. He put back the dark hood that had shadowed his face and his lips twisted in a smile.

"You are going far away. Who knows if I will see you again? Is it so unlikely that your brother should wish to bid you a more private farewell?" His voice was controlled, as always, but a muscle jumped in his cheek. She thought he looked older than his years.

"Godo or Gislahar I would believe"—she drew a deep breath—"or even Gundohar, still trying to soothe his conscience with apologies. But you have not come to seek forgiveness. . . ."

"I have heard that you fear to go to the land of the Huns with no treasure of your own." He watched her with head a little turned, keeping her within view of his good eye.

"Fafnar's hoard is my inheritance, but when I asked that it be loaded into chests for me to take with me I was told that you had the keys to the treasury."

"I will give you back your treasure, sorely though I foresee we shall need it, in exchange"—his gaze fell away from hers—"for the rune rod and the ring."

For a moment Gudrun stared at him, then she began to laugh.

Hagano took a step toward her, his usually impassive features lit by some passion she did not understand. "What do you need them for? They belong to the Rhenus, to this land!" he exclaimed. "They should not be taken away! Do you hate me? With the gold you can buy men to use against me—"

"And what would *you* do with them?" Gudrun shook her head. "Even had Brunahild not told me to keep them from you, I would refuse this simply because you ask. You destroyed the only man I will ever care for—at least I can keep you from picking his bones!"

"You do not understand—" he began, but she interrupted him.

"I will *never* understand!" He had hurt her too many times. "Now leave me, before I call Rudegar to throw you out the door."

"Is he so much your slave?" Hagano's sudden stillness was like a dash of cold water on Gudrun's rage. "One day he will regret it. But since your will is set, there is no more to say."

Shaking, she wrenched open the door and stood holding it until he had gone. It was a long time before she slept, and when she did her dreams were all of Sigfrid, and Hagano standing over him with a bloody spear.

* * *

They set out from Borbetomagus as the Hunter's Moon was waning in the sky; a skein of flatbottomed boats to carry Gudrun and her women, and the escort of mounted warriors and an impressive number of laden horses pacing them along the road that ran by the riverside. To the troop that had come with the Hun lords had been added Ecgward and his fifty riders. Tempting though the baggage might be, they had no need to fear attack from any band of masterless men that might roam the land.

The long oars pulled the boats a short way up the Rhenus to its confluence with the Nicer where it passed between the old Rufiniana fortress and the Holy Hill. Gudrun gazed up at the mountain as they crept slowly past it, remembering the many times she had climbed it when she was a girl. On those green slopes the chestnuts would be ripening. At the right time of year you could walk beneath the leafy canopy with skirts held wide and catch the spiky nuts as they fell. When they were fresh, the green husk and the brown skin inside peeled off easily to reveal the sweet, mealy nutmeat inside. But the girl who had gorged herself on the chestnuts of the Holy Hill was as dead as the black-haired Walkyrja maid who had once climbed this mountain at her side. When Sunnilda asked her mother why she was crying, Gudrun could only hold her close and weep the more.

Above the Holy Hill the Nicer had carved a gorge eastward through the hills. Here the river flowed strongly between steep slopes clad thickly with trees, their solid green splashed with patches of amber and bronze as the oaks and beeches began to turn and the occasional splash of scarlet where the leaves of the rowan trees vied with the crimson berries they bore. Though the nights could be bitter, for the most part the weather held fair, and the sun dried the world quickly after the brief showers.

Sometimes they would hear dogs barking through the trees and find beyond the next bend in the river a longhouse and a few cleared fields. Children dashed down to the waterside, waving until the flotilla disappeared. In the evenings, mournful ululations drifted from hill to hill as women called their cattle home. This was the way all of the Burgunds had lived until a generation ago, the way Gudrun herself had been trying to live in the forest. But that life, like the settlements they were passing, was behind her now.

Presently the river curved south, and the road the escort followed led from one gap in the forest to another where Sunnilda, running about when they pulled in and made camp for the night, would uncover the remains of Roman pavements and blocks of dressed stone. Long ago these had been the *limes* between the Empire and German lands. But the Romans were gone, and the Burgunds had rolled westward, and the boundary meant nothing anymore.

Presently the river grew too shallow for boats, and the women were mounted double behind warriors to continue south and east along a winding track through the hills. Even now, these lands were sparsely settled, but though the Romans were gone, the apple trees they had planted flourished in the wilderness, and the travelers ate the ripe fruit as they rode along. So much was past and done with, thought Gudrun, looking at those apples. What lay in the future? What was she going to now?

Then came a morning when the mists that lay along the mountainsides lifted suddenly, and Gudrun saw laid out below her the silver ribbon of the Danuvius and the rich plain beyond it, rising gently toward blue distances that glinted where mountains so high they surely must hold up the sky caught the sun. From here the trail dropped sharply, and before sunset they were dismounting in a meadow by the riverbank, where the barges Attila had sent to bring his bride to the land of the Huns had been drawn up on the shore, waiting in confident expectation that she would come.

The evening was mild; they sat by the cookfires, watching the golden haze upon the plain of Noricum deepen to flame and a purple shadow that darkened until the only light was on the distant rose-colored peaks of the great world-wall that separated the barbarian lands from Italia. As night fell, they did not so much fade as mist away, as if mountain and plain and Roma herself were an illusion, and the only realities the fire and the river and the starry sky. The whisper of the waters was a constant background to the hiss and crackle of the fire.

To Gudrun, sitting with her hand on the silken hair of her sleeping child, they seemed to be sharing some profound conversation she could not quite understand. The fire was brilliant, swift to seize the moment, consuming and consumed by its own need. The river murmured a soothing commentary, certain, however long it might take, of coming someday to the sea. She closed her eyes to listen, trying to shut out the human chatter around her.

"My lady—"

Reluctantly, Gudrun looked up. Ecgward was kneeling beside her, his back to the fire so that she saw only the backlit silhouette of his broad shoulders and fair hair.

"Ecgward, is all well?" She gathered her attention for the sake of politeness. "I have not thanked you for being willing to join me in this exile."

"Lady, your service could never be an exile for me," he said in a low voice. "But it is true that we are going far from our people. Gudrun—I must know—are you doing this willingly?"

Gudrun's attention focused. "Does it matter? It is done now."

"Across the river lie the Roman lands," he said in a rush. "If we went tonight, we could be out of their reach by morning—Huns, Burgunds, anyone. My men are oathsworn to me. We could keep you safe, I swear."

"Rome!" she exclaimed. "That would truly be an exile. You would do that for me?"

"My lady—Gudrun—" the words came hoarse with feeling, "I would go to the ends of the earth for you!"

"As my husband?" she asked with a detached curiosity. She had not realized that he, too, was in pain.

"As—whatever . . ." he stuttered like a youth, staring at

the ground as if even through the darkness she could see him blushing. "Whatever you wish me to be. . . ."

Gudrun shook her head. "Ah, Ecgward, I do not deserve such loyalty. If I had any love left to give, I might even accept your sacrifice. But for both of us, Ecgward, there is only duty. Come with me to the land of the Huns," she added grimly. "It will be harder, for both of us, than running away to Rome. But it will comfort me in that strange land to know that I have at least one friend."

"A friend I will be . . ." he echoed, "if that is what you wish of me."

"The man I loved was a hero, Ecgward. Heroes die. You will be better off this way."

"Lady," he smiled painfully, "have I ever led you to believe that I desired ease? Nonetheless, let it be as you say."

Physically, the journey grew easier now. They were floating downstream, and with each passing day the Danuvius grew broader and smoother, a great green serpent that wound slowly between marsh and meadow with the Suevian hills fading away toward the north on one side and on the other the broad Dacian plain. In the mornings, mist lay along the river and drifted in slow veils over the shores; the barges floated through a world as insubstantial as they. Cranes flew crying from the reeds as the flotilla passed, then settled back again. As the day wore on the mists burned away, revealing first watery glimpses, and then suddenly the whole land basking in the autumn sun.

Until they reached Castra Raetica, the north bank of the river was still, in theory, Burgund land. But the folk who dwelt here were already strange to her, some of them with heads flattened in the fashion of the Huns. Gudrun wondered why it mattered who ruled here, since the Huns were more than half-Germanic and her own people growing more like them the longer they lived side by side.

In this more open country the Hun horsemen began to demonstrate their prowess, dashing back and forth in intricate maneuvers calculated to display their skill. Ecgward and his men could only grit their teeth and express their admiration; they were good horsemen as the Burgunds counted such things, but no man among them could cling with one leg to a galloping pony and shoot beneath its belly, or toss a looped rope over a foe and disarm him without himself falling off.

The only difficulty the Huns were encountering was with one of Gundohar's gifts to his brother-in-law, a black mare whose dam had been of the big Tolosan breed and whose sire had been the great stallion Grani, who had burned on Sigfrid's pyre. And as for Grani, some said Sleipnir himself had fathered him. Certainly no one but Sigfrid had been able to handle the horse, and he seemed to have bequeathed his wild nature to the mare. To the Hun horsemen she was a challenge, and though the Burgunds might watch their struggles with amusement, they knew better than to say so. When a well-placed kick broke one man's leg, Gudrun splinted it without comment, and bound up another man's bitten arm. But she could not help thinking that perhaps Attila might find his new bride as difficult to tame as his men were finding the mare.

Sometimes Rudegar would ride with her in the barge, talking of his campaigns in the khan's service, of the lochagoi, the notable men who served Attila, of the many tribes and peoples who had been swept up by the advance of the Huns into Europe and become part of their confederacy. It was only gradually that Gudrun realized how valuable an education she was receiving and thanked him.

"I swore you an oath, do you remember?" he answered, smiling. "It seems to me that to prepare you to understand your new people is the first service I owe you. There are other things that my wife, Godelinda, will be able to tell you. I will bring her to you, and perhaps my young daughter as well. When I look at your child I miss my own, and remember how delightful she was at that age."

"I am sure we will be friends," said Gudrun, suppressing

a smile. It was hard for a little girl to sit still all day. Sunnilda had not quite managed to fall overboard, but at times it had been a near thing, and if Rudegar thought her delightful, perhaps he did not remember his daughter's childhood as well as he thought.

As they passed Castra Raetica, clouds began to cover the sky. Soon a thin rain was falling, which grew heavier as the day wore on. They stopped to make camp early, and huddled, damp and shivering, under the hide tents until the dawn. But they got into the boats again in the morning, though Sunnilda was sniffling and Gudrun herself had begun to cough. There was no place where they could shelter nearer than Batava, the old Celtic town where the blue waters of one mighty stream and the lesser, darker waters of another came down to swell the Danuvius into an even greater stream.

Even though it had ceased to rain by the time they got there, Gudrun was too miserable to appreciate the beauty of the buildings the Romans had built from the local stone. What mattered was the warmth of the house to which they took her, and hot herb tea, and dry clothes.

When she woke the next morning, the world was ablaze with sunshine. Despite her sore throat, Gudrun found her own mood brightening. When she opened the shutters of her window she saw that it was set on a height overlooking the confluence of the rivers. Houses clung to the curving banks like children to their mothers' skirts, and the waters were sparkling in the sun. Behind her, mountains dark-clad with forest marched down from the north. On the other side of the river she could see hills curving up from the southwest to contain the plain. She was still gazing at the view when the maidservant came in to summon her to breakfast.

The house was not large, but well built in the Roman style around an atrium. An old man in a worn white tunic with a shawl across his shoulders against the morning chill was sitting there, eating a bowl of porridge. He seemed oddly familiar, though she could not think why. When he saw her, he blinked as if he recognized her, as well.

"Indeed, child, I must have known you even without the escort," he said smiling. "You are very like your mother when she was young."

"You knew my mother?" asked Gudrun, sitting down. The tantalizing smell of new bread was coming from somewhere nearby. She heard Sunnilda chattering and guessed that her daughter had already made friends in the kitchens.

"I grew up with her—" The old man shook his head ruefully. "Did they not tell you? I am your uncle, Gudrun."

She stared. It must be true—he had the same deep-set eyes and noble sculpturing of cheekbones and brow. But why had her mother never spoken of a brother? Then he leaned forward and she saw the heavy silver cross he wore, set with purple stones.

"I did not know . . . she never spoke of you," she stammered.

"I suppose that I was the black sheep of the family, to her. She was the oldest, and from the beginning her mind was set toward the ancient ways." He sighed. "But we both had a great hankering after knowledge. Mine took me all the way to Roma to study with the teachers there. It is why, when they ordained me, I chose the name Peregrinus, the pilgrim."

"Did you like it there?" asked Gudrun, still trying to digest the fact that her mother's brother was a priest and a Christian.

"Liking is not a word one applies to the city of the Caesars. Roma is a place both wonderful and terrible, where one finds great beauty and the most sordid ugliness, sin and sanctity, side by side. I would have stayed there forever, seeking wisdom, but our Papa is greedy for the souls of our countrymen. So they made me a bishop and sent me back to minister to our little flock. I am afraid I am a disappointment to him, for I have not made many converts here. Is it different on the Rhenus, where you are so close to Gallia?"

Gudrun shrugged. "Father Priscus and Father Severian did their best to teach us, when they were not arguing with each other. My mother . . . followed another path. . . ."

Peregrinus nodded. "Did she find what she was seeking?"

"I think so—" said Gudrun carefully, remembering the dried herbs that hung from the rafters of her mother's house in the forest, and the clay pots labeled with runes.

"And did it bring her peace?" His voice grew softer, and she saw that he was holding on to his cross as if he found some comfort there.

"I don't think that is what she was looking for." Gudrun tried to shut away the memory of the ecstasy she had glimpsed in the Old Man's single eye. The god Grimahild had served gave many gifts to those who served him, but she did not think they included ease. Her mother had sought power, but had it brought her satisfaction? Gudrun could not say.

"And what are you looking for?" he asked.

"A husband," Gudrun said brightly, deflecting his question. "Didn't they tell you? Of course, he is a pagan. Father Priscus objected to that. Do you?"

Her uncle looked at her and sighed. "Attila is an interesting man. In his household Christian and pagan live together and follow their separate beliefs freely, a thing which will hardly be seen again. He will not force you to choose. And so I ask again, what do you want, Gudrun?"

I want Sigfrid alive again and safe in my arms! her spirit cried. But that was not what the old man was offering her. She shook her head. Since agreeing to this marriage she had been carried along with no more volition than a leaf on the stream. Gudrun the wife of Sigfrid was no more, and she did not yet know what Gudrun the wife of Attila would be. How could she decide?

Peregrinus patted her hand and began to talk of other things. But his question would not go away.

Chapter 3 ❧ The Burgund Mare

Near Vindobona
Blood Moon, A.D. 429

The sound of singing drifted over the waters, women's voices joining in close harmonies sweet to the edge of pain, bitter as tears. Gudrun shivered as the barge turned shoreward. In the afternoon sunlight, the Danuvius ran slow and shining as a river of bronze, pouring through the gap between two noble, tree-clad hills into a broad expanse of water edged by marsh and grasslands, startling after so many days among the trees.

"The Hun maidens have come out to welcome you," said Rudegar. "They are singing of love." Gudrun managed a smile. To her, they seemed to sing of loss, but in her experience the two had been the same.

She felt as if she had been traveling forever. Batava had seemed a great distance, but she knew now that it had been no more than the midpoint of her journey. But the second half had passed more swiftly, for as they moved eastward, the river flowed with greater power, speeding them downstream. The western marches of the territory ruled by the Huns were thick with forest. On the southern shore lay Pannonia, in theory, part of the Empire. But except for a few stubborn outposts, Imperial civilization in the province had been shattered by two centuries of war. On the Roman side of the river, as on the side ruled by the Huns, only the smoke from an occasional farmstead marked the presence of humankind.

41

But here it was different. Though the Roman town of Vindobona huddled behind its walls on the southern shore, on the Hun side of the river the only permanent structures were a scattering of timber houses where the ground began to rise. They had come to the first outpost of that ancient and mysterious Scythia which had cradled so many races. And today these meadows had sprouted round felt *gers*, covering the plain in their hundreds like mushrooms springing up suddenly after a rain.

As they drew closer, she could see the line of singers drawn up by the landing, standing beneath a white linen cloth which was held up by the women to either side. Their layered garments glittered with bits of gold. As the barge grounded, the singing surged in a sustained ululation that lifted the hairs on her neck and arms and then faded to silence.

Gudrun fingered her amber necklaces nervously and adjusted the drape of her veil, remembering the days when she had known her future might depend on whether a man found her fair. She did not see Attila among those waiting, but if she were to prosper here, it was as necessary to have the favor of the Hun women as it was to impress the khan. She whispered to Sunnilda to get the gift basket. It had been her practice on the journey to reward those from whom she received hospitality; a reputation for liberality was always useful.

"Say to them that I find their singing very beautiful. Give them my thanks for the welcome—" she told Rudegar as he assisted her to step out onto the land. "Say that I have brought gifts from the Roman lands, that I ask them to accept with my goodwill."

"We have heard of the beauty and the generosity of the Burgund khatun," the first of the women replied in accented Gothic. "She outshines the word that has come."

Smiling, Gudrun passed along the line of singers, giving to one a glass bangle, to another a square of fine linen or an ornament of jingling bronze. From their reactions, she judged she had guessed correctly—their princes had seen a great deal of Roman gold, but the little, ornamental things that women liked, common enough in the West, would, because of their rarity, be valuable here.

As she came to the end of the line, she had the sudden sense of being watched and turned. Where the road from the landing reached the first house riders were waiting, mounted on long-bodied, shaggy Hun horses, the harness of their mounts glittered with gold. There were Huns and Germans together, but it was not the tallest that caught the eye. It was the man on the bay horse who attracted Gudrun's attention. She had seen him when he came to confer with her brother, but then he had been no more than her brother's ally, and she, only the wife of one of Gundohar's chieftains.

Attila . . . my husband. . . .

The khan had never had reason to pay her any attention, but he was staring at her now. Fixed for the first time by the full force of that black gaze, Gudrun felt a tremor and did not know if it were excitement or fear. For a long moment he looked at her. Then, with the faintest of nods, he reined his mount away. The other men glanced back as they followed with more open curiosity, but no one lagged; men and horses moved together as if ruled by a single will.

"Come, Lady," said Rudegar at her elbow. "They have prepared a house for you. The marriage feast will be held tomorrow evening," he added, answering her unspoken question. "They did not know just when we would be arriving, and must bring in game. You will have time to rest and prepare."

A night and a day! thought Gudrun. *A night and a year would hardly be enough to prepare me to meet that man. . . .*

She slept badly and woke aching and congested from the close warmth of the house after so many days in the open air. If this was the dwelling that had been promised her she intended to make some changes, but most important was to get herself clean. With some difficulty, she managed to make the women who had been assigned to serve her understand what she wanted, and they gathered up towels and scented oils and trooped down to the riverside.

"They are not an unclean people by nature," said Locris, a Thracian woman who had been taken in a raid long ago and freed when she bore her Hun master a son. "But water to them is a thing to be revered, perhaps because there is so little on the plains. Even with the Danuvius before them, they would not insult the spirit of the waters by immersing their bodies. They use damp cloths to clean themselves, and the juice of herbs."

"I understand," said Gudrun, picking her way along the path that followed the shore. "But I grew up beside the Rhenus, and I must wash the dirt of my journey away!"

Near the settlement, the natural forest of the river flats had been cleared away, but upstream the shore was still fringed by poplar and pin oak and other water-loving trees. Presently they came to a backwater where an ancient stand of willows made a natural screen. Fallen leaves turned lazily in the slow eddies, and, in the depths, sunlight glimmered like amber. Chattering softly, the women spread out along the shore.

Briskly Gudrun stripped off her clothing and stepped into the water, gasping at its chill. In Borbetomagus she had bathed in scented water heated by the slaves, but in the forest she had washed herself at the horse trough. In any case, after having made such a fuss about bathing in the river, she could not allow herself to flinch now.

And the water was refreshing. After the first shock she felt her blood beginning to sing beneath the skin and scrubbed vigorously, willing all the strain of travel to flow away on the stream. Presently the small sounds of wildlife began to return. A mallard swam quacking from its hiding place beneath the roots of the willows, a heron eased through the reeds trailing ghostly white plumes.

"Mother Danu," Gudrun whispered, "give me your blessing as you flow through this land." Staring into the water, for a moment she seemed to see the shape of a golden woman with open arms and flowing hair. Then a breath of wind ruffled the surface, and, when it grew still once more, all she could see were her own white limbs and the reflected branches of the willow trees. She remembered the Lady she had seen in the saltwell at Halle when she was a girl, and the voice she had heard at the springs of the Mariae below the Donarberg.

"Are all your waters one water, branching like veins beneath the soil? Do all rivers flow at last into one sea?" She stilled, sensing with an awareness beyond hearing the Danu's slow song.

She understood suddenly what Hagano had tried to tell them after he came home from his sojourn here. The Rhenus was the Father of Waters, rolling ever toward the wild lands of the north. But the Danuvius did not flow north, or west like the rivers of Gallia to empty into the trackless ocean, or even into the safe and charted waters of the Middle Sea. Her waters flowed ever eastward, back to the center of Middle Earth, from which, in the beginning, all the tribes had come. The Huns were only the latest of many to whom she had shown the way.

When Gudrun returned to the settlement, clean and scrubbed with the blood flowing swift beneath her skin, she heard shouting.

One of Ecgward's men caught sight of her and ran forward, waving. "Lady—the khan is going to ride the black mare—come see!"

Gudrun allowed herself to be led past the buildings to the pen where the Hun lords had been keeping a few favorite mounts. Now, these were all tethered to the railing. The black mare stood inside, ears twitching nervously as she watched the man who stood with arms crossed near the gate, apparently interested in anything in the world except her. She was a lovely creature, long of leg and sleek of body compared to the sturdy Hun ponies tethered outside. With what seemed to Gudrun suspicious eagerness, someone found a wagon for her to sit on so that she would have a good view. Attila's glance passed over her without flickering, but she was suddenly certain he knew she was watching. She settled herself and folded her own arms as nonchalantly as he.

He was singing, or at least she supposed that was what the sound must be, though it was almost toneless, moving up and down within a limited range without ever quite becoming a melody, shaped by syllables in no language she knew. But the mare seemed to like it. Gradually she quieted. It was then that Gudrun realized that Attila had also gotten closer, without somehow appearing to have moved. He continued to drift toward the animal in the same imperceptible fashion, still singing, until he was beside her.

The mare still wore a halter of woven thongs. Before she could flinch, Attila grabbed the rope and held her. He did no more until she calmed again. Then he began to stroke her. At first she jumped and sidled, but he was relentless as the river, patient as the hills. He held her head and blew into her nostrils, stroked the soft nose and brought his hand up under hard cheekbones to the vulnerable throat, fondled the twitching ears.

He stroked down the mare's shining neck and combed his fingers through her thick mane, ran his hand down the sloping shoulder, the smooth muscle of the foreleg and along the slender pastern. To Gudrun's surprise the mare allowed him to pick up her foot and inspect it. Then he let it down and felt up the inside of the leg to the softness of the chest and repeated the process on the other side.

By this time the mare's eyes were half-closed, her head drooping. Gudrun realized that she, too, had relaxed, lulled by that monotonous song. She jerked upright, forcing herself to observe how the man used his hands to learn the mare's body, passing along the curve of the back and around the hard curve of her barrel, across shining flanks, stroking the spine so that the flowing tail lifted, probing down between the muscled quarters, down one hind leg and up the other side.

Gudrun shifted uncomfortably on the hard wood, watching those sure hands. What was wrong with her? He was only touching the mare. But she could not help remembering that tonight it would be her own body that those clever hands would be possessing. She must not underestimate him. This was a man of great experience, with women, and with mares. . . .

Attila worked his way back along the shining black side. This horse was of the Tolosan kind bred to carry Goths, several hands taller than the Hun ponies. Attila's head scarcely topped her spine. Gudrun was still wondering how he meant to mount her when he gripped the tangled mane, and with a spring almost too fast to follow had his leg across her back. Certainly the move had been too fast for the mare to avoid, but Gudrun was aware of a certain satisfaction as she saw that all that preliminary gentling had not demoralized the animal entirely. After a moment's atonishment, the mare's head went back and she reared.

It was no use; her rider swayed forward, and then back again as she reversed position and her heels raked the air. Gudrun contemplated the strength of leg and thigh that must be required to keep him so firmly seated as the black mare twisted and plunged, and shivered.

For a few moments Attila allowed the mare to rebel, then a steady pressure on the leadrope brought her head around until she was turning in a tight circle. Confused, she forgot to buck. When he loosened the rein she leaped forward unthinking. One of his men had opened the gate and the mare darted through it. Folk scattered as he gave the horse her head and she uncoiled in a breakneck gallop toward the riverside. Before they quite reached the water Attila brought her round again, managing her with subtle shifts of weight and voice so that by the time they returned to the pen she had slowed to a prancing trot. She was sweating profusely, but clearly she had no notion of rebelling anymore.

"And how do you like her, now that you have tried her paces?" called one of the chieftains, a Goth.

"Very well," answered the khan evenly. "I must send thanks to Gundohar. In the country of the Burgunds they breed good . . . mares."

Gudrun returned to her house to dress for the wedding feast torn between outrage and laughter. Custom forbade any meeting with her new husband until the feast in which his lords would witness their union. But she felt very certain that the episode had been timed so that she would see it. Had he meant to impress, to frighten, or to arouse her? She supposed that before the night was over she would know.

Attila's bride came to the feast escorted by wellborn girls in embroidered clothes who held a linen cloth above her head like a canopy. Fire burned in a long trench in the meadow, pale in the light of the setting sun. As Gudrun approached, she saw that the men were waiting on one side and the women on the other. Since this place, being a temporary camp, had not enough chairs or benches for such a company, they had laid out split logs for the folk to sit on, covered with furs and embroidered cloths.

She straightened her robes, all crimson, the fortunate color, but cut in the Roman style, and let them lead her forward. The khan had sent her ornaments to wear, a broad diadem set with garnets, heavy earrings with dangling pearls, a necklet with more jewels and chains of gold. As she moved she jingled like a walking treasury. Attila, she could see, had on a well-cut coat fastened to one side with ties, of the same crimson color as her own, but unlike most of his lords, he wore neither diadem nor jewels.

He did not need them. Even in so short a time, Gudrun had learned there was never any doubt who was in charge when Attila was near. It was she who had to be got up like a Beltane tree so that they would know she was a queen.

As she approached, the crowd fell silent. Attila got to his feet and the others, men and women, scrambled up after him. As they reached the foot of the fire trench, Rudegar came out to meet her, followed by a boy bearing a golden cup, who offered it to Gudrun.

Nodding her thanks, she accepted it. She had been told that the custom was for the guest to make a prayer, but to whom should she pray? They were all waiting—the very air had grown still as if the whole world was waiting to hear what she would say.

"To the High God who rules all and to the spirits of this place and to the ancestors I give honor," she murmured finally, "and ask their blessing on this company." She poured out a little on the ground in libation, then sipped from the cup, striving not to grimace at the sour taste. The stuff in the ceremonial cup must be kumiss, the drink the Huns fermented from the milk of mares. She wished they had warned her.

Rudegar smiled approvingly as she handed the cup back to the boy.

"My lord, to the land of the Burgunds you commanded me to travel—" he cried, "seeking the fairest and most gracious of women to be your wife. Great khan, I have obeyed you. I present to you the Lady Gudrun, daughter of Gipicho of the clan of the Niflungar, *hendinos* of the Burgund nation!"

Attila's own cupbearer brought him a cup, of polished wood, not gold, and he lifted it.

"You have done well—" Attila's voice, curiously deep for a man his size, carried easily. "I honor the Lady Gudrun and make her welcome." Drums thundered as he drained his cup.

Her maidens escorted Gudrun to a bench at the center of the women's side, cushioned with embroidered felt stuffed with down. She sank down in a flutter of crimson silk, smiling graciously as the chieftains who sat in rows to either side of the khan took the cups their own servants offered and drank to her.

Attila's cupbearer came forward once more. "Next in honor this night is Rudegar," said the khan, "who brings me this treasure." Rudegar stood up as Attila sipped from his cup, then sat in the place of honor on his lord's right as one by one the other notables saluted him.

Gudrun reached for her cup, and the woman beside her shook her head quickly.

"Be grateful. The women are not expected to join in the drinking."

"Thank you—" Gudrun said kindly, and the woman smiled.

"I am Godelinda, wife to Rudegar," said the woman as Gudrun continued to look inquiring.

"I had hoped to meet you. Your husband spoke of you often on our journey, and your daughter as well."

Godelinda's smile became even more complacent. She gestured to one of the girls who sat behind them, and the child blushed and bowed.

"Who is the man they are saluting now?"

"That is Edika, one of the wellborn Huns who advise the khan. He is a clever man, and has gained much wealth in Attila's service," said Godelinda. Rudegar's wife was a comfortable soul, and her daughter, just reaching womanhood, like a bud on the same branch.

"And the younger man just behind the khan? Why did Attila not drink to him?" Gudrun asked as the toasts continued. Even if they only sipped from their cups each time rather than draining them, it was clear that among the Huns, a good head for liquor was necessary for survival.

"That is his eldest son Ellak—" Godelinda gave her a quick glance. "The child of Ereka, his queen."

Gudrun smiled sweetly. "I have heard she is a noble lady." Did the woman think she did not know she would not be Attila's only wife? And indeed, she had seen Ellak before, when he came to Borbetomagus with his father. But he had been a boy then. Now he was almost a man.

"She has given him three sons—" Godelinda said wistfully, and Gudrun concluded that the other woman had not yet borne a male child.

"She is fortunate," Gudrun agreed. "But daughters are a comfort as well. My own child, Sunnilda, has come with me. Of course she is much younger than Diedelinda, but perhaps they can spend some time together while you are here." Now the toasts were being made to Thiudimir. "He was with the party that escorted me. He seems a noble man."

"For a Goth—" Godelinda gave her a flickering glance, and settled back, apparently satisfied that Gudrun did not admire the prince too warmly. She continued to provide a running commentary on the notables being honored as the drinking went on. Ecgward was not among them, but Gudrun could see him among the men who sat behind the leaders, watching her like a lost soul. Gudrun refused to meet his eyes, keeping her attention on the chieftains, matching faces to the names Rudegar had given her during the long days of their journey. Her own mother had made a point of knowing everything about her husband's counselors— more, said some, than their own wives did. Her own survival here might depend on doing the same.

There was old Kursik, whom she already knew, Kuridak, chieftain of the Akatiri, Ardaric, the Gepid king, and a man called Berik, battle-scarred and grim. Beside him sat a large man, solid rather than stout, with a grizzled beard.

"That is Heimar, who is married to a niece of the khan," said Godelinda. "He is of the Marcomanni, like my husband, but these days he stays mostly on his own lands. They say his wife is not well."

Brunahild's foster father, thought Gudrun. She wondered if it would be possible to speak to him, and if so, what she could possibly say.

"And who is this one for?" she asked quickly as the cup was brought forward yet again.

"Now they salute Eskam. He is the most powerful of Attila's *kams*, his men of magic."

The Marcomanni woman spoke with the faint air of disapproval appropriate to a good Christian, but carefully. Gudrun remembered what her uncle the bishop had told her—all religions were held to be equal here. Or perhaps, she thought, remembering something Brunahild had once said about Attila, the only power the khan wanted his people to fear was his own.

Gudrun considered Eskam with interest, since he was clearly a man of influence here. His tunic was of garishly embroidered Roman silk, trimmed with fur, but only a few odd necklaces indicated his calling. Still, his eye had a piercing quality surpassed only by that of his master, and she thought it would be better not to cross him.

"I will try to deserve the honor the khan has done me," said Gudrun meekly, "and I hope that you will advise me. I know that I have a great deal to learn." Godelinda flushed again, this time with gratitude, and Gudrun knew she had been right to make the other woman her friend.

Slave girls came down the path beside the fire trench, bearing platters of silver and copper laden with what proved to be some kind of spiced meat mixed with onion and herbs and wrapped in cabbage leaves. For Gudrun and her closest companions there was a benchlike table on which to set the platters; the others ate from cloths spread on the ground. Male slaves were doing the same on the men's side, but Gudrun noticed that Attila's platter was of wood, not silver, with a little plain meat rather than the delicacies the others were being served. A modified silence descended as people applied themselves to their food.

Presently the first set of platters was taken away. Once more the cupbearers came forward, but this time it was the turn of each of the honored guests to offer a toast to the health of their host and the success of his new marriage, a custom, Gudrun realized gradually, which was to be repeated after every course throughout the evening. The women lifted their own cups to drink to the khan, but were not, thank goodness, expected to say anything.

The next offering was wild duck, which appeared to have been baked in clay, also very spicy, and flaps of a thin fried bread to eat it with. There were bowls full of a sour creamy stuff to cool the mouth, and dried cherries stewed with honey. Presently these were followed by boiled mutton with millet and other dishes which Gudrun picked at while she listened to Godelinda, herself growing more mellow as the courses, and the drinking, went on.

Attila had invited most of his own lochagoi— the notable men who served him—to the wedding. But neither the overking, Ruga, nor the khan's brother Bladarda were there. The sullen child on Attila's left was his second son, Denzigik, and the fair boy sitting by Ellak was Aetius's son, Carpileon. He seemed to be quite at home.

By this time it was quite dark and torches had been lighted. The slaves brought in spit-roasted wild boar and stag, and the men, whose toasts were by now being made in unwatered Greek wine, roared their approval. But Gudrun had noticed that throughout the feast Attila had eaten lightly and taken no more than ceremonial sips from his cup. No fear that he would be incapacitated by bedtime, as her brother Godo had been at his wedding.

Gudrun supposed she should feel relieved. Despite the feast and the oaths, until Attila had lain with her there would be no alliance. Since it was inevitable, it were best to get it over with quickly. Gudrun took another long swallow of her own wine. If her new husband was not drunk, perhaps she should be. As the evening drew on she could not help remembering how she had sat with Sigfrid at her first wedding, wanting him without understanding what it was she desired. Perhaps wine would numb her memory.

It was certainly dulling her awareness of the evening's proceedings. During the courses there were various entertainments—more singing by the women, and later, wild dancing by tribesmen to the beat of drums. A Gothic skald sang of Attila's heroic deeds and Gudrun's beauty; a fool, dressed in skins and tatters, reduced everyone to tears of laughter with his acrobatics and his monologue, delivered in a mixture of all the languages spoken among the Huns. Attila listened to it all with what she was beginning to suspect was his habitual impassivity. Gudrun, who had caught only one word in three and suspected that the rest were equally indecent, adopted an expression of incomprehension and hoped they would assume she did not understand anything at all.

The last platter was taken away. Gudrun, whose eyelids had been drooping, felt the shift in atmosphere as the feasters grew silent and straightened. Attila had risen in his place, thumbs hooked into his belt, without a word commanding their attention.

"My friends, my honored guests, my kinsmen—" he was speaking in Gothic, so Gudrun guessed it concerned her. "I thank you for coming to this feast. Know this—with the *hendinos* of the Burgunds I have made alliance. In exchange, he gives me his sister, this royal woman of the Niflungar. I call you now to witness—I accept her as full and honored wife, with the rank of khatun among our people."

There came a jangling from the shadows beyond the fire. Gudrun shivered despite the warmth of her draperies as she glimpsed in the shadows something misshapen that grew no less monstrous as with a curious, hesitating step it danced into the light of the fire. There were human feet showing underneath the flapping leather, so she supposed a man was inside, but it was only when the figure whirled and she glimpsed a flare of bright brocade that she connected it with the shaman Eskam. His overgarment was a roughly sewn tunic of hide to which had been sewn clattering ornaments of iron and bone. The tails of animals tossed from the shoulders, and a fringe of braided cords flared as he whirled, brandishing his horse-headed staff. His face was masked by the fringes of a headdress crowned by branching antlers.

Father Priscus, thought Gudrun, striving to maintain her composure, *would definitely not have approved.*

With a motion at once both awkward and sinuous, Eskam approached, his progress punctuated with strange moans and cries. At times Gudrun seemed to hear the cry of the swift saker falcon, then a horse's whinny, or the deep grunt of a bear. Without apparent effort he sprang from one side of the fire pit to the other, and as his movements became more frenetic, into the pit itself to walk upon the coals.

As he drew nearer, Godelinda took Gudrun's elbow, whispering to her to stand. Attila was on his feet also. Now the shaman danced between them, motioning disjointedly. Gudrun found herself going forward. Attila extended his arm across the fire pit, and she reached out to take his hand.

Eskam was still gibbering, but now she could hear words, names, of ancestors or gods or spirits of the land—she did not know who they were, but she could feel them gathering in answer to his call.

"Tanri!" The shaman raised his staff to heaven, shaking it so the iron pendants jangled commandingly. Another string of syllables and he pointed to the earth. Then he produced from somewhere among his garments a flask of water and poured it over their joined hands. The coals hissed and steam boiled up in a white cloud. The staff tapped first Attila's head and then hers, then the shaman shouted and leaped up onto the women's side of the fire, in the same motion lifting Gudrun and pushing her into Attila's arms.

It was done too quickly for her to fear. She was aware only of the steely strength of the arms that held her, the scent of horse and herbs, the sound of men cheering and women's stylized lamentation as Attila bore her away. When they reached the dark beyond the firelight he set her down again, and she realized in some amazement that standing side by side, she was taller than he. Without speaking he drew her after him across the meadow to the largest of the *gers*, its white wool covering pale in the darkness. The door flap was tied open and lamplight streamed from within. Remembering Rudegar's teaching, Gudrun took care not to let her foot touch the threshold as she followed him inside.

She straightened, trying to catch her breath, trying to cope with a whirl of impressions. She had been promised her own household, but clearly that was contingent on this night's encounter. Attila had brought her to his own dwelling in order to make her his wife.

And yet, thought Gudrun as she looked around her, this was hardly the rude tent of her first imaginings. She had been thinking, she supposed, of the light *gers* the Huns in her escort had used while journeying. This was a more elaborate affair entirely, wider across than most Germanic longhouses. On the inside, hangings of embroidered silk concealed the flexible wooden frame, and rugs of thick felt covered the floor. Bags for gear and weapons hung from the posts and beams, and other belongings were stowed in chests of wood and hide. To one side stood a portable shrine with a rude carving in chalk of a god, before whom a bowl of kumiss had been set in offering. On the other was the bed, made up with silken coverlets and heaped with furs.

"Do you need women to help with your clothes?" Attila's voice startled her and she realized that while she had been studying the *ger*, he had been watching her.

Gudrun shook her head and with clumsy fingers began to undo the fastenings. Perhaps she should not have drunk so much wine.

She was relieved that he did not intend to rip off her clothing, but by the time she was down to her undertunic she found herself wishing he would help her. Sigfrid had kissed her, and assisted her, ever so gently, to disrobe. Her eyes filled with tears, remembering. With elaborate care she folded each garment and set it aside, stripped off the golden ornaments and bent to lay them together upon her veil. She could hear small rustlings on the other side of the *ger*. Was he disrobing as well? She dared not look to see.

Still kneeling, she began to remove the pins that held her hair. Suddenly she felt his warmth behind her, his clever fingers plucked out the rest of the hairpins and freed the long strands until they fell around her in a silken veil.

"Burgund gold . . ." his deep voice was scarcely more than a whisper. She stayed where she was, trembling, as his hands caressed her hair and then passed through it, sliding across her neck to loosen the ties of her undertunic and slipping it down over her shoulders. Slow and gentle, the strong fingers caressed her, moving at last to cup her heavy breasts, callused thumbs rotating lightly on her nipples until they grew hard.

Gudrun's breath caught. "Are you going to gentle me as you did the mare?" To her dismay, she was trembling.

"Ah—you understood me . . ." He released her and stood away.

She turned and saw that he had moved to the bed. The Romans said that the Huns never removed a garment once donned, but Attila was naked, and his skin, pale brown and seamed with old scars, was clean. It was only compared to the perfection of Sigfrid's body that her new husband was ugly, barrel-chested and long through the torso, his well-muscled legs permanently bowed. She swallowed, remembering how those legs had gripped the mare.

"There is no need. The mare had never known the weight of a man. But you have had a husband. I saw how you looked at him. You, I think," he added with infuriating confidence, "will only need reminding. . . ."

"As you say—" Gudrun felt the easy tears filling her eyes once more. She had hoped the wine would make her numb, but all it had done was to sap her self-control. "I had a husband. I loved him beyond what was proper, perhaps, but I will never be done with grieving. I will do my best to be a faithful wife to you, my lord, but do not expect anything more." She tried to blink the tears away. She had known this moment would be hard, but she had not intended to let it matter, to let this man have such power.

"What more should I ask?" he shrugged and beckoned. "Now you belong to me."

And the truth of that, she thought as she got to her feet, was proved by the fact that he did not need to take her by force, but only to command.

He stretched himself out on the bed and waited, pos-

sessing her with his eyes, as she wriggled the rest of the
way out of her undergown. She left it in a heap on the floor
and, obeying his gesture, eased down at his side. Sigfrid's
eyes had been luminous as sunlight in water; Attila's were
opaque and black; she could not meet them. She closed her
own and lay back.

All he wants is my body . . . she told herself. *He has the right
to use it, but he will never possess what I gave to Sigfrid so willingly.*

She sensed the leaping of the lampflame through her
closed eyelids, dark and bright, dark and bright. The
rhythm of their flickering matched the motions of the hand
that was touching her throat and her breasts, her arms and
down her sides. As he had hummed to the horse she heard
him singing. As he stroked her hips and the length of her
legs and then the tender skin of her inner thighs she felt
herself floating away on the song. And then it seemed to
her that it was not the lamp but her own pulsebeat that
made the flickering. With a detached amazement she realized that her breathing was coming faster.

There was a pause, and then Gudrun felt him probe between her thighs, his fingers slippery with oil. She started
to tense, but almost in the same moment she was pinned
by his weight and he entered her. Instinctively she tried to
break free, but another expert movement brought his legs
around hers, locking so that the curve of her own thighs
held him in place within. She bucked beneath him, but it
did her no more good than it had the mare. His strong
hands, imprisoning her wrists, stretched her out beneath
him. Torso to torso, their heights were the same.

Held beyond any possibility of rebellion, she could only
flex to his motion as his powerful thighs gripped her and
panting, he rode her as he had ridden the mare.

And in the end, responses she had thought extinguished
awakened, overwhelming both will and reason, and he
drove her to her own climax as well as his own.

Chapter 4 ❦ Birds of Prey

In the weeks after Gudrun's marriage, leaden clouds moved in from the north, bringing with them a fine mist of rain. It was dismal weather that turned the paths to mud and leached all the color from the trees. But Gudrun did not complain. The grey skies matched her mood, and every day, in rain or dry weather, she walked out along the bank of the Danuvius.

As she was coming back one afternoon something stirred among the willows. She sighed as she saw it was Ecgward, his hair dampened to unaccustomed sobriety by the rain.

"Lady—" he stammered, "is it well with you?"

Gudrun stared at him. "If I were ill, would I be walking in the rain?"

"You are pale, and your eyes are unhappy—" he said, flushing. "If *he* is cruel to you, tell me, and I will take you away!"

Gudrun shook her head. "The khan has not mistreated me." It would have been easier for her to bear, she thought grimly, if he had. "My grief would be as great if I had been married to you, or any other man."

The truth of it was that she should have stuck to her first refusal to marry. She had not expected to love her new husband, nor had she wanted to. What had come as a surprise was her physical response, unwilled and uncontrollable. Attila was not cruel to her, but he was quite aware of his power over her body, and for that, sometimes, she hated him.

She did not dream of Sigfrid when she lay in Attila's bed. Each time the man she had married forced her body to its consummation she betrayed the man she had loved anew.

"Ecgward—" she said sternly, "I honor your loyalty. But you must say no more of this to me. If it is too painful, I will send you back to Gundohar."

He shook his head, coloring once more. "If you can bear it, Lady, so can I."

Gudrun nodded and swept past him. She felt his unhappiness but could not pity it, being too occupied with her own.

They stayed by the Danuvius while the moon dissolved away to darkness and magically began to reappear. Each night, Gudrun was escorted to Attila's silk-lined *ger*, and each morning returned to her house in the village to weep alone. And then, on a morning when the sun shone through a break in the storm fronts in a widening azure sky, she emerged to see *gers* fluttering to the ground all around her, horses being driven in from the pastures and wagons loaded, men scurrying about in furious activity.

"Oh yes, we are going," said the slave who had come to escort her. "Did not the khan say? Your women are already packing. The khans will make a great hunting, far to the east of here. We will be moving before the sun is high."

Attila had said nothing. The night before, waiting for him, she had fallen asleep on the furs. When he came in he had taken her with brisk efficiency and gone to sleep himself. But he had not talked to her. He rarely did. Even if he had been disposed to confide in a woman, she had made it clear she had no wish for anything beyond the physical relationship her duty required. For him, it was enough that her body accepted his mastery.

So why, she wondered, did she feel so angry?

* * *

Gudrun had heard that the women of the Huns spent half their lives in their wagons—traveled, conceived their children and bore them on the move, cooked meals, and sewed the mouseskin garments their menfolk wore. After two days of travel in the wooden wheeled vehicle with its canopy of oiled hide, she was convinced that if so, the bones of Huns must be made of some more durable material than her own. If she had been pregnant, the constant jolt and sway would surely have made her lose the child.

That night she sent to Attila to request a horse, and the next morning they brought her a sturdy grey pony with a nose hooked like a Roman dowager and a disposition like a hungover Goth. But the beast could eat while moving, and keep up the same steady pace all day. Brunahild, she remembered, had ridden as if she and her mount were one being. No doubt the Huns laughed at her own horsemanship, but Gudrun discovered an unexpected pleasure in forcing the animal to obey her. She understood that this was in part a reaction to the way that she herself had been mastered, but it did not diminish her satisfaction.

And anything would have been better than the wagon.

She had the leisure, now, to look about her. They were moving slowly eastward along the north bank of the Danuvius. Sometimes there were gaps in the thick woodlands, long meadows and marshlands that heralded the plains. Cows grazed the naked stubble of harvested fields around the thatched houses. Sometimes they would meet a woman driving a flock of sheep with twisted horns.

The way was marked by posts and strengthened with hurdles where the marshes could not be avoided. The line of heavily laden wagons creaked painfully along the road, lurching as their solid wooden wheels caught in old wheel-ruts and carving new ones into the softened ground. Behind them came the herds of beasts for food and riding, grazing as they moved along. It was a leisurely progress; a man on foot could have moved faster. But the warriors, mounted on swift, wiry beasts that could run all day, swooped and flitted around the slow-moving column as freely as the waterbirds their passage frightened from the reeds.

Earlier in the season the wetlands beside the river had been even noisier, but the flocks that wintered in the warm Roman lands had already passed through, leaving behind them the permanent residents and those who found in the plain of the Danuvius a refuge from winter climates more unwelcoming still. Sometimes Gudrun would hear a harsher cry and look about her for the black blot of a raven, but she did not see any, and after a time began to hope that she had traveled beyond the range of Wodan's watchers at last.

The small folk of the marshes flew up, yammering, as the wagons neared, but the teal soon settled back to a pleasant chuckling chorus of low nasal calls punctuated by the "yeeb" of the male mallard and the indignant quacking of his drab mate as she challenged a competitor for waterweed. More wary were the grey geese, and the great white egret that moved like a ghost among the reeds. Farther out on the river she glimpsed the tapered white bodies and stiffly poised necks of a group of singing swans.

Gudrun had reined in to watch them when she saw Hun horsemen approaching. She stiffened, angry because she recognized Attila in the forefront with a certainty that owed nothing to the fact that he was riding the black mare. The last few nights, sleeping in the wagon with Sunnilda curled against her, she had almost forgotten that her body was no longer her own.

As the riders drew closer, she saw that most of the men bore birds on their fists—goshawks and gerfalcons, a saker falcon, and on Attila's arm, the great brown eagle of the steppes. They swept toward her and slid to a halt, mud spraying from beneath sharp hooves.

"So, you like the mare?" asked the khan.

"I think we have reached an understanding," said Gudrun dryly.

The egret feathers in Attila's cap trembled as he laughed.

"She is good stock, like you—bad temper makes her strong. Ride with us!" Without waiting for an answer, he darted away.

As if that had been a signal, the mare jerked into motion. Gudrun grabbed for the mane, swearing, as they galloped after him. Waterfowl exploded in a brown cloud as the horsemen thundered along the bank, each flock's alarm setting off the next—the mallards and the grey geese, and then with a sudden clap of wings, the swans. Attila slowed, gazing upward as the white shapes wheeled away, painfully pure against the leaden skies. The "hoop-hoop-hoop" of their cry rang in the air. For a moment he gazed, then, with a swift, efficient jerk, the hood was plucked from the head of the eagle on his arm.

For a moment the great bird balanced, taking her bearings. Then the falconer flung her upward. Gudrun watched, transfixed by the beauty of complete efficiency in motion as the raptor climbed the skies. Now the nearest of the swans had seen her, and his graceful flight faltered, wings larger than those of the eagle desperately rowing the heavy air. But strong though those white wings might be, they could not match the eagle's power. With a deadly inevitability, the dark bird sped after him.

The swan, knowing himself outclassed, dropped toward the rushes. The eagle, seeing her prey disappear into the tangle of reed, veered after the wavering chevron the others were lacing across the sky. Ever more rapidly her wings sliced the air. As the last swans scattered, the eagle fixed on the slowest and beat upward while the swan strained for speed. Gudrun tensed, muscles straining in sympathy. If the swan could reach the river—but even as she hoped, the eagle dropped.

White feathers sprayed as she struck, knocking the swan sideways in the sky. Locked together, the two birds fell. Even now, if they had landed in water, the eagle might have given up the game. But she had aimed her strike with a deadly precision, and they crashed in the coarse grass, wings battering the ground. The swan's whooping cry failed in a strangled squawk as the eagle's talons closed. By the time the hunters reached them, the swan lay still.

Attila slid from his pony's back and stalked toward them, murmuring softly, a piece of deer meat in his gloved hand. The eagle's sleek head swiveled, turned back to her prey, then to the man again. He held the meat just out of her reach until reluctant talons released and she sidled onto his leather-clad wrist. Then, still murmuring praises, he let her feed.

Gudrun, whose pony had come to a halt nearby, felt the color flame in her face. She had been seeing herself as the swan, but the words Attila was using to the eagle were the same endearments he whispered to encourage her in bed when he brought her a fulfillment she had not desired. As if he felt her gaze, the khan looked up.

"You have to rule everything . . ." she whispered. "Every instinct you turn to your will. . . ."

"She is empress of the skies," he answered. "The swan was bigger—she would not have attacked it, but she fears nothing, with me!"

That is so, thought Gudrun. *But she is not free. . . .*

The migration continued. When the river curved southward the forests that covered the flat plain grew sparser, the meadows extending into long vistas of grassland with occasional stands of trees, but farther out onto the plain there were no boundaries, only clusters of felt *gers* and drifting herds of sheep and horses. They paused for one night at a Hun settlement on the heights across the river from the abandoned Roman town of Aquincum, consisting, like the one near Vindobona, of a few permanent wooden structures and space for the *gers*. Gudrun had heard that Queen Ereka lived there, but she did not see her.

In the morning they were on their way once more, following a south and eastward course across the plain. The prairie was mixed with marshland, especially as they neared the Tisia. Sometimes they paused at settlements of Gothic or Gepid clans or at the winter camps of the Sarmatians and Alans and Huns. Gradually Gudrun realized that their apparently haphazard progress was in fact an ordered, if leisurely, sweep through the lands the Western Huns ruled.

It took her some time to notice that although the clan mothers held no official place in the Hun councils, Attila made sure that when their brothers or husbands reported, she could always see and hear. Gradually the names she had heard at her wedding became attached to faces, and she began to gain a sense of the shape and nature of the land. She realized, finally, that it was his Germanic subjects to whom he took particular care to introduce her, and when, one day, he asked her opinion of a petitioner, she found herself answering him. She was a sister and daughter of rulers, and growing up in a royal hall she had absorbed more of kingcraft than she knew. Despite her reluctance, she found herself growing interested, and now, when they were together in the evenings, it was not only her body's response that he drew forth, but that of her mind.

And so the autumn faded into early winter. In the settlements they visited, folk measured the hay in their stacks and the grass in the home pastures and slaughtered those beasts they would not be able to feed. The smell of smoking fleshmeat hung in the air. As they neared the Danuvius once more Gudrun wondered where Attila meant to winter. So far, the weather was holding hard and clear, but they would have to find some sheltered place before snow fell.

Toward the end of the Frost Moon, word came from the Roman fortress at Singidunum that a clan of the Iazyges, one of the few tribes of that Sarmatian people that still remained on the Hun side of the Danuvius, had crossed the river and overrun the farmlands of Valeria. Attila's response was immediate, and before the day's end he rode out with his comitatus behind him, armed for war.

For several weeks, they heard nothing. That was not unusual, said Locris. Attila often traveled faster than news of his movements, and indeed the first they knew of the outcome was the sight of the khan riding home. He was followed by a line of roped captives and a number of dispirited sheep.

"I assume that my husband was the victor," said Gudrun as they shambled by.

"Of course." Locris raised one eyebrow. "They took them by surprise. No doubt the heads of the Iazyge chieftains now adorn poles by the Danu. The rest will have been killed or made slaves and the livestock divided among the khan's men."

The Greek woman seemed to take this as a matter of course, but Gudrun wondered. What the Iazyges had done was no different from the habitual practice of the Burgunds and most of the other Germanic tribes when they needed more land, though the timing was unusual. She recalled some mention of rains in that area that had destroyed the hay harvest. If they had found themselves without enough feed to support even the minimum of animals needed to maintain their herds, she could well understand the lure of more fortunate lands. Why had they been punished so severely?

That night, after he had reasserted his mastery of her body, she ventured to ask. Attila raised himself on one elbow, looking down at her. Gudrun tensed, unsure, in the flickering light of the oil lamp, whether his flat regard hid anger or amusement.

"It is because they broke the treaty—" he said after a moment, and she realized he had hesitated because he was unused to explaining himself.

"Doesn't everyone?" she shook her head. "I cannot count the times my brothers have raided into Gallia."

Attila's face hardened. "They make the treaty, they choose to break it. But this treaty *I* make. The Iazyges are sworn to *me*."

Gudrun looked at him. He had shown her no anger, but suddenly she was afraid.

* * *

The next morning they were on the move once more, turning northward up the Tisia. As the plain narrowed, the mountains that had hung as a shadow on the horizon grew larger. Closest were the Iron Mountains, but beyond them she could see peaks still higher curving away to the east and south—the great bastions of the Carpatus range. Once or twice the grey skies released a scattering of snowflakes, but for the most part the chief hazard was the hard frost that each morning covered the ground. A chill wind hunted the last of the leaves from the willows, and Gudrun was glad of every layer in the Hun garments she wore.

The farther they traveled the emptier the land became. It grew colder as well, and Gudrun was glad to huddle in the wagon with Locris and Sunnilda and Bala, the Iazyge girl Attila had given her after his campaign. She was beginning to wonder if they meant to head northward until they ran into the mountains when the Tisia, which had been tending eastward as it grew smaller, made an abrupt bend to the south.

The ground rose here, sloping up toward the foothills. Whatever livestock had summered there had been driven down to warmer pastures long ago, leaving the uplands to antelope and other game. And so, Gudrun was all the more astonished when they came over a rise and found instead of trailing mists the darker smoke of cooking fires. Then they were sweeping around the edge of the woodlands that bordered the river and the full extent of the encampment became clear.

The *gers* of the Huns covered the plain. Like Attila, the other khans possessed permanent dwellings of wood at various places in the lands they ruled, but the portable *gers*, their pale felt edged and ornamented with woven bands on the outside and hung inside with silk, were nearly as elaborate. Standards marked the dwellings of the khans—Locris identified for her that of Bladarda, Brunahild's father, and those chieftains of the Western Huns who had already arrived. Gudrun told herself she should have expected it. The old trading road that followed the Tisia to its headwaters in the Carpatus continued toward the headwaters of the Hierasus and the Tyras that flowed through the lands of the eastern clans. This sheltered corner was an obvious meeting place.

They were grouped around an enclosure circled by a cloth barrier, where a standard of black horsetails, taller than the others, fluttered in the wind. Ruga, khan of khans, lord paramount of the Hun nation and all those tribes his people had mastered, was here.

By day, the Hun lords hunted or challenged each other to horse races or competitions with the lance or lassoo or bow, and at night they feasted. Each evening, a different chieftain hosted. When Attila's turn came round, Gudrun, who was just beginning to make herself understood in the Hun language and was still trying to comprehend their cooking, was grateful that he had his own officers to manage such affairs. Thus, she was surprised when Attila told her to bear in the drinking horn, German fashion, as the party began, and stay to serve the meal. Whether she was meant to see or be seen was not clear, but Gudrun dresssed carefully in the rich, layered garments Attila had given her, heavy with embroidery and glittering with stamped ornaments of gold.

She bent low at the doorway, stepping carefully out of her felt boots and ducking her head to avoid catching her conical headdress on the frame. She kept her eyes lowered in order to see her way, though she hoped they would take it for modesty, as she made her way around the left side of the fire to her husband. Firelight glanced off the hard planes of weathered faces, gleamed from jewels. Attila was plainly dressed as always, firelight coppered the silver threading the auburn in his hair. The man beside him was bigger, his beard heavy for a Hun, its black strongly mingled with grey. That would be Bladarda, whom she had only seen from a distance before. Gudrun watched him under her lashes, seeking some resemblance to Brunahild. It was hard to believe this man with his broad belly and puffy eyes could have fathered Gundohar's deadly queen.

She knelt on the patterned felt rug to offer the horn to her husband. It was one of the heavy dark wines the Huns took in tribute from Rome, strong enough to dizzy her just from breathing the fumes. He nodded, unsmiling, and gestured toward the man on his own left, who had been given the most lavishly embroidered of the cushions to sit on, and the richest of the furs.

In the first moment, Gudrun thought, *This is what Attila will someday be*—but then, as she looked again, she wondered. Where the years had given bulk to Bladarda, Attila's frame had grown more wiry. Ruga, at twice his age, seemed worn away to the most essential sinew and bone. His features, sharp beneath the tight-stretched skin, were an exaggeration of the younger man's. But the eyes were different. Flat and dark, both of them, but Ruga's were dead pools, while Attila's were never still.

Ruga reached for the horn she held out to him, drank, and returned it to her with a smile. But she sensed that he was not really paying attention. Perhaps his mind was simply on more important things, like Gundohar's when he was working on his poetry. But Gudrun did not think so. *He has ceased to care* . . . the knowledge came to her, and then, *he will not live long.*

Still kneeling, she turned to offer the horn to Bladarda.

"A fair woman, and obedient, but all your mares are well trained—" said Attila's brother in his own tongue.

"My brother was not so skilled with Hun . . . mares—" she answered sweetly in the same language. There was a brief silence. She sent a swift glance toward Attila, and saw his lips twitch. In the next moment all the men were laughing, and she drew breath once more.

"And a woman of wit," said a new voice, his words fluent, but accented in a way she had not heard before. "She has transplanted well." Gudrun looked at the man sitting next

to Bladarda, tall as a Goth, with close-cropped light hair
and a neatly trimmed beard and blinked, remembering him
suddenly on a spring day beside the Rhenus, clad in Roman
armor.

"Greetings, my lord Aetius," she said in Latin. "You, too,
are far from your home." She held out the drinking horn,
knowing better than to ask what the Master of Gallia was
doing here.

Her face composed once more, she waited for him to
drink, then offered the horn to the big blond man who sat
at Ruga's left hand. That would be the Gothic king, Walamir the Amalung, Thiudimir's brother. And the man next
to him was the Gepid king Ardaric who had been at her
wedding.

"You brighten our darkness, Lady." The Gepid smiled a
shade more warmly than the occasion warranted. Gudrun
raised one eyebrow—she had heard stories about the
man—saw his gaze shift toward Attila and then away. She
let him hand the horn to the next man himself.

There was a gleam of humor in Attila's eye, but he nodded in grave approval as she made her way back to the
women's side of the *ger*.

Once she had settled onto the cushions, the men appeared to forget her presence, scarcely noticing when she
received more food or drink from the servant who brought
it to the door and started it around. There was a skin bag
of kumiss for those who preferred the fermented mare's milk
of the Huns, and mead, but what most of the men were
drinking from their silver-banded beakers was more of the
heavy Greek wine. And gradually, as food blunted their
hunger and drink oiled their throats, Gudrun realized why,
against the usual custom, it was not Attila's slaves but his
wife who was serving them.

"You have dealt with the Iazyges?" asked Aetius. "We can
make no plans for joint action so long as they are still in
Valeria. The Imperium will never believe their foray was
against your will."

The others looked at Attila, whose expression did not change. "They will not trouble you. There is no people called the Iazyges anymore. But you know that Valeria cannot be defended. Someone will always be trying to take it—better you let me hold it in *feodus*. It will be safe then."

"—Said the fox as he looked at the henhouse." Aetius smiled gently. "Or at least that is how it would be perceived. As you serve the khan"—he nodded in Ruga's direction—"I serve the empress." Somehow he managed to convey a rueful commiseration. Gudrun wondered if Ruga could see.

"Or rather"—Aetius sobered—"I serve Roma." For a moment the name hung in the air like an incantation, ancient, powerful, transcending personality. Gudrun had always thought of the Empire as soldiers, clerks, and governors, laws and agreements like those her brother was continually trying to cobble together for the Burgunds. But such arrangements were not worth dying for. She saw suddenly that Roma was an Idea, older and greater than any of the men who struggled to control it. It was that Idea, glimmering from beyond the borders, that drew the tribes from the darkness of their forests again and again. They thought they were seeking plunder, but it seemed to her that the fascination went beyond riches—the Empire was might, but it was also order, and authority. Aetius had invoked Ruga's name as if the great khan were the equal of an emperor. But emperors could come and go—sometimes with bewildering rapidity—while the Idea of Empire remained. Attila had destroyed the Iazyges because their rebellion threatened *his* authority, not that of Ruga. He served Ruga, she saw with sudden clarity, because it suited him. And his loyalty would last until his uncle began to fail. Then Attila would be the great khan—she could sense that power in him, like a hidden flame. But after him was there another who could wield it?

Roma would win in the end, she thought grimly—the idea of the Empire if not the reality, when all the little nations whose identity depended on the authority of a single leader had passed away.

She looked up, and saw Attila's black gaze upon her, and thought suddenly, *This is what he wanted me to see.* A slave pulled at the door flap and Gudrun received a platter of sausages cooked with cabbage and apples. But as she served the men and took away the remains of the previous course she could not help but wonder why.

"Bonifatius served the empress too!" Bladarda popped a sausage into his mouth with a snort of laughter. "And now he is in bed with Gaiseric the bastard after all!"

"Do not laugh at Gaiseric," answered Aetius. "He may be lame and a slave woman's son, but that makes his achievement all the more impressive. They say he is easily angered, but his rages always have a purpose."

"He is a son of Loki," commented Ardaric, "a stirrer of strife."

"He rages, but he does not reveal his mind," Attila added. "He drops words into other men's ears, and they do his will without knowing. Your Bonifatius is a fool, but Gaiseric is dangerous. . . ."

So are you . . . thought Gudrun. He might have been describing himself, except for the rage. Did Aetius know?

"It is true the Vandali grow very powerful. They make alliances. Theoderid has given one of his daughters as a wife to Gaiseric's son," said Ardaric. For a moment Aetius's grey gaze lifted to Gudrun, but his expression gave nothing away.

He knows, she frowned thoughtfully. *The Huns are making alliances too . . . If one day Aetius decides that Attila is too powerful, what will he do?* The door flap quivered; silently she rose and pulled it aside to take a platter of mutton on a bed of millet, still steaming from the cauldron.

"Theoderid!" In Walamir's mouth it was a curse. "I ask him to send Wideric back, but he will not."

Bladarda's laugh filled the air. "You go fetch him yourself

next summer, eh? Not good for the king's cousins to go so far away!"

Gudrun saw Walamir's face grow red and remembered abruptly that Wideric was an Amalung as well, a descendant of Airmanareik in the senior line, with a claim to lead the Ostrogoths that some might consider better than that of Walamir. Carefully she set the platter of meat in front of Ruga and withdrew to her cushions once more.

"You wish us to fight for you in Aquitanica?" asked Attila, turning to Aetius. For a moment the Roman looked taken aback, then he smiled.

"But of course—" For a moment he held Attila's gaze, then he turned to Ruga. "Will you consent to that, lord? The Empire will provide the usual compensation."

Gudrun saw the focus come abruptly into Ruga's eyes. Clearly there was one thing that still could rouse him. But his gaze went first to Attila.

"If it is your will, great father, we will go. . . ." Attila's words were more respectful than his tone.

"You will want the western war-band to fight in Gallia?" asked Ruga. "You will pay how much for each thousand of men? And what if the Juthungi break out? Who fights them?"

Aetius grunted and took another drink. Alone among them, he was watering his wine. "I suppose we must expect it," he said distastefully. The Juthungi had lived on the plain of the Danu before the Burgunds passed through, and before the Huns arrived. In theory they belonged now to the Empire, but hidden in the folds of the lower Alpes, they were always ready to challenge Roman authority.

"Well then—" He straightened, lips drawn back in a grin that gave him suddenly an eagle's glare. "This year we will be ready for them both. Attila shall lead his horsemen to lie in wait at Arelas, and I will ask you, lord, to give me a commander of troops to watch the Juthungi!"

The others smiled, and Gudrun saw them suddenly stamped with a single identity. *They are all eagles,* she thought, *and when they have finished the only victors will be the wolves.*

The next morning, Gudrun saw Aetius's banner fluttering above the *gers*, and picking her way carefully across the frosty ground in the wake of the gathering crowd, found the troop of Huns who were his house-guard forming up in front of Ruga's pavilion. They were a fine-looking lot, all well armed and armored with mail shirts and good helms, the harness of their ponies bright with woolen tassels and ornaments of gold. But after a moment she realized there were no Goths, no half-breed Germans, among them. Every man of Aetius's guard was a Hun of the old breed, many of them with skulls deformed in infancy to the shape of a helm in the fashion of the more conservative eastern clans.

Gudrun found herself instinctively reaching to protect her belly. If she should bear Attila a son, she would never allow such a mutilation. But the khan's skull had been left as nature made it—he would never require—She stopped herself, astonished to find she had even been considering it. She had had difficulty enough in giving a child to Sigfrid, whom she had loved. Her courses had always been irregular. She was not going to bear Attila a child.

She looked at Aetius's escort again. Hun troops had served as Roman auxiliaries many times, but she could not help wondering what these men, scarred faces expressionless as they waited for their master, thought of the Romans, and the Romans of them. Father Priscus used to speak of the Huns as if they were less than human. But after some months among them, Gudrun suspected that she would find their ways less alien than those of the Empire, with their hard straight roads and rules that were more rigid still.

The door flap quivered and Aetius emerged, drawing on his riding gloves. In full daylight she could see clearly the lines of power graven from nose to mouth and across his brow. She knew he was younger than Attila, though in truth

he did not look it—but then, Attila would probably not
change much until he was Ruga's age. For a moment the
Roman general stood still, his grey gaze moving across the
encampment. Then he strode toward the horse that had
been held ready for him, mounting as easily as any Hun.

As the little cavalcade clattered off, Gudrun stood looking after them. There had been something in the Roman's
face that puzzled her. It was only when they were out of
sight that she identified it as regret. She frowned, beginning
to understand—for a time in his youth Aetius had been a
hostage among the Huns. It was not solely to impress his
own people that he affected his barbaric escort. Hard
though it was to believe, he liked them. If he had had his
will, thought Gudrun, he would not have been going home.

When she returned to her own *ger*, she found servants
busy packing. Aetius had only been the first to take his
departure. The khans had finished their consultations, the
royal encampment was breaking up, scattering to reach
their winter quarters before the first real storm closed the
paths across the mountains whose peaks were already white,
to sharpen their spears and their skills in preparation for
the campaigns that would begin with the spring.

Gudrun bundled Sunnilda into the wagon and mounted
her mare, bracing herself for another long, cold ride. But
after several days of travel she discovered that she was
bleeding, and unwillingly joined her daughter in the cart.
For a few days, she thought, she could stand it. But instead
of diminishing as her moonblood usually did after the first
day, this blood came in a dark, thick flood that continued
to drain, and with it fever. Gudrun fell into a long tunnel
of pain in which she knew only the need to keep from
frightening her child.

After a time she was vaguely aware that the tormenting
motion had stopped. There were voices. She heard Sunnilda's protests fade as the child was taken away. Then the
wagon began to move once more. Gudrun did not know
that it had changed direction; awareness was to come to

her only in confused flashes of consciousness for many days.

"Drink, it helps you heal—"

The face above her was pale; Gudrun saw dark eyes beneath blued eyelids, winged brows, and, beneath the headdress, a glimpse of dark hair. Gudrun frowned. She knew the soft voice, with its hint of exotic gutturals beneath the Germanic words, but she had never seen the face before. The woman was holding a beaker of something that steamed gently in the chill air. Giving up the struggle to understand, Gudrun opened her lips to drink. The stuff was bitter; she tasted willow bark, berry leaf, comfrey, other, less identifiable flavors. But its heat was comforting. She tried to speak but could not find the strength, and then she was asleep again.

When she woke, chill air was flowing into the warmth of the room. The door was open; grey morning light showed her a palisade surrounding a yard of trampled snow. Inside, firelight from an iron brazier flickered on a circular wall of finely planed and fitted planks hung with embroidered cloths. Thick felt rugs covered the floor. It was a *ger*, translated into the wooden construction of the Germanic tribes. A figure appeared in the entrance and closed the door. Gudrun tried to speak, though a grunt was all that emerged, and the woman came to her.

"Locris—"

"My lady! You are awake!" The freedwoman's face lit up as she bent over her. *Was I so ill, or does she really care for me?* Gudrun could not waste strength asking.

"Sunnilda?" she croaked. "Where?"

"Outside with the other children. There are many here—" Locris slipped another cushion beneath Gudrun's head. "This house belongs to Ereka-khatun. The queen herself has been nursing you."

Gudrun closed her eyes, remembering the face she had seen. At least one question had been answered. The khatun, or someone, knew her herbs. If Queen Ereka had felt ill will toward her husband's newest wife, Gudrun would not still be lying here.

She spent the next few days recovering her strength. Gradually it became clear that this was the queen's house in the village across the river from Aquincum, where they had stayed briefly before. Folk were beginning to call it Attila's town.

On the third day, the khatun came to visit her.

"So, you are better?" said the smooth voice Gudrun remembered. She looked at the ageless face, framed now by a headdress of brocaded silk from Byzantium, and wondered why, having this wife, Attila had ever sought another one.

"Much better, and grateful to you for your care." She inclined her head as well as she could from the pillows.

Ereka-khatun nodded. "Maybe soon I will take you to the hot springs on the island. The Romans made a bathing pool there."

"What happened to me?"

"You lost a child."

Gudrun gave her a quick look. "Is the khan angry?"

"He wonders . . . you did not tell him. He would spare you the journey." Impossible to tell whether that dry tone hid disapproval. With three strong sons of her own already half-grown, Ereka did not need to fear any offspring Gudrun might bear.

"I did not know," answered Gudrun. "Does he think I did this on purpose? I know many safer ways, if I did not wish to bear a child."

The khatun shifted position on her cushion and resettled her heavy robes. She was sitting cross-legged; the soles of her indoor slippers were ornamented with embroidery.

"I hear your mother was a wisewoman. I have women here who are herbwise; perhaps you would like to speak with them."

Gudrun nodded. *And what, my lady, are you versed in?* she wondered silently. Subtlety, perhaps, and the hidden ways of power. She sensed that Ereka-khatun was a match for the man whose bed they shared.

"Is it custom, with your people, for a man to marry more than one?"

Gudrun blinked, reconsidering the subtlety. "Only for kings," she answered, "and the Christian priests do not approve, so they are now called concubines." She drew a careful breath. "I consented to this marriage."

"But you love another man—" said the khatun.

Gudrun stiffened, wondering just how much she had babbled when she was ill. "Forever. But he is dead. Attila knows."

"Of course—" For the first time Ereka smiled, as if it were inconceivable that there should be anything that concerned him that the khan did not know. "You must see by now, our husband is unusual." Gudrun nodded. "One day he will rule Huns, and then, maybe, more." A flicker of those dark eyes gauged Gudrun's reaction.

Gudrun raised one eyebrow. Had she guessed all this, or did Attila actually talk to her?

"I help him—You stay here for the winter, and I show you."

"I am sorry my illness has caused you this trouble," Gudrun began, but Ereka shook her head.

"Do you think that is why? He sent message a moon ago. After midwinter he meant to bring you. This is sooner, that is all."

Gudrun considered this for a few moments in silence. "You must understand, I am grateful. But in the treaty," she said finally, "it was said that I should have my own place."

"Oh yes—" said Attila's queen. "In the spring. You are to live at Lentia, and speak for Attila there, as I do here. Did not you know?"

Gudrun shook her head, feeling the easy tears spill from her eyes. He had not told her. She wondered why that knowledge should give her pain.

Chapter 5 Yule Gifts

Borbetomagus
Yule Moon, A.D. 430

Sleet rattled against the shuttered windows of Gundohar's workroom like the hoofbeats of charging cavalry, like Hun horsemen swept along by a wind from the east, thought the king, putting down the tax roll he had been reviewing and reaching for the tablet he used to draft his poetry.

"*A storm from the steppes, stampeding ponies...*" His stylus pressed the letters into the wax one by one. "*Thundering hoofbeats—*" No, the accent would be on the wrong sound. "*Hoofbeats thunder,*" he corrected, "*hailstones harry... Against the storm the Goth-lords gather....*" Gundohar hesitated, the stylus poised in his hand.

What must they have felt, listening to that gathering storm? Had they understood at first that this was something more than another raid by the wandering peoples of the plains? There was a story that the Goths had driven out all their wisewomen onto the steppes when they became Christians, and these witch-women, the *haliurunae,* had mated with demons to produce the Huns. Brunahild would have pronounced their defeat a fitting punishment for having rejected their ancient wisdom. Gundohar winced, remembering the exquisite curve of her lips when they were curled in scorn.

In the first moons after she died he had been reminded

79

of her constantly, but it was getting better. Now he was only troubled at odd moments like this one.

He shook his head, taking refuge in the safe certainties of the past. From time's beginning, tribes had come out of the empty spaces beyond the known world to spend their strength against the settled lands—the Scyths, the Sarmatians, the Alans, and more. But the Huns were different; the Gothic story showed it. They lived like the other nomads, but they fought with a disciplined efficiency as effective in its way as that of the Romans.

It had fallen to Airmanareik, lord of more lands and peoples than any Germanic king before or since his time, to face them. Did he understand what was happening? Since Gundohar had first begun trying to make the verses that would tell the Goth-king's story he had often asked himself that question. And with it came another—would he recognize the great challenge of his own kingship when it came?

A chill draft fluttered the parchments and he went to the window. The shutter had come open. Through the gap he could see the square courtyard. A little snow was falling, barely visible in the fading light, frosting the dark stones. The trees beyond the wall were already edged and capped with white. Beyond the city walls the snow would be gathering in wheel ruts, smoothing the stubbled fields. Grandmother Huld was shaking out her feather quilts, and soon the world would be blanketed in white.

In Borbetomagus the snow came gently. On the plains of Hunland it would be otherwise, where there was nothing to hold back the wind. He had never been there, but he had listened to Hagano's tales. He closed his eyes, imagining those endless reaches of white, and wondered suddenly how his sister fared. That she was wintering with Queen Ereka his last messenger had told him, but no one could say if she shivered when the wind moaned around the houses, or if she wept when she was alone.

*   *   *

Hagano straightened as the wind rattled the door to his mother's rooms, turning his head to see. There was no one—a part of him already knew that—but since losing his eye he often had the feeling there were things happening just outside his range of vision, that if he could only look fast enough, he could see. He sighed and picked up the next packet of herbs. From the scent he guessed it was motherwort. He looked at the bindrune on the tag and made a note of it. Grimahild had used her own code for labeling herbs, and he was only beginning to translate it.

There had been more medicines, and writings, in the queen's house in the forest, that he had not been able to remove before Gudrun moved in. They were not there now, but whether she had taken or destroyed them he did not know. *Ah, sister,* he thought with unaccustomed sadness, *the children of Grimahild were stronger when we were united.*

The clamor of a gong, sweetened by distance, signaled the night meal. With a sigh Hagano pushed the bag of herbs back into its niche and went out into the gathering darkness.

These days, Gundohar and his brothers dined with the men of the comitatus. The Burgund kings had grown powerful. Their retinues were large enough so that only the basilica was large enough to seat them all. But there was no Lady of the Burgunds to bear the drinking horn around the hall.

Old Ostrofrid, who had come in from his villa among the vineyards, took care to point this out as he set his beaker down. Hagano caught his brother's goaded glance and smiled. That the old lawspeaker should harp on royal alliances was as predictable as darkness at the end of the day.

Gundohar shook his head. "My first marriage brought little good to me or to the Burgunds. I have no mind to try again."

"It is your duty to make an heir."

"I have brothers. Let one of them hold the high seat after

me. There are candidates enough within the kindred of the Niflungar."

"That is so, but your brothers have no children either. In these changing times the power will pass more peacefully if there is an acknowledged heir. Have we not seen enough such struggles in the Empire?"

That was true, thought Hagano. But Gundohar's reluctance to take a wife was also understandable. Godo used his own bereavement as an excuse not to marry again, but though he had liked his young wife, he was obviously more comfortable in a masculine establishment. Gislahar still had his illusions. Perhaps it would be the youngest brother's offspring who would carry on the line.

Hagano grinned sourly as he realized he had not counted himself in his figuring. But even when he had two eyes he had not had much luck with women. He did not think he would find one willing to live with him now, even if he had really been old Gipicho's son.

"And who would you have me marry?" Gundohar said patiently.

"You need alliances as much as you need heirs," answered the old man. "Your sister's marriage protects our eastern borders. You must look west, perhaps to the Visigoths, for a bride."

"I won't find her soon then," said the king, "unless I do my wooing sword in hand. I am sworn to aid Attila and Aetius if Theoderid tries to take Arelas again this year."

Ostrofrid shrugged. "The Visigoths will not hold that against you. They say Theoderid is looking about him for alliances. He has even been talking to the Suevi in Hispania. If the Romans win, you can ask for a wife as a part of the settlements. If they don't, the old man may be even more eager to court your friendship by making another kin-bond between you."

"Another bond?" asked Gislahar from his other side. "What do you mean?"

"You have a cousin among the Visigoths already, didn't

you know? The Lady Gundrada is married to Valobald the Balthi prince, and has given him a son."

Who is also within the eligible degrees of kinship, thought Hagano. But it was about as likely that the choice would fall upon Hagano himself as that the Burgunds would make little Gundiok their king.

"I'll consider it. Will that content you?" said Gundohar. "In the meantime, let us do justice to our meal."

As usual, Hagano finished eating before the others. Less concerned with food or conversation, he was the first to notice the growing clamor outside. Instinctively his glance went to the weapons on the wall, calculating accessibility and distance. But by the time the great doors at the end of the hall swung open he could hear singing, and settled back again.

The warriors stilled as the Roman priest, Father Priscus, appeared. His acolytes were behind him, armed with incense and torches. Marching with bent brow and stately, self-conscious tread, the priest led the little procession around the benches. Their hymn echoed thinly from the arched ceiling, and drifts of sweet smoke began to cloud the air. Hagano hid a smile as the priest paused before Gundohar, blessing him with great sonority and directing the acolyte to cense him thoroughly before they went on. He suppressed a sneeze as the little procession swept by him. The priests treated him with the same wary neutrality they had used toward his mother, his ambiguous position in the royal family protecting him at the same time as it allowed them to ignore him.

The season of Yule was beginning. All great changes thinned the barriers between the worlds, but at midwinter, when the winter dark threatened to eat the sun, the wild powers of the world were freed to make mischief. Wise men warded hearth and hall, barn and byre. In the old days each family's elders had performed the rituals, while the *sinista* protected the royal clan. The last high priest of the old faith had died when Hagano was a child. The priests of the

White Christ, always so eager to combat the powers of darkness, had willingly taken on the responsibility.

The people did not complain. They greeted the new procession with cakes and ale as they had the old. Christian folk took chalk and marked a cross upon their doors. Those who were less convinced, or more cautious, added a second cross at an angle to the first one and finished the ends with tridentine prongs, the eight arms of the new figure crossed with shorter strokes to make the symbol of the Helm of Awe that had been old before the Romans came.

Ward away, thought Hagano as he watched them pass. *But take care you do not create as many devils as you dispell.*

"Phew!" said Gislahar, grinning as the door closed behind the priest and his attendants. "You'll smell sweet tonight, brother. I should think the troll maidens would come flocking, not stay away!"

"Run after them and maybe they'll smoke you as well," put in Godo. "—Only way you're going to get a female to look at you!"

The warriors all roared with laughter and Gislahar blushed furiously. In truth, the girls found him appealing, but so far he had been too shy to take much advantage of his opportunities.

The exotic sweetness of frankincense was replaced by the honest savor of good beef as the food was brought in. Hagano shook his head. That the holidays were a time of peculiar tension he could not deny, but the only evil spirits he had ever seen were those men found at the bottom of a drinking horn. Still, the procession was a useful way to signal the beginning of the season. The chieftains would be coming in for the feast; he must remember to talk to Gundohar about what they were going to say about next year's campaign.

The weather held dry but chill as the moon waxed, old snow turning to hard ice on which men slipped and swore. As the hours of darkness lengthened folk huddled by hearthsides, finding in their fires a promise that the light would not entirely leave the world. But as the solstice itself approached folk grew more busy, food was readied for feasting, women hurried to finish their spinning before the days of enforced idleness when Huld and her maidens rode the skies.

Hagano strode through the streets in the gathering darkness of solstice eve, a lantern swinging from his hand. Westward the sun sank under low banks of cloud whose dull glow was slashed by guttering flames. Then the black hills swallowed the light. A chill wind hunted a few gusts of sleet down the streets and he shivered despite the heavy cloak he wore.

Ahead of him other lights were bobbing through the gloom. On this night, folk set lamps to burn for their dead kindred. In the little church the flames were already kindled, but the heathen dead lay in the grave field outside the town, equally honored, and perhaps more in need of appeasement than the Christian souls. When he reached it, many lamps were already flickering. On some of the newer graves food had been left in offering. But the weather did not encourage lingering; most of the people Hagano met were on their way back to the town.

Grimahild's grave mound had been raised a little beyond the others, on the side toward the river at the edge of the high ground. Old snow clung to the dead grass; crunched beneath Hagano's soles as he climbed the mound. But the top was clear; no doubt the wind had swept it clean. He tried to put from his mind the stories of howes on which no snow would stay. Gathering his cloak around him, he cleared dead leaves from the hollow in the center and set the lamp in its shelter. It flickered wildly, then settled to a steady flame.

Hagano sank back on his heels with a sigh. He ought to go now, but it was curiously peaceful here in the windy darkness with only the flame as his companion, as if his mother's spirit had come back to warm him. And as he observed its subtle changes, it came to him that he had meant all along to spend this night sitting out on his mother's howe.

Already it seemed to him the wind was weakening. His cloak was of tightly woven wool, shaggy on the outside as a wolf-pelt; it would keep him warm. He had stood watch many a night in worse weather, and in poorer company. He tucked the cloak more securely around him and settled back, cross-legged, facing the flame. Now night's mantle wrapped the world completely. Other folk had fled to the shelter of warm hearths. On this night, especially, the Outgard—the whole wild world outside the space enclosed by human walls—was open to realms beyond Middle Earth, whether hostile or benign. There were those, thought Hagano, who would say he belonged to Outgard already. But he was human enough for a shiver to walk down his spine when he looked into the darkness.

"Mother, I have come to see you," he whispered. "Will you not speak to me?"

In Grimahild's rooms he felt her presence, sometimes as if she had been there but a moment before. But when he called out to her there was only silence. He knew well enough the dangers of clinging to those who were gone, but her hold on him was too powerful. The queen had borne her other children to serve her husband. But when she knew herself with child by a man of the elder race she had herbs and arts enough to have gotten rid of it. She had given birth to Hagano to serve her own purposes, and except for those years with Attila, he had always done so. Even dead, she haunted him. He needed to confront her one more time or he would never be master of his own soul.

And I will face anything—wild weather or the Wild Hunt itself, he thought grimly, *to be free.*

As the wind died it had grown very silent. He gazed out across the grave field where the lampflames danced and guttered. Beyond them loomed the old Roman walls of Borbetomagus, featureless in the gloom. Only a few buildings, on the rising ground at the center of the city, showed above it. On the second story of the palace a light glimmered in one window; he thought it might be from Gundohar's workroom. The city seemed an illusory safety, surrounded by such a vast wilderness of darkness.

He turned his gaze from the city to the lands that surrounded it, lying still beneath the heavy sky. He thought of pastures where by day the cattle cropped the brown grass, vinelands studded with the skeletons of pruned vines. What walked there? In the hills snow blanketed the roots of the forest. What wights stirred now in those shadows, spiraling like smoke from rock and tree, growing solid in the chill air? His awareness spread outward, circling round toward the river, whose cold waters flowed leaden toward the sea. Did its nixies sleep, or were they, too, stirring in the depths and yearning for the warm flesh of men?

His thought came at last to the meadow by the riverside where they had raised Sigfrid's howe. It seemed to him that a light burned there also, kindled as such flames had always been for men of great fame, men who shone with some inner radiance that made them seem kin to the gods. Alive, they had feared him. Did they fear him dead as well and light the fires in propitiation, or to honor his sacrifice?

It is not only my mother from whom I must win free, he thought then. From somewhere across the river came a drawn-out howl. He waited for the rest of the pack to echo it, but there was only the one. A shiver walked his spine.

"Is that you, then, my hero, my enemy?" he whispered. "Men say you walk in the wild warg's hide. Do you wander those woods where your blood fed the ground, or will you wait for the river to freeze and cross to haunt us here?"

He stilled, listening. "We gave you arms and treasure," he said then. "No warrior ever came so well provided to Wodan's hall. You had a queen to lie beside you. What more do you want?" As if in answer a wind from the river ruffled his hair. "Leave us alone, warg!" he cried. "Your death was needful, and you accepted it."

Hagano had to believe that, or he was a murderer. There had been so many moments when Sigfrid could have turned to fight or run and he had not done so, surely he must have consented to become the offering. *And if the same sacrifice is required of me, will I know it?* Hagano wondered then. But that would never happen, he told himself. He was not a king.

He had relived the moment when Sigfrid went down beneath his spear in dreams; once more the memory came upon him, and he felt the pressure of the god's hands upon his own. *I served Wyrd, not Wodan,* he told himself, but at moments like this he could not help but wonder if they had been the same.

His memory of events fragmented into impressions and emotions, becoming ever more disjointed; imperceptibly, he slid into sleep.

In dream Hagano heard the wolf howl once more, and took up the king-spear to go after it. He passed across the leaden waters of the Rhenus like a spirit, and by that, some part of him knew he must be dreaming. But he could see through this dark dream forest sleeping better than his single eye saw the waking world.

There was a wolf—he started after it, for a moment he saw it clearly, then it seemed to dislimn into mist and flow away. There was a flicker of movement on his right—the same wolf, or a second? He glimpsed them, first to one side, then the other, and began to wonder who was hunting whom. But the trail was clear, and he moved forward.

Without surprise, he found himself approaching the house in the forest where his mother had brewed her spells. The place seemed larger than he remembered, though it lacked the housewifely touches Gudrun had added when she lived there. The door was open, and warm light spilled across the yard from the hearth. His steps slowed.

"Why are you waiting in the darkness?" came a voice from within. "Stupid child, come!"

Hagano grimaced, recognizing the tone. Out of habit, he started to duck as he passed beneath the lintel, but here there was no need. And yet, when he looked around him, the interior was the same as he remembered—or more so— more herbs hanging in bunches from the rafters, more scrolls thrust into shelves, more overflowing baskets and bags, the great chest carven with more intricate runes. And the cauldron in which he had enspelled the spear was large enough, now, to hold a man.

His mother was sitting at the head of the hearth, spinning. From the basket to her right a cloud of white wool floated between her fingers; from the basket to her left, black wool flowed like shadow. Hagano watched with fascination as her nimble fingers mingled the two into a single silvery strand.

"Black hair from Heide's goat and white wool from Fricca's rams. . . ." she said, looking up at him from beneath bent brows. "It is always from opposites that the strongest strand is twined."

He halted on the other side of the hearth, leaning on the spear.

"You can put that thing aside," she said then. "You will not need it here."

Hagano grunted, not so sure of that, nor was he entirely certain just who it was who was sitting there. It was his mother's shape, but as with the house, something had been added. Still, when dealing with the Otherworld, even in a dream, good manners were advisable. He leaned the spear against an upright where it would be ready to hand and eased down on a bench by the hearth.

"Are you hungry?" she asked then. "The cauldron is bubbling. I apologize that I cannot serve you. The hour grows late, and I must finish spinning by dawn."

The steam that drifted from the pot was fragrant with the scent of fleshmeat and herbs. Hagano felt his mouth watering, but he shook his head. The flickering firelight picked out the frame of the loom behind her. He could not make out the pattern, but the warp threads were weighted with skulls. He preferred not to ask what kind of meat had gone into that stew.

"My thanks, but it is not food I seek here, Mother, it is wisdom." He found himself flushing as she laughed. Always, she had had this power to confuse him.

"To seek wisdom, you must be wise. How can you ask when you do not yet know what you desire?"

"I desire to choose my own path—" he retorted. "Mother, set me free!"

Her laughter continued. "My child, it is not I who hold you. See—you have already bound yourself into the weaving—" She pointed, and Hagano realized with a ripple of shock that a silvery thread extended from beneath his breastbone to the loom. He started to his feet, but the strand remained taut; no matter how he moved it stayed the same. He blinked, for now it seemed to him there was a shimmer around the loom, as if a multitude of threads were raying out from it into the gloom.

"Can I see the pattern?" he asked hoarsely.

She nodded, and he moved past her toward the loom. The figures woven there seemed to move as he looked at them. But suddenly he recognized his child self, shouting insults back at the boys who taunted him so they would not see him weep, then teasing Gudrun until he made her cry. He saw himself holding the spear as his brothers swore the oath of kinship with Sigfrid, and swearing his own vows on the same spear before he killed him. He saw himself fighting Waldhari and felt a reminiscent throbbing in his missing eye. He saw a hundred battles in which he and Gundohar had fought side by side. And sometimes he saw behind his own figure a shape of shadow, cloaked and hooded, leaning on a spear.

He could see how the figures were woven, but their meaning he could not tell. And when he tried to follow the patterns of the others, he could not make them out at all.

"Very well. I accept the wyrd that I have chosen. But I

am also what you have made me. Therefore, I ask you, Mother, to give me a blessing, that I may choose wisely in time to come." He turned to confront her, and for a moment her fingers faltered in their swift twisting of the wool.

"That is well spoken, Hagano, Child of the Holy Grove. Come to me."

Hagano felt his gut tighten, but he had asked for this, after all. He made himself go up to her, and meet her gaze. *This is Grimahild, and something else,* he thought once more, for her eyes were filled with light. He had heard that human souls, when they passed from flesh, might join with the gods. In life, his mother had spun plots and twisted fates. It seemed to him that she was becoming very like one of the norns now.

"You have asked for the power to choose," she said softly. "Take hold of this strand." The spindle swung from the twisting thread as she lifted her hands, trailing clouds of wool.

Very carefully, he reached out and grasped the thread below the place where her fingers held it. Lightning shocked through his body; for a moment he could not see. When he focused again, spinner and fire and the house itself were gone. Hagano stared around him with a sudden ache of loss. There was only himself and the great loom, and the thread he grasped came now from beneath his own heart.

"*You see now what most men never guess at,*" came her voice in his ear. "*The gods warp the loom, but men weave themselves into its patterning. This gift I give you, to spin your own fate, understanding what it is you do. Thus, and thus only, shall you be free. . . .*"

He stared around him in sudden anguish. What he wanted was not freedom but to be assured of her love. But that was not what he had asked. The understanding she had promised came upon him suddenly then and he saw that if love was what he wanted, he had the power to choose it. If he wanted glory, or power—he could seek it, but only wisely. And what was wisdom?

I am wisdom . . said a voice that he had heard once before, when he grasped Sigfrid's death in his spear.

"No!" he cried, and that denial whirled sense away into a darkness beyond dreaming, and he knew no more.

When Hagano awoke, he found himself tangled in the frozen folds of his cloak, hugging his belly. Grunting as stiff and aching muscles reluctantly began to move, he sat up. The lamp had burned out, but east across the river the newborn sun was rising, its tender rays striking rainbows from the frost that covered the graves.

The Burgund lords had worn their best to the king's Yuletide feasting. Crimson cloaks vied with blues and greens in hues as rich as the polished stones set into the round golden headband Gundohar wore. And everywhere gold glinted from arm rings and belt-plaques and brooches. *Most of them are dressed better than I am*, thought the king, who had put on a dalmatic of a purple so dark it was almost brown, *except for my crown*. It had been Grimahild who chose what he should wear for these public occasions. He supposed he should pay more attention to his appearance, but since Brunahild died he had found it hard to care.

"Health to the land, health to the princes of the Burgund name, health to the king!" The chieftains raised their drinking horns with a roar that shook the rafters.

Godomar swung up his own horn in answer, grinning widely, and drank its contents down. A moment late, Gundohar lifted his own silver mounted horn in acknowledgment. The remains of a noble meal lay before him, crumbs scattered on the cloth, fat congealing on the bones. It was everyone's duty to feast to the point of gluttony at the festival to assure they would eat well throughout the coming year. The king had done his best, but the food lay leaden in his belly. As soon as the clamor quieted, he thought, he would stand up and speak to the feasters. He sighed, mentally reviewing the points that must be made.

The real planning would take place later, in private meetings with the most important men. But the momentum that would carry them through the coming year would be established by the speech he made today. To address his people was no longer the trial it had been when the king was younger. *With practice even I have learned kingcraft*, he thought in habitual self-mockery. *I can command an army or convince a council. I only wish I enjoyed it more. . . .*

Like a bird to its homing, Gundohar's thoughts returned to his epic. Before the feast he had been working on the part in which messengers brought the first word of the advancing Huns to the Goth-king. *Why is it so much easier to imagine the speech Airmanareik made to his council than it is to prepare my own? Perhaps*, his thought continued, *it is because they are all dead and will not dispute what I tell them to say. Living men have the uncomfortable habit of coming up with ideas of their own! But I should not complain. Kingship would be even more exhausting if I had to think for all my people too.*

He began to smile, saw Gislahar's look of surprise, and realized that this too was something he did not often do anymore. *Tonight we will get very drunk*, he told himself. *If I drink enough, I can laugh, because I will no longer care.*

Abruptly he pushed himself to his feet and stood leaning on the table, looking down at them. Men saw the movement and began to still. Smiling, Gundohar straightened and picked up his drinking horn.

"Burgunds, I salute you! In health and wealth, in faith and troth, may you dwell throughout the year!"

He set the horn to his lips as they began to cheer, swallowing until it was empty and reversing it so that the last drops fell upon the floor. They were not to know it had only been half-filled to start with—even that much of the heavy mead at one go made him blink, and the men, enjoying his momentary confusion, stamped and cheered. The king smiled widely, encouraging them to think him a little fuddled. A man who did not lose his restraint in the Yuletide drinking was suspect. People assumed your true thoughts would flow from an upended drinking horn.

Nobody had ever seen Hagano drunk. As he set down the horn, Gundohar wondered if that was why some did not quite trust him. His brother was sitting quietly at the end of the high table, looking into his horn. For the past week he had been more subdued than usual; perhaps when the feast was over Gundohar should talk to him.

"I drink to you, and I promise that as we pour out the drink this Yuletide, next summer we'll spill the blood of our enemies!" That brought another cheer, as he had expected.

"Whose?" shouted someone. "And where?"

"It looks like we'll be fighting again in Aquitanica—so tonight, when you've drunk up all the beer, you can slide under the tables and dream of good wine and willing girls and Visigothic gold!"

More cheering—Gundohar felt the warmth of the mead beginning to percolate from his belly to his brain and grinned back at them.

Now the cooler heads would be coming up with more questions, such as who was going to command, and how much they would be paid. The king gathered his wits to answer them.

Ordwini had just risen, pulling straight his tunic, when there came a great knocking on the doors. Benches crashed over as men lurched upright, clapping hands to their sides in search of the swords that had been prudently hung up on the walls. One of the warriors who watched the entrance went to the window behind the pillar. Gundohar heard laughter, and then the great double doors were pulled wide.

Torchlight streamed into the hall, accompanied by a mighty clamor of clappers and bells, rattles and whistles and drums.

"The knockers!" came the cry, and with it a tumble of men, or at least one assumed so, costumed though they were in furs and straw and painted leather till they scarcely seemed human. Some wore the masks of bulls, some bore he-goats' horns, while others were swathed in the skins of bears and wolves.

Braying with laughter, the mummers cavorted about the hall, a very different crew than the sedate psalm-singers whose procession had begun the season, though indeed, some of the performers might have been the same. Gobbling and screeching, they snatched food from the tables, drained horns and beakers, and no man courted ill fortune by denying them.

With a grin, Gundohar surrendered his horn to a wild-eyed figure clad in streamers and straw and stood with his thumbs hooked into his belt, watching the revelry. Nobody would expect him to make any serious speeches now.

More prancing figures pushed through the door and spread out to frame the entrance of three who were more richly dressed than any who had come before. First came a distorted creature with soot-blackened face and staring eyes, he-goat's horns poking through a floppy red cap. A patchwork of furs had been bound around him, ending in a wildly swinging tufted tail.

"Sooty-black, troll-clack, dwarf-man bring the sun back!" cried his companions, and more than one of the chieftains, taken by surprise, crossed himself as the troll man cart-wheeled down the hall, tossing handfuls of nuts from his pouch whenever he came upright again.

The angular figure that followed was dressed in a mockery of women's clothing, apron pinned to its shoulders by two horseshoes, bedecked in necklaces of garlic and onions, swathed in patched shawls. A tawdry veil was tied low over its forehead, and pillows had been stuffed under the tunic to provide an ample bosom, but no attempt had been made to hide the mummer's bristling red beard.

"Perchta, Perchta," came the shout, "sweep the dark away!"

Perchta glowered around her and hobbled into the hall, one hand grasping the spindle thrust through her belt as if it had been a sword, with the other grasping an upended broom as if it were a staff.

"Why should I?" she replied in a cracked voice. "Lazy

fools, all of ye—leave yer harness unpolished and yer spinning undone! I know you—" She flourished her broom at one of the feasters, a young cousin of Ordwini's who was here for the first time. "Tumble the girls and leave 'em weeping, eh? Cut off yer shaft, I will, and then you'll leave 'em alone!"

The young man, his face crimson, suppressed a move to protect his crotch while his companions roared with laughter. Gundohar frowned, for it seemed to him he had heard some tale of this lad and a Roman girl. The broom swept along the board, sending horns and trenchers rolling to the floor. Cackling, Perchta continued her awkward progress around the room, peppering her complaints with remarks that more often than not seemed to have meaning as well as malice. No one dared object to the insults flung out in the Yuletide mumming; if the chieftains were wise, they would take note of the sins which their people had picked out to parody. What was a cause for laughter at Yule could mean a knife in the dark by Midsummer if someone did not make amends.

Gundohar braced himself as Perchta limped up to the dais. For a moment she frowned up at him, then she made an abortive jab at his groin with the broom.

"Don't need to take yours away—ye don't use it! Need a good fat wife to warm yer bones!"

"Well, mother, shall I take you to my bed?" he replied, and heard approval in the laughter as she swore and turned away. But he had also heard the warning

Another group pushed through the door and Gundohar straightened, for although the noise had not abated, suddenly there was a shift in the quality of the attention. The troll servant had always been of questionable origins, and Christian fulminations against the evils of the goddesses had clouded Perchta's native brightness, but the figure they escorted was even now of a nobler kind, though perhaps the one above all whom the priests would rather have

classed with the demons their procession had been intended
to banish.

They had robed him in pieces of Roman silk cobbled
together with gold thread, from his shoulders dragged a
cloak of yew green wool, its patches embroidered over with
fruit and flowers. A wig and beard of fleece completed the
disguise, with a holly crown. He came leaning on a staff
bound with ribbons and ivy and sprouting stalks of golden
grain, and gradually the cacophony resolved itself into
song—

> *"Wish rides from the wood,*
> *Brings his sack of food,*
> *Knocks on every door,*
> *Giving to the poor . . ."*

"Hail, Yulefather!" Gislahar splashed mead into his horn
and ran down to offer it. Gundohar nodded his permission
as men picked up his royal chair and set it down between
two of the braziers that warmed the hall.

> *"He brings to those who lack,*
> *A bulging sack,*
> *To those who will not share,*
> *A storeroom bare!*
> *So give us meat and ale also,*
> *Halli, halli, halli, hallo. . . ."*

The Yulefather eased into the chair with a grateful sigh,
and no wonder, thought the king, for by the time they got
here the mummers had danced through every street in Borbetomagus, and drunk at every door.

"And what will you give us, good father, if we feed your
folk well?" asked the men who clustered around him.

Yulefather's laughter seemed to bubble up from somewhere around his toes, shaking his belly, quivering in each
hair of his beard. "I give you what you wish, eh? For I am

Wish"—he leaned forward confidentially—"but you have to know what you really want before you can ask. . . ."

Gundohar glimpsed movement from the corner of his eye and turned to see his brother Hagano on his feet and staring. Step by step, his usual deliberate tread wavering as if he were being drawn against his will, Hagano came around the table and down to where the old man sat throned between the fires. Curious, the king followed him.

"So, son of Grimahild." Yulefather looked Hagano up and down and the other men drew back, whispering. "Shall I teach you how to choose?"

His wreath had slid down over one eye. It ought to have looked ridiculous, but the mummer's dignity lent an unexpected splendor to his robes. The old man looked from Hagano to Gundohar, standing behind him, and once more he laughed.

"Bright brother, shadow brother! You must give my gifts to each other if you will not take them from me! You want to see your way?" he said to Hagano. "This one has vision—" He nodded, astonishingly, toward Gundohar, then fixed the king with his single gaze. "And you, teller of tales, you want to sing about heroes? Your brother is a hero—you will praise him, and maybe one day sing your own deeds too. . . ." His gaze grew suddenly somber, and Gundohar shivered.

"My dreams do not matter," he answered quietly. "My deeds must serve those to whom my vows are sworn."

The old man looked at him and shook his head. "Burgund king, what else does a hero do?"

Gundohar was still seeking an answer when Godo thrust past him, offering a brimming mead-horn. Yulefather's gaze brightened as he reached out for it, and in another moment he was laughing again.

Hagano looked at his brother, snagged another horn from one of the warriors, drank deeply, then held it out to him.

"Thank you—" said Gundohar, gulping down the fiery

honey of the mead. As it began to burn in his belly he sighed and passed it to Hagano again. Another drink like that and he would be tipsy. The more he thought about it, the better that idea seemed. He took Hagano's arm and led him toward the end of the hall where the mead-vats were waiting.

Behind him he could hear shouts of laughter as the Yule-father answered Godo's question. There was more merriment as the others came up for their prophecies.

"Good mead—" said Hagano, an unaccustomed brightness growing in his eye.

"Very. Let's drink some more of it," said Gundohar. "Poly—politically a good thing for the lads to see we can drink like men!"

And maybe if he drank enough, he would forget the vision that for a moment had flowered from the old man's words, not of Airmanareik, but of himself and Hagano, battling a horde of Hun warriors who came on and on.

Presently he heard the mummers preparing to depart, but he did not turn. As they went out they began to sing again—

> *"Man of the Holy Night,*
> *Bring us back the light;*
> *Join with kith and kin,*
> *Joy to all within. . . ."*

Chapter 6 ✶ Warrior Wooing

Castra Raetica
Summer and Winter and Summer Again, A.D. 430–431

At the beginning of summer, when the cattle had been driven to the hill pastures, the armies began to gather. In Tolosa the Visigoths polished their armor and scouted the roads to Arelas. In Ravenna, Flavius Aetius argued with supply clerks and flattered the empress. On the plain between the Danu and the Tisia, Hun horsemen exercised their swift ponies in maneuvers of increasing complexity. And in Borbetomagus, the Burgund king spent long hours in the practice yard, toughening the muscles of his bad leg so they would bear him into battle once more.

Eggtide Moon was nearing its end when the first Hun horsemen galloped up the road from the river to tell them that Attila was near.

"My sister is well?" asked Gundohar, leading the way toward the horse lines. It had rained the night before and the ground was muddy. As they passed the smithy he picked up a pole to use as a staff; his thigh was still aching from a practice session he had continued too long the day before and he dared not risk a fall.

"She is well enough when last I saw her," said Attila, walking with his odd, rolling gait beside him. Gundohar jabbed his staff into the soft ground. Bowlegged though Attila might be, he moved with a compact efficiency that had made the Burgund feel gawky even before Waldhari lamed him.

"She quickened to me, did you know, but she lost the child," his brother-in-law continued. "Ereka, my senior wife, nursed her. I wintered farther east, did not see her again until the wild geese winged north. I give her now a household in Lentia on the border, as the marriage treaty says. She has wisdom, your sister. She will serve me well."

Gundohar blinked, a little taken aback by this business-like approach to marriage. Perhaps it was custom among the Huns. He remembered how, even while she denied him her bed, Brunahild had been careful to fulfill all the public duties of a queen. The memory gave him less pain than he had expected. Like his leg, with time and good management, even his heart might heal.

Clouds lay heavy on the forested hills beyond the river, but over Borbetomagus they were parting to admit a little watery sunshine. Moisture steamed in thin curls from the drying ground. Scents of soil and growing things, and as they approached the pens, the rich smell of horses, weighted the wind. The king drew a deep breath. He was beginning to have a good feeling about the coming campaign. Even the air smelled wealthy.

"We put the big Tolosan mares we got five seasons ago to heavier northern stallions," he told Attila. "The colts from the first breeding are just coming now into the battle line. They have their mothers' speed, but more sense, and they can go longer on poorer feed. I think they will do well for us—the men of my house-guard are pleased with them."

Attila grunted. Gundohar felt a little foolish, boasting to a Hun of horses, but what he had said was true. They could see the proud heads of the young animals lifting above the poles of the horse yards to watch them.

Hold your heads high, my beauties, thought the king, *it is the Lord of Horses himself who comes to look at you.*

They came to the fence. The horses shied away, and then, when the newcomers only stood there, came sidling back, whuffling curiously. A sleek chestnut mare with a creamy mane and tail paused before Attila, nostrils flaring. He blew back at her, murmuring something in his own language, and Gundohar saw the wariness fade from her eyes. The khan reached out and began to scratch her head where the short hair grew in a rough whorl beneath her forelock, and the mare pressed against his hand.

Gundohar had a moment to wonder if Gudrun, too, had been tamed by a breath and a few words of the horseman's tongue; it was an oddly disturbing notion. But Attila was already beginning to evaluate the points of the horses, identifying a possible weakness in the pastern of one, praising the deep chest of another, and the thought was forgotten.

"So, on the whole, you like them?" he said at last. "I hope the Visigoths do not regret their horse-trading when stock of their own breeding comes charging down on them."

"Do not fear—" said Attila, giving a last pat to the mare. "You ride east, not west this year. Aetius has orders for me. He waited till now in Ravenna because the empress sends to make peace with his old enemy Bonifatius. But now Gaiseric has penned the Roman up in the city of Hippo, so Aetius thinks he can leave. He means to wait for Tolosans at Arelas, and wants me and my riders with him there. You and your warriors are to face the Juthungi in Raetia."

That summer, as Gundohar and his warriors hunted Juthungi rebels through the foothills of the great mountains, he thought with longing of the rich plains of Aquitanica. Supplies arrived regularly, but this enemy offered little in the way of plunder, and as for a bride, he was unlikely to find a lady out here who would meet with the approval of his counselors.

But he had to admit that the Commander of Armies understood how to use the forces at his disposal. The Juthungi were a forest folk, their steadings tucked into hidden valleys and folds in the land where watercourses came down from the mountains. In such country, the Hun horsemen would have been wasted.

In this terrain warriors were needed who could find a path through the woods without losing their way, who understood which berries and mushrooms could be eaten safely, who could extend their rations by tracking game. And above all, they must be men who would not panic when shut away from the open sky. But the king, bumping along on his stout hill pony, could not help regretting those fine half-Tolosan horses.

The Juthungi were descended from folk who had lived here long before the Romans pushed northward from Italia, mixed with tag ends of every tribe that had passed through since then. The Burgunds burned villages, but if the inhabitants escaped them, even their woodscraft was not sufficient to catch men who knew every deer trail and forest pool. There would be a few weeks of peace, and then the surviving Juthungi would regroup and make another foray against the villas of the plain.

Gundohar could not entirely blame them. When the tide of Roman conquest swept around them they had been given little choice in becoming part of the Empire. But he had cast his own lot with the Romans, and could not afford sympathy. And so the inconclusive warfare continued.

From time to time word from the west would reach them. Hagano, acting as regent for his brother in Borbetomagus, was developing a fine network of informants. They heard that Theoderid's war-bands had taken the familiar road to Arelas, only to find Aetius and a Hun army waiting for them. This year the Master of Gallia was pursuing the war with unusual efficiency. There were rumors that the empress contemplated sending a force to rescue Bonifatius. No doubt Aetius meant to leave the land secure behind him if he had to make a sudden return to defend his own interests in Ravenna.

For a while, then, the fighting in Gallia seemed as confused as it was in Raetia. Then a message came that Aetius had captured the Visigoth's commander, Theoderid's eldest son.

"That will settle them," said the tribune who was serving as liaison and advisor to Gundohar's forces. "They say the old man dotes on his sons. And this one is his heir. Mark my words, we'll see a settlement before harvest."

Gundohar sighed, wishing he had been able to bring his own campaign to as tidy a conclusion. And yet, though they had not succeeded in destroying the Juthungi, their patrols had seriously impeded rebel efforts to disturb the Romans. No doubt Aetius would find a way to make that, too, sound like a victory.

If the Roman commander painted a rosy picture in his dispatches to the empress, his messages to his Burgund allies were more realistic. The Juthungi had been suppressed, but would require watching. Gundohar was therefore directed to keep his men under arms and establish winter quarters in Castra Raetica. And while Aetius could not command that he himself stay with them, the advisability of his presence was strongly implied.

It was by no means so clear to Gundohar. However less official rumors held that the Master of Gallia himself would be passing through Raetia on his way home, and the Burgund king put off his own departure from week to week, hoping to speak with him. Around the equinox, the golden days of summer gave way to sudden storms alternating with days whose heat failed quickly when night fell. New white glimmered on the peaks that floated above the horizon, the lower slopes of the mountains blazed bronze and gold.

Then came a day when the wind seemed to blow straight off the snowfields, severing dry leaves from the oak trees and piercing like elfshot through every gap in one's clothes. Gundohar's lamed leg stiffened; he winced with every step and wondered if they could get the legionary baths going again. The hypocaust in the old commander's quarters did not work either. He was trying to warm himself at a brazier that had been set up inside when he heard trumpets. Excitement shocked through him and he forgot the cold.

He limped out onto the broad porch that faced toward the city gate, shading his eyes with his hand. It was Aetius for certain, the Roman standards that went before him flashing in the sun and horsetails tossing behind him as the Huns trotted after. But the procession, however well turned out, was not a long one. Gundohar sighed. He had hoped the commander would be bringing a force to relieve him.

He noted the bright cloaks of the officers, the wagons of the baggage train. One of them, he was surprised to see, had a tentlike canopy. It was a light, two-wheeled traveling wagon such as women might ride in, or a wounded officer. His household was gathering around him. Without taking his eyes from the newcomers, he gave orders for food and drink to be prepared. With an inward flicker of relief he recognized Aetius, his face bronzed by a summer's campaigning. If the commander had fallen ill, things would have been difficult indeed.

Gundohar adjusted the draping of his cloak and went down the steps to meet him. The cavalcade drew up in front of the building. Aetius swung a leg over his mount's neck and slid to the ground.

"My lord, you are welcome—" Gundohar reminded himself he was the host here, a king on his own land. "Come in and be warm. My people are preparing a place for your men. If you have sick"—he glanced toward the wagon—"there is a guesthouse next to the kitchens where they may be tended."

"That will indeed be useful," said Aetius, smiling oddly, "but we are all in health. The wagon carries a hostage. We gave Theoderid back his son and got in exchange a daughter, Galamvara."

Gundohar's gaze went back to the wagon. As it rumbled to a halt the curtain shivered, then was drawn back by a white hand. A face appeared, lightly freckled, her shawl framing red-brown hair. For a moment a pair of hazel eyes held his own, then the lady withdrew behind her curtains once more.

"Who—" The king coughed and tried it again. "Who is going to keep her for you?"

"That's not been decided." Aetius's eyes sparkled suddenly. "I was thinking that if I could persuade that bishop of yours down in Batava to spend the winter in Raetica and be her guardian, I might leave her here. . . ."

And thus, without ever having formally agreed to it, Gundohar found the Lady Galamvara and his uncle, Bishop Peregrinus, added to his household. After a time he sent word to Hagano that he would be wintering on the Danuvius after all. But that was the extent of his participation. If they were expecting him to court the lady, they would be disappointed. Royal marriages were made by go-betweens and counselors, and in any case, she had been entrusted to him to guard, not woo.

Galamvara was a neat, self-contained person, of no overwhelming beauty, but well-made and well-mannered. She dwelt in the guesthouse but took her meals with the king's household, where she held up her end of the converse with grace and wit. Gundohar found himself becoming uncharacteristically silent when she was there. His men teased and said he did not like her, but that was not the problem.

The king had been willing to consider a wife as a hypothetical provision in a treaty of alliance. But faced with this living woman, Gundohar became appallingly aware of his own deficiencies. How could a healthy woman accept a man past his first youth who walked like a lamed crane? What intelligent woman would marry a man whose first queen had killed herself rather than stay married to him? What decent woman would go into one bed with a man who had had to force himself on his wife the last time they lay together—and who had been unable to approach any woman sexually thereafter?

In the long watches of the night Gundohar wished he

had defied Aetius and gone home to Borbetomagus. He wished he had gone off to Britannia when Hengest the Anglian was recruiting men to serve as mercenaries for the British high king. He wished he had died with Brunahild.

By day, the Burgund king went hunting.

It was a good year for red deer, numerous because men had been too busy killing each other to hunt them, fat from feeding in trampled fields. The royal table had never been so well supplied. Gundohar went out even when no food was needed, seeking beasts for their pelts with the excuse that the winters were colder here than in Borbetomagus. But he did not care whether he came home with game, only that he returned exhausted.

It was inevitable, he thought afterward, that one day, a little past Yule, his bad leg should betray him on the icy ground, and they would bring him home on a hurdle alongside the dead deer.

But Gundohar had not expected the shock to his system to lay him open to a rheum that confined him to his bed, or that Galamvara, with an efficiency worthy of a daughter of warleaders, would take charge of the sickroom. If the fever was another defense against her, he thought in his more lucid moments, his body had no wisdom, for the longer he lay ill, the more vulnerable he became.

The king is hunting. Dimly he remembers that when he started out the day was warm and fair. Now clouds shadow the heavens, and darkness pools beneath the trees. It seems to him that the trail he follows once was clear; now undergrowth chokes the forest, and only an occasional track shows him his way. His legs ache with weariness from so long a pursuit and each breath burns in his breast. But he cannot stop running.

He has almost caught up with the creature he follows. He can hear her breathing, as labored as his own. He flails at the encircling vines.

"Please—" His own voice sounds very far away. "Wait for me!"

With an effort that leaves him gasping he breaks free. A dark shape wavers before him, veiled in dark hair, weeping.

"Forgive me," *he whispers, "I loved you. . . ." He reaches, grasps not hair but black feathers that come away in his hand.*

For a moment the face that turns to him is a woman's, a pale mask alight with a terrible beauty. Then it changes, and it is not a mouth but a raven's beak that gapes wide. The bird launches itself toward him. Dark wings expand to blot out the world, and he screams as the black beak stabs him to the heart.

"Gundohar!" The voice that called him was gentle, the hands that gripped his face soft but firm. "Gundohar, wake now. It is only a dream!"

He fought for air, and with each breath, agony stabbed his breast.

"Dear God, he is burning up!" He felt her movement, and then a blessed coolness upon his brow. "Be still now, my lord—lie still. . . ."

Gradually his racing heartbeat stilled. If he breathed shallowly, it did not hurt so much, and presently he was able to make out that he lay in his own bed, and the woman sitting beside him was Galamvara. The air had that stillness that comes in the deeps of the night. The flicker of lamplight showed him they were alone.

"Why . . . are you with me?" he whispered at last.

"You have the lung-fever. You are not in danger if properly cared for, but just now there is no one I would trust to watch you." Her words were calm, but he could see shadows beneath her eyes. And yet, though her blunt features at best might be called pleasant, at that moment to him she seemed beautiful.

"You are honest with me." He tried to smile. "Thank you."

She colored a little. "I am always truthful. Some call it a failing."

He drew a careful breath. "Not to a king." *Even Hagano,* he thought wryly, *only tells me what he thinks I ought to know.*

"Not to some kings." Galamvara flushed again, and Gundohar had a sudden intimation of why Theoderid had chosen this daughter to give as hostage. She poured tea from

the pitcher into a beaker and set it to his lips. "Drink this—
it will help to clear your lungs."

"It had better," he answered, grimacing, when he had
gotten the nasty stuff down. "I don't want to drink any more
of it than I have to. You are skilled in the sickroom."

"More with wounds than with fevers, though I have
nursed both. My husband never came away from a battle
without a gash somewhere about him for me to tend. The
last one was to the head," she added dryly, "and beyond
my skill."

Gundohar looked up at her, frowning. He had not known
she had been married. "I am sorry," he said finally.

She shrugged. "There is no need. We were only married
a few years, and he loved his sword and his war steed more
than he did me. I think that both our hearts bear battle
scars—" She looked down at him. "Who is the woman who
has wounded you so deeply that you shrink from a gentle
touch and cry out in your dreams?"

Gundohar jerked as if it were she who had stabbed him.
"I think . . . that is more honesty than I asked for!" He tried
to laugh, but her gaze held him.

"Until you have spoken it I think you will not rest easily."

She wants truth . . . he thought in confusion. *I ran away when
I thought she was a highborn maiden who would scorn me . . . but this
is a woman who can show me my soul. . . .* That ought to have
made him even more afraid, but something in the depths
of his spirit quickened to her challenge, as once it had on
the Longstone field.

"Galamvara," he said painfully, "I am in your hands, with
no defenses. I will speak, but I make a condition. When
you know the truth of me, say, with the same honesty I
gave you, if you will have me for a husband."

Her fair skin was truly crimson now. She started to speak,
but he shook his head.

"Only one woman ever had that power to hurt me, because there has only been one woman I ever loved, and
that was my wife, Brunahild. And I gave her good reason,

for she was a wild mare of the steppes, a raven of the skies, and I imprisoned her in Roman walls. Her faith was given to another man, and I forced them both into treachery. For nine years we tormented one another—" The words poured from him now that he had begun—all the anguished tale of Sigfrid and Brunahild, until she stabbed herself on her lover's funeral pyre.

"And so in the end I killed them," he whispered, "though my hand touched neither the sword nor the spear. But I bear the blood-guilt, and there is no one to whom I can pay weregild and be free."

Gundohar broke off, coughing, and she gave him more of the herbal brew. It loosened the phlegm in his chest, and as he lay back again it seemed to him that she had been right, and the confession had released something else, less tangible but more constricting. For a time he lay still, unable to speak, and Galamvara was silent as well.

"Something of this," she said finally, "I had heard, and I wondered. The tale of the death of Sigfrid Fafnarsbane has spread far. I see now that love can be more deadly than hatred. I am no priest to absolve you—" She bit her lip, but her gaze came steadily to his once more. "But I come of a royal clan, and know how to endure the sins of kings. If my father will consent to it, I will be your queen."

Gundohar's pent breath went out of him in a long sigh. For a moment she looked alarmed, but he managed to reach out and take her hand. And yet, even as joy and amazement warred within him, it occurred to him that it was neither Galamvara nor her father who would have to give permission for this marriage, but Aetius.

Whether it was love or Galamvara's herbal brews that cured him, from that night onward Gundohar recovered quickly. But he found that his return to physical health created new problems. Where before he had avoided Galamvara for fear he would repel her, now he feared to frighten her with too much love. At least he supposed that love was what he was feeling, though it was nothing like the exaltation of hope in which he had sought to win Brunahild, nor the despairing passion with which he had loved her afterward.

A detached observer would not have found his intended fair, but Gundohar took a constant pleasure in watching the deliberate care with which she did all things. When he met her calm gaze he, too, could be at peace. At other times, though, as he waited for the messengers he had sent to the Visigothic king to return, he wondered. He knew himself for a bad bargain as a husband. Was Galamvara taking him out of pity, or did Theoderid's widowed daughter need to escape her father's roof so badly she would have accepted any decent offer? He tried not to let it matter—after Brunahild, he ought to be satisfied with even a pretense of love.

While winter held the land in thrall he stayed more or less content by the fire. But when springtide sent sap bursting from every branch, old desires began to stir in his blood, as incalculable as the rising waters that were whirling the ice of the Danuvius away. But he dared not seek more than the touch of her hand. There were far too many folk around them, from his uncle the bishop to the women who scrubbed the floors, for them to meet in secret, and elopement was not an option for a king. If Gundohar wished to obtain the political advantages that would come with her, he must do nothing that would stain Galamvara's honor or his own.

When it was too wet for riding he walked, knowing that only physical exhaustion would allow him to sleep. From his rambles he would bring his lady small treasures—a speckled egg, a heron's snowy plume, a handful of flowers—and tremble when she smiled. Gundohar found it strange, for he had never thought himself a man of strong passions. He strode along, trembling when the damp breeze brought him the fragrance of apple blossom, laughing at the soaring flight of the lark, weeping at the beauty of its song.

And presently, conceived in springtide's splendor and gestated by those long tramps through the countryside, words began to shape themselves into poetry.

> *"Sun in springtime sweetly smiles,*
> *Frozen earth from ice is freed,*
> *Wind wings each bird to win his bride,*
> *Knowing nothing but his need. . . ."*

It was a beginning. Gundohar laughed at himself, feeling the need that surged within him subtly eased. He would pray to the Frowe for inspiration—folk said she liked love poems. For certain, the Christian god had nothing to do with what he was feeling now. Perhaps, if he could bring the poem to completion, he would even dare to show it to Galamvara.

He was still searching for the next line when he came back through the streets of Castra Raetica and saw a sweated horse with bloodstained saddle steaming before his door.

"The Juthungi are out—" said Sindald, coming down the steps to meet him. "We should have expected it, for we left them precious little to harvest. They've raided two villas in Lucius Alburnus's district—burned the buildings, run off the stock, and carried everything edible away."

Gundohar grunted, struggling with mental calculations involving horses and supplies. The roads were still muddy and it would be heavy going, but they must make some response or the next outbreak would be even more virulent. Absently he blessed those long walks he had been taking, for without them he would not have been in shape for fighting so early in the year.

Galamvara got to her feet when he came into the hall, her face a little pale, but composed.

"I have set your servant to readying your gear and armor,"

she said softly, "and Unald is gathering the men. I thought that was what you would want done."

"Indeed it was!" he said warmly. "And you are a jewel among women." He saw her flush as he kissed her hand. But now men were bombarding him with requests and information; he turned to answer a question, and when he looked again for Galamvara, she had gone.

The evening was hectic with preparations, but that night, Gundohar slept without dreams.

By the time they heard from Aetius, the Burgunds had been campaigning for a moon. As a postscript at the end of a letter otherwise entirely devoted to military matters, the commander had added a note to the effect that he approved of Gundohar's projected marriage in principle, but of course any formal arrangements would have to wait until the conclusion of the summer's campaign.

Gundohar, reading this by the light of a fire somewhere in the sub-Alpine forest, grinned mirthlessly. The Master of Gallia was a fox, using whatever came to hand to ensure his ally's loyalty. He supposed he ought to feel insulted that Aetius did not think his pledged word sufficient to make him pursue this war, but no one expected a Roman to understand honor.

But by now, the king's interest in the task of controlling the rebels, as well as his honor, were engaged. Better supplied and armed than their enemies, the Burgunds were gradually burning out the last pockets of resistance. It was hard luck for the Juthungi that their bodies must pave Gundohar's road to his bride.

That summer the Burgunds reaped a bloody harvest in the Juthungi fields. When folk in more fortunate lands were threshing heads of grain, the heads of rebel chieftains were being lopped to adorn the gate of Castra Raetica. If the Romans thought the display barbaric, the message was quite clear to the tribes.

Although Gundohar, as his uncle the bishop pointed out to him, had served only seven months, instead of seven years, to win his bride, he was rewarded by a message from Ostrofrid. Theoderid had sent to the Burgunds a formal offer of treaty and alliance, to be sealed by the gift of his daughter's hand. The tented cart was brought out of storage and refurbished with a new canopy of crimson felt ornamented with tassels of gold. Galamvara, while observing that red had never been her best color, had to agree that it should make a definite statement to anyone within view.

They journeyed through a land of ripe apples and golden corn. At every steading they passed, folk cheered them. Gundohar had not realized how sharply they felt the lack of a queen. And yet, the closer they got to Borbetomagus, the more anxious he became. He told himself that he should have married Galamvara in the spring, when his blood had been warmed by the returning sun. It was not that he had ceased to love her, he thought as they left from the old palace below the Holy Hill to begin the last leg of their journey, but rather that during a summer spent entirely in the company of men, the understanding that had begun to grow between them had been lost.

When Galamvara pushed aside the tent flap to view the countryside, he saw a stranger. Was he making a mistake in marrying—again? The political and dynastic arguments for such an alliance which had been discussed in council were still valid. But then his council had encouraged him to marry Brunahild. The fact was that with every turn of the road, he was remembering more clearly how he had brought his first bride home.

By the time they reached Borbetomagus, he hardly dared look into Galamvara's eyes.

But among his people, rejoicing was universal. There was no royal lady to greet the new bride, but Ordwini had brought his household to the city for the occasion, and his wife did her best to make Galamvara feel welcome. It was with relief that Gundohar let the women carry her away.

He himself submitted to the teasing of Godo and Gislahar with as much patience as he could muster. The bride was an Arian Christian, and the treaty stipulated that she should be married in that faith, which delighted Father Severian. Fortunately both sects of Christianity provided that a second marriage be celebrated with less pomp than a first.

Gundohar himself had only one order to give his household. He ordered the royal quarters to be moved to the other side of the courtyard. A new bed was constructed, with new hangings. They thought it was to honor his bride, but in truth, the king could think of nothing more likely to destroy his chances of happiness with Galamvara than to begin his marriage to her in the bed he had shared with Brunahild.

"Well, brother," Hagano's voice, soft as ever but with that edge that always suggested mockery, sounded in Gundohar's ear. "We have gotten you married once more. I wish you joy."

The wedding had been celebrated earlier in the evening, as was the custom among the Arians. Galamvara, unbecomingly flushed beneath her crimson veil, sat next to him, watching the chieftains who had come to feast them. On her other side, Ordwini was discussing the North African news with Ostrofrid. The empress had sent Aspar to aid Bonifatius and the Vandals had defeated them both. Now Gaiseric held Hippo, and with it the Province. At the news of his old rival's downfall, Aetius was said to have danced with glee.

Satisfied that his bride's attention was on the conversation, the king turned to his brother. "Don't you approve?"

"Well, she is not Brunahild . . ."

Gundohar twitched. "You wanted this marriage, all of you!" he said in a low voice. "Let me be—I will do the best I can."

Hagano touched his arm. "I meant that kindly. This bride is a very different woman from your last."

"But I am the same man—" Gundohar replied, reaching for his goblet and taking a long swallow of wine. The meats had been cleared away, and they were nibbling on sweet cakes. "Just at this moment I am wondering if I am fit to marry anyone."

"You are king of the Burgunds." Hagano's grip tightened. "You will do what you must . . . and for what it is worth"— his words became a whisper—"you have my loyalty . . . and my love."

Gundohar placed his hand over that of his brother. "I think that is worth a great deal."

Hagano sighed. For a moment they sat thus, while the other conversations eddied around them. Ordwini, seeing his king's attention otherwise engaged, had drawn the new queen into the conversation.

"They say that your father has been making overtures to the Suevi in Hispania. Does that mean he has given up on conquering Arelas?"

"I hope so," Galamvara answered him. "I would be grieved if my husband should have to face my father in arms."

"I do not believe he would have given you to our king if he had expected that," Ordwini said kindly. "There are rumors that he is looking southward for new lands, across the Pyrenees."

"Everything is changing," said Ostrofrid petulantly. "When will they all cease wandering about and settle down!"

"As we have?" Ordwini laughed.

"Why not?" the old man replied. "I was born in lands now ruled by the Huns. I do not even know who tills the soil that holds my father's bones, and no one knows where those of my grandfather lie. But when my time comes, my grandsons will pour out the offerings on my howe. That is how a land is claimed, by giving it our blood and our bones!"

"And by breeding children to hold it!" Ordwini grinned at Gundohar. "Well, my lord—we have drunk your health and feasted you. Our celebration is almost over, and it is time for yours to begin! You have waited patiently, but I think it is time for the bedding—what do you say, men? Shall we sing the bride and bridegroom to their chamber now?"

There was a roar of approbation, and Gundohar felt his skin chill. Galamvara shot him a quick glance, then looked away, her face flaming. It had needed only Ordwini's word to set things in motion. He sent a quick glance of appeal to Hagano, who shrugged as if to say that in this battle he could be of no assistance. Then the others, laughing, dragged him off while the women did the same to his bride.

Gundohar poured himself a goblet of the sweet wine that had been left in the royal chamber and drank it swiftly down. *Oh my mother,* he thought ruefully. *Where are your love potions now when I have need of them?* Galamvara, sitting up in the great bed, drew the coverlet around her and frowned. *She is wondering if she has married a drunkard* . . . thought Gundohar.

"I am sorry—" he began, but could think of no more words. Galamvara raised one eyebrow.

"But why? You have done nothing—" she said softly.

"That is why—" He slammed the goblet down. "And now I am wondering if I can. . . .It is nothing in you—" he answered her look. "I do not think the Frowe herself could stir me now. If we had married in Castra Raetica it might have been different. But here—" He shook his head. "You demanded truth from me, Galamvara, and I will tell you. Here, Brunahild still holds me in thrall—" He stared at the wall.

There was a short silence. Then he heard her sigh. "I wondered if it might be that, when you were so cold to me. Put out the lamps, Gundohar, and come to bed. Perhaps the flesh will have a magic of its own to undo this spell."

As always, the calm in her voice eased him. When he

lay down in the great bed beside her, Galamvara kissed him, and he took her in his arms. She was good to hold, warm and firm of flesh, and there was some sweet scent in her hair. But though Gundohar found peace in her arms, he did not feel desire. For a time he caressed her, but it made no difference—neither his hands on her body, nor hers on his own.

When he began to weep, she gathered him against her breast and stroked his hair.

"Never mind, never mind—" she said softly when he was still at last. "They say Queen Venus is the most fickle of deities. When you have healed, our time will come. For now, it makes me happy just to hold you, Gundohar. It is a good thing to cling close to someone you love when you have slept for long alone."

He lifted his head, though he could not see her features in the dark. "Do you love me?"

"Unwise for a princess, I know," she laughed a little shakily. "But it is true."

Gundohar eased down again beside her with a sigh. "Galamvara my wife," he whispered into her hair, "before the gods I swear that I love you as well, and whatever is in my power to give, you shall have."

He heard her breath catch, and her arms tightened around him. "Then hold me! My first husband used my body, but in three years of marriage, there was never a word of love. When he was done, he would roll away and snore until morning."

Gundohar gave a grunt of laughter. He straightened a little so that her cheek was on his shoulder. "Brunahild flung many insults at my head," he said softly. "But she never said I snored! Sleep, my beloved, and I will guarantee to hold you till the dawn."

Chapter 7 ❧ The Hunter

Hun Territories
Hunter's Moon, A.D. 433

Gudrun sat in the sunshine in front of her house in Lentia, wool flowing between her fingers into a taut strand while the herb seller spread out her wares. She was a woman of some Gallic tribe, left behind here when her people moved on and surviving because of her expertise. The names she gave the plants were often unfamiliar, but Gudrun recognized many she had seen in her mother's collection. She listened intently, memorizing the words so that another time she would know what to ask for. She had no time for herb gathering, beyond a few things that would grow in her garden. But ever since Sunnilda had been so ill with the cough last winter Gudrun had known she must get together a selection of basic cures.

From here she could see most of the settlement. She had been happy here, even though Lentia was hardly the noble establishment implied by her marriage contract, consisting of a few timber houses clustered in the semicircle carved out of the forest beside the river landing, with an additional open space for the Huns to pitch their *gers*. She and Sunnilda slept in the largest of the houses with the Iazyge girl Bala, who tended the child. One of the buildings was occupied by her women, under the direction of Locris, and another by Ecgward and the dozen men of her guard. Other buildings served as weaving sheds or for storage. For a while

119

there had been a priest, sent to her by Bishop Peregrinus, but when he died of a fever she did not replace him. She had had enough of gods.

The ground sloped gently down to the river. The reeds on the farther shore merged into the autumn mists. The plain on the other side was a dim memory. To either side the river curved away between stands of trees. Sometimes she felt as if she might as well have stayed in her house in the forest, as if Lentia were the only island of humanity remaining in a wilderness of wood and water.

But then would come one of the seasonal festivals when the folk gathered to trade, to arrange marriages, and to ask Gudrun to judge disputes that arose between clans or that could not be settled within a family. These people were used to respecting their clan mothers, so perhaps the way they had accepted her was not so strange. The first time she did so, Attila had been with her, making it clear that she spoke with his authority. But it had been almost two winters since she had seen him. She no longer thought about the way he made everyone around him come alive: She could pretend, even, that her body was her own.

It was quiet here now. She sighed, thinking that she had lost track of what the herb woman was saying, then realized that the old woman was still, listening.

"What is it?" Gudrun frowned.

"Horses—many horses coming—the earth tells me—" The herb seller set her palm to the earth. "It is the horse-lords." She sat back and began to gather up her wares.

Bala twitched nervously as she always did when Hun warriors were near. Gudrun patted her hand, then turned to the herb seller.

"Wait—I want some of the yearwe and the white willow. Give them to Locris and she will pay you." She bundled up her spinning. Now even she could hear something like distant thunder. At the edge of the village dogs began to bark.

"And blood-mint?" The herb seller smirked up at her.

Gudrun flushed. Did the whole countryside think that she

had intentionally miscarried Attila's child? But she need not worry this time. Queen Ereka herself, guarding the rights of her own sons, had made sure that if the occasion arose again, Gudrun had the herbs she would require. A beautiful, wise, and ruthless lady was Attila's first queen. Gudrun was glad she lived at the other end of the Hunnish lands.

"You heard me—" She stuffed her work into the basket and stood up.

Hoofbeats sounded clearly as a single rider galloped into view, no doubt a messenger. People were popping out of the houses, the whole place awakening from its autumn peace. By that alone, Gudrun thought ruefully, she should have known that Attila was near.

The Roman, Aetius, was with him. Gudrun eyed him curiously as she dealt with the problems of food and lodging. He looked older; his usual bland assurance a little blunted. She wondered what was wrong. Much of what they needed the Huns had brought with them, but the Roman would lie in her house while Sunnilda and Bala slept with the other women and she herself went to Attila in his *ger*, and it must be readied. There were sheep to slaughter for the feasting, and amphorae of wine to roll out from the storehouse.

Attila had brought a dozen men of note besides his escort of warriors, among them Rudegar, who greeted her enthusiastically, full of stories about his wife and his daughter, who was growing husband-high, but too finicky to accept any of the matches he had proposed for her.

"I ask her what she is waiting for—a hero out of legend?" The waves of grizzled beard quivered as he laughed.

I did, thought Gudrun. "Then she had better plan to live in a legend as well," she smiled sourly. "Heroes do not fare well at the courts of kings."

"If I can give Diedelinda to a good man who will love her, I will be satisfied," said Rudegar.

Even that may not be enough to keep her safe, thought Gudrun, but she said no more.

* * *

"You will serve us tonight," said her husband in one of the few moments they were alone. "Do not ask questions. Aetius takes refuge here—last year he had Felix killed, who was the empress's favorite. She made him Master of all the Empire's soldiers and Consul of Roma, but she did not like it. She called on Visigoths—the comitatus that took oath to her when she was married to Adaulf—to drive him out. Aetius goes first to his estates to wait until once more she needs him. But now Bonifatius is back from Africa—"

Gudrun nodded, remembering what she had heard before. "Aetius's old enemy."

"The friend of Galla Placidia. She gives him all of Aetius's titles and makes him the Patrician of Roma. So Aetius thinks it wise to winter with me."

His lips twitched beneath the trailing moustache. Attila, at least, had not changed. He was a shade greyer perhaps, and a little more sinewy. Gudrun watched his strong fingers unknotting a baggage strap and shivered.

"Will you help him regain power?"

"When the time is right. Bonifatius could not hold Africa. I do not think he will hold Italia. But Aetius has to pay for our help. When he finds the right price, we move."

Gudrun looked at him, wondering if this was how men who ruled empires had to think, or whether it was only the Huns who put self-interest above loyalty. She had always believed that Aetius was Attila's friend.

"Tomorrow we go north, hunting," Attila said, getting to his feet again. "You will come with us."

Gudrun shook her head. "It has been awhile since I did much riding. I would not last out the day. I will stay and make things ready for your return."

"No. We may not come back this way. You can rest after I have got you with child."

Her eyes widened as she realized it had not been a request but an order. She started to protest, but though he did not touch her, there was something in his face that stilled the words. She could feel the heat of his body, and as she thought about how he would use her this night and every night until he went away again, she felt the traitorous responses of her own body awakening once more.

Wind gusted through the branches, bringing with it a spattering of moisture from wet leaves, or perhaps it was more rain. The booming of the drums the Huns used to drive game echoed hollow from somewhere up ahead, like distant thunder. Gudrun dropped the rein to pull her cap down, then grabbed for it as the mare she rode sidled nervously. For the hunt, she had dressed in the clothes Hun women wore for riding—a lapped, fur-lined tunic over breeches, and a pointed hat with earflaps that tied under the chin. It was warmer than riding in women's clothes, but the wind was probing with icy fingers.

For two weeks the hunting party had worked its way northward, riding, and resting, and making a hunt where they found plentiful game. Sometimes they stayed in tent camps, and sometimes they guested with families that had carved farmsteads out of these hills. She almost hoped for pregnancy so that he would let her go home. Her courses were late, but until she was certain she dared not tell him. That morning it had seemed better to ride with the hunters than to wait with the servants to be summoned to whatever campsite they had found when evening arrived. But that morning there had been no more than a few clouds hovering on the horizon. Now the storm curdled the sky, darkening the air.

Horsemen crashed through the undergrowth nearby, too intent on the chase to care about the weather; Gudrun held her pony back from following them. Since dawn the circle of beaters had been pushing though the forest, contracting inward, driving before them all the game caught within their deadly sphere. To Gudrun, accustomed to the wild chase after the hounds of her homeland, there was something inhuman in that inevitable constriction. But it was undeniably effective. Anyone waiting within the circle was assured of a clear shot at something. There was even an element of risk, for the noose was not selective, and a hunter might as easily find himself face-to-face with an angry bear or boar as a frightened doe.

Her pony twitched again as the booming of the drums grew louder. *I will wait until the beaters draw near and let them pass me*, she thought as she reined the animal down. *I have no desire to end up in the killing ground.*

Thunder boomed overhead; her mare reared, ripping the reins from her hands. In the next moment two deer exploded through the hazels beside her. As they bounded past the horse stampeded after them. Gudrun slid backward, then managed to grab a handful of black mane. She struggled to pull herself closer to the mare's neck, her long legs clamping the heaving sides. An arrow streaked past her; she crouched low, ceasing the efforts she had been making to stop the animal and urging her to greater speed.

Too late . . . Thoughts flickered like the images that were flashing by. *Now I am the doe. . . .*

The horse ran faster. There were no more arrows, but she glimpsed other shapes, unrecognizable in the gloom, galloping near. They were all around her—the mare must have bolted into the very midst of the hunt.

A sword of light flared, left a tumult of images imprinted on her vision. She saw tossing antlers, but it was a spectral elk that ran beside her, bearing a rider whose face was a skull. Beyond him loped a skeletal stallion, its rider encased in black armor. She had a confused impression of others and of the wolves they followed, was glad the light had not lasted long enough for her to see. She tried to pull up, but the mare was past reason, her breath coming in great whuffling gasps.

Then came the thunder. The horse, driven beyond endurance, stumbled. Gudrun grabbed once more for the mane, but the beast had run out its strength. She felt the animal falter, but could only try to throw herself clear as it went down.

She hit hard, rolling, crashed into a tree trunk and clung there, feeling rather than seeing the Hunt as it swirled past. Once more lightning split the heavens; in that sudden radiance she saw a rider on a horse of ghostly grey. He turned; it was Sigfrid, his tawny hair flying, his eyes alight as they had only been when he was in the forest, running free. She scrambled to her feet, shrieking out his name.

Her cry rang through all the worlds, louder than the thunder. Or perhaps it was only the sound of the hoofbeats returning, circling and slowing, that she heard. Gudrun stood utterly still, her heartbeat outdrumming the hooves. Wind rushed suddenly through the treetops and it grew lighter, as if the clouds had thinned. She heard howling and horncalls, the sounds of the chase seemed to near. But shadow still surrounded her. Only the space just ahead was illuminated, and as she focused on the shapes that filled it she regretted losing the darkness.

But Sigfrid's grey horse was among them. More softly this time, she called him. A cloaked shape slid down from the stallion's back and moved toward her; she strove to make out his features in the gloom. Was this death? Had she broken her neck when the mare went down, and died so swiftly she had not felt the pain? At the thought that she had escaped them all and found Sigfrid again she felt a fierce exultation. She stumbled forward, reaching out to him.

There was a crashing in the undergrowth behind her; a deer leaped past, flanks heaving and nostrils spraying a bloody froth, trailing a tangle of snarling wolves. Gudrun screamed; strong arms closed around her, snatching her out of their path. In another moment one of the wolves had got the deer by the throat and dragged it down.

Gudrun hid her face in the folds of her rescuer's cloak, drawing in the familiar scents of horse and wolfhide in great gasps.

"They will not hurt you if you stay still, if you stay with me. . . ."

Gudrun tensed. Surely Sigfrid's voice had never been so deep. But the man who held her *smelled* right, and she had seen his face not a moment before. The deer still twitched and struggled, but the wolves had it pinned and were already beginning to feed. She shuddered, and the arms tightened around her.

"Sigfrid—" she whispered. "Take me with you! Every day since you died I have wept inside. Whatever you are now, wherever you are going, take me too—"

She felt him sigh. Then he released her and went to the deer, drawing his knife as he moved. An old, floppy hat hid his features. She frowned. Sigfrid had not been wearing a hat before. The man snarled at the wolves, who backed away, whining. He bent over the deer. Then he was upright, the heart, still red and pulsing, in his hand. He held it out to her. Involuntarily she stepped back, bumped into a tree, and stood at bay against it.

"You must eat, Gudrun, if you wish to ride with me. . . ."

She recoiled as if the flesh he was offering her was her own. He stood tall as Sigfrid, balanced and powerful, with the look that Sigfrid might have come to wear if he had lived to be old. But the hair and beard were grizzled, and the one eye she could see beneath his hat brim glinted like moonlight on a steel blade. She had seen that sardonic gleam before, in the eye of an old man standing in a newly harvested field. Her breath caught as she recognized the god.

"Why do you draw back? This is no worse than the cutting of the grain. Come, wife"—she could not tell whether he was pitying or laughing at her—"eat the harvest my hounds have brought you."

"Don't call me wife—I am married to Sigfrid—" Gudrun found her voice at last.

"Attila would not say so," Wodan responded. "But who shares your bed, or gets you with child, does not concern me. Through you I am wedded to this world—"

"I was tricked at the harvesting. I never consented. . . ."

"You are the Holy Queen. You agreed to serve the land."

"Gundohar has his own queen now—let her do it!"

He shook his head. "His bride listens to the priests of the Christos, who say that the earth must not be loved, but left behind."

"My happiness was sacrificed for the Burgund land!" she shouted. "Haven't I suffered enough, Old Man?"

"It was not you, but Sigfrid who made the offering." Wodan's voice grew grim. "And since that time you have hoarded your sorrow as a dragon hoards gold. You think you have suffered? That was only a foretaste of what you will endure if you think of yourself alone."

"I defy your curses and I deny your claim!" The reference to Sigfrid had enraged her.

"I do not curse you—" This time what she heard in his voice was sorrow. "You deceive yourself, Gudrun. I only see what is coming to pass."

A fury too great for containment boiled in her blood; she found herself in motion. Branches clawed at face and hands as she plunged through the young trees, unseeing, unhearing, knowing only that she must get away.

Gudrun ran, pursued by the Wild Hunt and her own fears. Shadow shapes of wolves loped before and behind her; she sought the deepest tangles of undergrowth, ran till her lungs burned, but always they were there. Sometimes she would turn to face them, shrieking defiance. They pulled back then, tongues lolling in mockery. Eventually she realized they did not mean to devour her. She was being herded.

With that, awareness of her own weariness swept over her. She tried to go on, but legs that a moment before had been impelled to a wild scramble by terror would no longer obey. A wet feather kissed her cheek; a star of frozen white clung for a moment to her outstretched arm. Snow . . . She looked over her shoulder at the wolves and her lips drew back in a rictus of a grin. *Perhaps you won't kill me, but the weather will. . . .*

She stumbled, reached out, and clung to a tree. More snowflakes drifted downward, starring the cold ground. Here was as good a place to die as any, and she could run no more. She sank down with her back to the hard trunk and closed her eyes.

She heard hoofbeats, men shouting and the cries of hounds. *The wolves have called their master*, she thought dimly, *but I will make no more sport for him today.* Her eyes stayed closed.

Hard hands closed on her arms. She felt them lifting her to a horse's back; someone gathered her under his cloak, holding her against his chest with one arm while the other managed the reins. He smelled wrong. She turned her face away. There was a time of jolting. Gudrun was scarcely aware of it. She did not rouse until the motion stopped. She was manhandled some more, and then, suddenly a blessed, unbelievable warmth flowed around her and she was laid down.

"Drink this—"

Instinctively Gudrun opened her mouth, tasted a fiery sweetness and the tart strength of herbs. She swallowed, choked, and struggled to sit up, coughing. A thin arm went around her shoulders. The beaker was set to her lips and she drank again. A warm glow settled in her belly and began to spread through icy limbs. She opened her eyes.

She was in a box bed with furs heaped around her. Through the opened curtains she could see carved house-posts, the gleam of weapons hung on the wall. The hall belonged to a chieftain of the tribes, but she had never seen it before. She turned her head. An old woman, as bent and twisted as an ancient yew, and as strong, was holding her. Gudrun wanted to ask where she was, but her teeth were chattering, and her nurse pushed her down among the warm furs once more.

"Sleep, my child," said the crone, "all will be well."

Gudrun tried to shake her head, images of spectral hunters and wolves with bloody jaws flickering behind her closing eyelids. But the woman was tracing a bindrune on her brow, and exhaustion drew a black wing across her memories.

When she woke again she ached all over, but the paralyzing chill had gone. She heard the rustle of cloth as the curtains of the box bed were drawn back and opened her eyes. A girl was leaning over her, fireglow backlighting fair hair. Golden eyes—wolf-eyes—met her own, bright with curiosity.

"Sunnilda," said Gudrun. "I must have been sicker than I thought if they sent for you, but I am better now, truly. How long have I been lying here?"

The girl drew back. "No more than a night and a day, lady—"

In the light, Gudrun could see that she was taller than Sunnilda, with the awkward grace of approaching womanhood, her hair a ruddier blond. But the voice, accented in the way of the Marcomanni, had already told her this could not be her child.

"Who are you?" Gudrun strove to gentle her voice, but the girl recoiled. There was something familiar about the way her head was poised on that slender neck, but it was the eyes that made Gudrun shake despite the warmth of the furs. *Sigfrid's eyes. . . .*

"I am Asliud. Are you sick again? Shall I call Huld?"

Gudrun stared, the voice bringing memories of Brunahild, understanding striking like a sword to the heart. She fell back with a groan, and the girl darted away.

Presently the old woman returned, frowning.

"I know you," said Gudrun before she could question. "You are that Huld who was Brunahild's teacher. That girl is her daughter, isn't she? And . . ." Her voice cracked. "Sigfrid's. . . ."

"And how would you know—" Huld's eyes opened wide.

"You are Gudrun! They said that you were the khan's woman, but gave no name."

Gudrun lay back, feeling the easy tears well from beneath her eyelids. "Sigfrid never told me," she whispered. "He never told me he had another child."

Huld grimaced. "You must not blame him, at least not for that. Brunahild did not wish him to know. You would never have been able to bewitch him into marriage if he had known Brunahild was with child."

"I did not—" Gudrun felt the old grief tightening her throat. "My mother made the magic. I never knew—" But that was not entirely true. In the depths of her soul she had always sensed there was something wrong. The old wound ached anew; Sigfrid, no matter how dearly she loved him, had never truly been hers.

"Brunahild left the child here to be fostered by Heimar. I have nursed her since she was a babe."

"And have you taught her the Walkyriun magic?" Gudrun eyed her curiously.

"Asliud would rather be ranging the woods than studying spells," she said finally, "and I do not press her. Her mother got little good from her magic." Gudrun frowned. She thought it more likely that the girl took after Sigfrid, who had always been impatient with such things. The magic of the Wolsungs came from within.

"And what of you? Did Grimahild teach you her skills?" Huld eyed her with professional curiosity.

"Do you think I would have been wandering the woods in a snowstorm if she had?" Gudrun answered bitterly.

"You were not wandering," Huld's voice went flat. "The trackers said you had been running as if the Wild Hunt were on your heels."

Gudrun could not keep from jumping. Her gaze met that of the old woman and she shivered, remembering. "It was. . . ." she whispered.

"You say you have no magic, but you hid your spirit so that even I was hard put to find you." Huld stopped, realizing what Gudrun had said. "Now I begin to understand. . . ."

"Did you search for me on the spirit roads? Brunahild told me once how you saved her from the snow. If Attila had not asked you to find me this time, I would have died."

"The khan?" Huld shook her head, sighing. "No, it was I who sent to him when I knew you were lost. He was not the one who sent me walking the spirit roads to find you, it was the god." Gudrun jerked, and Huld's attention sharpened. "What does Wodan want with you, that he should hunt you with his hounds, and then seek to save you?" The old seeress glared at her.

"He calls me his bride. . . ." Gudrun said bitterly. "You know the Walkyriun magics—teach me how to keep him away!"

For a moment Huld stared at her. Then she began to cackle. "You have vastly overrated the Walkyriun if you think that I could stop that one from going anywhere he wished to go. I have served him for more than fifty winters, and I know. Even if I could, I would not. No one can fight the wind. You can bend to it, or be broken like Sigfrid and Brunahild, but one way or another Wodan's purposes will be fulfilled. And he loved them, as I suppose he must love you—" She shook her head, as if she found that hard to understand. "It is Need that drives him—the Need of the world. He has not spared himself in that service. Why should he be kinder to you?"

"And do you love him?" Gudrun exclaimed. "Wodan is a god of death and terror—"

"He can be . . . if you see him so. . . ." Huld's gaze went inward. "But—have you ever stood in a meadow in the springtime, when the scents the wind brings make you dizzy with desire? You don't know what you want—the world is part of it, but you want more—and then the great wind sweeps you out of yourself, and you are carried away by joy. . . ."

Gudrun stared at her. Her own mother had served the

god. Had Grimahild ever been so transfigured by his rapture? Her daughter could not even imagine it.

Huld gave herself a little shake and the light went out of her eyes. She frowned at Gudrun as if regretting her words.

"You must regain your strength quickly," she said briskly. "Before the moon is old the khan will come for you."

Gudrun nodded. "I will keep your secret, but you must hide Asliud when Attila arrives."

"Hide her from the khan?" Huld laughed. "You do not know him if you think we could do so. But there is no need. He was here when Asliud was born."

Gudrun shut her eyes and turned her face to the wall. But she could not shut away the sound of Huld's laughter.

Attila knew all the time, she thought as she heard the old woman moving away. *Why should I be surprised?*

In that moment there seemed to be little to choose between her mortal husband and the god who claimed her— both of them were devious and tenacious, willing to sacrifice all to achieve their goals. How could she hope to stand against the man or the god? But somewhere there was a magic that would serve her. Somewhere she would find the power. . . .

Gudrun had half feared that Attila would think she had lost herself on purpose, but when he came at last he only asked her if she was fit to ride or required a horse litter. Fortunately, once she got warm she had recovered quickly. She did not know what Huld had told him, but he did not ask why she had fled instead of waiting for someone to backtrack her horse and find her. That night her husband took her body with his usual expertise, but for the first time, Gudrun did not fully respond to him.

After that, the hunting was not so good as it had been. Dealing with the game that had been taken already was more than enough to occupy the men, and Attila left them to smoke the meat while he rode with his bodyguard and his honored guests to Ruga's encampment on the Danu. Gudrun asked to return to Lentia; after seeing Asliud, she needed to hold her own daughter close once more. But she was not much needed there at this season, and Attila refused her. The truth, thought Gudrun angrily, was that he had not yet gotten her with child.

Often, as the days grew darker and folk spent more time inside the *gers*, Gudrun found herself in talk with Aetius. He amused her with gossip of the Imperial court; the young Valentinian was a handsome child, but spoiled. His household denied him nothing, and his mother, who might have curbed his self-indulgence, had always been too busy trying to preserve his inheritance to prepare him to rule it. The daughter, Honoria, seemed to be more intelligent than her brother, but was already promising to be quite a handful.

Aetius was quite at home with Hun customs; it was only sometimes that an intonation or a gesture would remind her that he was not one of Attila's Gothic chieftains but something entirely different, dangerous because it was unknown. She knew that the Roman was worried about what was going on in the Empire. Just how worried, she did not realize until one afternoon she came back from riding along the river and found her servants setting up a fence of birch poles to make a shaman's enclosure in the space beside Attila's *ger*.

Aetius was standing with arms folded, his features still as a Roman marble, watching the preparations from beneath half-closed eyelids. Gudrun eyed him curiously.

"Do you disapprove of our pagan superstitions?" She stopped, surprised at her own words, but in truth, she was not sure what she believed in now.

As he straightened and turned to look at her his gaze kindled. Gudrun twitched her cloak straight, suddenly acutely conscious of how she must look to him, with her hair blown to tangles and her cheeks flushed from her ride. Seeing her confusion, he smiled.

"Has no one told you that you are a very beautiful

woman?" he asked as if he had not heard. "In Roma you would be a sensation, as nobly formed and white of skin as one of the old goddesses, with no need to buy a wig of glorious golden hair." He reached out to take a silky strand between his fingers, and she found herself trembling.

What would it be like, she wondered, to lie in his arms? Did the Romans indulge in strange practices with their women? Would he take her with Attila's authority, or his skill? She did not compare him to Sigfrid. Only in height were they the same. Other men might be able to arouse her body, but no one else would ever possess that unique combination of innocence and power that had ravished her soul.

"Don't be afraid—" He let the curl fall. "This is only a game, such as they play in Roma. I would not touch Attila's woman."

Gudrun drew a deep breath. "Because you are loyal to him, or because you fear what he would do?"

For a moment something steely glinted in his gaze, then it was veiled. "How could I betray him? Attila is my brother, my ally."

It was not really an answer, but she could hardly expect a candid response when what she had really been asking had been "Which of you is stronger?" At the moment the obvious answer would be Attila, but Aetius, exile though he might be, was still powerful. He was Attila's brother in more than name. If his enemy Bonifatius thought him defeated, he was a fool.

She shrugged. "My brothers betrayed my first husband, after they had sworn brotherhood in Earthmother's name."

"Ah—" said Aetius. "I had forgotten you were married before. You hate them, don't you . . . ?"

Gudrun smiled vaguely and looked away. The slaves were preparing a fire in the midst of the circle. The sun was already setting. If they followed custom, the ceremony would begin when darkness fell.

"Perhaps it is superstition." Aetius's gaze followed hers.

"Certainly the priests at home would say so. But I have seen the *kams* of the Huns do some strange things. I must make a decision soon, and I need counsel."

"Good fortune to you—" she said politely, the moment of intimacy gone. "I had best go and change these muddy clothes for something warmer before we begin."

Gudrun came out of the *ger* when she heard the drumming. Among the Huns the *kams* could be male or female. This one, she saw, was a woman, sitting in a huddle of robes with closed eyes while one of her helpers, probably a relative she was training, warmed up the drum and the other built up the fire. Aetius was already seated in the place of honor, well wrapped up against the chill. She returned his nod of greeting and took her place on the women's side of the circle, fastening her hood of marten fur beneath her chin.

There was a little stir as Attila arrived. The shamaness seemed to take this as a signal. A tremor ran through her body, and she opened her eyes. It was quite dark now, a few stars peering through light cloud cover overhead, the fire a red eye blinking in the shadows below. The drummer pounded commandingly, and conversation ceased.

The other helper assisted the *kam-kadin* to rise and handed her a horseheaded staff. Leaning on it, she limped around the circle to Attila and looked down at him. Her garment was stitched together from many kinds of hide, fringed with the tails of animals and strips of Roman silk and ornaments of iron and bone.

"The Lord of Horses calls, and I come to him. What does he seek to know?"

Her voice creaked like an ungreased wagon wheel. Her weathered skin looked like old leather in the flare of the fire. *She should be sitting by somebody's hearthfire, wrapped in shawls,* thought Gudrun. *What is she going to do here?*

"It is my brother who questions," Attila replied gravely.

"He wishes to know if he should return to his own land, and will he defeat his enemy?"

With a little birdlike tilt of the head the old woman considered Aetius. He met her gaze unflinchingly, and after a moment she gave a cackle of laughter.

"This one, he is a man of power. I think the spirits like him. But we shall see—" She gestured to her helpers, who untied a young ram from one of the posts and led it forward. Attila murmured something to the Roman, who set his hand on the animal's head. The helper handed him the beast's tether to hold. "The bones, they do not lie. I am the White Heron, the Mistress of Spirits, and with their aid I will hunt the secrets you would know. . . ."

The drummer began a lively beat and the other helper assisted her mistress to put on a cap formed from the plumage of the bird. As the strings were tied the *kam-kadin* jerked, feathers quivering. Then she began to sing. Her voice, at first thin and quavering, grew sweeter as her chant continued. It was in a dialect Gudrun did not know, but she thought it was about a heron. And then, apparently from the air above them, the bird replied. The shamaness called out in greeting, and the bird called again. She jerked once more and suddenly she was dancing, her first wobbling steps becoming a mincing stalk, fringed arms beating the air like wings.

Well, that is magic anyhow, thought Gudrun, *for an old woman to dance and sing like a girl.* But why should she be surprised, who had been married, however unwillingly, to a god?

The *kam-kadin* took a birch branch and swept it along the sheep's back, still singing, then danced off around the circle again. Two times this procedure was repeated. When she came to the sheep the third time, she was holding a crude hammer of stone. With a practiced swiftness, the shamaness brought the weapon down between the animal's ears. It gave a grunt and collapsed. Before it had stopped twitching, the old woman had slit open the skin above the foreleg and was stripping back hide and muscle to reach the shoulder blade. With the skill of long practice, she sliced tendons and snapped joints, popped it free, and, muttering fiercely, brought it to the fire.

Pungent smoke swirled up as the White Heron cast handfuls of herbs upon the fire. She poked at the logs with her staff, then laid the bloody triangle of bone upon the coals. The flames hissed at the moisture, the smell of roasting mutton mingled oddly with the scents of the herbs. The old woman bent over the fire pit, watching intently as fire began to glow through the thin plate of bone.

There was a faint crack, hardly distinguishable above the sound of the fire. Instantly the *kam-kadin* reached out and plucked the shoulder blade from the flames. It was still smoking, but she handled it without apparent pain, turning it back and forth to examine the runes scored there by the fire.

"Tell us, Wise One, what do the spirits say?" asked Attila at last.

The old woman's head turned at the sound, but her eyes were all pupil; it was not Middle Earth that she was seeing now.

"The Golden Eagle soars far from his home . . ." Her voice was a whisper, but the drum had stilled and no one made a sound. "He flies towards his nest, but the other eagles gather. They are many, too many, and an old bird leads them, prideful and strong. They fight; the Golden Eagle is overwhelmed and must flee once more. But I see— ah, I see now, that the old bird is wounded. He has been hurt in the fighting . . . he fails now . . . he falls."

Aetius, who had begun to frown, sat upright, staring. "And what then, Bird of Wisdom? What then shall the Golden Eagle do?"

"He shall return—" She gave a harsh cry that might have been laughter. "He returns, and there is no one who can stand against him. The she-eagle bows before him. He perches upon a housepost of white marble; he is master in the land."

"How long?" Attila said softly. "How long does the Eagle rule?"

The Roman stilled. Among his people, even emperors sometimes counted their lordship in days; perhaps he did not want to know.

The *kam-kadin* swayed. Her fingers twitched as if she were counting. "I see . . . ten winters, and ten again shall pass . . . before he is struck down. . . ."

Aetius sat back with a great sigh. Attila was still watching the *kam-kadin,* his gaze unreadable. "Our thanks to you, Mother, you have done well," he said. "Let the spirits go now, and rest."

She looked back at the sheep's bone, and for a moment it appeared she might say more. But Attila's words had power over spirits as well as men. A shudder ran through her body, and the shoulder blade slipped from her hand. Her helpers scurried to her side, plucking the hat from her head, supporting her as she slumped sideways, and after a moment blowing some evil-smelling smoke into her face to bring her around.

The ritual was over. Aetius and the others, talking with the rather frenetic speed of men who have been more shaken than they would like their fellows to know, strode off to drink and discuss strategies over Ruga's fire. She supposed they would continue until dawn. But Gudrun was glad that this night she would sleep alone, for she, too, had much to think on.

The *kam-kadin* had skills as great as Huld's, but different in style. Different enough, maybe, to defeat a god. What gift, she wondered, would persuade the old woman to teach her Hunnish sorcery?

If it was not quite dawn, it was late enough when Attila came back to the *ger.* Gudrun roused as the door flap was lifted, listening as he moved deftly about in the darkness, and knew that he had drunk with his usual discipline. He slid under the sleeping furs beside her and she began to drift off again. But presently she realized he was lying too still for sleep and her own eyes opened. She turned on her side to face him.

"I found the ceremony interesting . . ." she said softly. "Your sorceress has great skills. Do you believe her prophecies?"

Attila grunted. "I believe . . . in the luck a man makes for himself. A strong man wins luck from the gods. Aetius is strong. . . ."

Gudrun had not dared to ask the Roman which of them was the stronger, and she did not ask Attila now.

With an abrupt movement he reached for her and yanked her sleeping shift above her thighs. She stiffened, and then, as his hand thrust between them, understood that he was answering her question. This time there was none of the careful courtship she was used to, and yet, surprisingly, she found that like a mare when the stallions fight, in moments she was ready for him. Her body arched instinctively as he entered her, and he laughed.

"I want the witch-woman . . . in my household," she gasped as he began to move within her. "I want to learn your people's sorcery. . . ."

His fingers tightened in her tangled hair, stroked lightly down her long throat to close on her breast, squeezing hard.

"Give me a child—" Amazingly, his voice was as unsteady as her own.

He is asking me . . . she thought in wonder. *This one thing, even the Lord of Horses cannot decree,* and then. *This is my husband now, not Sigfrid, and not the god.* . . . She released her grip on the furs and set first one hand, then the other, on his shoulders, stroked along the hard muscles of his back to his buttocks and pulled him closer.

And in that movement of assent, she felt something opening within her that had resisted all his skill, and knew that this time she would conceive.

Chapter 8 Imperium

During the week that followed the Ostara feasting, it was the custom for the *hendinos* of the Burgunds to
sit in judgment beneath the great oak tree in the meadow
outside the town. During the year, the lesser cases would
have been heard by the chief men in each district. They
saved the thorny problems, the ones that involved conflict
between Burgund and Roman, for Gundohar.

He was not without assistance—Father Priscus sat on one
side behind him to advise where the Church was involved,
and Father Vidulf, who had been sent to be Galamvara's
chaplain and had replaced the ailing Severian, represented
the Arians. Junius Desiderius, head of the oldest equestrian
family left in Borbetomagus, spoke for the Romans. Once,
old Ostrofrid had been his mentor in Burgund law; now it
was Hagano. Sitting here in the dappled shade, Gundohar
could almost imagine himself a king in the old style, with
his council around him. But though his chieftains still ad-
vised on war and peace and policy, these days the responsibility for giving justice lay with the king alone.

But he wished he could have set someone else to judge
the case before him now.

The plaintiff, a lesser chieftain called Skarilo who was
some kind of cousin to Ordwini, had charged his wife with
desertion.

140

"The law of our people on this matter is clear." He sent a murderous glance toward the woman, who sat with her brother, a man called Arpagius Cestus, on the other side of the circle. "She has broken the marriage, and the punishment for that is to be taken to the marshes and smothered to death in the mire. . . ."

Cestus jumped to his feet and strode forward. "That may be the Burgund way, and a barbaric custom it is, but my sister is a Roman, and I demand that she be judged by Roman law!" The toga he had dug out for the occasion flapped awkwardly around him as if he rarely wore it, but there was an honest outrage in his face that demanded respect.

"Now I begin to see why the Visigoths have forbidden marriage between Romans and barbarians . . ." said Hagano in his ear. Gundohar sighed and looked over at Cestus.

"According to the Law of Honorius, there are three cases in which divorce is permitted—for a crime, for bad character, and without reasons alleged. In the first case, the woman may recover her dowry and eventually remarry; in the second she may not remarry but she may separate from her husband; in the third case she must go into exile."

"That may be the emperor's law, but it is not God's," Father Priscus exclaimed, and for once, Father Vidulf nodded agreement. "Divorce is permissible only for adultery."

"Arpagia became a Burgund when I married her!" exclaimed Skarilo. "I demand justice according to our customs!" He glared at the woman who had been his wife, and she, though her face was colorless, met his gaze defiantly.

Had she loved another man, wondered Gundohar, feeling his own gut twist as he remembered Brunahild. Or had her crime been to shame her husband by leaving him? At least Brunahild had spared him that dishonor, until the end, when crime and punishment became one on Sigfrid's funeral pyre.

Stop! he told himself sternly. *That is all over, and you have a good woman now who loves you. . . .* As always, the thought of Galamvara eased him, even though, in a way, he had failed her as badly as he had Brunahild.

"That law may run east of the river," said Desiderius, "but here you are ruling a Roman land—"

Gundohar grimaced, remembering the interminable debates to which Ostrofrid and Priscus had subjected him when he was a boy. The law of the people or the law of the land—which took precedence? The branches above him quivered and he looked up, saw a flicker of buff belly and the flare of russet by the blue-grey wing, then, from the narrow black mask, a bright eye gleamed at him. A nuthatch . . . he remembered some tale of how the birds had counseled Sigfrid. But a cheerful chirrup was all this one could give him. The birds, like the gods, no longer spoke to men.

Gundohar cleared his throat, aware that they were all watching him.

"Circumstances may mitigate a crime, even in customary law. What reason does Arpagia give for leaving her husband's hall?"

Everyone looked around, as if in their debate they had forgotten the woman who was the cause of it all. Arpagia stood up, her pale cheeks flaming.

"I am a free woman, and he treated me like a slave! Is that the custom among your people? Worse than a slave, even, for a master is obligated to feed and provide for his servants. This man who calls himself my husband has wasted his own wealth and my own portion. Sometimes I have had nothing to buy food with, and then he beat me when I complained."

"Has he committed adultery with other women?" asked Father Vidulf.

"How should I know what he does when he is out drinking?" she flared. "But if he has lain with them, that is more than he has done with me!"

Every man there winced, so perhaps, thought Gundohar, his own reaction had not been noticed. *How can I judge her?*

he asked himself. *If I am harsh, I will wonder if it is the pain Brunahild caused me that is speaking. And if I am merciful . . .* but even to himself, he could not admit that there was a part of him that still remembered her with love.

"She has not deserted her husband to go with another man," said Hagano, taking pity on him. "She has returned to the roof of her kindred, and that is proper according to the customs of our folk as well as hers."

The woman's gaze turned to Gundohar. Her eyes were dark, like Brunahild's, but Gundohar's wife had never begged him to pity her.

"Because she is Roman-born, I will judge her by Roman rules," he said finally. "No crime is proved against her husband, but she is justified in leaving him for bad character. He shall keep the *witimon* that she brought him at their marriage, and she shall dwell in the house of her brother."

The brother looked sour—no doubt he had been hoping to recover her dowry, but Arpagia's face was for a moment beautiful.

Gundohar did not return her smile. He had gotten through this one, but he was not happy. One day this tangle of custom and precedent would have to be sorted out, when he had decided whether law was dependent on place or person or some other principle that transcended both of them.

He looked up, gathering his strength for the next challenge. But everyone was looking past him. A horseman, decked out in shining Roman parade armor, was trotting up the road. As he drew closer, the king could see that his lance bore Aetius's emblem. His heartbeat sped. The last he had heard, Aetius was fleeing a lost battle. He got to his feet, and the others, remembering their manners, did likewise.

"This court is adjourned—" he said in a loud voice, as happy to see the Roman commander's colors coming to the rescue as ever he had been on a battlefield.

*   *   *

"Bonifatius is dead—the Roman general who beat Aetius—" Gundohar announced as he came into the women's quarters in the hall. Galamvara paused in her spinning to smile up at him. Spring sunlight, shining over her shoulder, struck coppery sparks from her hair. The king gazed at his wife with the bittersweet pleasure the sight of her always aroused in him. There was love in their bed, but no passion; he tried to pretend it did not matter. He cleared his throat and began again. "The wounds he got at Ariminium went bad on him. He won the battle, but he has lost the war."

"I was surprised to hear that Aetius had challenged him," Galamvara replied. "I met Bonifatius once, when I visited Roma with my father. He struck me as the kind of commander who could be very effective when he had superior strength, but not a man of much imagination." She wound the spun yarn around the shaft and handed it to the lad who attended her, a child called Andulf, who gazed at the king with an awe that he found embarrassing.

"Whereas Aetius is a fox." Gundohar nodded. He had wondered how the politics of the north would change when he first heard how the empress had demoted the Master of Gallia, and found it difficult to imagine. But the wily Roman had managed to transform his disaster into a triumph.

"What does he want from you?" Galamvara raised a knowing eyebrow. Gundohar grinned back at her. "He is marching on Roma—or rather, Ravenna—there is no one in Italia now who can oppose him. He calls me to join him; Walamir of the Goths will be there as well, the Gepid, Ardaric, and some of the Huns. He will come to the empress with an escort of kings, and though she may still hate him, Galla Placidia will have to restore his honors."

After a winter cooped up in Borbetomagus, he had found his thoughts turning more and more to the summer's campaigning. But he would see the land of Vergilius and Horatius, of Tacitus and Caesar, and he was not even going to have to do any fighting!

"The homeland of the Empire has many wonders," Gal-

amvara said mildly. "It is understandable that you should
want to see them. I will watch over things here while you
are gone."

He blinked at her assumption that he would leave her in
charge, but it was not unreasonable. The land was at peace,
and after all, he had given the same authority to Brunahild.
He shook the memory away.

"Yes—well—I must go and tell Hagano!"

As the moon of Ostara faded, the Burgunds set forth for
Italia. Their baggage train was larger than usual, for they
came prepared for fight or festival. They encountered no
resistance; the garrisons of Raetia knew Aetius well, and
were more inclined to come to his aid than oppose his
allies. Slowly, suiting their pace to that of the mules, the
Burgunds chased the receding snows of winter up the slopes
of the Alpes until the frost giants turned at bay to strike
them with a final storm. Feast cloaks added their warmth
to riding gear then; they lost some mules and two men
disappeared beneath an avalanche, but when the clouds,
defeated, rolled away at last, the young men laughed and
began to pelt each other with snowballs.

They came down from the Pennines into the fertile plains
drained by the headwaters of the Pagus, where the rest of
the barbarian army Aetius had raised for his triumphal return was waiting for them. They had to face a certain
amount of chaffing from Aetius's other allies, for while they
had been fighting the snows in the Alpes, the Goths had
been helping the commander to defeat Bonifatius's son-in-
law Sebastian.

"Why, I wonder, does Aetius not seek to become emperor?" asked Thiudimir. He and his brother the Goth-king
had fallen into the habit of riding with Hagano and
Gundohar. "They say that in former times any man who
could command the army could be raised to the purple,
and that is why there were so many emperors."

"Maybe in those days the emperor actually commanded his armies," answered Hagano, "but I think the Magister desires rank only because it is the road to power. He would not enjoy being imprisoned in a palace as they say the child-emperor Valentinian is now."

"We'll see for ourselves soon enough," put in Gundohar. He strove for dignity, but there was a spot of bright color in each cheek, and his eyes were as excited, thought his brother, as a child's.

A habit honed by many seasons of campaigning brought Hagano's gaze back to the land around them. Reason told him there was no danger in the rolling Ligurian countryside, but there was no point in allowing himself to become careless. That much he had learned from Attila.

The khan was not with them, although he had sent some of his men. Hagano wondered if the decision not to come had been that of Aetius or his own? It made sense, he supposed, not to bring the Huns. The people who came out to watch them pass were used to Germans, who had been the backbone of their armies for a century or more. Huns still struck them as aliens, and probably demonic to boot. The tribes were at least nominal Christians.

Hagano adjusted his eyepatch and grinned sourly. He had thought he would leave the god who haunted him behind in Germania; it was one of the reasons he had agreed to come along. But since they had come down from the mountains, he had at times noticed a presence like a faint pressure at the back of his head, felt someone using his senses to see and hear, especially when they encountered something new. A priest would have said he was being haunted by a demon, but he had been called by that name himself often enough not to care.

What surprised him was that Wodan should be interested, for he had not expected to be impressed by Italia. He had seen Treveri, after all, and Arelas and Tolosa. Aquitanica had been Roman for a very long time, richly benefiting from the obligation of the noble classes to compete in public works and civic benefactions. He was no stranger to the marble columns of temples inherited by Christian saints along with the attributes of the old gods, to aqueducts and amphitheaters and red-tiled villas now the proud homes of Visigothic lords.

But in Italia, the transformations of civilization had been in progress for much longer. The earth itself, tame with centuries of cultivation, offered itself to the moist furrows of the plow, and the plow turned up timeworn images carved by nameless ancestors among their bones. Even in the springtime, the air seemed golden, especially in the long evenings, when the poplars cast blue shadows across the road and the cows wound slowly homeward over the hills.

They had come, he suspected, at the most auspicious time of the year, when the streams ran high and the meadows were lush with new grass. The very trees had decked themselves with blossom as if to welcome them. Hagano saw the strain go from the eyes of his companions, heard their laughter grow louder with each passing day. A country made to be conquered, they were thinking, the peasants who tilled it as docile and uncomplaining as their cows. Here, one could live at ease and never have to fight again.

Which was no doubt why Hagano felt vaguely uncomfortable.

Of course, the peace through which they rode was ephemeral. The Galli had invaded these lands before Roma was even an empire. Hannibal had marched through it, and Alaric. These plains had provided battlefields for the Romans' innumerable civil wars. This holiday march to reinstate Aetius was surely not the last, only the most recent, invasion.

"Yes, this is a good country," Thiudimir echoed his thought. "A good base from which to rule the world. It is only the people who are worn-out—"

"Like Aetius?" his brother Walamir snorted.

"The Magister is half-Goth. It's our blood that gives him

his vigor. Stilicho was a German, and Sarus, and many another. If all the tribes could work together, we could make an empire greater than that of Augustus."

"With the Amalungs as Caesars?" Gundohar raised one eyebrow. "Have you told this to the Balthis in Tolosa?"

Thiudimir flushed at the reference to the other princely house whose bloodline went back to the time when the Goths had been all one people, before the coming of the Huns.

"Your Gothia is a fine dream, brother, but I do not think it will come into being in your lifetime or mine," said Walamir peaceably.

"Perhaps our sons will do it—" Thiudimir replied.

That was it, thought Hagano. Thiudimir's lady had given him a fine boy-child the winter before. Fatherhood could do strange things to a man.

"It is true, though, that when we add our strength to the skills of the Romans we can build something better than either," said Gundohar thoughtfully. Hagano turned to look at him. Apparently his brother had more on his mind than the *Eclogues* of Vergilius, which he had brought to read on the journey.

"Myself," he said repressively, "I would rather avoid coming to any conclusions until we have seen the heart of the Roman power in Ravenna."

The city, seen across the lagoon, was a mirage of white walls and red roofs and domes and towers. Riding back and forth through the encampment while they waited for the ceremonial entry, Gundohar had had time enough to consider it from every angle, until he almost feared to come nearer, lest a closer encounter should reveal it less fair.

Ravenna was said to be impregnable. Riding out beyond the camp to the edge of the solid ground, one could see the port of Classis, where the fleet still found good harborage, though that harbor was no longer part of the town. Therein lay its strength. The meandering waters of the Pagus had surrounded the city with a maze of open channels and marshy islets. It could be besieged, and indeed, Aetius's forces spread out in a broad crescent on the high ground beyond the marshes looked remarkably like a besieging army. But an enemy would need to control the sea as well as the landward approaches to completely contain it. Gundohar could see why Emperor Honorius, fleeing Alaric and the Vandali, had taken refuge here a generation ago, and why the Imperial court had remained here ever since. It could not be captured by force, only by trick or treachery.

Messengers trotted back and forth along the narrow causeway that was the only visible approach—most of the city's provisions must come in by sea—but no one seemed to know when they would make their ceremonial entry. After a week of this, it occurred to Gundohar that far from threatening the city, they were deliberately being kept outside until the empress judged them to have thoroughly understood their own unimportance. The other kings laughed when he suggested this, and made plans to go hawking in the marshes. Only Gundohar held back from the sport, preferring to sit on a grassy knoll where the wind stirred his hair, and where he could look up from reading the *Histories* of Tacitus which Aetius had lent him, and see the city.

Of them all, Aetius himself showed the least impatience. He had waited a long time for this, and he could afford to let the empress salve her pride by making him wait a little longer. At times, there seemed to be something almost superhuman about his calm. Hagano, who talked sometimes with the Huns in the commander's bodyguard, said there were rumors that a *baliuruna*, a witch-woman of their people, had foretold the first lost battle, and the death of Bonifatius, and Aetius's eventual victory. It is easier to be calm, thought Gundohar, when you know that the gods are on your side.

The long-awaited entry did not take place until the feast of Pentecost, but indeed, when the day arrived, it did not fall short of expectation. Clothes and jewels long prepared were shaken out, chests ransacked for last-minute changes. Even Hagano was persuaded to add a silver circlet and arm rings to his somber attire. Gundohar looked at his brother and smiled. If the folk of Ravenna had known who Wodan was, surely they would look at that grim mouth and dispassionate, one-eyed stare and say the god himself had come to them.

He told himself he should repent thinking such things on a holy feast day, but no matter what blessings the bishops might dispense inside those walls, this occasion had little to do with Christianity. Though Aetius had put aside his gilded parade armor, there was nothing humble in his dalmatic of sun-colored silk woven with figures of eagles and lions, or the mantle, of a fine crimson wool barely a shade off from purple, bordered with a brocade so stiff with gold thread and pearls and couched jewels that its base color could not be seen. This was about power.

He surveyed his own azure gown wryly. Galamvara had known what would be needed, and prepared his festival attire with her usual efficiency. In Borbetomagus the marten furs that bordered his deep blue cloak had seemed very splendid. He had seen enough by now to know that he would be unlikely to impress the Romans even had he worn the whole contents of Sigfrid's hoard. But that was not his purpose. He was intended to blend into the procession of royal personnages, no more and no less splendid than Walamir, or Ardaric, or the other kings.

They knew already of the narrow causeway that led to the city, wide enough for no more than two horses to go abreast; any army that had tried to pass that way would have been strung out for miles, hopelessly vulnerable to missiles shot from the walls. He devoutly hoped they would perform the whole entrance on horseback. Mounted, he could be reasonably imposing; his limping gait afoot would not add to Aetius's consequence.

Much of what they had seen since crossing the Alpes was ancient and crumbling, thought Gundohar as they drew closer. But the walls of Ravenna were new, arrogantly towered, presenting a smooth white face to the world. Gold glinted from some of the rooftops inside them. Classis had been no more than a naval town a generation ago when Honorius took refuge here. No doubt many of these buildings would be new as well, built since his time.

Some of his following had been surprised to learn the Imperial family did not dwell in Roma. But since the time of Constantine the court, with its hundreds of chamberlains and *comites* and secretaries, had been constantly in motion, settling temporarily in the great Imperial residences at Mediolanum or Sirmium or Augusta Treverorum and then moving on as the needs of the Empire required. Now it was the great generals who ranged the Empire, while their sacred ruler stayed safe behind these marshes.

The walls loomed above them. Gundohar glanced at his brother's impassive profile and tried to summon up some protective cynicism. He had seen the great works at Treveri, where the Imperium had lodged when the emperor ruled in truth as well as name. How much could thirty years have done for Ravenna?

They passed beneath the massive arch of the gatehouse, hooves ringing hollow on stone, came out into sunlight. Horns blared commandingly and his horse tossed its head and sidled. The Burgund king blinked, trying to take in the confusion of light and color that suddenly surrounded him. People were shouting—he hoped they were cheering. He caught Aetius's name.

In that first blazing moment inside the walls he understood that Treveri, however magnificent, had been a shell of past glories. Ravenna was the living incarnation of Imperium.

By the time the barbarian kings had endured the splendors of a solemn high mass in the cathedral and been conducted to the Palatium even Hagano was fighting to preserve his detachment. Gundohar, a quick glance told him, had succumbed long ago, and was gazing about him with the wide-eyed wonder of a child. Hagano was surprised to feel a surge of protective affection. To defend his brother had become second nature, a commitment made when he went up against Waldhari if not before. But he was not accustomed to tenderness.

Enjoy it while you can, brother. He tried to keep from blinking at the dissected splendors of the mosaic floor over which they were passing. *It will be long before such riches are seen in Burgund lands.*

The corridor was faced in colored marbles, pink and black and green. Statues looked down at them from the embrasures, the same sneering smiles with which the emperor's household had greeted them immortalized in cold stone. Goldwork gleamed from the capitals of the columns that supported the arched doorways. It was wonderful workmanship, but he told himself it would be wearing to live with. The forest, with all its infinite variety, was more beautiful. For a moment the marbles before him were overlaid with a vision of living green, and that in turn by the image of Sigfrid.

Hagano shook his head, saw gold and stonework and the bobbing headdress of the chamberlain who was conducting them. Sigfrid should have been walking at Gundohar's other shoulder. . . . But he could not even imagine Sigfrid in this jeweled cage.

From ahead came a murmur like that of a distant waterfall. The carven doors ahead of them were flung open. The sound swelled to a roar, then stilled. He was relieved to see that Aetius, who had been taken ahead when they entered the palace grounds, was there already, unruffled and unharmed. The cut of his beard reminded Hagano of a statue of the Emperor Marcus Aurelius that he had seen, but there was a gleam in the commander's eye that was far from philosophic. It suggested that whatever business had taken him away had been successful. Hagano told himself he should not have worried. Galla Placidia might be vindictive, but she was not a fool. She sat safe in Ravenna, but the rest of Italia was at the mercy of Aetius's army.

The hush became a silence so profound it brought him to attention. More dignitaries were appearing between the pillars at the other end of the hall, peeling off and taking up position to either side as if the notables portrayed in mosaic behind them were coming down from the walls. There was a sudden, nerve-shattering clamor of clarions. Three figures appeared, blazing with a sunburst of jewels, and all that great assembly bent like a cornfield in the wind.

Straightening from his obeisance, Hagano found that the Imperial family were now seated. His head throbbed and he felt once more the touch of that Other, observing from within. *Look your fill, Old One,* he thought then. *These are the gods who rule Middle Earth now.*

Valentinian, a half-grown youth with a face that would have been pleasing if not for his sulky expression, sat on a raised chair of ivory. On the dais below him two chairs of carved and gilded wood were occupied by his sister and Galla Placidia. In front of the dais was another, empty chair.

The empress was older than he had expected, and smaller, armored in stiff brocades riveted with pearls. She surveyed the assemblage and Hagano stiffened, for in that moment she had looked very like Grimahild. That steely gaze went to Valentinian, who straightened from his slouch, and Honoria, who was eyeing the tall German warriors with an appreciation beyond her years.

A glittering functionary paced forward, unrolled the scroll he was carrying, and began to read. Hagano, whose command of the Roman tongue was not so good as his brother's, struggled to follow the Latin words.

"*Magister Utriusque Militiae . . .* " So, they had given Aetius the supreme command he was demanding. The spate of verbiage flowed on. There was a pause, Aetius was moving forward, abasing himself before the Imperial family like a priest at the altar, rising as the empress rose from her own seat and came down from her dais to meet him.

"*Patricius noster—*" At her words there was a little hiss of indrawn breath from the Romans. The empress-mother had made him a patrician, then, *the* Patrician of Rome, and they had not expected it. She lifted her hands to his shoulders, brushed his cheek with a dry kiss, stepped away again, her face unmoved. If she blamed him for the death of Bonifatius, who had supported her throughout her early tribulations, had even, it was said, sent money for her support when she was in exile in Constantinople, she did not allow it to show. Aetius bowed. Galla Placidia gestured toward the empty chair and took her own place once more. The commander straightened. He was not smiling either, but as he turned, his cloak flared out triumphantly and he took his seat as if he were claiming the world.

And so he is, thought Hagano, watching him, *or at least of the half of it the Western Empire holds. He is the Master of Rome.*

A half a moon later, the Master of the West rode out from Ravenna with his retinue of kings, made captive not by his sword but by the idea of Imperium. To Gundohar, the homeward journey passed as a dream. In the great trees of the mountains he saw columns of porphyry; polished marble in the eternal snows. Even the bright noonday blaze of the heavens reminded him of the dome in the cathedral, where jeweled priests moved like apparitions through clouds of incense like the mists on the hills. When they came down from the mountains of Raetia, he saw in the dimpled waters of the Rhenus a mosaic of gold.

He had thought, in those moments when the smell of horse or the taste of porridge recalled him to ordinary reality, that coming home might be a disappointment. After the burnished splendors of the Palatium, surely the cracked plaster of his own basilica would seem tawdry, and his tribesmen uncouth and barbarous after the devout functionaries who had looked down their noble noses at him in Ravenna. But when, as high summer was ripening the fields, he rode through the gates of Borbetomagus, all he could see was possibilities.

* * *

"Travel agrees with you," said Galamvara, pouring more wine. "You are brown as a nut and as fit as I have ever seen you."

Gundohar grinned up at her. Tomorrow, they would hold the feast of welcome, and he would try to capture in words the glories that still blinded his imagination. But tonight she had ordered a simple meal brought to their chamber for himself and Hagano. Galamvara herself had bloomed in the warm summer weather, thought her husband. She was a little flushed, and a curl of bronze hair clung to her neck below her veil.

"I don't mind long hours in the saddle; on campaign it's the people trying to spear you that wear you out. If looks could kill, that young senator"—he looked at Hagano, who murmured, "Petronius Maximus"—"might have been a danger, but he's only a cockerel, and we could afford to let him crow."

Hagano grunted. His estimate of the young senator had been less sanguine, but Aetius was the man of the hour. He had to agree that Petronius could do little against him now. Indeed, the senator had merely been the most obvious in his scorn. Most of the Romans, from the emperor's officers to the servants, had maintained a similar pose of superiority.

"Did that trouble you?" asked Galamvara.

"It made Thiudimir wild." He grinned again. "He wants to come back with an army, take the city, and rub their noses in their own weakness. And then he will show them how much better the Goths can rule. . . ."

"And can they?" She sat down and picked up her own wine. Gundohar's eye followed the movement, lingered for a moment on the shape of her breast beneath the fine linen of the loose gown.

"Not Thiudimir," rumbled Hagano. "Not any of the Ostrogoths. Attila is a mountain and they cannot see past his shadow. These are only dreams." Gundohar found it interesting that Attila was perceived as the leader even though Ruga still lived.

"The Visigoths can . . ." said Galamvara. "But my father looks toward Aquitanica."

"And I can—" Gundohar found himself saying. "Though what I see is Belgica Prima. We have the example of Alaric to show what happens to those who attack Roma directly, but now I have seen how glorious a kingdom can be when it is supported by Germanic strength and adorned by Roman skill."

Hagano's lips pursed. "Have you been talking to Ordwini?"

"Not recently, but isn't it obvious?" Gundohar replied. He had not known he was thinking about expansion, but now that the words were said, he was surprised he had not articulated it before. Galamvara was watching him with shining eyes. He would show her he was worthy of her, that he was truly a king. "Those lands are destined to be ours, I am sure of it. With Attila to guard our backs and Theoderid our ally and Aetius our friend, how can we fail?" He set the silver cup to his lips and drained it.

"If we start carving chunks out of the empire Aetius has just been given to defend, I am not so sure he will still be our friend," muttered Hagano, but Gundohar kept his gaze on the the curve of his cup, which the lampflame was turning to gold.

"Just now, what we need is for you to carve this goose which has been so beautifully roasted," said Galamvara peaceably.

He looked up, nostrils flaring as the scent of the bird the slave was bringing in reached him. He realized suddenly that he was very hungry—during the last days of their journey they had been pushing hard to get home and had skimped on the cooking. Suddenly both he and Hagano were laughing, and forgetting their fine Roman manners, they tore into the fowl.

When they had eaten Hagano left Gundohar and his wife alone.

Lamplight had always been kind to Galamvara's blunt features; now they were beautiful. While they had been eating he had been watching her, and found another kind of appetite growing. He thought ruefully that Hagano, not knowing how matters had been between them, had realized before he had that he wanted her. He stood up abruptly, staring at her, and saw the color come and go in her face as she looked back at him.

The journey had altered more than his coloring, he thought in wonder. Somehow, his immersion in all that power and beauty had healed him of his fear. Galamvara began to tremble as he dealt efficiently with the pins that held her clothing; she stood unresisting as the garments fell away and he stripped off his own. He laid her upon the bed then, his long fingers, trained equally to the delicate manipulation of the stylus and the hard grip of the sword, moving over her body. Presently she began to sigh, and he stretched himself above her, possessing her with the same easy strength with which they had taken Italia.

For two years Galamvara had been his queen, but for the first time since their marriage, Gundohar came to her as a king.

Chapter 9   Funeral Games

Flavius Aetius celebrated his accession to power with a swift and effective campaign against the Franks, who had begun to make themselves a nuisance in northern Gallia, then returned to Roma to make sure Galla Placidia appreciated the virtues of her new defender. In Borbetomagus, Gundohar took up the reins of government with an unaccustomed vigor. Clearly the journey to Italia had been good for him. As for his queen, folk rejoiced at her obvious happiness in his return. Galamvara had ruled temperately and well while he was away, but so had Brunahild, and they had never loved her. Perhaps it was because Gundohar's Visigoth queen was someone they could understand.

In the land of the Huns, Gudrun studied magic with the woman called White Heron, and contemplated the ripening curve of her belly as the summer sun ripened the fields. She found she had absorbed more than she knew of her mother's magic. It was interesting to see where the magic of the Burgunds and of the Huns differed, and where they were the same.

Her mother had always worked her spells through singing; the White Heron, though she chanted, used the drum as well, riding its beat as the Huns rode their ponies to reach the Otherworld. Like Grimahild, the *kam-kadin* used herbs for healing and magic, though some of them were different from the ones that grew by the Rhenus. The Huns had learned some rune lore, but in that area the old queen had been far wiser. But the White Heron knew the ways of every creature that lived in these lands.

"You learn to listen, and Earth herself teaches you—" said the *kam-kadin*. Light, reflecting off the river, underlit her seamed features so that she herself looked like some wight of the Otherworld. "Everything you see, every beast and bird, speaks to you. And some things you see are spirits— they, too, take animal form. Every person has a spirit shape, that you can use when you journey. You see it yourself, is a warning, but others, those with Sight, can see."

"Is that the creature you call on when you dance for vision?" asked Gudrun, trailing her feet in the water.

"I call on my helpers. I am White Heron, but there is another heron, greater, that helps me. Also sometimes I call wildcat and the siga, which is like a goat and like a deer, that runs on the great plain beyond the Euxine Sea." Some of the *kams* boasted loudly of the numbers and strength of their allies. The White Heron spoke of them like friends.

"And what of me?" Gudrun asked then. "Can you See the shape my spirit wears?"

For a moment the old woman looked at her, pupils dilating as her eyes unfocused, even the fringes on her headwrap still. When she spoke, her voice had the slowed, distant quality of trance.

"White shape swimming . . . grace in air and water . . . she moves from land to land . . . the silent swan. . . ." The *kam-kadin* let out her breath in a long sigh, twitched and blinked, and suddenly was herself again.

Gudrun shivered, whether with fear or excitement, she could not tell.

"Show me how to see as you do," she whispered. "Help me find my own allies. . . ."

"It is harder, when you are with child," said the shamaness, "but we will see."

It was not only the spirits from whom Gudrun learned. Until now, Attila's need to prove his mastery by getting a child on her had been her protection. Success might well diminish his fascination with her body, and if so, she would have to use her mind to intrigue him. Only by holding his interest could she protect the interests of her new child.

Lentia was the logical place for any messenger going east or west to pause, and Gudrun was careful to make them welcome. They betrayed no secrets in telling the khan's wife what was known, east or west, to everyone. But what she learned, she remembered, setting fact to fact to build a picture of what was passing in the other lands. In this way Attila himself had made his reputation for omniscience. His sources were of course far more extensive, as was his knowledge, but she persevered.

Messengers from the lands of the Huns told her that Ruga had threatened to break the truce with the eastern emperor if the Romans did not send back the Amilzouri, the Tonosours, Boiskoi, and other tribes which had taken refuge on the Roman side of the Danuvius. Theodosius had chosen two former consuls to negotiate a settlement, probably in gold, which would be more useful to the Huns than their fugitive tribesmen had been. More recently Plinthas, one of the Romans, had sent an Alan renegade called Sengilach to plead his cause until the Roman embassy could get there. Ruga, it was said, was temporizing, hoping to raise the price by playing one negotiator against the other.

Messengers from the Rhenus told her that Gundohar wanted to build a new palace modeled after the Imperial residence in Ravenna. It had not been made clear where he was going to find the funds to pay for it; according to rumor, he meant to use Sigfrid's hoard. At that point Gudrun's informant had halted, frightened perhaps by something in her face that he had not been meant to see. That night she slept badly, haunted by dreams in which

Brunahild was trying to speak to her. But no matter how she listened, she could not understand her words.

And toward the end of the harvest, a messenger from Attila came pelting into the village with the news that Ruga, the khan of khans, was dead, and the chieftains and locha-goi were gathering for his funeral.

"Lady, if you go to the funeral, you endanger your child," said Locris as Gudrun directed Bala to pack her crimson overgown.

"Perhaps, but I think he will be in greater danger if I stay here." She massaged her belly. She had been having a few warning cramps lately, and knew she was near her time. "I am far enough along so that the babe could survive. My first child was late and large. I do not fear this one arriving too soon. The White Heron has read the bones for me, and sees no immediate danger. If my time comes while we are on the journey, we will stop, that is all."

Locris shook her head, as she always did when Gudrun referred to the *kam-kadin*, who had become part of the household, by Attila's order, when she informed him she was with child. But Gudrun knew this journey was no fancy of pregnancy. With Ruga gone, there would be a major readjustment in the balance of power. She needed to be there to represent the interests of her son. It did not occur to her to doubt that the infant would be a boy. All of Attila's children that she knew of were male. Ereka was still first wife and queen, but any woman who gave the khan a son acquired a status which a mere junior wife could not claim, no matter how powerful her relatives.

Gudrun would not have taken such a risk with a child of Sigfrid's, but if she did not take a chance with this one now, his life might be at greater risk later. She had thought long and hard about her future when she first realized that she was carrying, and decided not to abort the child. She considered her situation no less dispassionately now. The danger to herself if she should have a difficult labor she discounted, finding a certain justice in the prospect of dying for having conceived another man's child. She was not doing this for love of Attila or the unborn babe. This son would give her power.

Despite Locris's dire prophecies, Gudrun had not completely left her senses. She knew well that in a jolting, wooden-wheeled Hun cart she would not have survived a day. But much of the journey could be accomplished by water, and earlier that summer, when her pregnancy began to make riding uncomfortable, she had instructed the woodworkers of Lentia to craft a horse litter to her specifications, like the ones she had seen the Roman ladies use. It was portable enough to be carried with them.

Three days after she had gotten the news of Ruga's death, Gudrun set out in three flatbottomed boats with Locris, the White Heron, and three slave girls, leaving Sunnilda weeping behind. That parting had been the hardest, next to persuading Ecgward to stay behind to guard her, and if necessary, to take her back to the Niflungar.

Her escort of warriors trotted along the path beside the river, keeping pace with the barge. The heat of summer's ending still lay heavy on the land, and heat haze shimmered on the hills. Even through the awning that shaded her Gudrun could feel the sunlight boiling the moist river air. The sweat ran down her face and her sides and between her thighs in such streams she thought that if her waters had broken she would not have known. She lay, breathing slowly, hoarding her strength against the need that would come.

"How do you feel?" The voice of the *kam-kadin* roused her.

"As if I were being boiled in a cauldron," Gudrun answered her. "How do you stay so cool?"

The White Heron grunted. "You're still young, still part of the world, now more than most times, because of the child. When you get old like me, your body is weak but the spirit gets stronger. More so when you follow the spirit path."

Gudrun turned her head to observe the Hun woman. She seemed ancient, to be sure, but not aged. *Like my mother, until she gave up, toward the end.* She had come the long way round, resisting her mother's ways, but now it seemed to her that her feet were on that path as well.

"Now I ask you a question," said the shamaness. "Which is stronger, the mountain or the river?"

Gudrun thought for a moment, rejecting the obvious. "The river, because it wears away mountains?"

"That is a good answer, but think. Where the Danu flows into the plain it grows broad, marshy, hardly a river at all. The mountain gives shape to the water—when the channel is deep, the river flows fast. They need each other."

Gudrun blinked, glimpsing for a moment a reality in which there were no certainties, only patterns, relationships. It was certainly not the way the Christian priests had taught her to look at the world.

"Is that how it is in the land of the spirits?"

Once more the old woman gave her grunt of laughter. "You begin to learn. For you, now, this sun is too hot. Is the sun then bad? It is the same with spirits."

Gudrun nodded. "My mother had a rune for that—*Jera*, the rune of the circling seasons, everything coming to pass at the right time." For a moment that memory evoked, like a shadow, an awareness of the god who had given the runes, the god who had taken Sigfrid. She shook her head and made herself look at the bright glitter of the river.

"I know the runes, a little," said the White Heron. "The *baliurunae* of the Goths are not the mothers of the Huns, as some people say, but we sheltered them when their own tribe began to follow the new god. Our *kams* learn from them. Words are different, gods are different, but many magics are the same."

Was that good or bad? wondered Gudrun. She had sought this woman's teaching partly as a protection from the god who gave her own people magic. At first, much of what the White Heron had to say had seemed strange, but sometimes now there would be a moment when it made sense to her.

She closed her eyes, directing her attention to the vibration of the current through the wood of the boat. It was all part of the pattern—the flowing water and the beating sun and the child floating within her warm body. . . . And for a moment, though she still felt the heat, it was not uncomfortable.

The final stage of the journey was the hardest, when they left the river and Gudrun had to lie in the swaying horse litter for the three days it took to reach the encampment of the khans. The hooves of the horses ground the hard earth of the road to a fine powder that worked its way through every covering, even if one could have borne to wear more than the necessary minimum of clothing. Though the counsels of the old *kam-kadin* eased her, it grew harder to attain harmony. Her belly clenched with contractions more often now, though they never lasted. If she did not bear her child on the road, surely the birth must be soon.

"The warriors of Ruga are as many as the stars in the heavens; they cover the plains like the grass . . . " So chanted the praise-singers of the khan. When the encampment came into view at last it seemed to Gudrun that the horde was, if not countless, at least beyond any ability of hers to reckon. The smoke of their cookfires veiled the sky. And here, at the death of their ruler, it was the Huns themselves, not the peoples they had conquered, who were in the majority. For the first time she had a sense of her husband's people as a nation.

The other thing that became clear as she recuperated from her journey and began to move about the encampment was that these people had come for something more than their khan's funeral. Ruga had been a great lord and worthy of honor, but his death was not an occasion for undue sorrow. The tribal kings and clan chieftains had come here, as she had, to see who would inherit his power.

The camp was full of rumors. It seemed impossible that so mighty a ruler could simply die of natural causes like any other man. The khan had been in the midst of negotiating with the Romans over the return of several clans which had fled the Hun hegemony. Among the refugees were Mamai and Atakam, two great-grandsons of Balamber. Some said Ruga had intended to execute them, and therefore he had been killed by their supporters, while others thought he had meant to make them his heirs, and therefore been murdered, if not by poison then by magic, by followers of Attila or his brother. These stories and more Gudrun heard, in infinite variation, as she moved through the camp.

Ruga's sons had died in battle; his surviving grandsons were children. Attila and Bladarda were his obvious heirs, but among the Huns the succession did not always follow strict bloodlines. If another leader arose with sufficient following, he could challenge them. Gradually, as the clans came in, their alignments became more visible. Bladarda and Attila, having been for so many years the warleaders for their uncle, had large followings, well armed, well trained, loyal to their leaders. The king of the Akatiri, Kuridach, seemed to be making a bid, feasting the chieftains, and walking about with a brightly dressed retinue. Anagai of the Utigur was less obvious about his campaigning; the word ran that he was prepared to throw his weight behind the most likely candidate. So far, the chieftains of the Utzinzures, Bittugures, Angisciri, Bardores and the others were keeping their own counsel.

So much Gudrun learned, but one thing she did not know, and that was whether her husband approved of her coming. Edikon, who ruled Attila's household, had made room for her *ger* in the khan's enclosure. Locris was given food for them from his stores. She reasoned that she would have known if he were greatly angry. No doubt the actions of one junior wife, even pregnant, were of little moment to him just now. Since her arrival, she had only seen him in passing, and he had sent no word.

But three days after her own arrival, when the child pressed so heavily she began to consider taking a ride in a Hun wagon to shake him loose, there was a stir outside the enclosure. Gudrun came out of her *ger* to see just such a wagon as she had been thinking about, but larger, more heavily carven and more brightly painted than any she had yet seen, curtained with embroidered linen and with fittings of polished bronze. The driver seated on the first of the three horses that pulled it reined his team to a halt in front of Attila's *ger*.

A second, more modestly appointed, wagon came after. When it stopped, a slave girl jumped out of the back, carrying a stepping stool. An impressive number of servants followed. They began to unload the wagon and erect another *ger* next to that of the khan; Gudrun recognized some of them from her stay with the queen. But by the style and substance of the entourage she had already realized who this must be.

The curtains of the painted wagon quivered. A figure emerged, swathed in veils despite the heat. She stepped onto the stool, and looked around her. Gudrun straightened, abruptly conscious of the bovine swell of her belly. But then she usually felt like a cow in the presence of Attila's queen. Ereka's dark gaze moved over her figure; for a long moment their eyes met. Then the queen completed her descent and disappeared into Attila's *ger*.

Ereka had arrived just in time. That night, the last tribe came in, and in the morning runners passed through the encampment calling the people to offer final honors to their lord at the *strava* of Ruga, khan of khans.

Gudrun angled the polished bronze face of her little hand mirror so that she could see to adjust her headdress, holding it by the knob at the back through which the cord ran, then let it drop to hang upon her breast with her necklaces of glass and amber and gold. She was dressed entirely as a woman of the Huns today, in a pieced tunic of saffron linen ornamented with embroidered and beaded patches and bands. The beadwork on her headdress suggested a round diadem without quite being one, with strings of beads hanging down to either side. She had pinned her hair up, and a sheer veil would give her some protection from the sun.

Only in one thing was she still a Burgund. Now that she no longer wished to hold off labor, she had put on the Frowe's neck ring, the ring that Sigfrid had given her, that had once lain in Andvari's hoard. The ring, and the rune rod that had also come from the hoard, always traveled with her, but until now she had not touched them since Sigfrid burned on his pyre. The sweetness she felt at the warm weight of the gold brought with it the pain of memory; she tasted it like a sore tooth, wincing, but unable to keep away.

Gudrun shook herself and gave a final twitch to her veil. She still had not spoken to Attila, but Edikon had informed her that there was to be an enclosure from which the ladies of the royal house might watch the proceedings. She came out of her *ger*, blinking, and saw Ereka, looking cool and slender in green silk. The queen beckoned. Gudrun took a deep breath and moved toward her, Locris at her shoulder. She had hoped that by the time she emerged, Attila's first wife would already have departed. Now Gudrun would appear to be part of Ereka's household. But she could not refuse the invitation without discourtesy.

In order to preserve the body until all the chieftains who might want to assure themselves that the khan was truly dead could see him, the body had been wrapped with herbs and placed in a wooden sarcophagus. Watching from the women's enclosure, which was shaded by a linen awning and had, thank the gods, benches for them to sit on, Gudrun wondered if anyone had taken advantage of the opportunity. The curtains of the silk tent which sheltered it had been tied back so that the coffin could be seen. Behind it gaped the grave pit, dug deep into the loamy soil and braced with stout timbers.

"You are very near your time," said Ereka quietly beside her.

"I am past it," answered Gudrun. "But it was so with my daughter as well."

Drums boomed insistently, or was it hoofbeats? Both women looked up as the crowd gave way before a score of horsemen, who whipped their mounts into a gallop as they burst through. At full speed they charged the funerary tent, swerving at the last moment with no visible sign from the riders into a tight circle around the pavilion and the grave. They were armed with swords and the small round shields of horsemen, but they wore coats of Roman silk instead of armor, in their caps nodded white egret plumes, and everywhere, on garments and horse trappings, glittered plaques and pendants of gold. Nine times they circled, chanting the khan's titles and victories, then came to a halt beside the grave.

As the dust settled, the sound of the drums became audible once more. The great lords of the Huns were coming, their shamans dancing around them. Attila's somber grey silk stood out among the gaudier garb of the others, but for the occasion even he had put on a round diadem of gold set with garnets and almandines. His face, as usual, showed no emotion, but his eyes were never still.

"I was surprised to hear that you were carrying," the queen said then.

Gudrun bowed her head demurely, not asking how she had known. "It was the will of our husband that I bear him a child." That, of course, was unanswerable, though there was speculation in Ereka's frown. Her dark gaze rested for a moment on the neck ring, as if she sensed the power locked within.

A man called Eslas, who had been one of the most trusted of Ruga's ministers, stepped out from among the others, and the people became still.

"Ruga, the khan of khans, is dead—" he cried. "Chief of the Huns, Ruga, the son of Uldin, who ruled first with Oktar his brother and then supreme. Mourn him, men of the Huns! Cry out for the mighty leader!"

From the gathered people came a ululation of mourning. Men began to gash their cheeks with their knives. The drums pulsed like a giant's heartbeat as Eslas went on.

"The Goths and the Gepids were his servants, the Romans of the East and of the West bowed before him. In his time the pastures have been rich in grass, and the tribes of the Huns are rich in sheep and horses. We are grown wealthy in wine and silk and gold, and the peoples of the earth fear us. All this comes to us in the time of Ruga. Shall we not weep for him? Who will give us gold and victory now?"

That was certainly the question, thought Gudrun. The chieftains went into the tent and carried out the coffin. There were ropes around it. Carefully they lowered it into the burial pit. One of the shamans jumped down into the pit to receive the platters of food and drink, the arms and horse trappings and other grave goods that had been stacked waiting. New shouts and cries broke out among the people, as if they saw the good life they had gained going into the grave with the offerings. More of the warriors slashed at their cheeks so that blood ran down with their tears.

"Why are they so afraid?" said Gudrun, so softly that only Ereka could hear. "Don't they know it is Attila and Bladarda who have been winning those victories?"

"It was wise to give credit to Ruga," said the queen in the same low tone. "I counseled him to say more of his own deeds, but Attila goes his own way always."

"Will he win?"

"He cannot fail!" Ereka answered fiercely. "That Kuridachos makes a great noise, but he is weak inside. He will give way when my lord faces him. Bladarda is strongest, because he has had equal power."

"And he is Attila's brother," observed Gudrun, remembering how Grimahild had raised her sons to support Gundohar.

"By a different mother—" Ereka's glance flicked scornfully across Gudrun's belly. Her son need expect no support from the queen's children. The message was clear. Gudrun found that she had reached up to grip the smooth gold of the neck ring and took a deep breath to regain her composure.

"Bladarda looks backward to the old days," the queen went on. "Always does the old things in the same way. He holds Attila back, I have said so, but he only smiles."

Gudrun looked at her curiously. "Do you doubt his wisdom? I think he will act when he is ready, when he is sure he can win."

The other *kams* were drumming and chanting, invoking the protection of the spirits. The grave goods had all been put into the chamber, and now they were setting in place a roof of stout timbers. The khan's favorite horses had been brought up. They stamped and sidled nervously at the scent of death. Gudrun closed her eyes, remembering how Grani had fought when they brought him to Sigfrid's pyre.

But the shamans had their own magic that held the animals entranced as they were led to the edge of the grave to have their throats cut. In turn each of the three was killed and toppled in. Each of the chieftains took a handful of the earth that had been heaped up beside the pit and cast it in, Attila and his brother first of all. Then they turned away and slaves came out with shovels to finish the job.

Cow horns blatted and the people began to edge back. Riders cantered back and forth, setting up poles a-flutter with brightly colored strips of cloth to mark the boundaries for the games.

Horsemen were forming up for the first races already. The judge's lance swung down, and the riders were off, the angular shanks of the Hun ponies churning with surprising speed. The Hun horse was a surprising creature, thought Gudrun, watching them run, long bodied, big boned, and heavy headed, with manes like hanging fleeces and long, bushy tails. They looked like bone-bags, some of them, but they were capable of a surprising turn of speed, and as she had seen, they could keep going long after a more esthetic beast would have given up and died.

Their masters had braided up the manes with ribbons for the racing, each plait finished with a little bell; above the drumming of the broad hooves came a faint silvery shimmer of sound. Dust billowed behind them. She tracked them by it as they disappeared beyond Ruga's mound, which was growing steadily but surely as the slaves added more dirt and stones. Sound faded and then swelled once more. In another moment dark shapes of men and horses shot through the haze, outrunning their dust. A dark beast whose rider wore a green coat was in the lead.

Ereka frowned. "One of Bladarda's men," she observed softly. Some of the women began a shrill ululation as the green rider thundered between the endposts to victory.

They watched the next race in silence. One of the Akatiri warriors won it and another group of women cheered him. When the third race went to a man of Attila's guard they smiled.

Slave girls came around with baskets of fruit and little cakes and flasks of mead. Gudrun waved them away and drank from the waterskin she had brought with her. The races had ended and the men were shooting at targets from horseback now. The powerful Hun bow sent the arrows drilling into their targets with a thunk audible across the field. Here, and in the lance work, Attila's men won more often, but his brother's warriors were very good. It was not surprising, for these two commanders had seen the most action in recent years. Gudrun watched the competing warriors, and the warriors who were watching them, and thought that it was here, rather than at the council fire, that the decision would be made.

She was not surprised when the competitions ended with the men who served Ruga's two nephews almost even in score.

"It will not be long now," she said, rubbing her aching back as they prepared to go. "The assembly is called for this evening, I understand." She bit her lip as her belly clenched in a particularly strong premonitory pang.

"Many things may happen this night," said Ereka, watching her. "Soon, I think, you will bear your child. Every time a woman gives birth is like going into battle, not so? Anything can happen. I am told that with your first child you nearly died."

The queen spoke sweetly, but Gudrun heard the warning. She had eaten nothing that did not come directly from Attila's stores since Ereka arrived. Was the queen powerful enough to ill-wish her by looking? Her hand went to the neck ring again.

"It was Brunahild, I believe, who saved your life then? It is a pity she cannot help you now."

Gudrun stared at her, wondering if the other woman had known how much that remark would wound. With an effort, she kept her face serene.

"Indeed, she was skilled," she said carefully. "But I am fortunate to have the services of a powerful *kam-kadin*. She says there is no great danger to me just now. And indeed, you should wish me well. Think what an evil omen it would be if even the most junior of the khan's wives should die giving birth to his child."

One winged eyebrow rose as Ereka acknowledged this response, and she smiled. Gudrun hoped she would see the truth of it, and forbear to attack her or her child at this moment of their greatest vulnerability.

That night a great fire was built on the plain before Ruga's kurgan; his wood-carved image presided from the top of the mound. The lords of the Huns gathered around it with their picked men behind them to choose their new king. Gudrun could hear them shouting even from Attila's enclosure, but she would not have gone to observe even had she been welcome. On the way back to her *ger* her pains had come upon her in earnest. While her husband strove to win a high king's diadem, she labored to bring forth his child.

"We must send to tell him," Locris had said when it began, but Gudrun, between pangs, shook her head.

"He does not need to know that the battle has begun, only that I have gained the victory." *If I do. . . . Don't even think it!* she told herself then. *Attila will be lord of the Huns, and I will bear this child alive and healthy.* Then another pain took her, and for a little while she did not think at all.

At least this labor was going faster than her first. Standing seemed to ease her. Naked except for the neck ring, she clung to the framework of the *ger*, panting, while Locris rubbed her back between contractions and the White Heron chanted softly, watching her with bright dark eyes. With Sunnilda, it had been the length of the labor that had exhausted her, before Brunahild had turned the child in the womb so that it could get free. Could a birthing go too fast, she wondered? She did not remember having felt so much pain before.

Presently her strength gave out and she dropped to her hands and knees, gasping.

The *kam-kadin* moved around the *ger*, drawing symbols in the air with her horse-headed cane. To Gudrun, watching in a moment of respite, they looked like the *tamga* marks with which the Huns branded their horses.

"The spirits gather—" said the old woman, squatting beside Gudrun, who was lying now on her side. "They come always to a birth, but this time there are very many. There is much power here, I am not sure from where—"

Gudrun gripped the neck ring and for a moment was eased. "Some of it is here. . . ." she panted. "The ring . . . belongs to our goddess. It helped me before."

"So—" The *kam-kadin* held her hand over the gold, not quite touching it, and peered at the runes. "I see it is true." She set her hand on Gudrun's convulsing belly, then bent to check the opening of the womb. "Call on your goddess," she said when she had finished her examination. "I think it will not be long now."

Gudrun closed her eyes, directing her awareness inward. For so long, the only god she had thought about was the one she was fighting. But of all the others, it was the Frowe whom she had especially avoided, for from the Lady came the joy she had shared with Sigfrid. She whimpered, remembering the warmth of his body and the light in his eyes when he made love to her. *Lady, how could you betray me? How could you allow me to bear another man's child?*

Since that afternoon she had been fighting to bring forth the baby, body and soul united as horse and rider when they charge the enemy. But now, all the grief she thought she had forgotten rose up to ambush her spirit, and as her will failed her body convulsed in terror and she was overwhelmed by the pain. They were calling her name, but all she could think of was to get away.

"She has fainted! Take off the neck ring—" cried Locris.

"No," came the reply, "then she is lost indeed. We call her goddess to help now. . . ."

The hollow thunder of the *kam-kadin's* hand drum filled the *ger.* Gudrun jerked and moaned, trying to escape that insistent throbbing, but it followed her even into the darkness. There was something familiar about that rhythm, for a moment curiosity overcame her fear. It was a heartbeat, but not her own frantic fluttering. This booming was deep and regular, it filled her awareness as the heartbeat of the mother fills the world of the unborn child.

Gradually Gudrun's panic eased. She was safe here, secure in a way she had not known since she lay in her own mother's womb. At the thought she felt a flicker of unease—wasn't she the mother now? The space around her was suffused with a warmth like laughter. *"You are still My child . . . "* her mind, trying to understand, interpreted the response as words.

"Let me stay with You!" Gudrun cried.

"How can you be anywhere else?" She sensed indulgent amusement from the Presence that surrounded her. Suddenly the warmth she felt was sunlight; she heard birdsong and running water, the air was scented with new grass, all bound together by a circle of gold. But it was more than hearing and seeing. The songs were coming from her own throat, the waters ran through her veins, and the grass— she could feel the roots drawing strength from the earth, feel that strength surging through her, growing, growing. . . .

Gudrun felt power swelling within her, bursting forth in a song that was a shout. And abruptly she was back in her body again, her legs drawn up, her belly heaving. But the music was still with her.

"Push!" came the cry from without and within. Once more, the power peaked and passed through her. She felt as if she were being split in half, but it did not matter, the pain was part of the circle too.

"At last . . . " came that inner awareness, *"you begin to understand!"*

The *kam-kadin* was still drumming, a triumphant pulsebeat that lifted Gudrun out of herself; the energy was too great, she could not breathe. For a moment her sight darkened. Then a sudden wind swirled around her; she gulped air, and with it a power, cool and silver as that of the goddess had been warmly gold, that shocked through every vein.

In that moment of balance she was acutely and simultaneously aware of everything—lamplight flickering across the *ger's* round ceiling, Locris's bony knees digging into her back, the *kami-kadin* kneeling before her, and the impossible pressure of the child whose body was splitting her own, caught between the worlds. Gudrun held her breath, held all existence within her own fragile boundaries. Then a still voice like the first shifting particle of snow that releases the avalanche said, *"Now . . ."*

She exhaled, felt herself whirled in a long spiral inward and downward, every part of her united in one last explosive effort that thrust Attila's son squalling into the world.

Gudrun's next coherent thought was that everything had stopped. Logic told her that could not be true; she felt the moist rasp of the cloth with which Locris was cleaning her up, and heard a thin mewling from somewhere nearby. But the forces which had raged through her body had departed, leaving her emptied of energy. Her womb was no longer occupied, and she was alone in her head once more. She opened her eyes as the White Heron laid the child in the crook of her arm.

Swaddled, all she could see was his head. His skull had been compressed by the birth; she knew it was often so, and with time the soft bones would round out, but he appeared to have come into the world with the helmet-shaped skull traditional Hun mothers bound their babies' heads to attain. She tried to speak, coughed, and tried again.

"He is whole?" Better to have the baby born dead than to give Attila a flawed son. Locris grinned broadly.

"He is a beautiful boy!"

The baby sneezed and turned his head against her breast. His features were crumpled, wisps of hair still plastered darkly to his skull. His opaque gaze wandered vaguely to her face and away, as if he were wondering how he had gotten here. Gudrun found herself wondering too. He did not look like anyone she knew. With a sigh she lifted her nipple and poked it into the pink mouth so that the child could feed.

Gudrun knew that she had slept when she woke to the sound of distant cheering. Her muscles were stiffening from her labor, but in the crook of her arm the baby was sleeping peacefully. The door flap opened and the lampflame wavered as the White Heron came back in. Gudrun raised an eyebrow inquiringly.

"They have decided," the old woman squatted beside her. "It is to be Bladarda and Attila in joint kingship, like Ruga and Oktar were before. They are all getting drunk now."

Gudrun nodded. That was only to be expected. A wave of relief made her cold. Attila was still in power. She and the son she had just borne him would be safe. Seeing the shiver, the *kam-kadin* tucked the blanket more closely around her and she slept again.

The next time she woke, morning light was streaming through the opened doorway of the *ger* and Attila was there. Almost immediately he met her gaze. At first Gudrun had thought him unaffected by the night's events, but as he turned the light danced in his eyes as if a fire were burning within.

"So"—he looked down at the child on her arm—"we have both been busy this night."

"And both victorious, as I hear," she answered him.

"The child is healthy—" It was not quite a question.

"Indeed he is, my lord," exclaimed Locris. "Would you see?" She plucked the child from Gudrun's arm and peeled back his wrappings. At the touch of the dawn-chilled air the baby began to cry. Attila nodded, and still kneeling, the woman rewrapped and handed him the child. The baby was still mewling, but as the khan began that odd humming which was so effective with horses, he stilled. Gudrun supposed she should not have been surprised at Attila's expertise—he had a great deal of experience with sons,, after all.

"You have done well. What do you want?" The khan settled the baby into the crook of his arm and looked back at her.

Gudrun blinked, and her hand went to the neck ring she still wore. *I want Sigfrid, and Sigfrid's child . . .* she thought grimly. *I want to be your queen. . . .* One was as likely as the other.

"I am still too tired to think." She managed a wavering smile. "Must I tell you now?"

Attila shrugged, then glanced toward the doorway. Gudrun realized that she could hear a murmuring from outside, as if a great many people were gathered there.

"I will show him to the people." Attila ducked through the doorway, still carrying the child, and there was a sudden roar of acclaim. It took a few moments for it to quiet again.

"My wife has given me another son—" the khan's voice rang out, and it became quite still. "I show him to the earth, I show him to the Lord of Heaven. I name him Apsik son of Attila son of Mundzuk of Balamber's line! We are sons of Tanri, we lead tribes, rule nations. Child of kings, he is born to royal inheritance."

Apsik—"little horse" in the language of the Huns. It was an appropriate name for the son of the Lord of Horses, thought Gudrun as the people outside began once more to cheer.

Chapter 10 ✿ Warsongs

Barbetomagus, Treveri
Spring to Summer, A.D. 436

T he king's long fingers strayed over the harp-strings, wandering through variations on the harmonies with which he had supported his song. Young Andulf stood enraptured beside him, the wine he was supposed to be pouring forgotten in his hands. The boy was still officially in the queen's household but somehow, especially when the king was making music, he seemed to spend most of his time near Gundohar.

Galamvara sat beside the window, talking to her cousin Valobald, who had arrived from Tolosa the day before. When she moved, the sunlight struck bronze sparks from her curling hair. As always, when he watched her, Gundohar found himself beginning to smile. He thought, *I am a fortunate man*, and then, *why isn't this enough for me?*

Nearby, Gislahar had set up the board for "tables" and persuaded Hagano to give him a game. Gislahar was in his mid-twenties now, tall without Gundohar's angularity and strong without Godo's overdeveloped musculature, but he still crowed over every capture like a boy. Hagano played, as usual, in dour silence, though from time to time he would frown at their visitor, who had not yet explained why he had come. Bent over the board, it was obvious how his hair had thinned across the broad dome of his skull, but then so had Gundohar's. It seemed to the king that his brother's

179

features had been ennobled by the rising browline, whereas his own could only suffer from the additional elongation.

Through the window the king could see tiled rooftops, and in the distance, the new green of vineyards planted beyond the city wall. When the sun shone brightly he sometimes thought he could see a shimmer of light above the leaves, as if the spirit of the grape was dancing there. A fair prospect, as goodly to the eye as Galamvara, whose spirit glowed like a steady flame. He had no interest in any other woman, but when he looked at the city his father had left him he remembered the glories of Ravenna, and he was no longer satisfied.

He had been singing to them of the conquests of Airmanareik and how he had made from the tribes and peoples of the Eastlands an empire. It was all from his earlier work, for since his journey to Ravenna he had composed nothing new. The Goths still dreamed of empire, he thought, remembering how Thiudimir had spoken at Ravenna. And so, he supposed, did he. But when he remembered Italia it was not so much the power of Roma that he longed for, but its beauty, like song preserved in stone.

Was it because he had begotten no child that he sought some other form of immortality? Since his return from Ravenna, it was not for lack of trying. He felt himself responding even to the thought of Galamvara's soft skin against his own, but despite the delight they found together, she had not conceived. He thought that perhaps the fever in his groin after he was wounded by Waldhari had killed his seed, and he would have to seek an heir among his kin. But none of his brothers was married; the only nephew he had was the child Gudrun had borne the summer before, and what care would Attila's son have for the Burgund lands?

Sigfrid's son would have been a worthy heir . . . came a still voice within him. But he himself had made that impossible. Sigfrid had left only daughters, but up and down the Rhenus he was gaining another kind of immortality in song. The

king had heard one already about how Sigfrid killed the
dragon on Wurm Fell and bore away his hoard of gold.

But who remembered the men who wrote the songs?
Even if he could write an epic worthy of the Goth-king, it
would be Airmanareik whose name would survive, not Gundohar. Among the Romans it was different, where men's
names were written with their words on parchment rolls.
But parchment was ephemeral—look how many works had
been lost when the Library of Alexandria was burned. To
survive, you had to write your name in stone.

He had begun, modestly, with a new church for the Arian believers, their numbers swelled by the queen's household so that Arianism had come to be accepted as the
religion of the Burgund court. Her father Theoderid might
tease the Romans with intermittent support for the Catholic
form of Christianity, but most of his people still followed
the Arian faith they had been taught by Ulfilas when the
Goths were still one people. It made little difference to
Gundohar whether the Christos was of one substance with
the Father or only his most perfect creation. What mattered
was that to profess the latter aligned him subtly with the
Goths. And with that, he realized that he, like Hagano, was
watching Valobald.

As it happened, Galamvara's cousin was actually already
Gundohar's cousin as well, at least by marriage, but his
uncle's daughter Gundrada had been married off when he
was a child, and he hardly remembered her. Her husband
was a stocky, good-humored man in his middle forties with
a luxuriant brown beard. He was said to be one of the men
most trusted in negotiation by King Theoderid, despite, or
perhaps because of, his apparent simplicity. Surely he was
making more than a family visit now.

The king's fingers twitched, striking an unexpected twang
from the strings, and everyone looked at him. Carefully, he
set the harp down.

"I am glad to hear that your uncle is well," he said gen-
ially, "but what of Theoderid's armies? Are they well fed

and well found and eager for the summer's campaigning?"

Unspoken, the question hung between them—"*Who are the Visigoths going to fight this year?*"

Gislahar and Hagano looked up, abandoning all pretense of interest in their game. Valobald smiled.

"Tell me," he said conversationally, "what news have you heard from Gallia?"

Gislahar blinked at the apparent irrelevance, but the king frowned.

"Not much—" he said slowly. "There is still trouble in the north, in Armorica, some kind of uprising among the slaves." He knew that after the Gallic tribes were conquered the Romans had divided the best farmland into great estates, the *latifundiae*, worked by slaves from all over the Empire.

"More than an uprising," said Valobald. "A man called Tibatto leads them, and he has built an army. Since last year his *bacaudae* have ranged the land like wolves, burning the villas and killing any Roman who cannot reach the safety of the towns. Now the troubles are spreading eastward into the lands between the Liger and the Sequana."

Everyone frowned. Conquest was one thing, but not willful destruction of property which they might one day want themselves. But what did events in Armorica have to do with the Burgunds?

"The Empire is built on slavery, and more than anything else—more than us, even—the Romans fear a slave rebellion. Aetius and his best general, Litorius, have both gone to fight them."

"The First Flavia out of Constantia, I heard—" said Hagano reflectively. The legion stationed in Armorica was supposed to keep the peace there.

"And from the Seventh Gemina, the Septimani Juniores." Valobad's smile deepened as he named the legion stationed in the south. "They both fought in Armorica last year. They weren't enough to do the job. Now"—it was definitely a grin—"I have heard that some of the units from the Second Flavia are also going to be called. . . ."

"From Belgica!" Gislahar whistled. "They really are scraping out the barrel for this one."

Hagano looked at their visitor. "I begin to see what you mean."

Gundohar took a moment longer to see all the implications, but the tactical situation was quite clear. The Romans used their own troops against *bacaudae*. Barbarians they set against each other, with a few cohorts in reserve to stiffen them and keep them honest. But not this year. He was surprised, really, that he had not heard from Aetius, but perhaps the Master of the West was hoping to quash the slaves and get his legions back in place before his loyal feoderati noticed they were gone.

"Don't tell me—" he said pleasantly, "Theoderid has finally decided to actually take Arelas."

"Will there ever be a better opportunity?"

"And he wants us to pledge not to attack him while he's doing it?" Gislahar asked eagerly.

"Oh I think Valobald is suggesting something a little more ambitious," Hagano said dryly. "I think he is pointing out that any troops that do remain in the south will be even more hopelessly overextended if at the same time we attack Treveri."

"There is only one effective force unaccounted for." Valobald's smile faded. "Aetius could hire the Huns."

"But Attila is married to our sister Gudrun!" Gislahar exclaimed.

Valobald shrugged. "That doesn't always signify. Aetius married Theoderid's oldest daughter, after all. Now that I think about it, I suppose that makes him your brother-in-law. But that was a long time ago, whereas I understand your sister has just given the khan a son. If Attila refuses to attack you for her sake, then there is no one to oppose us at all."

Gundohar sat back, thinking furiously. Of course he

wanted Belgica. The Burgunds had tried to take it several times before, but could such a project possibly succeed?

Valobald rose to his feet. "No doubt you will wish to discuss it. Galamvara, my dear, would you like to show me your gardens?" Andulf pushed his straight hair out of his eyes, topped off everyone's goblets, and followed them.

When he had gone, the king let out his breath in a long sigh.

"Interesting, isn't it," said Hagano dryly. "He expects Attila to keep his oaths to us while cheerfully counseling us to break our pledges to Attila's ally."

"I don't like oath-breaking either," said Gundohar, and saw his younger brother's eyes widen. "But our people are growing. At some point our territory is going to have to grow as well. The question is whether this is the time."

"Do we have enough resources to field the full war-host?" asked Gislahar uncertainly.

"If we empty the treasury," Hagano replied. He looked back at the king. "Valobald is right—we will never have a better chance. But it is still a gamble. You must make the decision, brother." He grimaced. "Whatever other oaths are broken, you have mine."

"And mine!" exclaimed Gislahar, apprehension giving way to excitement. "Do we need to consult with Godomar?"

"Don't worry—he will like it. It means more fighting," Hagano answered him.

Gundohar rubbed his eyes. "I think we must . . . take the chance. We need the land."

But the visions that filled his mind were not of tilled fields, but of the marble columns of the city that had once been called Augusta Treverorum. Borbetomagus had only been a garrison town. Treveri had been home to emperors. If he could carve his name into those imperial stones, it would never die.

Hagano was always surprised by the way stone could burn. Flames were shooting from the villa's roof by the time he caught up with his war-band, filling the night sky with a ruddy light which at least made it possible to distinguish friend from foe. Several bodies, both Roman and Burgund, littered the ground. He ran toward the closest conflict, but before he could get a blow in, the Romans broke and made a dash for the church beside it, where the surviving members of their troop were still holding the door.

"Get men around back, there may be another exit—" he snapped, and two of his warriors trotted off, grinning.

The roof was beginning to smolder already; the church would not be a refuge for long. Firelight flickered on an arched doorway, touched the faces carved on the pillars with a premonitory agony. Some of the men formed up in a loose circle in front of the door, waiting like dogs begging scraps for their dinner, while others began a more careful search of the remaining buildings. This fight was the most fun they had had for some time.

Belgica Prima had been taken by surprise, the skeleton garrisons left behind in guardpost and camp helpless against the numbers coming against them. The province was used to being raided, but this was no swift blow against a specific target, leaving everyone outside the line of march alone. Gundohar's goal this time was conquest, and he was moving his army through the countryside with the deadly deliberation of a Roman war machine, reducing all resistance. Many, of course, escaped, fleeing before the advancing horde to the shelter of Treveri. That too was part of the plan, for the storehouses of the city were not what they had been in the days of the soldier-emperors. When he laid siege to the city, hunger would be his ally.

In a few places, though, the local magnates had armed their slaves and fought for their homes. Clearly the man leading this bunch had military training; his people had fought well and retreated in good order. It would not do them much good, though, thought Hagano, once the roof of the church began to burn.

"A pity about the church," said Hanno, beside him.

"That's where all the good stuff will be stored. There won't be anything left of the vestments, but I suppose we can sift the ashes for melted gold."

"Later—" Hagano gave him a sour look. By this point in the campaign most of the men had some scrap of looted silk draped over their clothes. "Or the line of advance will leave us behind."

A flicker of light caught his eye; from the church roof darted a tongue of flame. Smoke was beginning to drift from the doorway. The air in there must be getting bad now. He shifted his grip on his sword hilt; the men inside must make their break soon. From the direction of the villa he heard a woman's scream and then men's laughter. He started to turn, frowning, for he had specifically forbidden rape, but at that moment there was a flash from the church doorway as a sword caught the light. The Romans stumbled into the open, coughing, and with a yell his own men closed in.

Two were cut down almost immediately, another surrendered, but the last man had some notion of sword work, and had spitted Hanno and wounded one of the others when Hagano finished the man he was fighting and came at him. He was young, with aquiline features and waving dark hair; gold thread glittered from what had once been a good tunic. Hagano feinted, drove the Roman's sword aside, and with another blow knocked it from his hand. Though the man was reeling, he managed to recapture it before Hagano could, and still on his knees, brought it up to guard.

"Yield," growled Hagano. "You won't survive another blow from me!"

"Better dead than to live as a slave—all my property you've destroyed, and we've no other family to send ransom." The screaming in the villa began once more, and his anguished glance flicked away and back to Hagano. "Damn you murdering bastards! May God damn you to eternal torment and shame!" With more strength than Hagano would have expected, the boy lurched to his feet and drove at his enemy.

Better dead fighting than by the lash, thought Hagano, knocking aside the first blow. *This one would never endure slavery.* The boy groaned, swinging wildly. Hagano stepped to meet him, his own blade wheeling round as the Roman neared, to cleave the joining of neck and shoulder and pull free in the same smooth movement as spouting blood, his enemy fell.

He stood panting as the boy's body rolled to rest. For a moment, nothing moved. Then with a groan the arch of the church doorway cracked and came crashing down.

Men leaped backward, curses mixed with laughter. Hagano glared at them, then remembered the villa and started toward it at a run.

It was easy enough to find his missing warriors. The cries had diminished to a desolate whimpering, but the men's laughter made up for it in volume. With a roar, Hagano used the flat of his blade to knock the lookout aside and drove the point into the pumping buttocks of the man on the floor before him. The fellow screeched and appeared to levitate off of his victim's body. A well-placed kick sent the second rapist rolling. He took a deep breath and looked around him.

The room reminded him of a barracks—a row of beds, no ornament but a crucifix on the wall. On four of the beds, women were lying, hands folded as if they were sleeping. But the blood that stained the neat slits in their tunics on the left side of each body, just below the heart, told him otherwise.

"They were dead, sir, when we got here—" one of the men said unnecessarily. He flinched as Hagano's cold gaze went past him to the women on the floor. One of them, still sobbing, had curled herself into a tight ball. The other was sitting, not deigning to pull her tunic down over blood-stained thighs. Hagano felt a chill, for she glared at her tormentors with the dead Roman's eyes.

At first, because of the coarse tunic and cropped hair, he had taken her for a slave. But there was no mistaking those fine features.

"I am sorry, Domina," he said in his clumsy Latin. "This was against my order, but they will not hurt you anymore."

She spat. "What more could they do?" Her eyes fixed on the bloody knife that lay in the corner as if it had been kicked there in the first struggle when the soldiers came in. Hagano sighed, bent to pick it up and thrust it through his belt, and saw the fire in her eyes begin to fade.

"At least some of us are free. . . ." she whispered. She shuddered suddenly, and dragged the skirts of her tunic back down.

"Did you kill them?" he asked gently, squatting down beside her. Her unseeing gaze moved from the beds to the woman on the floor.

"It was my responsibility . . . to send them unstained to the Lord. We were a sisterhood, vowed to live together in holiness as they do in Egypt and other lands." For a moment her eyes closed. "Are there other prisoners?"

"There was a young man—a relative? He refused to surrender and died like a warrior. You can be proud."

She sighed. She had known it already, for she was the same.

"My brother." She crossed herself. "May the Christos receive his soul."

Hagano cleared his throat. "What is your name?"

"Casta—" she looked at him, and her face contorted suddenly. "Casta! Do you know, barbarian, what that means?"

Hagano nodded. *The one set apart, the pure.* "It is still true." He could see her unsullied spirit clearly, though she obviously thought herself forever stained. Meeting her eyes, his breath caught, as if she had pierced his soul.

The woman began to laugh; he caught the undertone of hysteria building and slapped her. She gasped and caught her breath, staring at him once more. Hagano reached out and grasped her hand. He had killed her natural protector.

By the law of the tribes it was his right and his responsibility to claim her.

"Get up. You will not be a slave. Since you refuse the name of Casta, you shall be Kustubaira, the bearer of my choice. Come with me."

Hagano had never asked for anything for himself before.

Every time Gundohar looked at the Roman woman his brother had claimed as a wife he felt the same amazement. It was not that she was unsuitable—the girl was handsome, or at least she probably could be if she would ever smile, and wellborn. But he had never expected Hagano to marry at all.

There were no relatives left with whom to negotiate the marriage; but since the woman had been sworn to the Church, they would have to find a bishop to grant a dispensation. Hagano could have her lands in place of a dowry, but until the conquest was achieved there was not much he could do with them. In the meantime, he seemed quite satisfied with a betrothal that would grant his Kustubaira the protection of Burgund law.

Gundohar could see why a woman, especially one who had just been assaulted, would not want to sleep with his brother. What he did not quite understand was why Hagano was willing to put off lying with her.

But that was really the least of his worries. The first part of the Burgund invasion had gone well, a broad sweep that sent hundreds of useless mouths hurrying to drain the resources of Treveri. But the Romans were not out of food yet; though they were cut off from the river, the city's wells gave them a dependable water supply, and for the moment, the city was well defended. He had now to feed and control his own army until he had starved the people of Treveri into submission.

Siegework was not a skill for which the Burgunds, or indeed any of the Germanic tribes, were noted, their warriors being best at exploits which could be accomplished

before hot blood cooled. But Gundohar was not too proud
to ask the advice of his father-in-law—certainly the Visigoths had plenty of practice sitting down in front of Arelas.
At the moment, they were said to be advancing on Narbo.

But things were apparently going well, for it was less than
a moon after he had sent his message that Valobald and a
small party of Visigoths rode in. Gundohar went out with
his brother Godo and Hagano to meet them. Valobald had
a boy with him, and another man, whose broad shape
against the sunlight made him blink with sudden memory.

The riders drew to a halt. "You healed well, I see," said
a deep, rumbling voice above him. The rider swung one
leg over the pony's neck and slid down. Waldhari was as
solid as ever, the king observed, though his red hair was
beginning to grey. A metal cuff capped the stump of his
right arm.

"I still limp," Gundohar shrugged. "I hear you have
learned to fight with your left hand."

Waldhari grinned. "What a lot of trouble we could have
saved ourselves if some seeress had told us we would be
allies one day!"

Interesting, thought the king, that the wounds they had
given each other eight years before should have made such
a bond between them.

"Very true," he said. "And how is Hildigund?"

"Blooming—" Waldhari began. "We have two sons—"
His gaze shifted as Hagano shouldered forward, weathered
features creasing in an unaccustomed smile of welcome.
Gundohar stepped back as they met, clapping each other
on the back, like bears embracing.

"Those boys of his are the terror of Theoderid's court,"
said Valobald behind him. "And my own cub is scarcely
better, though I am trying to teach him some courtesy—
come here, Gundiok, and greet your cousin."

Still smiling, Gundohar turned. He saw a thatch of white-
blond hair, and as the child rose from his reverence, a boy's
face whose roundness was already beginning to lengthen.

Not a child—he realized, looking at that gangling frame— Gundiok must be nearly fourteen.

He reminds me of Gislahar at that age, a true Niflung, thought the king, and then, as wide grey eyes met his own, *he is like me.*

"My lord, my mother sends you her greetings," said Gundiok.

Gundohar mumbled some inane politeness, still staring at the boy. How strange that his cousin Gundrada, whom he scarcely remembered, should have produced this child whose features recapitulated his own.

He found himself watching Gundrada's son often during the days that followed, his attention drifting from the interminable discussions of strategies and supplies.

"I thought the point of a siege was to starve out the people in the city," said Godo plaintively. "But Treveri's storehouses are legendary, while we are eating the countryside bare." He looked wistfully at the age-darkened sandstone battlement of the Porta Nigra, the northern gate of the city. The dome of Constantine's basilica, beyond it, was just visible above the wall. The Empress Helena had given the Treveri a piece of the Christos's seamless garment. The people said it was protecting them.

"There is food to be had if you can buy it," said Valobald. "Lay in more supplies and settle in. The Romans thought that one campaign would smash Tibatto, but the man is a crafty fighter, and he is likely to keep Aetius busy in the north for some time."

"Aetius, yes," Waldhari put in, "but what if the *Magister* sends the Huns to fight for him as he has before?"

Gundohar shook his head. "Not this time. We were right to marry our sister to Attila. He has promised not to ride against us as his gift to her for bearing him a son."

"How convenient . . ." Waldhari lifted one eyebrow.

"Very," Hagano said dryly. "Especially since at the moment the khan is busy setting his own house in order, and needs his men at hand. You have heard, I suppose, that

Ruga was negotiating for the return of his errant tribesmen? Attila and his brother have been in Margus, making a new treaty with the Eastern Romans. They will get back the fugitives, or a price of eight solidi for each one who stays, and the Romans will accept no more—" He grimaced. "They surrendured Mamai and Atakam. . . ."

"The Huns crucified them—" said Godomar.

Waldhari nodded. "Attila is disposing of rival claimants to the leadership. I am not surprised."

"His people should be pleased with him," said Gundohar. "The Romans will make alliance with no people with whom Attila is at war, and most important, they are setting up new markets where the Huns can freely trade."

"Don't forget the gold," added Godomar.

"Seven hundred pounds a year," said the king.

"That's twice what they were getting before!" exclaimed Waldhari.

"Indeed. So I do not expect to see our brother-in-law in arms this summer. He will be busy enough at home." Hagano allowed himself a sour grin.

"Then there should be no problem." Valobald sat back, smoothing his beard.

"Not from that quarter," answered Gundohar, "but the plunder has not been so extensive as we expected"—for a moment his gaze wandered to the burned-out shells of the villas in the hills overlooking the town—"and it will cost a great deal to feed so many men."

"I fear Theoderid has spent all the gold I brought from Hunland," Waldhari said ruefully, "but what about using the treasure your sister's first husband left you, since her second husband has agreed to leave you alone?"

Gundohar looked at him in shock. He had not realized that the tale of Fafnar's hoard was so well known. No doubt it had grown in the telling, too.

Hagano was shaking his head. "That gold is held in trust for Gudrun!"

"Pay her back when you take the mint at Treveri," suggested Valobald. "You have risked too much to hold back anything now."

Gundohar shook his head. Valobald shrugged, and the conversation moved on to the possibility of breaching the walls.

That evening the king asked Gundiok to accompany him as he inspected his lines. It was the still hour just after sunset. In the west the clouds still glowed in banners of gold and flame, shedding a deceptively tender light across the ruined countryside. But the Imperial palace of which Gundohar had dreamed was in shadow.

Gundiok followed the king's gaze. "Is your city like this one?"

Gundohar shook his head and smiled. "It is smaller, built of warm red stone. There are vineyards around it, but across the river you can see the forest where we hunt stag and wild boar." *And sometimes*, he remembered bitterly, *men*.

"It sounds nice," said the boy. "My mother told me about the river."

Gundohar looked at the green waters of the Mosella and saw the silver ripples of the Rhenus, as he saw it sometimes in his dreams. "Perhaps one day you could come to see it . . ." he answered.

Perhaps one day you will rule it, he thought, but it was too soon to speak of that. Still, Gundiok was reaching the age when boys went to other households to learn man's skills and cement alliances. He wondered if Valobald would consider sending the lad to him as a fosterling.

Hagano sat on the rim of the dead fountain, sharpening his sword. The villa where the Burgund princes had made their headquarters was alive with lamplight, and the sounds of other men preparing for tomorrow's battle, but he preferred the darkness of the inner garden. A week ago he had expected to spend this week on the road to Borbetomagus, planning how to make the best use of Sigfrid's hoard. At least he had been spared that decision, he thought grimly.

No sooner had Valobald and his party left the Burgund camp than word had come that Litorius and the Second Flavian Legion were on their way.

They had been preceded by a messenger ordering the Burgunds to lay down their arms. The Burgunds had responded by asking that the Treveri lands be added to their *feodus*. The Roman's next message had been more aggressive, and Gundohar's reply had been a demand for gold. It had worked for the Huns, after all. But the treasury of Theodosius apparently held more than that of Valentinian, and Litorius had rejected his demand. Gundohar did not much like the idea of fighting Romans, but Litorius, though an effective general, was not the equal of his master. And the Burgunds had risked too much on this game to give up now.

Scrape . . . scrape . . . the strokes of the whetstone echoed from the columns of the colonnade and the walls of the rooms behind them. His blade would have to be sharp to bite through Roman armor. Not for the first time, he wished that Sigfrid's god-forged sword had not perished on his pyre.

Something pale moved in the deeper shadows beneath the roof of the colonnade, and Hagano's stroke faltered. He took a deep breath and began again, as careful to show no awareness of the woman who stood there as a hunter afraid of frightening his prey. He did not need to see to know when she drew near. Though she wore no perfume, to him it seemed that with Kustubaira there always came a breath of fragrance in the air.

"I could not sleep . . ."

She had spoken to him. It was permissible to look up at her. Kustubaira had her own rooms in the villa with a stout freedwoman to guard her, but neither he nor any other male entered there. The luminous oval of her face was framed by a white palla—she would not wear colors, though she no longer considered herself worthy to dress in the coarse garments of a nun. Hagano gazed for a moment, unable to reply.

"The men are singing, out there on the hill," she said then. "Are they always so eager for battle? Have they no fear for their souls?"

"They believe that by fighting bravely they will save them—" He kept his deep voice soft.

"A pagan Roman commander faces a Christian barbarian king—" she shook her head. "How will God know which side to favor?"

Hagano shivered. It was not the Christian god to whom his people prayed, even now, for victory.

"The side that fights best," he answered her. "It will not be easy. Litorius is a good general who does not give up —" Indeed, he must be, to have resisted baptism for so long. "I served under him when we fought the Visigoths. But our force is larger, and we are not exhausted by marching. And we have staked a great deal on this campaign.

"Whatever happens, you need not fear," he added. "If your people win, you have your family's land and the gold I have given you. And if the Burgunds are victors but I fall, you will still have the status of my widow."

The edge of her palla trembled. "I should be praying God to drive you from this land. But among my own people I am shamed forever for surviving what was done to me." She crossed her arms as if she were cold. "I will pray for peace . . ." she whispered. He reached out to her and saw her flinch; then with a flutter of robes, she was gone.

It took a long time for Hagano's heartbeat to slow. He had thought it would not matter if Kustubaira ever turned to him, that it would be enough simply to protect her. But that moment of recoil had been like a spear to the heart.

Abruptly he sheathed the sword, gathered up his cloak, and strode out into the night.

The Burgund watchfires circled the beleagured city with a garland of light, spreading out upriver and down. There was a concentration at the bridge, over which they would march before the sun rose, and a thin line on the northern bank. Farther upriver, the Roman watchfires had blossomed beyond the band of darkness that tomorrow would become a battlefield. At least the problem of food was no longer so pressing. If they lost, they would not need it, and if they won, the folk of Treveri, seeing their rescuers defeated, would lose heart and surrender. For a moment Hagano looked at those defiant flames, anticipating already the dust and stink of the fighting, then he headed up the hill.

A clean wind was blowing from the summit. Hagano took a deep breath, then stilled, for the wind carried the sound of chanting. Instinctively he began to move as if he were hunting, flowing silently between the trees. His stalk brought him to a hollow surrounded by hawthorns. In its center a small fire cast a dancing light across the faces of men from Godomar's band, and the king's, and his own. Some of them he had thought to be good Christians.

A calf had been tethered to a post whose top was roughly carved to indicate a bearded head with a single eye. It lowed again and tossed its head as some of the men began to punctuate their invocation by slapping their thighs with their hands.

"Wodan . . . Wodan . . . Wodan . . . Wod. . . ."

Hagano felt the fine hairs on the back of his neck begin to rise. Frowning, he pushed through the screening trees.

For a moment they stared in appalled silence. Then one of his own men recognized him; he heard the murmured echo of his name. Faces changed from terror to shame or a kind of hunger that filled him with unease. It was one of those, a man named Hanulf who carried his standard, who first stood up and saluted him.

"Lord, we wish to offer to Wodan for victory. It would be most fitting if you performed the sacrifice."

And it would certainly prevent me from reporting them, Hagano thought wryly. As the wind stirred his hair, that strange shiver chilled him once more. Wordless, he accepted the knife Hanulf held out to him.

The calf stamped uneasily as Hagano approached, but he had learned at his mother's knee the runes to quiet it.

"What else will you offer?" he looked at the men around him. "What pledges will flow with this beast's blood to the god?"

Hanulf's lips drew back in a feral grin. He took up a drinking horn that had been stuck point first into the ground, filled already with the dark local wine. "To Wodan!" he lifted the horn. "If we win the battle, I will rebuild my father's shrine to the holy ones and every year the god shall have another such beast as this one." He passed it to the man beside him.

"I have no shrine," muttered his companion, "but I pledge to dedicate my next son to the old gods."

From man to man the horn went round, evoking promises of honor or offerings, until at last it came to Hagano. The air around him seemed suddenly heavy. For a moment he held it, staring at the men from beneath bent brows.

What do I possess? A woman who will never love me; a guilt that will never leave me . . . and my oath to serve the Niflungar. . . .

The pressure grew; he felt upon his own hands the grip of others, as he had once before. Wordless, he untied the tether, poured the contents of the horn over the calf's white poll, and while the animal was still licking at the drops that rolled down its face, felt gently for the jugular, lifted its head, and drew the knife through the softness there.

The knife was so sharp, and his touch so sure, that the beast did no more than wheeze as the bright blood gushed out. Hanulf bent to catch it in a helmet. Hagano held the calf against him, still singing in that strange undertone, until it sank to its knees, then laid it, twitching and trembling as the last of its life pumped away, on the ground. Presently the spurting fell to a dribble and it lay still. *It is not enough,* he thought, *not this innocent blood.*

With the same cool deliberation, he pulled open his tunic, and holding the skin of his solar plexus taut, took the bloody knife and drew two crossed lines there. There was only the faintest sting, but in another moment his own blood welled up in thin bright lines to mark the rune he had made.

"*Gebo*—" Hagano whispered. "This is my gift, Old Man. I will no longer fight you. My life is yours if you will give us victory."

Wide-eyed, Hanulf took the helmet full of blood and poured it over the godpost. The knife dropped from Hagano's hand, his sight darkening as if his own lifeblood were flowing from the mark he had made. Against that shadow the image of the rune glowed like fire, and to his inner ear came words—"*I am the one who offers, and I am the Offering. . . .*"

Dizzied, he sat back on his heels, trying to understand. A part of his mind was gibbering at the thought of the doom to which he had just consented. But another part was soaring, freed at last from both shame and anger, on a tide of ecstasy.

Chapter 11 ⚇ The Spear of Wyrd

Treveri
Haying Moon, A.D. 436

The king of the Burgunds reined down his roan war-horse, swearing softly. He suspected that the animal was only reflecting his own nerves, but it made everyone feel better to pretend it was the beast which was misbehaving.

"Impatient, is he?" said Dancward, beside him. "Well, it won't be long now. . . ."

Gundohar grunted and continued to survey his chosen battlefield. The long valley of the Mosella looked deceptively peaceful; early sunlight glittered from the slow ripples of the river, carved sharp shadows in the line of hills that rose to the north and glowed in the grassy flats between. Beyond those hills ramparts of cloud were building, but the sky over Treveri was bright and clear.

Since shortly after midnight he had been moving his forces into position—that was always the most vulnerable phase of a battle, when a surprise attack could panic an army. He had thought he would be sick then, with the waiting. But by sunrise the Burgunds were as ready as they were going to be—arrayed in three columns on the northern side of the river, cavalry on his right, led by Ordwini, foot on the left, led by Gislahar, and the center with Godomar in the fore and himself with a small mounted force at the rear. And now his belly was griping once more.

Gundohar told himself they made a fine array, with the

sunlight striking points of flame from spears and spangen-helms, and their shadows elongating across the grass as if their spirits sped before them to attack the Romans, who were now moving into position a double arrow shot away. His gaze moved onward to the patch of woodland at the base of the hillside ahead of them, where he had hidden Hagano and his men.

They had been the first to move into position. Gundohar wished there had been time for more than a few last instructions before they marched away. Hagano had been . . . strange, and there had been a smear of blood on his brow. The king would have thought that odd exaltation came from drink, but his brother's step had been steady and his speech clear. Perhaps it was only that he was unused to seeing Hagano smile.

In any case, it was done. And it ought to work. It had to work. The Romans were outnumbered, still tired from marching, and they would have to advance against the sun.

But now, when there was no changing his dispositions, Gundohar could not help wondering whether he might have done better to wait for his enemy on the other side of the river. No doubt that was why his belly still churned. He remembered how he had chanted poetry when he had fought at Treveri before. But it would appear that the poet in him had been killed by the king.

Godomar and some of the other chieftains had argued in favor of the southern bank, where they could have positioned themselves on a hillside and gained momentum for their charge. The last battle they fought at Treveri had been won that way. But last time their army had consisted of a fraction of the men. There was no ground on the other side of the river where they could have made full use of the nearly fifteen thousand men on foot and the four thousand riders that stood here today.

Roman clarions called, their brazen challenge made sweet by distance. Gundohar repressed a nostalgic pang—the last time he had heard those horncalls the Burgunds and the

Legions had been fighting on the same side. A shimmer of light ran through the mass of armor ahead of him. The Romans were moving; he felt, as much as heard, the vibration as thousands of hobnailed sandals crushed the grass.

"Litorius has put the Second Flavia in the center," said Dancward, whose distance vision was better than his own. In another few moments the king could make out the pattern of the shields with their concentric circles of yellow and white and red.

"The Auxiliaries are coming up behind them," the other man went on. "The Mattiaci and the Bructeri, by their colors."

Gundohar nodded. Those units had been raised originally along the Rhenus, though they now were as Roman as any other division in their training and arms. When he was in Ravenna he had seen a copy of the *Notitia Dignitatum*, the great roll of Imperial forces for all the provinces of the Empire. There had been Taifali, Mauri, Bucinobantes, and Tervingi, Transtigritani and Scythae, tribes who still fought Roma and others whose names, outside the army, were only memories. There might be men over there whom Gundohar had fought at the Longstone field when he was a boy. If he succeeded in establishing his people within the Empire, there might be a Burgund Auxilium one day.

"He has placed his heavy cavalry on his right, facing ours. From the standards I think they're the Taifali." The cataphracti bore no shields—they did not need them. Sunlight blazed from segmented steel armor on men and horses, and glittered from patches of mail.

"Ordwini won't like that," said Gundohar. By this time most of the Burgund chieftains rode in mail, but they had none to spare for their horses. If the Taifali were allowed to gather any speed they would roll right over them. "Wolcgar, ride to Ordwini. Remind him that he'll need to get up to speed right away when we advance. If he can reach the point where the flats widen first, his lighter horses will be able to outflank the cataphracti."

Without a hill to give them momentum, he anticipated that his center might be driven back after the first encounter and had planned for it. If Ordwini could hit the cataphracti from one side and drive them in on their own troops, and Hagano's ambush smashed the other, the Romans would be helpless. It all depended on their speed.

Giving the order had helped a little, but now he had to fight back the nausea again. Why was he so surprised? He had felt sick before every battle from the fight at the Longstone field until now. After each battle he forgot the fear, but like a woman in labor, he had no choice now but to go through with it, no matter how much he wanted to run screaming from the field.

Now he could see faces framed by steel helmets, breastplates of molded leather, brown-clad legs moving in unison. He calculated distances, momentum against exhaustion. Behind him he heard the rustle of stiff fabric as the Gundwurm standard that Deorberht was holding stirred in the wind. *Is it time, old dragon? Are you eager for the fray?* Instinctively responding, Gundohar raised his hand.

Burgund cow horns blared a sour challenge to the brazen music of the clarions. Like an echo made visible, a shiver ran through the ranks before him. The horse tossed its head as the men ahead began to move. Again the horns brayed, and again; Gundohar's body jerked reflexively, he took a quick breath and found his nausea had gone. The roan horse, catching the excitement, leaned into the bit, and the king let him go. Space between the men ahead of him was lengthening as the leaders began to run. Gundohar felt their war cry rather than heard it, opened his own throat and joined in their defiance as the Burgund army charged the foe.

Feet pounded the earth; war cries assaulted the air. Hagano felt the vibration through the earth on which he lay, in the trunk of the tree against which he was pressed, in his very bones. An answering shout built in his own belly and he bit his lip to stop it, glared at his men to keep them quiet. He had not known it would be so hard to sit still until the Romans were at his mercy. Patience had always been easy for him before.

He supposed the change had been caused by last night's ritual. He had assumed that the exaltation would wear off, leaving him to face in cold blood the doom to which he had bound himself. But he had come to this battlefield ready to embrace death like a bridegroom, and by this he understood that his offering had been accepted. He found in the situation an unexpected irony. The danger that most men feared was what he longed for; the safety in which he now waited the burden he must bear. But it was his duty to choose the moment when he could make the Romans pay most dearly before his blood fed the ground.

The Burgund vanguard were running at full speed now, spears ready. Ordwini's riders streamed out along the riverbank, racing to reach the flats before the heavily armored Roman cavalry. Hagano realized that he was pounding the earth, urging them on, and dug his fingers into the ground.

The Roman central column was advancing steadily, maintaining their line. His lips drew back in a feral grin when the shields of the Guards, marching in parallel formation, came into view. The cream of the army, every man of them destined for an officer's crest if he survived, they would be worthy foes. He marked the commander, his breeches a little cleaner than those of the others, with gilded armor. They moved over the uneven ground in perfect order, and if their white breeches were muddy and their tunics ragged from the hard campaigning they had left behind them, their breastplates and helmets shone.

The Burgund line was less precise, but louder. When barbarians won, it was through numbers or luck or sheer courage. His side had the first and the last for certain, thought Hagano, and the god would grant the second, when his price was paid.

He saw Godomar pounding along in the lead, eyes glittering beneath the rim of his spangenhelm, mouth open as if he were giving voice to the roar of the entire Burgund army. *In this moment it is true.* Hagano's own throat ached with the need to join in that cry. *He is their soul.*

A ripple ran through the Roman line, they slowed, the second rank holding back to let the first fling its lances. Oncoming warriors swerved to keep from stepping on the men who went down. The first rank of Romans halted while the second advanced and released their own throwing spears. A third rank started to move forward, but the Burgunds were too close.

The two lines shocked together with a thunder of crashing shields. Back and forth the warriors swayed, darting spearpoints caught the sunlight like tongues of flame. Soon, some of them began to come back red; gaps opened in the lines. Shields locked, the Romans pushed forward. A Burgund dropped to one knee, thrusting upward; his foe fell backward, knocking his companions off-balance. Burgund warriors seized the chance to spear them and gain another few feet of ground, but the legionaries in the next rank were already filling in the gap. Inexorably the Roman line began to advance once more.

Hagano realized he was grinding his teeth. He told himself that Gundohar had expected his center to be forced back, but the sight of that retreat filled him with rage. He could see Roman backs now as well as faces. He forced himself to count the ranks as they struggled forward, gauging their progress by the movement of the standard as if he were checking a river's current by the speed with which a leaf bobbed downstream.

The center gave way further. Over the seething mass of helmets he could see horsemen skirmishing in the shallows. As the column of Guards, coming up on the left of the Legion, began to increase their own speed, the movement of the battle was beginning to mold the Roman line into a ram. But the Burgunds were wolves. He caressed the hilt of his sword. *Batter away—I have a tooth that will hamstring you!*

For a moment the scene before him dimmed. Hagano

blinked, was it the dust of the battle or his own sight betraying him? He looked up and saw that a brisk wind had
driven clouds halfway across the sky. Above him the leaves
fluttered, wind stirred his hair. He took a deep breath of
that wind and blinked again, dizzied by a rush of something
he could only call joy. Always, before, he had fought with
a dogged efficiency born of necessity. But in giving up his
life to Wodan it seemed he had also shed his old sorrows.
Not yet, Old Man, not until my enemy is within my grasp—he
thought, but the battle-fury was rising within him, and
he did not know how much longer he could hold it in. If
he had known it would be like this, he would have given
in to the god long ago.

They were in front of him now, he could see the white
horsehair crest of the commander in the midst of the first
rank. But they were slowing! Hagano slammed his fist against
the ground, then froze as the white crest turned and the Roman looked toward the woods. Was it the instinct of an old
campaigner that had warned him? For the space of a heartbeat the only thing moving was the raven that beat upward
from the trees. Then a shiver ran through the ranks of the
Guards and shields began to turn toward the hill.

Hagano hardly saw them. His gaze was on the raven
whose wingstrokes assaulted the sky. His spirit rose with
it, he leaped to his feet, grabbing shield and spear. Without
looking to see if anyone followed he burst through the
screening branches and down the hill. His mouth was open
so he must be yelling, but all he could hear was the roar
of blood in his ears.

A pilum thrummed past, he paid it no attention. A
painted shield loomed up before him, red, its blue border
gleaming with golden arabesques. Hagano smashed it aside
and its owner with it, bowling him over to be spitted by
the next warrior who came along. His own spear was already darting toward the unprotected side of the soldier
ahead. He felt the shock as it screeched across metal armor,
then the point found the seam between front and back

plates, and he drove it into the Roman's side.

He jerked out the spear, blood spurted after; there was blood everywhere. All awareness narrowed to the next stroke, the next enemy. His shield was hacked to pieces, spear and sword scythed men all around him, but nothing touched Hagano. Screaming, he struggled toward the officer with the white crest, and where he passed, men died.

Gundohar heard the shouting on his right, looked just in time to see the Guards' commander fall. From the Romans came a cry of dismay. For an instant the fighting wavered; he glimpsed Hagano in the midst of it. Somehow his brother had lost both helm and shield, but he was laying about him like a berserker with his sword. There was no time to fear for him—in the next moment the Roman line began to recoil.

"They flee!" he shouted, sweeping his arm towards the opening. "Onward the Gundwurm!" The cow horns blared wildly and Burgunds, cheering, stopped giving ground. For a moment the combatants swayed in place, then Hagano's impact on their crumbling flank began to make itself apparent. A tremor ran through the Legionary line, and the Burgunds gripped their spears more firmly and started to push them backward.

But the Romans, though they were retreating, had not lost all discipline. The Guards were trying to form up again, curling around into a defensive line. The Legion's center formed a solid block, and after a few moments, they began to hold their ground. A cold wind blew out the stiff folds of the Gundwurm banner. Armor that a moment before had blazed grew dim as the moving clouds darkened the sky.

There was a shout; a shower of Roman lances burst toward the Burgunds who were surrounding them.

"Burgund dogs, feel our teeth! Worms, see how our serpents can sting!" came a shout from the line. It was followed by other insults in Gallic and Latin. Those that the Burgunds understood were sufficient to inflame them. A growl of outrage became a roar, and in answer, the air trembled to the terrible ululation of the legionary war cry.

It was the defiance, thought Gundohar, of men who see their death upon them. Grinning savagely, he urged his horse forward.

Hagano jerked his sword from a Guardsman's belly and looked up, for a moment without another foe before him. Across the seething mass of helmets he glimpsed the Gundwurm, searched onward for the gleam of his brother's gilded spangenhelm, and saw brightness flare from its curve as lightning flared overhead. If there was thunder, the clamor of the battle was too great for him to hear it, but every hair on his body lifted as power crackled through the air.

"Wodan! Wodan!" he cried, and saw the eyes of the Roman who had turned to face him widening in fear. His sword swept out as the man lunged toward him, batting the thrusting pilum aside and continuing around to bite deep into his side. Above, the sky was curdling, roiling clouds in every shade from slate to silver colliding as if the battle had spread to the heavens.

Hagano knew he was continuing to move forward, felt the shock as his blade connected once more, but his awareness surged toward the storm. It seemed to him that his dead eye had somehow opened, and with that expanded vision he saw shining shapes darting among the clouds, distorted female forms with staring eyes who rode gaunt wolves. Froth spattered from their gaping jaws; hailstones scattered where their paws scored the air. Shrieking, the war-hags swooped above the battle, shaking their spears. For a moment he thought he saw Brunahild.

Again came the lightning. Clouds boiled as if the bowl of heaven had become a cauldron from whose cobalt depths a great horse was emerging, its grey hide strained over white bone. On its back, a rider cloaked in shadow, a dull gleam of blue-black mail, a great spear brandished in his armored hand. . . .

"Victory Father!" Hagano cried, "Spear-thruster, father of hosts who puts armies to flight!"

Two legionaries came against him; a single, blinding stroke took off both heads; blood sprayed as he raised his sword in homage to the skies.

Shadow swirled above him; single eye met single Eye, and Hagano flinched from that grim gaze. The point of the Spear swung around, left the god's hand in a trail of searing radiance as it flew over the heads of the Burgund host, leaving darkness behind it. Blinded, Hagano heard above the thunder of battle a new challenge; from the edge of the field came the blare of more Roman horns.

The ground beneath his feet was trembling. A hand closed on his arm and hauled him backward. Returning sight showed him the Romans gleefully waving their spears and beyond them, a moving mass of riders. A shock wave rolled through the Burgund host as a new wing of Roman cavalry hit their right flank. Hagano fought to keep his feet as panicking warriors tried to escape, too paralyzed by disbelief to rally them.

"You promised!" he shook his sword at the skies. But the clouds had closed. The god was gone. "You promised—" he whispered, "to take me and give the Burgunds this battle. . . ."

He was still alive. He took a new grip on his sword, and snarling, plunged into the oncoming Roman horde, seeking the death that would force the god to grant his side the victory.

"Aetius! Aetius has come!"

The Roman shout was like a blow. Gundohar reined his horse in a tight circle, smashing aside the lance that stabbed up at him, seeking to rally his men. He had never believed the Magister could get reinforcements here so soon. At the thought of facing Aetius he had to fight back despair. But he had no choice now.

The mobility of the reinforcements, Alan light cavalry from what he could see of their gear, had given the cataphracti the breathing room to regroup. Now they were putting their weight to good use, pressing inexorably into the Burgunds, whose spears were useless against the bronze scales that protected the horses from poll to croup. Some of them had already been pushed into the river, where they flailed against the current, casting arms and armor away.

"Form a line!" he yelled, "we've got to pull back in order—" His words were whirled away. The Burgunds still outnumbered their foe, even with reinforcements, but they were hampered by their very numbers, and they were tiring.

"A time will come when your enemies surround you, and then you will miss the strength of Sigfrid's arm. . . . " Gudrun's curse was coming true. Surely he had never needed a hero's courage as he did now.

His horse reared and he wrestled it down, looking for Godomar. But it was his youngest brother who fought his way to the king's side. Deorberht was still with him. More men joined them and they began to get some kind of control over their immediate area, though the staff of the Gundwurm banner was like a branch that snags in a flooding river, buffeted this way and that even as it catches other debris, liable at any moment to be whirled away.

"Gislahar—" he gasped, "get to the rear. Gather whatever unwounded men you can and hold the bridgehead. Make them cross in order or no one will get to the other side!"

A thrown pilum smashed into his battered shield, and Gundohar swore and tossed the dangling fragments away. A man of his house-guard held up his own for a replacement, the king started to refuse but in that moment the warrior was speared. Instinctively he grabbed at the strap as the man fell and shrugged it onto his arm.

They were very near the river now. A quick glance showed him men marching across the bridge in good order, but there was fighting at the other end; Treveri had opened its gates and those citizens still strong enough to bear arms were streaming out to help their rescuers, but Ordwini and some of his men had gained the farther bank and were holding it.

"Deorberht! Some will have to swim for it—give me the banner, and get men into the water to form a chain."

"Lord, you must go first"—Deorberht paused to slash at the legionary who thrust up at him—"go ahead, and I'll cover you."

"Not yet—" gasped Gundohar. "None of them will hold if they see the Gundwurm flee."

"We'll stay on the bank of the river, then," came the reply as they were driven a little farther. Foot by foot, and life by life, the nucleus of the Burgund host retreated. Men began to move into the river, and Ordwini, seeing what they intended, sent horsemen to aid them. Many, the king saw, had crossed the bridge in safety and were fleeing around the city toward the eastern hills, striking down any man of Treveri who got in their way. How many had fallen? How many, he wondered, could he still save?

Men came singly and in clumps, escaping from the knots of struggling soldiers that still twined and twisted across the field. But more of the approaching helmets were Roman now.

"My lord king, you must come—" Dancward, dismounted, grabbed Gundohar's rein.

"I will stay," said Deorberht, seeing him waver.

Gundohar cast a last look across the battlefield. Burgunds were still out there, fighting, dying. But more had reached the other side of the river.

He shook his head. "The Gundwurm has never been captured—" he said dully. "We will go together."

Taking that for assent, Dancward began to pull the roan toward the water, and Gundohar did not resist him.

A few spears flew past his head as they struggled across the river, but the Burgunds who remained had drawn together to cover his retreat. As they breasted the far bank Gundohar turned in the saddle. His impromptu rear guard was plunging into the water behind him, but most of the fighting had ended. He saw a few survivors standing at bay or already prisoners, and the dead, many of them, both Burgund and Roman, sprawled on the field.

The walking dead man stumbled through the dusk. As he moved past the walls of Treveri, dogs nosing at corpses whined and slunk out of his path; human scavengers who had come out from the city to plunder the slain crossed themselves. The walker ignored them, and none ventured to attack him. He was not surprised. Once he had been Hagano, their enemy, but now he was dead and they could not harm him. Once this valley had been a fair setting for a noble city. Now its beauty was trampled and its river ran with blood and the souls of slain warriors gibbered on the wind.

On the banks of the river a Roman camp was rising. The commanders had entered Treveri with cartloads of food. Tonight the living would feast and thank their god. Only ghosts walked without comfort now.

He thought that perhaps his destiny was to wander, a fit punishment for sins he could no longer remember, but which weighted his soul. Only once or twice, when he recognized among the slain some man he had hunted and eaten and camped with, did he remember who and what he had been. But he did not see his brothers. Perhaps, if he remained dead, his sacrifice might still be accepted and they would survive.

Without decision, he found his steps carrying him away from the city and up the slope beyond it. A villa rose before him, its whitewashed walls, untouched by war, glimmering in the gloom. He recognized it as the place where the Burgund kings had been quartered, and that, too, seemed fitting, for did not ghosts haunt the places that had held happiness for them when they lived?

The door was open. Clothing and other gear lay scattered in the hall and the atrium, as if the inhabitants had left in a hurry. He slowed. What was left for him here? But he kept on moving, through the second corridor to the peristyle and the fountain.

And there, at last, he halted. The place was empty. Kustubaira was a sensible woman; she would have fled with the others. But the detachment that had sustained him was departing, and with it the last of his strength. He groaned.

I must be dead indeed, he thought, for another ghost was coming out to meet him, and she looked like the woman he had come to love. But it must be an illusion, for Kustubaira would never draw his arm across her shoulders and grab him, swearing, as he began to fall.

After a time without thought, Hagano found himself awake. He no longer thought he was dead, for the dead did not lie beneath fine linen in a goosefeather bed, but for the first few moments he could not imagine where he might be. A lamp was burning in the alcove; by its light he saw a woman sewing, and his breath caught. She looked up at the sound. He met her shadowed gaze, and memory came flooding back.

"Kustubaira . . ." he whispered, "why are you still here?"

"Where should I go?" She crossed the room and laid a hand on his brow. "I have no place but here, and I thought"—her gaze fell—"that if you lived, it was here you would return."

For a moment his heart did not beat, then it began to race, so furiously that surely she must feel it. He tried to speak, croaked, and tried again.

"How badly am I hurt?"

She looked at him, her lips curving in an odd smile. "It is exhaustion that has felled you, Hagano. The blood I washed off of you was not yours. Bar those scratches on your breast, there is no mark upon you at all."

Hagano groaned. *Like Sigfrid,* he thought, *whom the god also protected,* remembering how the men had murmured at his unscarred hide.

"The god deceived me. . . . I gave him my life . . . for victory." Wodan had accepted him—surely he had not imagined it. He tried to recall the exact words he had heard.

Kustubaira drew a quick breath. "Now you understand!" She spoke with bitter satisfaction. "I would have welcomed a martyr's death, but my Lord rejected me. We have both been abandoned by our gods."

Abandoned? Remembering what had been said on the hill, Hagano was not so sure. It was he who had assumed Wodan was agreeing to the terms he offered. The fact that he had come unscathed through such a battle was proof that the god had claimed him. But what unimaginable fate was Wodan saving him for?

Hagano took a deep breath and felt the *Gebo* rune beneath his ribs smart anew. *That was an exchange, Old Man!* he said silently. *My life belongs to you, but you still owe me a victory!* And somewhere, in the depths of his awareness, it seemed to him he heard a laugh.

Kustubaira offered him a beaker. "You did not drink for a day. Even without blood loss, you must replenish your body's water."

Hagano gulped it down. The stuff was some kind of tea, tart with herbs and sweetened by honey. *Like Kustubaira . . .*

"Are we quits, then?" he said quietly when he had drained it. "I cared for you in your extremity, and now you are tending me. You owe me nothing more."

She sighed, twisting her long fingers together, her gaze fixed on the flicker of the lampflame. "I am your wife . . ." she said softly.

"My betrothed," he corrected. "We have not come together. The Church would not hold you to that bond."

She gave him a quick, evaluating glance. "Do you wish to break it?"

Hagano tried to reach out to her and found that he could hardly move. What had she put into that brew? He was helpless, both body and spirit, in her hands, but he found it hard to care.

"Indeed, the gods are playing with us, both yours and

mine. In my life I have dared love no woman until now, when I am cursed—or blessed—with love for a Christian woman who would fear my touch even were I whole and handsome. I might pluck out my other eye, Kustubaira," he said slowly. "But I cannot pluck from my heart what I feel for you. . . ." He tried to see if her face held patience or scorn or pity, but he was too tired.

"Sleep now," she whispered, stroking his brow, and more softly still, "perhaps in the morning I will know how to answer you."

Hagano slept that night through and well into the following morning, and it was Kustubaira who awakened him. He heard hoofbeats and the clink of harness and sat upright, wondering, in that first moment, if she had betrayed him.

"There are soldiers outside," she said in a low whisper. "I must hide you."

Awareness shocked through him, he gave a quick glance around the room.

"Not in the chest," he said. "If they are looking for plunder they will open it. Nor under the bedstead." He rolled out of the bed and pulled it away from the wall. "Push the bedclothes back as if you had just gotten out of it and I will slide down behind them. Do you have any weapons here?" His sword, along with everything else, had been lost somewhere on the battlefield.

"Only the dagger you gave me." She handed him the blade, its sheath set with Frankish enamelwork and on its pommel a golden dragon, and snatched up a shawl to cover her gown.

"Just as well they should not find this," he grinned. "It might make them wonder."

Someone began to beat on the door. From the shelter of the bedclothes Hagano heard Kustubaira call out a reply and the creak of the door.

"Domina!" the man's surprise was clear. He sounded like

a young officer, with an escort of rankers, by the noise their hobnailed sandals were making on the stone floor. "We thought—we were told the Burgund kings had been quartered here."

"God be thanked for your coming!" she said fervently. "They were here indeed, but they fled. That was a great battle!"

"God favored us," came the reply, and Hagano nodded, though he would have disagreed on which god. "By our count the barbarians left five thousand dead, many of them drowned trying to cross the river, while we lost no more than six hundred men."

Hagano stifled a groan. He had known it was bad, but not this great a disaster. He could guess what Gundohar, if he lived, must be feeling now. *I must go to him!*

"Did you kill their king?" she asked, as if she knew what he was wondering.

"His guard got him away," the officer said sourly. "Apparently unwounded. We are searching the area for stragglers and I was ordered to come here. . . ." His embarrassment was obvious.

"Well, you must do your duty—" Her own accent had become perceptibly aristocratic. The footsteps drew nearer. "I was so relieved to be free at last I am afraid I outslept the sun!"

"My apologies, Domina, for disturbing you—" The door to the bedchamber was opened. "They did not—" The young man dared not ask the obvious question.

"The kings treated me with respect," she said truthfully.

"Of course," he answered quickly. "They would want your ransom. I'll inform the Magister you are here when I return, and he will send a litter to bring you to Treveri. He brought more supplies, and there is food there now."

"That is very thoughtful. Will they be coming soon?"

"I'll send a messenger as soon as we leave here," the officer said helpfully. The door closed.

"You are very thoughtful," he heard her saying as the footsteps retreated across the atrium.

In a few moments Kustubaira returned.

"We must be quick——" She pulled the bedclothes aside and he uncoiled from behind them. "I have found servants' clothes that you can wear——" She paused, obviously wondering if she had insulted him.

"It is all right—I have gone in disguise before." His grin faded. "But there is no need for you to come with me. They do not know what happened to you. As you said, you are free."

She looked at him and shook her head. "We are both maimed," she said slowly. "I, in a way that no one can see. This is the answer I did not give you last night. If it is as you say, and you would give no other woman what you are offering me, then I will give you all that I can give a man. Is that enough for you?"

Hagano stared at her. When he was younger, he had gone to slave girls or whores when he could not deny his body's needs. But he had not done so since losing his eye. The release of the flesh was not a necessity. What he could no longer live without was love.

"It is more than enough," he said hoarsely. Gently he kissed her hand.

By the time the horse litter arrived at the villa, attended by an escort of soldiers eager to see the lovely lady who was waiting there, she was nowhere to be found. One of them, it is true, glimpsed for a moment what he took for a pair of country folk on the crest of the hill, but he did not mention it. The people of Treveri had a right to whatever they could scavenge, and besides, he was tired of climbing hills.

In another moment the figures had disappeared. The soldier turned back to see whether anything of value had been left in the villa. On the other side of the hill, Hagano and Kustubaira began their journey back to the Burgund lands.

Chapter 12 ☥ The War-God's Sword

Hun Territories
Spring, A.D. 437

Rain drummed monotonously on the curved dome of the *ger*. That was nothing new, thought Gudrun. It had been raining ever since an early thaw began to melt the snow. And ever since then the Danuvius had been rising. She and her household had already had to abandon the buildings at Lentia and move into *gers* set up on higher ground. It was hard on the humans, who could at least see the danger coming and flee. But it was worse for the stock. Instinctively seeking the nearest high ground, little groups of sheep or cattle sometimes found themselves surrounded by the rising waters. When the wind was right, you could hear the hollow echo of their lowing across the flood. And from time to time the bloated bodies of those that the waters had overtaken came bobbing downstream, stiff legs accusing the leaden sky.

Pitched on a ridge and surrounded with ditches to carry the runoff away, the *gers* stayed almost dry. But food was always short at the end of the winter, and the floods had drowned the greens with which, by now, folk would normally have begun to supplement their cheese and gruel. When the rains began Gudrun had been generous in sharing out her own supplies, perhaps too much so, though in any case the storehouses were half underwater now. But by her fault or not, their own food was beginning to run low.

Sunnilda, now a great girl of ten, bore her hunger patiently and did her best to keep her little brother amused. But Apsik was only two and a half, and he did not understand why he could not have more goat's milk and gruel.

"Look—" said Sunnilda, curving her fingers in front of the lampflame, "there's a shadow pony, trotting across the wall!"

Apsik's eyes followed the movement; they were dark eyes, like his father's, though his hair had come in flax-fair. His gaze narrowed, and for a moment he looked more like Attila still. Then he lunged for the shadow. His sister caught him, and laughing, the two rolled on the felt-covered floor. Gudrun sighed. Apsik was not a bad child, though willful, but she found it hard to love him as she should. Whatever he did, she could not help comparing it to the imagined progress of a son of Sigfrid. His very existence was a reproach to her.

Sunnilda tried to make the boy sit still so that she could repeat the shadow play, but suddenly he began to kick and flail. The first time he had done this, Gudrun feared he was having some kind of fit, but it had become clear that it was neither illness nor temper, only an explosion of excess energy. Remembering how Attila seemed always to be in motion, Gudrun was not surprised.

"Is it a fight you want, cubling?" cried his sister. "I can play at that game too!" She plopped down onto all fours and began to growl, burying her face against his belly and worrying at his tunic with her teeth until his wails changed to shrieks of laughter.

Gudrun bit her lip and looked away. She had forgotten how Sigfrid used to play "wolf" with his little girl. She had wondered, sometimes, if Sunnilda retained any memories of her father, but this game, at least, the girl remembered only too well. Gudrun went to the door and lifted the flap. Outside, nothing moved but the slanting lines of rain.

She sat back with a stifled groan. It was not only Sunnilda and Apsik who would explode with frustration if the sun did not shine soon. She herself might very likely go mad, cooped up with two children and her memories.

She had almost decided to send Ecgward over the mountains to see if her uncle the bishop would take them in when a troop of Attila's men, mud-spattered to the thigh, came riding in.

"The lands around the Danu, all underwater," said young Onegesh, the *tzur* who comanded them. "And the lower Tizia—all the plain. The khan says bring you to the winter pastures up where the Tizia rises. If the flooding reaches the Carpatus mountains, then the Christian priests are right and their god is ending the world." He grinned through his moustache.

"Oh, I don't think even the Christian god would drown all the lands under Attila's protection." Gudrun smiled tightly. "He wouldn't dare."

For a moment Onegesh looked at her oddly, as if wondering whether he was supposed to laugh. Then he shrugged and began to give orders for packing up their gear.

The mountains were not underwater, but by the end of each day of travel Gudrun felt as wet as if they had been. Water splashed upward from the pony's hooves to soak her legs and seeped downward through her hood, and swinging branches showered everything between. And that was when it was not storming. The children, wrapped in cloaks and held in the arms of strong warriors, fared a little better, but by the third day Apsik was not only whining, but sniffling as well. Each night they tried to get dry beneath the shelters of oiled hide that the warriors set up for them, but their garments were always still damp in the morning.

The trails had been bad going west, said Onegesh. Returning they were even worse. Mountainsides gave way and slid down to block the paths, and streams that could be spanned in a step during the summer were rushing torrents. One man was swept away trying to break the force of the water so the others could cross; a pony broke a leg and several others went lame. But the troop had brought spare mounts, and the Hun horses, sturdy and sensible, continued to pick their way along, now and again shaking the water from their heavy manes.

As the journey went on Onegesh grew easier with Gudrun, and they talked sometimes when the rain was not so heavy, huddled steaming over a little fire. Things were bad everywhere, said the warrior. Farther down the river in the land of the Eastern Huns, where the Danu split into many channels that emptied into the Euxine, everything was underwater, and one could no longer tell where the shores of the sea began. The higher ground was filling with refugees weeping over their lost herds. This year's crop of lambs had almost all been lost.

Already, said Onegesh, folk were beginning to say that the gods were angry. The khans had offered up some of the precious beasts in sacrifice, but neither the rain, nor the whispers, came to an end.

"Is there sickness?" Gudrun asked then, remembering the year that the Rhenus overflowed.

"There is some," the *tzur* said unhappily. "Maybe there will be more. The khan Bladarda is sick, they say." He stopped, staring into the fire.

"And I suppose some of the whisperers say he is old, and should not have been granted the rule . . ." Gudrun thought aloud. She saw the conflict on the young man's face and laughed. "You do not need to answer me. I know you are sworn to both khans."

She frowned into the fire, wondering how Attila was handling the situation. Was he trying to turn suspicion in some other direction, or was he making use of the rumors to bring his brother down? It was rather remarkable, really, that with so many other matters to occupy his attention, he had bothered to send for her.

But I don't suppose he is taking all this trouble out of love for me, she thought, looking at the muddy warriors around her. *It is for Apsik, his son, and because Attila will not suffer anything, even the rains of heaven, to harm what belongs to him.*

* * *

The moon, which had just begun to wane the last time Gudrun had glimpsed it, was swelling toward the full once more when the clouds parted at last on the evening before they rode down to the encampment at the headwaters of the Tizia. Attila's household said that she brought the sunshine with her, for from the moment of her arrival the skies began to clear. Gudrun shook her head and said nothing—to her it seemed that mud was the only thing she had brought with her, so much that she wondered if anything she had worn on that journey would ever again be truly clean.

While the camp steamed gently in the strengthening sun, Gudrun washed clothes with the other women and listened to their chattering. Though the rain had stopped, the sickness was spreading; folk already weakened by cold and damp and short rations were easy prey. Bladarda was not dead, but he grew no better. Some said it was not the plague that had brought him down, but Queen Ereka's poison. Gudrun doubted it. Bladarda might be protected by the magic of every *kam* in Hunland, but if Attila's senior wife wanted someone dead, he would already be in the ground. In any case, Bladarda was being tended in his own encampment on the Hierasus, and Queen Ereka was still in her house on the height across the river from Aquincum.

Folk seemed surprisingly untroubled by the prospect of losing Bladarda, whether from natural causes or by design, from which Gudrun gathered that at least in the west, the shared kingship was becoming increasingly illusory. At the moment, Attila was keeping everyone far too busy searching for lost families and their livestock and distributing food for many to question his authority.

But though Bladarda lived, others continued to die. There were some who said that the powers of heaven were displeased because the sons of Mundzuk had crucified Balamber's other heirs. No good could come of a kingship that had begun by shedding the blood of kin, they murmured, ignoring the fact that half the royal houses in the known world had started out that way. If things did not improve,

Attila might find his own power crumbling. Gudrun scrubbed at her stained garments and wondered if she would have done better to flee to the west after all.

Every evening the khan took his meat with a different family. It made good sense politically, and in truth, Gudrun had not expected him to welcome her with open arms. She was still his responsibility, but whether he was angered because she had come to the king-making without an invitation or had simply lost interest now that she had given him the son he wanted from her, they had had little to say to one another since Apsik was born. But it would have appeared strange if he had avoided her entirely.

When the message came that the khan would honor her with a visit she gathered the ingredients to make a stew that he had liked, put on her cleanest robe, and instructed the children sternly on how to behave.

The word had spread to others as well. It was amazing, or perhaps amusing, how many of the people who had ignored her before, perhaps uncertain regarding her status here, found an opportunity to stop by her *ger* to pass the time of day and incidentally favor her with some tidbit of information they wanted the khan to hear.

Ecgward, who was a clever hunter, brought in a barren doe just beginning to fatten up on the greenery that was appearing everywhere after the rains. Of stored food there was little, but many of the herbs Gudrun knew from her homeland were already sprouting in the foothills above the encampment, and on her walks with the children she had noted where they grew. Deer meat stewed with wild onion and spear-leek and spring greens should make a welcome change from the old goat and older cheese on which most of the camp had been subsisting. By the time the khan arrived, the stew in the Hunnish cauldron that stood on its pedestal in the midst of the fire was boiling merrily.

"You cook well," said Attila when she had served him. "I forgot that." His black stare rested on her and Gudrun found herself flushing. "You still surprise me."

Gudrun's eyes widened. From the lord of Hunland, that was an unexpected admission. Up close in the firelight, she could see that despite the new silver in his beard he looked not older so much as fine-drawn by poor food and strain. The wounds where he had gashed his cheeks in mourning for Ruga had made additional furrows in his lean cheeks, and there was new silver in his beard.

She strove to keep her voice steady. "Does that displease you?"

"Not always." His gaze moved toward his son, who was gnawing on a deer rib under his sister's watchful eye. "Apsik grows well. He is big enough now to begin to ride. I will send a pony and a man to teach him."

"In height," she said carefully, "he seems to take after my kin." She herself had forgotten what Attila was like, she thought then. This conversation in front of the children, so full of overtones and implications, was making her head ache.

"It is well that he should look like a Burgund, so long as he rides like a Hun. It is a pity," Attila added, "that none of your brothers have sons to follow them."

Gudrun's breath caught. Was *that* what he had had in mind when he got her with child? There was a certain justice in the idea that a child of hers might be Gundohar's heir, but she was not so sure she wanted him to do so as under-king within a Hunnish empire.

"There is still time. Godo and Gislahar may still take wives. And I hear that Hagano is married." That news had come the previous fall; the thought still amazed her.

"To a Roman woman. But he does not sleep with her," Attila replied.

Gudrun blinked. She would not even ask how he knew. He held out his bowl and she filled it with more stew. *You do not sleep with me.*

"Will you stay here this night?" she asked, one thought leading inevitably to the other. "The children can sleep with their nursemaid."

Attila's eyes gleamed appreciatively, but he shook his head. "After such a winter you would not bear a healthy child."

Considering how long it had taken her to conceive the first one she was not sure that was a compliment. She did not want to think about whether his answer relieved or disappointed her.

"Very well," she said equably. "Let me know if you wish more of my cooking. It is not a condition that you share my bed."

Again that odd gleam, but if she had been expecting some apologetic gallantry she was disappointed. "I must go soon. Tomorrow will be busy," he said then.

"Because of the Sword?"

"What do you know of it?" His gaze focused suddenly and she knew she had surprised him once more.

Gudrun shrugged. "It was one of this morning's more interesting rumors—Folk say it is an ancient weapon that a herdsman found when one of his heifers stepped on it and cut her foot. It must have been uncovered by the rains. Some say it belonged to an old king in these lands, and others that it is the Sword of the God of War."

Attila did not seem disturbed by her words. What, she wondered, was he up to now?

He nodded. "Word travels well. What other stories do they tell—over the washing at the stream?"

She told herself there was no reason to be surprised he should know how she had been spending her time.

"The women wonder what they will eat this year, with so many animals gone. They say that in the lands of the Romans there is still food, and ask if you will send the warriors to fight for it there. They wonder if you and your brother have offended the gods."

He nodded. "They will see that is not so, for the blade that has been found is a god-sword, such as the tribes worshiped in the eastern lands. It will be good for the people to have a god that is greater than their family *eidola*, not so? I think we will honor him with a festival."

A god whose reappearance confirms his favor to the khan ... thought Gudrun. "I look forward to it greatly," she said aloud.

He had not answered the other questions. In past years, Aetius had hired Attila's men to fight the Visigoths. But now Theoderid and her brother were allies. The thought of the Huns coming against her people made her feel ill, but the prospect that the brothers who had killed her first husband might have to fight the second husband to whom they had given her was different. Upon reflection, she thought that what she was feeling might be satisfaction.

For a night and a day the heights across the river from Aquincum had pulsed to the sound of drums. The place had grown since she wintered here the first year of her marriage. More wooden structures stood now on the summit above Queen Ereka's dwelling, two or three buildings where men of note could stay, and Attila's new hall. Below them, where the ground grew more even, the *gers* of the Huns and the tents of their allies flowed away toward the plain.

Gudrun could feel the vibration in the earth on which she stood, like the beating of a great heart. As the strengthening sun dried out the land, the leaders of the Huns and the Goths and Gepids and Sarmatians and all the other peoples swept up in their migration had come to the meeting Attila had called there, to eat the food he had purchased with Roman tribute and honor the god whom he had found, and the people were dancing. Rudegar had set up a pavilion of silk for his wife and daughter; Heimar was there as well, though he had not brought Asliud, a dozen other chieftains she had not seen since her wedding had answered Attila's call.

It had taken most of a moon for the clans to come in; the household of the khan had been here only a few days. Whether everyone believed in the story of the Sword was uncertain, but after this deadly springtide, they would have rallied to anyone who promised them a good meal. It seemed to Gudrun that Attila was staking a great deal on this ceremony, and that surprised her. She thought he only wagered on certainties, and who could be sure of any god's favor, even if the Sword really was a hallow from ancient days?

And yet, perhaps the khan's confidence had some foundation. As Gudrun walked through the camp with her children beside her, she saw cheerful faces where before there had been frowns or the dead stare of despair. Miracles, it appeared, could be worked by food and drink and the excitement of the drums. It was not only the Huns who had come in. That morning she had been astonished to learn that Aetius himself, the Master of the Empire, had slipped across the river from the Roman fortress for the festival. Had he come in answer to some desperate plea from Attila, or was it the Roman general, facing another campaign against the Armorican *bacaudae* and possibly a fight with battered but by no means beaten Visigoths and Burgunds, who was desperate?

Just at the moment of the sun's setting the drumming ceased, and the bitter music of cow horn pipes and birch bark flutes summoned the people to the ceremonial ground. Once again, the wives of the khan sat together. Instinctively Gudrun placed her own body between her son and Attila's queen, but in truth, she did not much fear for the boy here, where so much depended on good omens. And perhaps she had been mistaken about the queen's intentions. No child could be guarded all the time. If Ereka had wished Apsik dead, she could have sent someone to kill him in Lentia.

Men were marching in with torches, stationing themselves around the circle. The platform that had been built of brushwood hurdles in its center looked much more solid in their dancing light. There was a little stir at one end of the circle; Attila appeared with Eskam behind him, and another man. The khan had put on a tunic of silk the color of old blood, and his diadem. The murmurs stilled.

"Listen, people of the hill and plain! Listen, men of the stag and the wolf and the stallion! And lords of the Gepids and Goths, for this concerns you too!" His black stare, that made everyone within range think he was its object, swept the circle, then he nodded, and Eskam came forward.

The *kam* wore his ceremonial robes, jingling with bits of metal and brightened now with streamers of colored cloth, but he had not put his headdress on. A clever touch, thought Gudrun, to enlist the support of the shamans for what was not, properly speaking, one of their mysteries. Eskam stalked around the circle, speaking in a conversational tone that nonetheless reached everywhere.

"Long and long ago, when our people still pasture their herds far to the east of here, there were mighty warriors on the Sea of Grass—" his trained voice rose and fell. "The Royal Scyths, the golden princes, rich in metal and magic . . . They had sorcerer-smiths who forge swords that would never break in battle. The greatest was Kurdalagon. Seven swords he made, from metal that fell from the skies, seven swords for the God of War."

Gudrun frowned. She had heard something like this once, when her brother was telling over the old tales. The Goths had had such a sword, the blade of the Tervings that was borne by Ingentheow the berserker and later by his daughter Heravar. But in his version the magic sword of Heathoric was forged by dwarves. Perhaps they were earth-folk like Ragan, Sigfrid's fosterer, who had been a smith of surpassing skill.

"Time passes"—Eskam gestured broadly, his ornaments clinking—"the Swords go from hand to hand. Only a great king can unsheathe them or they bring disaster. If you bury such a sword, someone always seeks it, and then its power is a curse. If it is not held by sworn priests and given worship, it must be drowned beneath the waters. One of these Swords the Alans held in the time of our fathers. They say another went with the Iazyges to Britannia. The Swords of Kurdalagon come and go at the will of the God of War."

He fell silent, and the people waited, expectance rising. They had all heard rumors enough to guess what was coming now.

"When the Powers of Heaven curse they also grant blessings. We are all half-drowned beneath the waters, this spring—" he paused for the murmur of laughter. "But the water washes away mud that filled a marshland. A sword, flung in when it was still a lake of water, rises into the light of day. On its hilt is gold. It has been in the mud, but it is not rusted. This is a mighty magic!"

Old Kursik led forward a man even older, bearing something swathed in silk in his arms. Eskam gestured toward him.

"We find a priest of the old blood of the Sarmati who knows the ceremony. He holds this Sword now."

The old man moved slowly around the circle, bearing his burden as if he feared the wrath of heaven would indeed strike him if he let it fall. He was richly dressed, but his face was seamed and weathered, and Gudrun guessed that he had been something more humble, perhaps a herdsman dreaming of his family's past glories, before the Sword was found. When he had completed his circumambulation, Attila strode across the grass to meet him.

"Set up the Sword so we see it, honored one." The khan's voice had that same singing tone he used to gentle frightened horses, and the old man straightened. "I am with you. Do not be afraid."

The old priest's eyes widened, but the reassurance seemed to steady him, and he clambered to the top of the platform. An iron pot filled with coals already sat next to the altar stone. Laying his burden carefully down, he took herbs from a pouch at his waist and cast them into the pot. In moments white smoke began to spiral upward. The old man lifted the pot and fanned smoke in each direction; Gudrun caught a whiff of something sweet and harsh at the same time and coughed. He purified Attila, then set the pot back down, ceremoniously washed his own hands in the smoke, then rose to face the people.

"I am Amaguz son of Zarmihr of the line of Urs-Barag, Servant of Batradz like my fathers before me, from generation to generation, until our last king was killed, and the god-sword cast into the sacred pool. Now the Sword comes once more to the light of day."

The guard of warriors who stood between the torchbearers began to strike the ground with the butts of their lances. The vibration came through the earth to the wood of the bench. There was a note in the old man's voice that made Gudrun shiver. He believed what he was saying, whatever the truth might be. Now he had bent once more to unwrap his burden. He straightened slowly, as if the thing he held were heavier than any mortal sword ought to be, and held it high. Torchlight flared from the polished blade like sunset from lake water, casting red lightnings across the grass.

"Behold the Sword of War!" The blade swung through the air, drawing the old man's arm after it. He staggered from side to side, striving to maintain his balance. "God steel, star steel, fire from heaven. Spell steel, forged by ancient magic. Not breaking, not bending, not rusting or tarnished, this immortal blade we honor!"

The priest swayed as the Sword curved downward, but whether he was too old and unaccustomed to such weapons to direct it, or whether he was unable to control the power in the blade, it missed the altar and slashed through the woven withies of the platform. The shock drove the hilt from the priest's hand, but Attila grasped it before it could fall.

All around the circle, pent breath was released slowly as the khan straightened with the Sword of Kurdalagon in his hand.

"In earth and water you were hidden—" There was a tremor in Attila's deep voice. *He did not plan this!* Gudrun thought in amazement as he lifted the blade. "Now you come to the hand of a Ruler of Peoples. In this land I inherit the power of your ancient kings. With your aid we go out and conquer." The murmur of awe that had swept the crowd became a roar. "When I am Lord of the World, you go before me! I call you, God of War!"

She could see his arm trembling, but he never faltered, as he brought the blade down with a deft twist to plunge into the slot prepared for it in the stone.

They brought up a white stallion, the finest in Attila's herds, and cut its throat. Its blood was caught in a golden ewer and poured over the stone that held the Sword. Gudrun rubbed her eyes; was it only her fatigue and the torchlight, or was the blade truly haloed in a golden glow?

"The Roman does not show what he is thinking—" observed Queen Ereka. "Will he tell his little emperor, I wonder, that a new Lord of the World rules here?"

"What about Bladarda?" Gudrun raised an eyebrow.

"What about him?" The queen's shrug was eloquent, and Gudrun smiled. Bladarda had lain sick in his *ger* while his people suffered. If Attila could bring them prosperously through the next year, he would be, in fact if not in name, supreme.

They left the blade in the altar stone throughout the evening for the people to honor, while the *kams* drummed and sang to bring the blessing of the spirits on the tribes. The women brought out skin sacks of kumiss, amphorae of Roman wine, and wooden casks of mead and barley beer, passing beakers and drinking horns from one to another until everyone grew merry. Gudrun took the children back to Bala to be put to bed. When she returned, having, for courtesy's sake, swallowed more mead than she intended, the White Heron, whom she had not seen since the year before, was dancing.

Gudrun stood at the edge of the crowd, watching. When she studied with the shamaness she had begun to learn some of the chants, and she found herself swaying to the beat of the drum, whispering along with the singer. Her skin prickled, then sensation left it and awareness narrowed to the words. She thought vaguely that perhaps the mead had dissolved her control, for she was half-tranced before she quite realized what was happening.

"What is the witch-woman singing?" said a quiet voice beside her in the Gothic tongue.

It was Aetius, with his servant behind him. Swathed in his cloak, to ordinary vision he might have been any of the German chieftains. But as she looked at him, Gudrun realized that just as the dancing shamaness trailed a haze of light behind her, the Roman leader moved in a kind of violet vortex of power. If she did not blink, she could even see his spirit shape hovering like a great eagle above him.

"She sings . . . the names of ancestors. . . ." Words came from her lips.

This was not the voluntary alteration of consciousness in which the *kam* commanded spirits, but the passive trance of the seeress, for without having willed it, she was answering. *This is not right*, said a part of her mind that was as yet unaffected. *My teacher told me not to do this alone. . . .* But while the trance held her that did not seem to matter.

"She sings . . . the spirits of the land. . . . All come to see . . . the sword. She calls them to protect the people . . . to help the khan. . . ." Speaking seemed to deepen the trance, as if Gudrun had become a channel for images and information beyond the words.

Aetius seemed to realize that she was not her ordinary self, for he motioned to the slave, spoke softly, and sent him away.

"They come, see how they come—" she gestured widely, for now the stag and the bear, the wolf and the eagle and the stallion, all the tribal totems whom the *kams* had called seemed quite visible. They leaped and soared, hovering over the people, and swirling around the Sword. To her inner sight, the blade blazed with blinding intensity.

A part of her awareness knew that people were making a circle around her; someone brought a bench and guided her to sit, but no one was commanding her to come back to her ordinary self. She laughed, pointing to the shapes that only she could see. Even the black she-goat who was her own ally had come to her. She wanted to speak to her, but the Roman's questions held her.

"You didn't tell me the woman could do this—" she heard Aetius say, and another voice, whose resonances held mingled amusement and danger, answering, "She is full of surprises. And yet maybe not. Her mother was a sorcereress."

The White Heron was drumming furiously, foretelling great blessings for khan and people. As she spoke, Gudrun saw them—women shining with golden ornaments and healthy children, flocks and herds filling the plains, and babbled of what she saw.

"Turn your gaze westward, seeress," said Aetius then. "There is a city called Narbo, which men of the Visigoths are besieging. Has the city fallen?"

For a moment awareness swirled in dizzying spirals. Then Gudrun's vision cleared. Words came with the images—a Roman army attacking the flank, breaking the Visigoth line, driving the warriors away.

"Litorius was in time, then," breathed Aetius. "But what of Armorica?"

This vision, too, came with the words, and she saw the *bacaudae* taking advantage of the Roman distraction to reconquer lost ground.

"You see my problem?" Aetius was saying. "We can control the Germans, or we can contain Tibatto and his motley crew, but not both of them simultaneously. I fear that if the Burgunds make another try for Treveri, we will not be able to stop them."

"You need more warriors?" Attila responded. "That is easy. I have many hungry men. You pay us, we will fight who you say. You see how we need the gold. . . ."

"Even the Burgunds? I thought they were your allies. . . ." Aetius spoke very softly, but Gudrun heard. It did not seem to matter.

"With the kings I swear oaths of kinship, not the army. Separate the men from their leaders and it is not treachery."

Aetius gave a grunt of laughter. "And of course to separate them from their leadership would make them more vulnerable. Could it be done, though? Before the summer campaigns?"

"Maybe . . . if I invite them to feast with me . . . if the woman asks them to come. . . ."

"You are still owed a blood-price for the death of your niece, Brunahild, are you not?" Aetius added more softly still. "And your wife—does she possess Sigfrid's gold?"

"You reason well, my friend," answered Attila. "But gold is only good when used—"

"I understand . . ." There was a silence, then, "You will have food for your people, Lord of Horses, and arms for your warriors. Will that content you?"

Attila laughed. Even Gudrun, floating in her tranced haze, found it an uncanny sound. She felt him move closer.

"What do you see, seeress, when you look at the Sword?" he asked.

Obediently, Gudrun turned her awareness to the blade still standing in the block of stone. It shone silver now in the light of the rising moon. But she saw that surface for no more than a moment. She felt her awareness altering even further, and gasped as light fountained upward from the point of the Sword in the shape of a man with one hand. Suddenly she began to laugh.

"What is it?" his voice was harsh in her ear. "Tell me!"

"You thought it was a story! You thought the old legend would serve you, when the herdsman found that sword. But it is true! There is a spirit in that steel—you felt it when you grasped the hilt! I see the God of War Himself arising from the blade. . . . He gazes toward the west. Fight for your people, khan, fight for Justice, and you shall have victory. . . ."

"Victory . . ." breathed Aetius. "My brother, that is what I offer you—if you will help me, beyond the borders of the

Empire you shall be supreme as I am within it. Together we will rule the world!"

Gudrun woke groaning. By the glow in the felt of the *ger* she could tell it was morning, but she had only the haziest recollection of coming to bed the night before. She shut her eyes again and started to pull the covers back over her, but there was a weight holding them. Her eyes flew open. She was not alone in the bedding; her husband was lying with his back to her, breathing quietly as he always did in sleep. She sat up abruptly and felt the unaccustomed soreness between her thighs. At the movement, Attila woke as well.

"What was it like, sleeping with the dead?" she asked bitterly. Her breasts were tender too.

Infuriatingly, he grinned. "You seemed to enjoy it. You don't remember?"

She shook her head. She had gone back to watch the dancing, and the White Heron had sung to the spirits. She remembered *seeing* them, and other things, or had that all been a dream?

Attila's gaze became even more opaque than usual. "I have many worries, but not so much anymore, because of the Sword. I was not kind to you when I ate at your hearth. It will be better now."

Gudrun eyed him suspiciously. What *had* she done the night before?

"Your brothers have not seen Apsik. A man should know his sister-son. I will invite them to feast with us here."

She stared at him, wondering why that should set off a chorus of warning howls within.

"When you left them you were not friends. Maybe you send them a gift with the messenger so they know you wish them to come, too?" He reached out to fondle her breast, and smiled as her flesh responded.

"I suppose so—" she began, but any other thought she might have had was lost as he pulled her down against him.

And whatever it had been like in the night, this time her body was alive and eager, caring nothing for her fears.

But later, when Attila had left her, the White Heron came to call.

"You are well?" she asked. "I know the confusion that comes after, until you are accustomed to trance."

So *that* was it. Gudrun rubbed her eyes, remembering visions of blood and victory, though they were hazy, like dreams. It seemed to her that Aetius had been there, and they had talked about the Burgunds. . . .

"It took me by surprise," she said carefully. "Is it usual not to remember?"

The shamaness nodded. "Unless you are reminded."

Gudrun sighed. Somehow she did not think Attila was going to tell her what she had said. But she could recall enough now to know that more than brotherly love lay behind this invitation to the Burgund kings.

When Berik came to receive the gift she had promised Attila she would send, Gudrun handed him a golden arm ring to take to them. But she had wrapped it in a piece of wolfhide, and in a gap in the design she had scratched the runes ᚹ ᚩ ᛁ—WOE!

She wondered if her brothers would understand and heed the warning. She wondered if she cared. As Attila had said, Grimahild's sons and her daughter had not been good friends when she left the Rhenus. Fury still writhed in her belly when she remembered Hagano and Gundohar standing together at Sigfrid's funeral pyre.

It came to her then that she had been right to warn them, for it was she herself who might prove to be their greatest danger if they came.

Chapter 13 ✿ Whispers on the Wind

Borbetomagus
Eggtide Moon, A.D. 437

"**B**ut why do you make a song about Airmanar-eik?" Andulf took a quick step to catch up with Gundohar's long stride. The wind, tossing the leaves of the beech trees toward the morning sun, dappled the muddy path to the horse pens with shifting patterns of shadow and light. "He didn't stop the Huns. He died."

"All men die." Gundohar looked at the boy and smiled. "Both thralls and kings. It is how you die that makes the difference."

Andulf had gotten leggy as a colt over the winter, as if all the rain that had fallen was making him grow. His mind was growing, too, thought the king. He asked awkward questions and argued with the answers. If Galamvara had given the king a son, they might have had such conversations. Or perhaps not—Gundohar would have had to train a Burgund prince in the craft of kingship, whereas young Andulf had the makings of a bard, and so long as the boy learned to fight as well as Wolcgar, no one would object if Gundohar taught him to use a harp as well as a sword.

He supposed that other boy, his cousin Gundrada's son, must be growing as well. He had hoped by now to have young Gundiok here as a fosterling, but since last year's disaster at Treveri, both Burgunds and Visigoths thought it politic not to make too great a show of their alliance.

"Like the saints in Father Priscus's tales?" asked the boy.

"Like the heroes," said Gundohar, thinking of Sigfrid. "The death of a hero gives life meaning, lets us feel we are more than playthings for Wyrd."

"What did Airmanareik's death mean?"

Gundohar sighed. "I don't know. I think that is why I am making the poem. Do you think the story flowers full-blown in my head before I write it down?" He went on as the boy looked uncomprehending. "Parts of it I know, but there is a thing that happens in the setting forth, so that by the time I have got the lines right there is more in them than I intended."

One day, he thought, he would understand. He had filled many tablets with writing as the story grew, but its ending still eluded him. The deeds of the Goth-king were known to all and should have been easy to chronicle. Since the Burgund defeat at Treveri, the gods of song, as if in compensation, had given back to Gundohar the power, or perhaps the need, to work on his poem. He had had a great deal of opportunity, for it had been a long winter and a rainy spring, though the flooding had not been so bad here as in other lands. One day, the answers would come.

When he understood the truth of Airmanareik's kingship, he might find it possible to write about Sigfrid.

From beyond the trees came a sharp whinny and Andulf's attention focused abruptly on the horses.

"Oh see—the grey colt is on his legs already!" A quick glance of appeal brought a nod from Gundohar, and the boy ran forward.

The colt's dam was one of those sired by Sigfrid's horse Grani, swift and tough and willful. *Like his master*, thought the king, wishing that the horses had been Sigfrid's only legacy.

The hero had been a royal sacrifice—an offering, self-offered, Gundohar told himself, for the man had had so many chances, so many warnings; surely if he had been unwilling, he could have run away. The king shook his head;

that was a road his thoughts had traveled too many times already.

Did Airmanareik kill himself as an offering, to buy the lives of his people? he wondered then. It was a thing that had been whispered sometimes when the Rome-priests could not hear.

He had heard another rumor, a new one. They were saying that Aetius meant to crush the Burgunds before they could threaten the south of Gallia again. Rome had offered gold to the Huns to go against Borbetomagus and Attila had accepted it.

Suddenly the wind felt cold.

The sighing of wind in the leaves was like the whisper of flowing water, thought Hagano as he looked upward— a river of air flowing through the forest. The riffling of the surface of the Rhenus hinted at the currents in the depths. In the same way, he saw where the wind passed through the forest by the movements of the leaves. It was not only air and water whose sounds could be so confusing—he had heard the flap of wind-whipped banners in the crackle of a fire. And what was fire but light whose life was in its motion? It was the movement that mattered, the invisible passage of something which could only be felt, not seen.

Hagano drew a deep breath and felt the air tingle through him; his solid flesh a mass of motes in frenzied motion. For a moment he understood everything. Then the breath rushed out of him, and he was only a man once more. But he could still feel the prickle of power lifting the hairs on his skin.

He shook himself, fixing his gaze firmly on the surfaces of things. The shadows were growing longer. Before the sun went down he must find the Cornelian boundary stone; he did not have time for foolish notions about the wind.

A year ago, he thought as he trudged onward, no one would have worried about where one estate ended and the next began. A year ago they had all been dreaming of the fertile hillsides around Treveri. Now that the Burgunds were confined once more to Germania Secunda, their lands seemed suddenly constricted. This was the third boundary dispute he had been asked to investigate this year. But if the records were right, he should find the marker soon. He hoped the flourishing new growth, result of the recent months' abundant moisture, had not overwhelmed it. It had been placed, according to the charter, near a small spring.

A breath of wind lifted the leaves and ruffled his hair. He paused, frowning, as the sound deepened. For a moment he heard the river of air he had imagined, then, as he went forward, realized that the sound was the rush of a stream. He pushed aside a branch of low-trailing willow and saw the glitter of water splashing down from a rockfall. Above it, the spring had formed a small pool.

Holding on to branches, Hagano began to clamber toward it. The rocks were slippery with damp moss, demanding all his attention. Panting, he squatted at the edge and bent to drink. A woman's face, framed by waves of shadowed hair, gazed up at him.

Kustubaira . . . his heart spoke, but in the next moment noted the attenuated features, the huge green eyes. The beauty of the Roman woman was human. This was something other. And in that moment of recognition, the nixie smiled.

Hagano jerked backward, swearing. A dislodged stone skipped into the water and the image dislimned like a shattered mosaic. It was gone so swiftly that he wondered if he had really seen it. But in the gurgle of the stream he heard a voice that called, *"Hagano, the world of men will betray you! Stay with me!"* and then a ripple of mocking laughter.

As his breathing returned to normal, he glimpsed the boundary stone he had been seeking poking from among the roots of an oak tree. That was all he needed to see here—he got to his feet and backed away. Among his mother's people it was considered dangerous to see such wights as the spirit of the spring. Perhaps for his father's kin it had been different, but he had never learned their mysteries.

He hurried homeward, wanting food and fire and Kustubaira's warm and human embrace.

"I have heard both your claims," said Gundohar, considering the two Romans who were glaring at each other across the green turf beneath the Oak of Judgment, and the Burgund chieftains who stood beside them. "And my brother has investigated them. Hagano, say now what you have seen—"

"I took the charter offered in evidence by Julius Cornelius Florus"—Hagano's gaze went to the older of the Romans—"and examined the description of the boundaries set forth therein. It is the contention of Gaius Turpilius that the charter has been altered, and that the original boundary ran along the ridge above the vineyards?" He raised an inquiring eyebrow at the other man, who nodded dourly.

Turpilius did not look nearly so confident as he had earlier, the king noted with interest. Had he expected Gundohar to find in his favor merely because the Burgund who was the "guest" sharing his estates was Dancward, who served in the royal guard?

"I walked that ridge, and saw no sign or marker." Hagano went on. "But the stone described in the charter is still there by the spring."

"He put it there," Turpilius began, but Hagano shook his head.

"The root had grown around it. That stone has been there since before we came into this land." Wind stirred the young leaves and Hagano's gaze flicked upward uneasily.

"Are you sure, lord, that it was a dressed stone?" asked Dancward. "I have found Turpilius to be an honest man, and I will take oath to support his claim."

"As I swear for Florus!" exclaimed Walest, son of Ulfar, who had inherited his father's share of the allotted lands after the battle at Treveri.

"Silence, both of you!" Gundohar rose from his chair, staring them down. "These boundaries were established by the law of the Romans, and the matter must be decided according to their customs, not ours!"

"Why?" asked Walest. "I was born on that land. Am I not a native here? I remember going with my mother to make offerings at the sacred spring when I was only a child, and seeing the stone."

Gundohar sighed. The boy had a point, but it was one that could be made to favor any of the peoples who had tilled this land. Who did the earth belong to? The spirits of hill and stream? If they had a law, he did not know it. He could only go by the words of those who had set him to govern here.

"The root of justice may be in the earth itself, but my authority to decide who uses it comes from the emperor. Be silent or pay the fine for interfering." Walest reddened, but he held his peace. "I refuse your oath," Gundohar went on, "but in confirmation of what Hagano has told us I accept your evidence, and I find in favor of Turpilius."

Dancward looked grim, but he held his peace. The king sat down again, suddenly weary. Beneath the babble of commentary and congratulation he could hear the the murmur of wind in the leaves. It occurred to him that he had spoken more truly than he knew. In that moment, if he could have gotten law from the landspirits he would have done so. But according to the Church, the purpose of Justice was to please God, not the earth and those who dwelt there. Perhaps in the old days, when the Burgunds lived on the other side of the Rhenus, things had been different, but he had to look westward now.

The feast of Pentecost came to the lands along the river with skies swept clean of cloud by the wind. The Burgund princes feasted their warriors and sponsored competitions, rewarding the victors with arm rings and consoling the losers with horns of mead. Clearly the men had expected the festivities to close with some announcement about the summer's campaigning, but Gundohar kept silent. Until he had certain knowledge that Attila's warriors were headed elsewhere, he dared not commit his own.

A week after the feast, a message came that a party of Hun horsemen were waiting at the ferry. It had come, then. Gundohar found his own reactions compounded equally of relief and dread. But he had been king of the Burgunds since he was fourteen years old, and had learned how to maintain his mask; he allowed no hint of either hope or fear to show as he sent word that Attila's messengers were to be honorably escorted to the town. He had half expected a line of Hun warriors on the other side of the river to announce Attila's intentions. One could negotiate with an ambassador.

That night the Burgund princes sat up late, drinking with their brother-in-law's messengers. The torches had burned out; the lamps on the wrought-iron tripods Gundohar had brought back with him from Italia cast circles of light on the table and the men who sat around it, with only an occasional flicker to conjure the faces in the frescoes out of the darkness behind them.

"Your crops are growing well," said Rudegar, holding out his beaker to be refilled. Galamvara smiled and poured him more of the pale sweet wine that came from the vineyards behind the city.

"The rainfall this year has been generous," answered Ordwini. "It swells the grapes and thickens the grass."

"Generous!" Berik snorted. "You are lucky to say so. In Hun lands, the water was our enemy."

"Some word of that came to us," put in Gundohar. "They say the Danuvius overflowed its banks and filled the plain. Eleven years ago the Rhenus flooded—I understand something of what you have endured."

"Maybe, but here the hills are near, you can drive cattle to high ground," the Hun lord answered.

Rudegar nodded agreement. "My own hall is in the hills, and we were not much harmed, but farther east, in Hunland, the plain of the Danu is very wide. The animals scattered, but wherever they ran the waters followed them. The plain looked like the Euxine Sea."

Gundohar frowned, understanding what the Marcoman chieftain did not say. Even more than the Burgunds, the Huns lived on the beasts they herded. He himself had been desperate for gold with which to buy new animals for the Burgunds the year they lost so many to the rains. It would be far worse for the khan.

"Your lord was not harmed? Or my sister and her child?" he asked. Attila would be looking for wealth from somewhere, but Gundohar had spent all his own riches on last year's campaign. There would be little plunder here.

"The khan is well, and the khatun." Berik straightened. "He sends you greetings. He says you have not seen his new son, your nephew. It is time you and your brothers paid him a visit. The floods are gone now, and like here, the land is very fair."

"Attila may wish to welcome us, but what of Gudrun?" Hagano asked then. "Is she eager to see us as well?"

"Surely she must miss news of her homeland," answered Rudegar earnestly. "She has sent a gift for you—" he turned to Berik. "Where have you stowed it?"

Berik shook his head, and reaching into the breast of his tunic, brought out something wrapped in grey fur. "I carry it so long I forget. Here, lord. This is for you to wear when you come."

Gundohar took the package and untied the thongs, nostrils twitching at the rank smell of wolf. Inside lay a golden arm ring incised with a design of leaping stags. He turned it, admiring the workmanship, and marked the glint of scratched runes that were not part of the design.

"Look, she has sent us a message." ᛈᚾᛁᛈᚱ—WEAL! He passed the arm ring to Hagano.

"So, will you come?" asked the envoy. The Huns were a dour people. No doubt that accounted for the strangeness of Berik's smile.

"It is an honor for you to ask us," Hagano answered smoothly, setting down the arm ring. Galamvara picked it up and began to turn it this way and that so that lamplight pooled and sparked on the bright gold. "But the king cannot leave his people without the consent of his council. We will call them in tomorrow, and give you our answer as soon as we may."

Gundohar raised one eyebrow, but why was he surprised? This would not be the first time his brother's thinking had anticipated his own. Hagano's reaction was clearly to refuse the journey. Gundohar could see the same dangers in this story of Attila's difficulties that his brother had, but he also saw in it an opportunity.

"You want to go to Attila? To leave us when there may be danger here?" exclaimed Desiderius. "With all respect, lord, have you gone mad?"

Hagano, seeing Gundohar's face pale in the light of the high windows, cleared his throat. "I believe it is in hopes of preventing that danger that he proposes the journey. It is for us, his counselors, to weigh the advantages and hazards of all courses open to us now."

The Roman magistrate nodded with the same faintly dyspeptic frown as the faces in the fading frescoes on the basilica wall. Looking beyond them to the figure of the throned Jupiter in the apse, Hagano wondered if the Roman god had the same kinds of discussions with his counselors.

"It is only a rumor that the Huns will be sent against us—" Garo observed. "We don't *know*—and if we insult Attila, won't we risk bringing on the very thing we want to avoid?"

Deorberht leaned forward. "Attila is our ally! He refused to fight against us when we attacked Treveri. Why would he betray us now?"

"When I first heard the rumor I wondered that, too, but his messengers have told us that the floods hit them hard this spring," said Hagano patiently. "I think they would fight for anyone who offered them enough gold to replenish their herds."

Ordwini pulled at his beard. "That's true. I remember how it was when the Rhenus flooded here."

"You make it sound inevitable." Junius Desiderius looked from one to another. "Why are we discussing it? We should call out the warriors and prepare our defenses now!"

"I'm ready!" exclaimed Godomar, who had been chewing his moustache impatiently. The king looked at him with weary affection.

"You are always ready for a fight, Godo, and it may come to that whatever we do." Gundohar turned to the others. "But if our course had been clear, I would have answered the envoys last night. I keep thinking there has to be another way. If I go to Attila, speak to him as one king to another, perhaps we can find it. The Romans only win because they set us against each other. If all the barbarian nations cooperated as King Theoderid and I did last year, what could Aetius do?"

Hagano started to speak, then paused. Since last night he had feared Gundohar was thinking of something like this, but it would be better to let the others argue him out of it.

"And who would be emperor? Theoderid? You?" Ordwini shook his head. "We would all be at each other's throats before five years had passed. We need at least the dream of Empire. Since your father's time our goal has been to find a place within it, not to destroy it. Destruction is Attila's way."

"He loves his people. He is a king," Gundohar said stubbornly. "If I talk to him—"

"You will have to buy him, brother," Hagano interrupted, remembering things he had heard when he was Attila's hostage.

"With what?" Garo snorted. "Treveri took everything we had."

The king looked at Hagano, who sighed. "Not quite everything. There is still Sigfrid's gold."

"That belongs to Gudrun—" Ordwini began.

"True, or we would no doubt have spent it long ago. But she is Attila's wife. One might argue that if we give it to him, we give it to her. . . ."

Godo shook his head. "I wonder if Gudrun will see it that way?"

"I am willing to ask her," said Gundohar. "I will get down on my knees to ask her forgiveness if that is what is required. There is risk on all roads. But we will never know safety unless the alliance with Attila is made secure."

"Godo has a good nose for danger," Hagano said then. "In the land of the Huns, our sister may pose the greatest threat of all. You might think that marriage and a new child would console her, but the Niflungar have long memories. I believe that she hates us still."

"She sent the arm ring to the king, does not that suggest a desire for reconciliation?" Garo asked.

"She sent it wrapped in wolfhide," answered Hagano. "That suggests something rather different to me."

"Such suspicions as yours are likely to reawaken her hostility—" said Gundohar.

"Lord, you have been a good ruler." Junius Desiderius rubbed his eyes, then looked squarely at the king. "Send a representative to speak with Attila, but stay here to lead your people—both Roman and Burgund—if he fails."

Gundohar's face grew very pink suddenly and Hagano raised an eyebrow. Had his brother not known he was loved?

"The invitation was for the king specifically," said Deorberht. "If he sent someone else, Attila might be insulted."

Gundohar cleared his throat, coughed, and tried again. "In a battle . . . you give the best archers arrows, and the best swordsmen good blades. I am not the general you need if it comes to open battle; my weapon is words. Would it content you if I left Godomar here to lead our armies? To persuade Attila to side with me against Aetius will take all a bard's skill."

"I don't like the idea of you going into danger without

me!" said Godomar. "And what about the rest of it? I haven't been trained to rule."

"I won't like leaving you to face danger here," Gundohar forced a grin. "But I know the men will follow you into battle if it should come. As for the rest of it, my queen ruled well when I was away before. I propose to leave her in charge of the government and you as warleader."

"If you are bound on going, take a strong force, well armed," said Hagano.

"You are determined on this course?" asked Ordwini. Gundohar looked at him.

"I see no other way. Guard our western gates while we are gone."

"It is not from the west that the danger will come to us." Ordwini shook his head, but he said no more.

Laidrad sighed. "I will go with you. I was one of those who sought Sigfrid's death, and I must make my peace with Gudrun. My nephew can lead my men."

"And I—" said Garo. Others spoke up after them.

"And what about you, Hagano?" asked Laidrad. "Or are you too wary a wolf to run your head into this noose with the rest of us?"

Hagano felt his throat tighten. The god who owned him had been hanged, upon the Worldtree, or so ran the tale. *Is this how Sigfrid felt when the noose began to tighten?* At the thought, he seemed to hear a whisper of laughter.

"You will need someone who knows the Hun lands and language to guide you. When was a hero ever stopped by the threat of danger?" He laughed, and saw men's eyes flicker uneasily. "Never fear, my heroes, I will be there."

Gundohar got to his feet and the others pushed back their benches and rose as well, talking excitedly. Hagano wondered if those who had volunteered truly believed in the danger, or if it was that which had attracted them. The god in the fresco looked down at them sadly. When all courses were evil, how did the gods decide?

The door at the end of the hall was opened and a warm

wind filled the hall with the scents of woodsmoke and grass.

"Do you mean to bring the gold with us?" Hagano asked his brother as they came out into the brightness of the day.

Gundohar shook his head. "That would be foolish. Why should Attila negotiate for it when he has only to stretch out his hand? Nor will I leave it here for the taking if they should attack us after all. Find a hiding place, brother." Turning, he shaded his eyes against the golden spangling of sunlight on the river. "Sink it in the Rhenus, somewhere only we can find it again."

Gundohar had thought sleep might come hard that night, but it seemed that making the decision had also made away with his apprehensions. He slept almost as soon as he lay down. It was Galamvara's nightmares that woke him, not his own.

"'Vara, wake up!" He tried to comfort her, but she struck at him. "Galamvara!" Gundohar grasped her wrists and held them until she stilled and collapsed against him, sobbing.

"Oh my love, I have had such dreams!"

He gathered her closer. She had gained flesh since their marriage; he loved the solid weight of her in his arms.

"Let it go, beloved. I am here."

"For how long?" She shook her head. "I thought a bloody sword was brought into the hall and it ran you through, and wolves drank the blood that flowed from your back and your breast."

"Well you know dogs don't like me." Gundohar forced a laugh. "Bloodstained weapons often stand for their snarling, they say."

"That was only the first one. Then I dreamed there was a storm, and nine women all clad in black came riding through the skies, and they were weeping. It seemed to me that they all had the look of the Niflungar. I think they were your idises, Gundohar."

He nodded. This dream of the spirits that warded his

line would not be explained away so easily, and he felt his skin grow cold.

"They came into the hall and claimed you, and though this dream was not so bloody as the other, I was terrified. Don't go to Hunland, beloved, not when you have been given such a warning!"

Gundohar sighed, stroking her hair. "I never heard a tale yet where a man could evade his wyrd by heeding an omen. It only works itself out in some other, and usually worse, way."

"Why should I have such dreams if not to save you?" she exclaimed.

"Perhaps the warning is so I may prepare—" he began, but she interrupted, clutching at his arm.

"If you will not believe my dreaming, perhaps the runes will convince you! I took a close look at that arm ring your sister sent, and it seems to me the last two runes were crammed in later by another hand. It is *woe*, not *weal*, that your sister wrote on the ring!"

"Do you think so?" Gundohar felt his heart lightening. If Gudrun had tried to warn them, perhaps she no longer hated him after all. "Then I can hope that she will be our ally—nay, do not cry," he added as she began to weep against his shoulder. "Even your priests say that God foreknows all that will befall. You did not try to stop me when I rode off to war. This is the same. If there is a chance that by talking to Attila I can save the Burgunds, then I must go even if Wodan himself should try to bar my way."

Galamvara shook her head. "What use to save your people if they have no king?" she murmured.

"The king exists for the people, not the other way around—" Gundohar realized he had always known this, though he had never been able to find the words before. "They will choose another when I am gone."

"Another man may be able to sit in your high seat," she said, wiping her eyes determinedly, "but no one will fill your place in my arms." Fiercely she kissed him, and Gundohar, abandoning words, did his best to comfort her in the only other way he knew.

As always, Hagano came awake instantly when Kustubaira entered his chamber. "What is it?" he whispered as she hesitated in the doorway, her pale bedgown glowing in the light of the lamp she bore.

They slept in separate rooms. He said it was to give her the privacy she needed for her prayers, but in truth, he feared it was her need for him that was too often their cause. As soon as they could get a dispensation from the bishop at Mogontiacum she had insisted on completing the marriage, but though her own saint had said it was better to marry than to burn, whenever his wife came to his bed she punished herself with penance and fasting after.

"I dreamed."

He rose from the bed, took the lamp from her hand, and set it on his table. For a moment she leaned against him, and he could feel the tremors that ran through her body beneath the thin gown.

"Don't go on this journey with your brother, Hagano. I dreamed a raging river swept in and smashed the pillars of the hall; it shattered the benches and swept your brother's legs out from under him and broke them, and then yours. Surely that means disaster. . . ."

"It is your fear speaking, dear one," he said, desperate to console her. "I will not expect evil of people without cause."

"I dreamed a bear came in, shattered the high seat with one blow, and opened his mouth to devour us all," she said then.

"The bear is a storm," he began, but Kustubaira shook her head.

"A human storm—God's tempests do not fill me with fear." It was true, she was courageous, and already he could feel her calming. He must talk to her, then, until she had command of herself once more.

"If the danger is here, then it is not in Hunland." Hagano

sat down on the bed and after a moment she seated herself, not quite touching, beside him. "But if we go to Attila, perhaps it will not come here."

"I dreamed an eagle came flying through the hall and splattered us all with blood. But it had the face of a Hun with a golden diadem. I think it was King Attila's fetch I saw. Will you not believe me now?"

"You are remembering the game our birds brought down the other day when we went hunting. Surely it is a horse shape that Attila's spirit wears—" Hagano forced a laugh. That was true, but what if that spirit were allied with Rome? The Lord of Horses might indeed appear as an eagle then. Hagano found it hard to argue against her, when he himself had given the same warnings to Gundohar without the excuse of a dream.

Kustubaira sighed. "You do not believe me. I suppose I should not expect it. And I cannot ask you to stay here because I am afraid. It is bad enough that I should be forsworn without asking you to forsake your oaths as well."

"My wife—" His voice cracked, forgetting, in his awareness of her pain, his own. "You are not forsworn to me."

She looked up and laughed with a familiar self-mockery. "Am I not? A good wife shares her husband's bed."

She stood up suddenly, pulled off her sleeping robe and dropped it, drew the chain that held her cross over her head, and let it fall atop her gown. Reflexively Hagano rubbed the rune scarred into the skin beneath his breastbone, wishing he could take it off when he wished to forget the god. But at least Wodan allowed him to lie with his wife without shame. He stood as well, knowing what would happen now, what always happened when she came to him.

Kustubaira finished unbraiding the heavy masses of her hair and laid herself down upon his bed, eyes closed, thighs parted in passive offering. On their wedding night he had tried to court her, and felt a wondering triumph when she clutched at him and cried out in his arms. It had been as great a surprise to her, he thought, as it had been to him.

But the next day her back had been bloody from her own self-imposed penance. After that he had tried to find his own release as swiftly as possible on those occasions when she was unable to separate her duty from her desire.

He lay down beside her and stroked the softness of her breast. She trembled, and a quiver of response ran through him like flame. Between times he tried to forget her beauty. In the lamplight her flesh was like a Roman marble, but despite her pretense of detachment, her skin was warm, her nipples rising to his touch, her breath coming faster as he caressed the secret place between her thighs.

"Kustubaira," he whispered into her hair. "I love you!"

She whimpered and pressed her body against him, but he held back, worshiping her beauty with mouth and hands until she moaned.

"Do not fight it, woman—this is how it is supposed to be!"

She shook her head. "It is . . . sin for me to want you so. . . ."

"I was prepared for you to recoil from me . . ." His voice grated with the strain of waiting. "If it had been so, after our wedding night I would not have troubled you. But to deny *this*"—she gasped as his hands possessed her—"is a sin against *my* gods! If I return from Hunland, you will live as my wife or I will end the marriage. But I think it more likely your warnings are true, Kustubaira, and you will have plenty of time for penance when I am gone, so tonight I am going to make you accept this joy!"

Hagano lifted himself above her, and slowly, so slowly that she clutched at his shoulders and tried to pull him down, he made them one.

In the moments that followed, his own control left him and he found himself in a place beyond words. But it seemed to him, as his completion followed hers and he sank to peace in her arms, that she was whispering words of love for him.

* * *

Hagano woke again in the still hour before dawn. Kustubaira still lay sleeping peacefully beside him. That surprised him. She had always gone back to her own chamber before. Would he listen to her now, he wondered, if she begged him to stay? He sat up, rubbing his eye, and saw the last of the lamplight glinting on her silver cross. She might try, he thought then, but both she and he were bound already to other masters.

He had been dreaming of mighty waters. Was it Kustubaira's dream, transferred to him? But the river she described had been destructive, while the images he was remembering had been of power, of a great river whose relentless current could sweep whole cities away. But beneath its surging waters he saw the gleam of gold.

Hagano remembered then what his brother had asked of him, and he understood how to fulfill that command. Silently he rose and began to pull on his clothes. Kustubaira stirred a little as he drew the blankets more warmly around her, but she did not wake as he went out into the dawn. It was better so, he thought as he walked through the sleeping town toward the treasury. Perhaps it would be better still if he did not see her again before they set out for the land of the Huns.

By the time the sun rose he had opened the treasury and with the help of the warriors who guarded it, packed the hoard that Sigfrid had won from Fafnar into a stout chest and loaded it upon a sturdy mule. But no one went with him as he left the ferry that had taken him across the Rhenus and disappeared into the Charcoal Burners' Forest on the other side.

It took him most of the day to reach the spring where Sigfrid had died, for the mule moved at its own pace, and it was heavily laden. A long time ago he had explored the stream that flowed from it all the way to the river. The backwater he remembered, sheltered by a fallen tree and the debris it had trapped and scoured to form a deep pool by the outflowing stream, was still there. He wondered if in those depths some trace of Sigfrid's blood hung still.

As the sunset began to reach with long fingers of light and darkness through the forest Hagano unloaded the mule and hauled the chest, testing the limits of even his great strength, to the edge of the pool and slung it in.

When he was done, he sat for a long time on the bank. It seemed to take as long for the ripples to fade as it did his pulsebeat to slow. But gradually he realized that he could hear the deep music of the river beneath the silvery song of the stream, and with them the whisper of the breeze that was cooling him.

"Have I done the right thing?" he asked aloud. "Are you satisfied?"

Throughout the labors of that long day he had not allowed himself to think of Kustubaira. Now, memories of the night before overwhelmed him, and from his single eye came tears of gratitude for what he had received and of grief for what he had lost. But he knew that if he returned to her they would only begin to hurt each other once more.

After a time Hagano bent over the water and splashed his face to wash the sweat, and the tears, away. The trees were stark silhouettes against the afterglow, the backwater a black mirror. His own reflection glimmered up at him, becoming clearer as the ripples stilled. He forced himself to contemplate his blunt nose and heavy brows, the strong line of his jaw and the ruined orb of his dead eye.

Then the image quivered and dislimned, though he had not touched the water. For a moment he glimpsed a long silver shape, as if some great fish were swimming there, and though he had bound the chest securely, gold gleamed from the depths. The water began to still, and now the face he saw was thinner, framed by silvered hair and beard. But it was still missing an eye.

For a moment only he saw it, then the last of the light left the sky and he was alone with the wind.

Chapter 14 ⚍ Riding the River

The Danuvius
Litha Moon, A.D. 437

Though the rains had ceased, the melting water from the snows those storms had brought to the Alpes were still swelling the mountain streams that fed the Danuvius. When Gundohar and the hundred men who rode with him, having followed the Moenus eastward to the borders of their own lands, turned south and crossed the Suevian hills, they found that the great river, if not quite a sea, had overflowed its banks in channels and backwaters that twined like a braid of silver across the plain. On the far side the old Roman road was still visible, built on an earthen dyke over the marshes and cut straight as a spearshaft across the fields, but there was no trace of the ford.

"Can we continue along this side and cross farther down?" asked Gundohar, reining in beside Hagano.

"There are roads, but none that will get us there so quickly," he replied, remembering his journeys through these lands when he had served in Attila's army. "The Danuvius bends northward between here and Batava. If we cross into Raetia, we can cut across the plain."

Gundohar sighed. "We have been on the road twelve days already. My heart tells me that if we want to reach Attila before the ground dries enough for him to move his horsemen, we cannot afford delay."

"The river is too wide to make a ford with brushwood,

but there used to be folk hereabouts with flatbottomed boats that could get us and our baggage across," said Hagano. "Make camp on the high ground here and I will scout ahead and see if I can find them."

"Watch out for snakes," said the king. "Many have been flooded out of their holes."

"Adders?" asked Dancward. "They won't strike at anything as big as a man."

"Any threatened creature will fight back," Unald disagreed. "But it's true that a bite to hand or foot won't kill a healthy man."

"I still don't like them," answered Gundohar. "Be careful."

Despite the delay, and the days of travel that had preceded it, the king looked more rested and, oddly, younger than he had seemed when this journey began. *It is because his decision is made,* thought Hagano as he reined his pony down the trail. *Whatever happens, he will not turn back now.*

But he himself felt no such peace, and he wondered why. Was it because for him the question was not whether he should risk his life in Hunland, but whether he would find there the battle in which Wodan would accept his life in exchange for victory?

High though the river was, earlier in the year it had clearly been higher. As Hagano reined the pony across the water meadows, he saw the carcass of a carp that had been stranded when it came to spawn in the shallow water that covered the field. But from death came life. The rich silt left by the receding river had borne an unexpected treasure of golden flowers, jeweled by the sapphire flicker of damsel flies.

It was good, he thought, to ride alone after so many days in the company of other men. Perhaps it was his father's blood that spoke to him in the song of the birds and the humming of the bees, for he felt at home as he never did in the cities of men. He understood suddenly why Gudrun had gone to live in the forest. He wished now that he had let her stay there.

A shadow flickered past and he looked up to see an osprey patrolling the meadow. Gazing back along the bird's line of flight he could make out a tangle of sticks high in an oak tree where the eagle's fledglings, as big by now as their parents and almost ready to fly, were waiting with gaping beaks for their next meal.

Death feeds life . . . Hagano thought once more, and the things that were most deadly were sometimes the fairest of all. He kicked his pony in the ribs and the animal began to trot across the luxuriant grass.

As he moved on, he began to wonder if the floods had washed all of humankind away, as the Christians said their god had done in Noah's time, for he found neither ford nor ferryman. Water lilies grew in the backwaters, pale flowers opening to the sun. From time to time a fish would break the still surface to take a fly, and young grass snakes hunted tadpoles across the green lily pads.

The day grew warm; Hagano pulled off first his cloak, then his tunic, and tied them to the saddle, absorbing the golden light of the sun through his bare skin. Presently he realized that he was smiling, as if he had shed more than his clothes. In this moment, he could even remember Kustubaira without pain. For a time he rode as if in a dream, one with the beauty around him. But as the day passed its nooning his stomach growled and he realized he was hungry. He began to look about for some place with water and grazing where he could rest his mount and eat the dried meat he had brought along.

There, perhaps, where the willows overhung the river, the water might be still enough for the silt to have settled. He reined the pony that way. But as he neared, the sound of splashing came to him from beyond the trees and with it the sweet trill of women's laughter. Frowning, he slid down from the saddle and tethered his mount to one of the outlying trees, then, using a hunter's skills, he crept forward, spear in hand.

The surface of the pool was a blaze of light, within which

figures moved. Hagano slitted his eyes to see. Piled clothing was lying on the bank; he eased through the bushes to get a better look, saw feather plumage and painted leather. The leaves screened the brightness; in the water women were bathing, two of them still young and one older, blunt-featured and broadly built as he was himself, with slanting greenish eyes and brown hair.

Earthfolk, he thought—though there was a look of the water wight he had seen in the spring as well. He had never met a woman of his father's race before.

Though he made no sound, he was not surprised when one of them turned, head tilted as if she felt some distur-bance in the air. Grimahild had possessed that gift also, of always knowing when a stranger was near. He wondered if it was his father who had taught her to sense the invisible currents that flowed between living things this way. The woman started wading toward the shore, and Hagano slipped through the leaves and took his stand between them and the clothing piled there.

Her start of surprise brought the others around, eyes wid-ening as they saw the man. The two young ones sank back down until only their heads were above water, their long hair swirling around them like waterweed. The third re-mained standing. Her breasts, supported by the strong arch of her rib cage, were heavy, the nipples staring back at him like dark eyes. The water lapped at the tangle of hair that covered the joining of her sturdy thighs. Across back and belly, along her arms and around her thighs, her pale skin was covered with blue tattoos. She spoke in some language whose vowels were like music and seemed surprised when he did not answer her.

"Who are you? What are you doing here?" His voice was harsher than he had intended. "Are you water wights or *baliurunae?*"

She looked at him and laughed suddenly. "We are magic people, yes—we know many secrets," she answered in the tongue of the Goths. "Give me my plumage . . . Hagano. . . ."

He blinked at the use of his name but he did not move. "Tell me how we will fare in the land of the Huns."

"Like heroes. . . . It is Haduberga who tells you so—no warriors that come to any land will win such fame as you."

"A fair prophecy, but I would know more," said Hagano. "Give me my clothes."

Grinning through his teeth, he stepped aside, spear poised in his hand. Wolund had bound a swan-may to be his wife by stealing her plumage, but what he needed was information.

Haduberga eyed him for a moment, then ascended majestically from the pool. Hagano blinked as she wrapped a doeskin skirt around her hips and slid the cape, in style much like those he had seen worn by Hunnish *kams*, over her head. The designs painted on the leather were like those tattooed on the women's own hides, but they were hard to see, for over breast and back had been sewn the white plumage of a swan.

"Go now, with words of glory." Wind ruffled the plumes around her and for a moment he saw not a woman but a bird.

"I will go when I have truth from you," he replied. Almost casually, the spearpoint swung toward her breast.

"My mother misleads you—" One of the girls grinned maliciously, coming up the bank behind her, though she made no move to put on her clothes. Her breasts were pointed, tipped with rose, and drops of water clung to her pubic hair like pearls. "You go to Huns and death waits for you. My sister and I have no husband—better if you stay here."

"I have a wife already," he began, but fell silent as the second girl rose halfway from the pool.

"But she gives you no child. Come to me, son of Ragan, and I make you a child of the old blood to carry on your line—" She lifted white arms, and he felt his flesh stir in response. He took an involuntary step backward, and they laughed. He stopped where he was, leaning on the spear.

"It is so," said their mother, frowning. "You wish to live, lead the Burgund warriors home while you can. You go to the Huns, and only the Rome-priest who rides with you comes back again."

"That is ill news to take back to my king," said Hagano.

The girls were dressing very slowly, teasing him. As his pulse quickened he wondered what it would be like to go with them, to leave behind that world in which he had never quite belonged. In truth, what remained for him back home? If he disappeared, his wife would be freed from her torment, and the Burgunds would no doubt breathe easier as well. As for his brothers, the only one who might actually miss him was Gundohar. If he could not save them, why should he die with them?

Because, the thought came to him from somewhere even deeper, *this witch would have to brew a potion more potent even than my mother's to make me forget Gundohar's trust in me.* Sigfrid had allowed himself to be deluded for the sake of a girl's sweet smile; only by holding to his own oaths could Hagano justify having been his executioner.

He cleared his throat, shaken more than he wanted to admit by that moment of indecision. "I must find a ferryman to take us across this river."

"Go back upstream to where river bends. A man with a boat lives across the water there," Haduberga said slowly.

Hagano's heart began to pound as he met her green gaze, more potent than the silly seductions her daughters had tried. He brought the spear up until its point brushed the feathers that covered her breast, but she did not stir. With an oath, he turned away.

"You ask no more? Foolish man!" said the girls. "That ferryman is fierce, and has evil master. If he does not answer your hail, say you are Amalricus come home!"

More laughter followed as he pushed through the willows. The branches swung back behind him as he came out into the sunlight, breathing hard. He turned his face to the light and abruptly his panic receded. What was he doing? There must be more those bitches could tell! He crashed back through the greenery.

But the banks were empty, the surface of the pool dark and still. Only the branches behind him were stirring. Then he turned his gaze toward the river and saw, flying low above the water, three white swans.

The longer Hagano thought about that encounter, the more his anger grew, but woman or water wight, in one thing at least Haduberga had been truthful. An hour's ride back up the river he saw smoke rising on the farther shore. There was a hut by the Roman road, and a flatbottomed boat drawn up below it. He reined his horse down to the water's edge and began to yell for the ferryman.

His broad chest gave him plenty of wind, and he needed it all to send his deep voice across that expanse of water. After a time he saw a small figure come out of the house, look at him, and wave him away. Swearing, Hagano pulled off his arm ring and lifted it on the point of his spear till it caught the sun. He saw the man hesitate.

"Amalricus!" he cried then. "Amalricus is here!"

At that, the ferryman came down to the boat, cast off, and began to scull across the current, correcting for the drift of the boat with each powerful stroke of the oar so that the barge left a serpentine wake behind. He was big, with a bristling black beard that flowed into a thick furring of body hair, and as he saw Hagano waiting alone his face grew red.

"Where's Amalricus?"

Hagano shrugged. "In hell, for all I know. This ring for your fee and more to ferry my lord and his men across to the road—"

"You lied about my brother—" The ferryman glowered at him. "Why should I believe you about the gold? I'd have to get permission from my master to bring over a whole company anyway. But before I go I'll take that arm ring for my trouble—" The powerful muscles that had conquered the river swung the oar toward Hagano's head.

The pony shied at the shouting, and the first stroke glanced off Hagano's shoulder. Roaring, the ferryman leaped from the boat, and brought the oar around for another blow. But by this time Hagano was on his feet again, and the rage which had found no outlet against the swan-women surged through him as he drove his spear up through the ferryman's belly beneath the ribs to the heart.

The oar flew through the air toward the river and Hagano leaped after it as the ferryman fell. He grabbed the oar as it hit the water, then saw that the boat had begun to drift away. This close to shore the current was weak, and the barge was slowed by the sandbars over which it slid as it was pushed along. Cursing, Hagano splashed through the shallows after it, but it had gone nearly a bowshot downstream before he was able to grab the rope and haul it up on the shore.

He leaned against it, gulping air, and as his pulse began to slow, heard men's laughter. The Burgunds had come down and were resting on a wooded point just downstream. He swore at them, wishing he had gone with the swan-wives. By the time Gundohar and the others reached him he had recovered some of his composure, though a look at his face was enough to discourage anyone who might still be amused.

"I see you've found a boat," said Gundohar carefully. "Where's the ferryman?"

"Holding my spear," Hagano said shortly, pointing upstream where his spearshaft jutted from the sprawled body of the man he had slain.

"Now you see the evil of wrath!" exclaimed the priest who had come along with Laidrad's household. "How will we get across?" He fell silent at Hagano's glare.

"I think I have lived long enough on the Rhenus to scull a barge," said Hagano tightly. "Bring down the baggage, and let one of you go for my horse and my spear. By the time you are done I will have my breath back, and then I will get you across, never fear."

It took nearly a dozen trips to ferry all the men and their gear over the river, with the horses swimming alongside, but Hagano was not the only one among them with experience as a waterman. The sun was setting, its passing hailed by a swelling chorus of frogs from the reeds that edged the shore, by the time they were done. It was on the last trip that he found himself sitting in the stern with Laidrad's chaplain.

He had caught his breath, but a black anger still boiled within him. They had reached the deepest part of the river and the boat was pitching as the oarsman fought the current that strove to whirl it away. As he looked at the priest he remembered the swan-wife's prophecy. There was one test, at least, that he could try. As the ferry lurched, he grasped the man's leg and tipped him over the side.

The priest had time for one shout before he went under. Then everyone was shouting, in the dim light unsure just what they had seen. In a moment the fellow bobbed up again, buoyed by his robes. Someone tried to throw him a rope, but it went wide. But he had gone in upstream and the current was carrying him closer; Hagano thrust out the butt end of his spear as if to let him grasp it and pushed him under once more. When he surfaced again, the ferry had passed beyond him and the current was bearing him toward the northern shore.

"Turn back!" cried some, but Hagano gripped the shoulder of the man at the oar.

"Go on—" he said grimly, "before darkness falls!" Peering through the dusk he could see the dark blot that was the priest appearing and disappearing in the water. But presently he saw him clamber ashore, stand up, and began to wring out his robes.

"That poor man—" said Gislahar, who was crossing on

the last trip as well. "Do you know, for a moment it looked as if you were trying to push him in."

"Don't pity him." Hagano sat back with a sigh. "He is safer than we will be."

He had tried to dismiss his own doubts and the women's dreams, but the swan-wives' prophecy was harder to ignore. Certainly they had been right so far. The men who had gone over first were already making camp on the nearing southern shore; fires flickered bravely as darkness fell. *We will all die,* he thought grimly, *every man of us except that priest who even now is cursing us in the name of his god.*

As Hagano had promised, they moved faster once they had passed into Raetia, following the Roman roads cross-country over the rolling plain. In theory, these lands were still part of the Empire, but as Gundohar had learned when he fought the Juthungi, the peoples who dwelt in the foothills of the great mountains were only superficially Romanized, and *bacaudae* and other robbers lurked in the tracts of wasteland surrounding the slave-farmed estates on the plain. The Burgunds rode in close order with scouts ahead of them, and when they made camp at night they posted guards.

Nonetheless, on the first day two men were wounded by arrows from ambush, and on the second they heard hoof-beats behind them on the road and turned just in time to receive an onslaught of armed men.

"It seems that ferryman's master has come to collect his weregild," said Gundohar, drawing his sword.

"I will gladly pay him in the same coin in which I paid his man," answered Hagano, leveling his spear.

Then the first of the attackers crashed into their rear guard, wiry men on scruffy horses, all the swifter for being unarmored as they laid about them with lance and sword. The clash was as brief as it was furious, but when the *bacaudae* drew off, they left a score of their men upon the ground while the Burgunds had lost only one.

After that, they saw riders in the distance several times,

but no one opposed them and they came to the confluence of rivers at Batava without further difficulty.

"I would have visited you, sir, as soon as we were settled here! You did not need to come to me—" Gundohar ran his hands through his hair. Bishop Peregrinus smiled at the confusion of men and horses and gear in the camp that was taking shape in the meadow and shook his head. Though the king had not seen his uncle since before he married Galamvara, the old man did not seem to have changed at all. He still looked upon the world with the delighted wonder of a child.

"You have much to do here," said Peregrinus. "I would not take you from your men. I only wish I had room to entertain you all."

Gundohar looked across the green waters of the Danu, swift flowing as its channel narrowed and the rivers that joined it here swelled the stream. The old Roman town had been built on the point of land where the Inn flowed into the larger river, but the bishop's house was in the quarter that clung to the heights on its other side. The stones of the buildings glowed warmly cream and gold in the morning sunshine. He remembered the peace of the bishop's house and wished he could stay there for a while.

"We had trouble enough crossing the Danu the first time. I am in no hurry to do so again."

One of his men dragged over a chest and laid a saddle-cloth across it for the bishop to sit on, while another poured ale.

"You will have to cross the Inn," said the bishop, "but its current is gentler. I will send boatmen to help you."

"You think the southern way is still the fastest? We have seen no Roman troops in Raetia, but I do not know about Noricum."

"It is true then? The Romans are your enemies?" Peregrinus shook his head unhappily.

"We fought Aetius at Treveri . . ." said Gundohar grimly.

"I am making this journey so that we will not have to fight the Huns as well. You must get news, here on the border. Has Attila sent out his men?"

"Attila?" Peregrinus shook his head. "The Huns move across the plain like wildfowl through the heavens. By the time I heard of their passing, they would be gone. They have not troubled us here, but they are strange folk. In Rome they call them demons. I know better, but I could wish your way did not lie eastward."

Gundohar grimaced. "Uncle, I do not make this journey for pleasure!" He shut his lips—no need to burden the old man with all the arguments that had brought him here.

Peregrinus straightened, suddenly a priest instead of a fragile old man. "My son, we must all go where God sends us. All I can do is to hear your confession and give you my blessing."

Gundohar looked at him. "The errors with which I reproach myself are not those the Church condemns," he said slowly. "I might have been a better king if I had sinned more boldly. It seems to me that my failing was to be neither one thing nor the other, not fully a doer or a thinker, a warrior or bard."

"But surely that is what is required of a king—" said Peregrinus gently. "In that way, kingship is a priesthood. It is as the apostle tells us, '*I am under obligation both to Greeks and to barbarians, both to the wise and to the foolish*.' You must understand everything, for you mediate between the peoples you rule, and between different sorts and conditions of men, and you stand for them all before God."

Gundohar frowned. He had complied with the formal rituals of the new faith, but given little thought to them. Was it dishonest to pretend piety now?

"Kneel—" The old man pulled his stole from the breast of his tunic and slipped it around his neck. Dancward, seeing what was going on, was already motioning the others away to give them privacy. With a sigh, Gundohar eased down onto his knees and bent his head.

What could he confess? That he had been tempted by ambition, put dreams of glory ahead of his people's good? Tried to make Burgunds into Romans? He muttered disjointed phrases, striving to turn his thoughts toward God, but the image that came to him was not that of the stiffly carved Christos in the little church, but of the one-eyed Jupiter in his feasting hall. He shook his head.

Lord, I do not know what to call you, he spoke to the darkness, *but if you care for my people, help me to serve them.*

He felt the old priest's hands on his head and heard the words of absolution, and though he could not say whether the comfort came from God or the old man's compassion, when he rose to his feet he did feel as though he had laid a burden down.

The bishop spent the rest of that day with the Burgunds, talking to the men. Some wished to make formal confession, while others seemed to find comfort simply in talking. The next morning he said mass for the Christians among them. When it was over, they moved down to the banks of the Inn to make their crossing, and continued their journey eastward across Noricum.

At Lentia the Burgunds crossed back over the Danuvius, which was shrinking at last as summer came on, and entered the land of the Huns. As they rode into the village, Gundohar looked around him with interest. The country here was not so different from his homeland, but something was strange. After a moment he remembered that he had felt this dissonance when he had traveled in Gallia and Italia as well. Perhaps Bishop Peregrinus had been right, and this was what he had come here to learn. However pleasant, these were not his lands or his people. Here, he was not the king.

But Gudrun was a queen.

As they pulled up in front of the largest of the houses, a rider came trotting down the path toward them. He looked familiar, with the characteristic lean profile of a Burgund despite the Hun pony and clothes. He reined in, staring, his hand moving instinctively to his hip, where an armed man would have carried a sword.

"Ecgward!" cried Gislahar, booting his pony ahead of the others. At that, an image of the youth the king had known overlaid itself on the gaunt features of the man before them and recognition came.

"The Lady is not here—" stammered Ecgward. "She's with *him*, in the house he has in the hills across the river from Vindobona. They're waiting . . ." He broke off, flushing.

"It's all right, man. I did not expect they would come to meet us," said Gundohar soothingly. He remembered Ecgward as an ardent youth. What had happened to turn him into this hag-ridden man? "How many days will it take to get there? We must find somewhere to rest and freshen our garments before we meet with the khan."

"Not here! She took the servants, and there are no supplies!" He steadied a little, frowning. "Four days' ride from here, where the hills come down to the river, is Rudegar's holding. He is a great lord and wealthy. He'll know how to welcome you."

Hagano moved his horse up beside the king. "And you'll come along to guide us, won't you, Ecgward? After having journeyed so far, we would not want to lose our way."

There was an edge to his brother's tone that Gundohar found disturbing. The next morning he was even more disturbed when they found a man lying dead in the road. Ecgward grew so white the king thought he would fall.

"What is it?" he asked. "Do you know who has done this thing?"

"I did—" said a voice behind him as Ecgward kept silent. It was Hagano, who had insisted on standing guard the night before. "If he was your man, I will pay his price to you."

"Brother!" exclaimed the king. "You have been as bloody-minded as a troll since we reached the Danu! We will not win Attila's friendship by killing his men!"

"Ecgward was sending this messenger to Gudrun," Hagano answered coldly. "I think the less time she has to prepare a welcome, the better off we will be."

"You still feel the guilt for Sigfrid, don't you?" blurted Gislahar, "and so you accuse our sister of wanting revenge!"

Hagano turned, his eye blazing, but Ecgward was shaking his head, still gazing at the corpse of his messenger.

"I do not know her mind," he whispered. "But I have heard her women say that in her dreams, Sigfrid's wounds bleed as red as these."

Gislahar swallowed and fell silent.

"Bury him," said Gundohar at last, "and we will ride to Rudegar's hold. He, at least, is an honorable man."

"From here we can see up and down the Danuvius," said Rudegar, taking Gundohar's arm. "It is a good spot. The Romans thought so too—over there lie the ruins of their signal tower."

The king nodded. Rudegar's holding was set on the knees of the mountain that overlooked the river, the highest for many miles. The river was a shining silver serpent below them. At the base of the bluff meadows edged the water, and on the other side a rising plain merged with the easternmost Alpes, diminishing into gentle hills. Beyond them, the world dissolved into silver distances. This must be how the gods felt, he thought then, looking out from heaven upon the world.

For a few moments they contemplated the vista before them, then turned and began to pace back again. In its way, the place that Rudegar had built here was as remarkable as his view. His hall was long enough so that a hundred warriors could feast by the hearth, not so large as the basilica in Borbetomagus, but one of the largest wooden buildings the king had seen.

"A Greek slave designed it," said the Marcoman chieftain.

"They are very clever people, the men of Byzantium, and know how to build in wood as well as stone. In the land of the Burgunds I have enjoyed your hospitality. Come, and let me show you mine."

As they turned the corner, they heard a girl's laughter and a man's low-voiced reply. From the back he recognized his brother Gislahar. The girl who was pinning the flowers he had given her to her mantle was a head shorter, round-faced and buxom, with hair the color of polished oak and snapping brown eyes. He lifted one eyebrow and Rudegar grinned, a broader, bearded version of the maiden's smile.

"My daughter Diedelinda—the delight of my heart," he confirmed Gundohar's guess. "I see that she has coaxed your young brother out of his shell."

Even at a distance, her merriment was contagious. Gundohar could see why Gislahar, who was usually too shy to notice the arts women used to attract him, had warmed to her.

The delight with which Rudegar had showed off his possessions was displayed even more fully in the feast he provided. The food, like the hall itself, was a study in contrasts, a rude vigor that reminded the king of his childhood in the lands east of the Rhenus coupled with the most sophisticated wares of the Empire. But despite the luxuries, he was surely in the old world of his ancestors now. After so many days of hard fare on the road, Gundohar found the rich food and freely flowing wine a bit overwhelming, but when he tried to thank his host, Rudegar tried to offer him more.

"I have feasted Aetius and the khans, I have welcomed the kings of the Goths and the Gepids to my hall. But this is the first time that I have served the kinfolk of my lady Gudrun."

"Is her power in the land so great then, that you wish to please her?" asked Hagano. "I thought that Ereka was still Attila's queen."

Rudegar shrugged. "Gudrun has given him a son, and she

has ruled wisely in the western lands. She is a noble woman, and the khan is too wise not to value her."

Gundohar and his brother exchanged glances. *You see,* said the king's, *Rudegar knows of no treachery.* But more interesting still was the fact that their host seemed to think that favor showed to her kinfolk would please Gudrun.

"Your own lady is worthy of honor as well," said the king as Godelinda came toward them, carrying the great silver-mounted drinking horn. Her daughter walked behind her with the flagon so that it could be refilled.

"If I were of kingly breeding," said Wolcgar expansively, "it is your daughter I would go after." He held out his beaker for more wine. "Don't know when I've seen a lovelier girl."

Gundohar looked from the bard to his young brother, who was staring very fixedly at the rib of venison in his hand.

"A prince for the daughter of a Hunnish chieftain?" Rudegar shook his head, but his gaze had gone watchful. "I suppose I will have to give her to one of Attila's captains some day." His wife filled up his cup and he drank it down.

Gundohar leaned toward Hagano. "He is Gudrun's man," he whispered. "Suppose we make him ours as well?"

His brother glanced at Gislahar with a sardonic smile, then nodded. "Your Diedelinda is as wellborn as any girl in the Burgund lands. If my lord king and I did not have fair wives already, we would be making you offers for her hand." He sipped wine, still smiling. "But Gislahar here is unmarried. Suppose we make a match of it between them?"

There was a moment of startled silence. Then all eyes turned to Gundohar. Both the girl and Gislahar were blushing furiously, but neither looked unwilling. At this moment, full of Rudegar's meat and wine, it seemed to the king that if they could make this alliance, his brother might even live to enjoy his bride. It was not often, he thought ruefully, that inclination matched so well with policy.

"If you will give us Diedelinda," he said to Rudegar, "I

will assign her lands of her own as well as those she shares with my brother."

"If you agree, my lord," said Laidrad, supporting him, "I can assure her that the Burgund lords will honor her."

Rudegar's eyes glistened and he reached over to squeeze Gundohar's hand. "It is more than we could have dared to hope for," he said tremulously. "But she will have a worthy dowry in gold and silver, for my master has been generous to me. Let this feast serve to celebrate the binding. The girl will need a little time to prepare her bride-clothes and linen, but she will be ready to go with you when you return."

The men, who had been listening avidly, began to cheer.

"What does the maiden say? Will she have him?" cried Wolcgar.

Shouting, the warriors made a ring and the girl was led inside it. Gislahar, still red as fire, was dragged into the circle with the others, who were making all the remarks customary on such occasions, and begging Diedelinda to let them show her what a real man could do.

"No, no," said her father, laughing, "take the noble Niflung, he'll make you a good husband."

The young woman, recovering her self-possession, pretended to be considering the other young warriors. "I'll set you a riddle," she said finally, "and marry the man who can tell me how I came by these flowers." She came to a halt in front of Gislahar.

He straightened, cleared his throat, and after a second try, managed to get out her name.

"I gave you the flowers, and I give you my heart—" Something in his brother's voice made Gundohar wince inwardly. He had been just as ardent, and as innocent, when he courted Brunahild. "Will you accept the one as you did the others?"

Diedelinda looked down at the blooms, a little wilted now, that lay on her breast, then pulled one spray from beneath the pin and held it out to him.

"If you will take mine in return, lord Gislahar. . . ."

Joy flamed in his eyes. He kissed her with clumsy fervor while his companions cheered.

Gundohar kept a smile fixed on his face. He would have felt better about this if everyone else had not been quite so ecstatic. He hoped Rudegar would not regret becoming his ally, and that if things did go wrong, that Gislahar would forgive him.

It occurred to him then that one thing his uncle Peregrinus had said was wrong. Priest and king might both be mediators, but Peregrinus had viewed the world with a shining innocence, despite his age. Gundohar could no longer afford that luxury.

Chapter 15 ☩ Midsummer Fires

The Huns had slaughtered a dozen sheep to prepare a feast for the Burgund kings; Gudrun could still smell the sweet stink of blood in the air. Though Ecgward had failed to send warning of their arrival, faithful Rudegar in his innocence had dispatched messengers when the Burgunds reached his holding, and others, four days later, to tell the khan his guests were on their way once more. As she climbed the hill toward the new wooden buildings of Attila's Town, she noted the signs of celebration, dust being beaten from felt rugs, embroidered hangings airing on the branches of the willow trees.

Attila's hall stood on the highest point of the bluffs above the river. Queen Ereka's house was to the north, a little separated from the others. The new dwellings had been built closer to that of the khan, forming a rough circle that sloped slightly downward toward the eastern plain, scattered with clusters of pale mounds where the clans had set up their *gers*, and the moving dots of their herds. There were fewer than there had been at the festival of the Sword—Aetius had sent them beasts to replace some of those lost and many clans had moved out. She supposed they needed new pastures.

It was fortuitous that this visit should coincide with Midsummer, when the native peoples of this land celebrated

their festival. Already, a tension that could have been excitement or apprehension sang in the air.

My brothers are coming, she told herself, *despite my warning.
It is Wyrd, not I, that will decide what befalls them here.*

She adjusted the folds where her wrap was pinned at the
shoulders and straightened her necklaces. In this bright
weather she wore only the single garment, but it was of
finely woven linen, heavily embroidered around the hem,
and her ornaments were worthy of a queen. A silk veil covered her head, shading her face from the sun. While Bala
watched Apsik, a new crop-headed slave girl followed a step
behind her, carrying her basket with spindle and wool.
Since the night on which Attila had claimed the Sword of
War, it had been clear she was in his favor, though only
rumors mentioned the prophecies. He had given her
lengths of cloth and jewels, a new and larger *ger,* and servants to take care of it.

What else will he give me, she wondered, *when the lives of my
brothers are in his hand?*

A woman who had bowed in greeting backed away uneasily, and Gudrun realized that she had laughed aloud.
From the direction of the river she heard the sound of cow
horns, their dissonance sweet with distance, and her heart
began to pound. She hurried up the path.

Attila's new hall stood near the edge of the bluffs. The
Danu glittered blindingly beyond. Its eastward facing door
was closed and she could not see the khan, but his house-
guard were already gathering, and with them the young
women who sang welcome, the long linen cloth which
would shade them gathered in their arms. Seeing Gudrun,
they held it up so that she could stand in the shade.

She saw Hun horsemen cantering up the path. As they
passed Queen Ereka's house they blew their horns. Behind
them, a cloud of dust gradually resolved itself into the figures of men on horses. The sky seemed immensely wide
and blue. Sunlight sparked from shield bosses, from mail
links and the curve of a polished helm, and the Gundwurm

standard, scarlet and gold, uncoiled above them as the wind carried the dust away.

"So, your brothers come," said a cool voice behind her. "You must give them a good welcome." Attila slid his arm around her waist with casual possessiveness.

Gudrun grew still within the circle of his arm. "How happy I must be to see my kinsmen with their bright shields and polished armor. But just now it is the grief they caused me that I am remembering."

The dazzle of sun on metal made distance deceptive; when the Burgund warriors came to a halt before them it seemed too soon. She smelled dust and horse sweat. People were talking in a babble of tongues. Gundohar was bowing before her. Attila let her go and she submitted to her brother's polite embrace. He looked thinner than she remembered, his face longer than ever beneath a receding hairline and his fine skin browned by the sun. Then Gislahar hugged her, saying something about a girl.

"You know her—Rudegar's daughter—" he repeated, his gaze openly joyous where the king's had been wary. "I never thought I'd find a girl I liked so well."

Gislahar was getting married to Diedelinda; the sense of what he was saying penetrated finally. At least that explained his radiance. But why had the king consented to such a hasty matching?

"She is a lucky girl!" Gudrun patted Gislahar's cheek and saw him blush. Then another figure moved into view behind him and she stilled.

"Don't trouble yourself to bid me welcome," said Hagano softly. Unlike the others, he still wore his helm.

Where Gislahar had grown golden, Hagano had weathered. More than any of the others, she thought numbly, he looked at home in his armor. Instinctively defensive, she avoided his gaze. She remembered the sardonic tone, the ugly features; she did not remember the aura of power. It reminded her, with a shock she realized, of Attila, who was measuring his guests in his own way at her side.

"You ride far," said the khan. "You must be thirsty. We will go into the shade and drink wine."

Hagano lifted his cup to his lips, resisting the temptation to gulp it down. Even though they sat beneath an embroidered linen canopy, the day was warm for armor. He was thirsty, but the khan had given them unwatered wine, and he wanted to keep his wits about him. He knew Attila of old, and suspected that the khan's cup held only water, but the time had not yet come to challenge his host's notions of hospitality.

The linen cloths stretched above them filtered the sunlight into a kind of luminous shadow that illuminated the features of those below with pitiless clarity. Gislahar had drunk freely, and was laughing too loudly at the king's account of their journey. Gundohar himself, more temperate if equally unsuspecting, had grown somewhat pink and was speaking with unusual eloquence. Gudrun listened, but it was hard to tell what she was thinking. When she was Sigfrid's wife, her face had been as unlined and her manner as unsure as a maiden's, but in the past nine years she had grown into her bones. She was solider in body than he remembered, with an uncanny look of their mother about the eyes.

Her greeting had left him with no illusions about her attitude toward *him*, but if Galamvara's interpretation of the runes scratched on the arm ring was correct, she had tried to warn Gundohar. Love was not an emotion one associated with Attila, yet Gudrun was richly dressed and the khan appeared to value her. Hagano wondered if her feelings, either friendly or hostile, would influence her husband's decisions at all.

"And so," said Gundohar, concluding, "we have come to feast with you as allies and kin. I had heard that your people suffered badly from the floods this year, but I see that you are prospering, though there are not the numbers of warriors here I would have expected to see attending so great a king."

He gave the khan a straight look, and Hagano realized his brother was not so drunk as he had appeared. Attila shrugged delicately.

"The clans must follow their herds to the summer pastures. But as you say, we lost many beasts this spring. Our warriors guard those that remain."

"How will you replace the animals you lost, my brother?" said Gundohar softly. "Is the tribute the Romans already pay you sufficient to buy new stock, or must you hire out your young men to fight their wars?"

If Gundohar had hoped to surprise the khan into some admission he was disappointed. Attila was still smiling as if he had meant the conversation to go this way. Perhaps the time to be more specific had come.

"You know how rumors spread among the people when times are hard," said Hagano, leaning forward. "We have heard the Romans are paying you to fight against the Burgunds. We did not believe it—you and my lord have sworn the oaths of brothers, and when we fought at Treveri you refused to join Aetius in his wars."

He sat back again, and saw that Gudrun had gone suddenly pale. His heart lifted; surely if the story were true, she would have known.

Attila sighed. "Last summer, our herds were many, now they are few. You are king—when the people hunger you feed them how you can. If Romans offer gold, can I refuse? I must find money somewhere!" He looked at Gundohar expectantly.

"That is why, brother, I have come to you . . ." Now the color had left the king's face as well, but his gaze was steady. "What do you need?"

"More than you have. You spent all your treasure to fight at Treveri, I hear."

There was a short silence. Gundohar's glance slid toward Gudrun, then away.

"Not quite all," Hagano said then. "There is one source we have not touched, but it is Gudrun who must give her permission for us to use it."

"Sigfrid's hoard!" Gudrun was on her feet, livid and staring. "All that he left me? You would dare to steal it from me?"

Gundohar looked at her sadly. "We have not stolen it, sister, though God knows there were times when we had need. Is it so unreasonable to ask that you give it up to save your husband's people and your own?"

"Do I have a choice?" she asked bitterly. "You took the gold from me and locked it in your treasury. Do not mock me by asking my permission to use it now!" She glared from one to the other, then turned on her heel and strode away.

"You are her husband! Surely you can persuade her!" exclaimed Gundohar.

Attila raised one eyebrow. "You did not do so well, I remember, with Brunahild." As Gundohar sat back, paling, Attila got to his feet, signaling to his servants to take away the table and the wine. "You are only just come here. You do not yet even see the house where you will sleep. Go and rest. Tonight we feast for Midsummer. We will talk of this again. . . ."

The house assigned to the Burgunds was one of the newer buildings. Slightly down the slope from that of Attila, and farther from the river. From the style, it was clear that some of Attila's Germanic tribesmen had had a hand in its building, but the wooden walls were hung with lengths of felt appliquéd and embroidered in the fashion of the Huns, and felt rugs covered the floor. There was room for the princes and a score of their men. The rest of Gundohar's warriors had been given a place to pitch their tents near the *gers*. The arrangement made Hagano, who had expected they would all be sleeping in tents together, uneasy, but Gundohar judged that to refuse the lodging would insult the khan.

Hagano spent the afternoon with Thiudimir, who was eager to show him how things had progressed since the days when they and Waldhari had all been young together in Attila's house-guard.

"Does the khan mean to move on Noricum?" asked Hagano, watching the men who were bringing in wood for the bonfire. They were farmers, folk who had lived by the river before the coming of the Huns and who now raised grain for their new masters, their ways much like those of the peasants in his own land. "When we passed through on our way here it seemed an empty land."

Thiudimir laughed. "The soldiers are all gone to Novidunum. You remember Walips of the Rugi, whom the Romans made a chieftain of foederati down there? The floods hit his people as hard as they did our own. He seized the town, and now the Romans are besieging him there. They say he ties up the children of Novidunum on the walls to prevent the Romans from using their ballistas. I do not think that tactic will work for long."

Hagano nodded. Sentiment was for men at peace. He supposed that if his own childhood had been more protected, he might have felt differently, but as the slayers of Sigmund the Wolsung had learned, young wolves were as dangerous as old. It just took them longer to bite.

The sun was beginning to cast long shadows when a slave girl appeared at Hagano's elbow with a summons from Attila's senior queen.

"I will not try to delay you," said Thiudimir, smiling. "You do not want *her* as an enemy."

He turned away, and Hagano frowned. Thiudimir was a good man, honest to a fault and close to Waldhari's level as a warrior, but he left to his brother, King Walamir, any task requiring subtlety. Hagano had known better than to pump him for evidence of treachery. If even Thiudimir could sense the tension around them, matters were serious indeed. Queen Ereka was another matter entirely. He would have to be careful, he thought as he reached her door, that she did not learn more from their encounter than he.

"In Christian lands, a man has only one woman, is it so?" Queen Ereka poured wine into a silver cup and offered it to Hagano. "My lord has many. It shows his greatness. I am still first, the queen."

Hagano sipped his wine. "He seems fond of Gudrun."

Ereka shrugged with delicate disdain. "She is useful."

"To seal the Burgund alliance?" Hagano let disbelief edge his words.

"To give him a son," said the queen.

Hagano raised an eyebrow. The khan had many women, but few offspring. Rumor had always said that the queen had made sure of that through her herbs and spells. "I am surprised you allowed it."

There was a short silence. "Do you know why he wants a Burgund child?" she asked. "Your king, your brothers, have no son. A sister-son can inherit, yes, by the old law of your tribes? He will make Apsik king in Burgund lands."

It made too much sense, thought Hagano numbly, to be invention. *Poor Gislahar*, came his next reflection. His marriage to Rudegar's lusty daughter, far from becoming a useful alliance, might well be his doom.

"I have not yet seen my nephew. I will look forward to meeting him."

"An energetic child." said the queen. "Will you have more wine?"

As the last light of the long Midsummer Day began to fade from the sky the khan called his guests to the feasting. In this fine weather they had spread the cloths outdoors on the grass above the fire circle for the warriors, with low tables and cushions for their lords. Nearby, the Midsummer pyre awaited the torch, its logs adorned with masterwort and vervain, sweet stalks of fennel and wreaths of bright summer flowers. Just so they had decked Sigfrid's pyre. Was it the sight of her brothers that had caused Gudrun's memories of the past seven years to fade so that his death seemed only yesterday?

His murder, she corrected. *And there walk his killers, who have offered me neither compensation nor apology.*

"Want meat an' honeycakes—" came a soft chant from behind her, "want meat an'—"

"Apsik, be still, or you will be sent back to eat with the slaves!" exclaimed Sunnilda. The boy was overexcited. He had been whining almost since they sat down.

"But I want to eat *now!*"

Gudrun turned and glared at her son. It was an empty threat, for Attila had commanded his presence. Sunnilda had pleaded to come as well, and offered to keep an eye on the boy. At her mother's look she grinned, for a moment looking so like Sigfrid that Gudrun's heart skipped. The girl was a leggy ten-year-old now, though with the promise of great beauty. Perhaps her uncles would find it equally hard to meet that golden gaze.

Apsik subsided, though he was still muttering about honeycakes, and plopped down on the felt-covered cushion beside his sister. She had dressed him in a gown of crimson with a design of running horses; his cheeks were so red with excitement they almost matched the cloth.

The Burgunds, splendid in tunics of Roman silk with goldwork on their belts and the hilts of their swords, came to a halt before Attila's table. It was set with a plain wooden cup and trencher as always, but Thiudimir and Widimir stood ready to serve him, and they were the sons of kings.

Tuldik offered the golden cup of greeting to Gundohar. Thoughtfully the king poured out his libation, then raised the cup, saluting east and west and the ceremonial pyre.

"To the sun, which rises in the land of the Huns and sets beyond the Rhenus; to the holy fire, which will light us through the dark; to the land wights and the ancestors I give honor; let those who guard the bonds of blood and oaths sworn to the gods watch over us now."

Gudrun stiffened. *You swore an oath in blood to Sigfrid!*

Attila lifted his own cup in reply. "All honor to my brothers, who have come from the place of the light's ending to its source. Be welcome here."

The Burgunds took their places on Attila's right. As Hagano sat down, Gudrun glimpsed beneath the grey silk of his garment the gleam of mail. She smiled sourly, wondering if he was right to be afraid. She had been unable to find out Attila's true intentions. This talk of an attack on the Burgunds disturbed her—though she had refused the role of Sacred Queen, she could not forget how she had once been goddess to her people. If Sigfrid's hoard would save them, she would give it. But it must be *her* gift, bestowed when those who had killed its master were humbled and in her power. And for that to happen, she must turn Attila's heart against them.

In the space before the bonfire, a line of young girls moved out and began to dance with arms linked behind their waists, heads turning, skirts swaying in unison to the music of their own song. The slaves carried in the food; upon a bed of barley the head of a ram with gelid eyes and asters twined around its curving horns; more mutton cooked with carrots and cabbage, savory flesh dropping from the bone; wildfowl and waterfowl, fish from the river, flat breads and sauces, all to be washed down with mead and Roman wine.

The maidens finished their dance and were replaced by other dancers, groups of men or women, or even little girls. As the remains of the meat were taken away a group of young warriors entered, and the people began to cheer. Musicians with drums and clappers set up a lively rhythm, accompanied by the bika, a pig's bladder stretched over a drumhead through which a horsehair strand was pulled to make a humming sound. As the music grew louder, the dancers advanced in a series of dips and spins punctuated by mighty leaps into the air. When all had entered, they faced inward, drawing their swords with a harsh hiss of steel.

Apsik tried to make a dash for the circle, but Sunnilda caught him and hauled him back as the dancers began to sing. Their movements were those of battle, advancing, brandishing, clashing blades in pairs. Torchlight flickered on steel as chorus followed chorus; swords were tossed from one hand to another, under a leg and around the head, beating the earth or driven into the soil, only to be snatched up again. It was a dance of death, swordplay made into an art. Those young men, displayed in all their pride and skill, were beautiful. Why, wondered Gudrun, as they finished and marched away, did watching them make her want to weep?

As course followed course and flagons were emptied, voices grew louder. It was almost dark now. Apsik, who had at first gorged, had begun to whine once more, fighting Sunnilda's attempts to keep him still.

Surely, thought Gudrun, Attila would react if the Burgunds were harsh to his child.

"Let him go," she told her daughter. "Listen, Apsik— there is your uncle Hagano. Go and see if he will laugh if you pull his beard."

"He does not look to me like a man who loves children," said Sunnilda as the boy trotted across the grass.

From the fire circle came singing. Men with torches began to dance around the waiting logs; a fitful flicker of light glanced from swordhilts and drinking horns, brought features into momentary relief, then cast them into shadow. Light gleamed from Apsik's pale hair. He had almost reached the Burgunds; Gudrun strained to see.

With a great shout, the dancers cast their torches onto the pyre. For a moment the flames sank; she heard cursing, and then as the Midsummer fire flared skyward, saw Hagano rise with Apsik in his hands and fling the boy to the ground.

Suddenly everyone was shouting. The Burgunds were on their feet, swordblades flashing back the fire. Gudrun ran toward the motionless body of her child.

"Hold!" cried Gundohar in a great voice, and for a moment everything was still. "Hagano—what have you done?"

Gudrun bent over the boy, feeling frantically for a pulse. There was nothing, and his head flopped when she gathered him into her arms. Such a little head, and such a slender neck, to snap so easily. . . .

Again! Before her Sigfrid's pyre was burning. Anguish tightened her throat, *Again Hagano kills what I love!* She staggered to her feet, face contorting, the hands that reached toward her brothers stiffening to claws.

"Take them!" Attila's deep voice broke the spell. As the Hun warriors closed in Gudrun began to scream.

"My Lady, stop!"

A hard hand closed on her arm, spinning her around. It was Thiudimir. For a moment Gudrun stared at him, then realized that she had been running toward the fray. The Burgunds were standing back to back, using the small tables for shields. The Huns were better armed, but their numbers hampered them. Already several bodies sprawled on the ground.

"Give me a sword!" she muttered, but Thiudimir was pulling her away.

"No, Lady, the khan wants you and the girl to stay in your *ger*."

Sunnilda! Gudrun looked wildly around her, saw her daughter safe in the shelter of Ecgward's arm.

"Very well—" she croaked. "Ecgward can escort us. . . ." She allowed Thiudimir to pull her away.

Behind her, the night resounded with the cries of dying men. It was hard to think, but Sunnilda's embrace steadied her. It would only grow worse here; she had lost Attila's son, but Sigfrid's daughter must not die. As the sound of the fighting faded behind them she stopped.

"Ecgward, you have said you love me. Is it true?"

"Gudrun—my whole life—" he looked back a moment, then tried to take her arm.

"If you love me, then take Sunnilda away from here now!"

"He told me to protect you!" Ecgward's face worked as he looked from her to the girl.

"Mother, I won't leave you!" Sunnilda echoed his cry.

"I will take care, I promise!" snarled Gudrun. *Until I have my revenge.* "Take my daughter to Bishop Peregrinus at Batava, and I will come as soon as I may. If there was ever truth in your vows of service," she added, holding his gaze, "I order you to do this now!"

She had thought her brothers must be overwhelmed immediately, but the battle was still going on when at last she made Ecgward swear to do her will. It was the work of moments to throw extra garments for the girl and some food into a saddlebag. Then they were gone.

For a long time she stood staring into the darkness where Ecgward and Sunnilda had disappeared. When she turned back toward the fighting, the bonfire was blazing. Silhouetted against its red glow she saw the contorted shapes of struggling men.

And from peak to peak the dark hills behind them were blossoming into points of brightness, as if the Midsummer fire had been a beacon calling men to war.

It was like fighting in a nightmare, like those endless battles one fought through the grey world, without cause or reason, and against faceless foes. Gundohar had had that dream too often; for the first few moments he stood frozen, trying to awaken, then the hot kiss of a swordblade along his thigh released the battle madness and he fought without thinking at all, swinging instinctively as new shapes loomed, recovering with the reflexive skill honed by years of war. Someone moved in to guard his back—that made it easier—he caught his breath, hit harder and laughed when his enemies went down.

"Back to the house!" "Get to our weapons!"

He heard the shouts without understanding. Then the man at his back pushed him. The warriors around him were moving; instinctively he went with them, and as the motion awakened a familiar pain in his thigh a measure of understanding began to return. The men who had been attacking them had fallen back, or fallen to the ground, but he could hear the sounds of hard combat from the other side of the fire, where the rest of the Burgund warriors had been feasting with Attila's men.

He tried to speak and felt someone take his elbow; it was Gislahar, his face so grim the king hardly knew him. Gundohar realized he was limping, but that was not why he had groaned. Men—his men—were dying out there.

The sounds of battle drew closer; there were shouts of greeting, new foes to swing at, and then the shape of a building black against the stars. Gislahar pushed him through the door and he stumbled into the darkness within. Outside he heard the sounds of battle; more men came through. Someone managed to kindle a lamp and the room sprang into visibility.

With sight came reason. Gundohar straightened, looking around him, and began the weary task of trying to think like a king once more. On every side he heard the heavy chink and jingle of mail as men scrambled into their armor. He tallied names in his head, realized many of those who had been quartered here were missing, while some of the lesser warriors had fought their way to his side.

"Dancward, take Unald's arms, you are much of a size—" he spoke to the nearest. "Laidrad, you know who else we have lost; match their gear with these men."

"Don't forget yourself, brother," said Gislahar. His byrnie of iron rings riveted to boiled leather was on already, though the straps at the back were still undone. Gundohar sighed. No doubt the lad who usually helped him with such things was dead or a prisoner.

His brother handed the king his padded arming tunic and helped him lace it, then lifted the fine mail shirt that had been Rudegar's gift when they left his hall. The king bent to let him lower it over his head and arms, the cold rings making a deadly music around him as he got his head through and stood up again. When Gislahar offered him his sword belt he waved it away.

"Do you really think we will have time to sheathe our blades?"

"No, but the belt shows your standing—" said Gislahar. His own belt, set with roundels of Frankish enamel, and the weapon it supported, were also a gift from Rudegar.

"And all we have left to us is our pride?" Gundohar shook his head, but he put it on, then made his brother turn and did up his buckles.

Hagano, who, as he recalled now, had never taken off his mail, had removed the silk overtunic and put on his spangenhelm. Now he stood by the door, leaning on his spear like an image of the god of war.

As the king put on his own helm, a fine piece of the armorer's art adorned with gold plaques portraying warriors and gods, that should leave no one in any doubt about his identity, he heard voices outside.

"Hurry up, now, lads, and get ready for company," he said loudly, and some of the men laughed. He motioned to Laidrad. "How many have we lost?"

"I saw Garo and Deorberht go down," came the answer. "As for the others, I don't know. Some of them might be prisoners."

Twenty-three men had made it back to the guesthouse. When the Burgunds arrived, they and the Huns had been more equal in forces, but he had now lost three-quarters of his escort, while Attila could summon more men from the surrounding countryside. They were not good odds.

He stiffened as a spear butt hammered on the door.

"Come out, Burgund worms!" cried a Hunnish voice. "Come out, seek mercy from the khan!"

Hagano gestured to three of the men who had their spears and the others stepped back to give them room.

"We are content where we are," he shouted back. "Come in and we will return your hospitality." He jerked open the door.

The first enemy fell forward and was speared before he hit the floor. Like adders striking, three spears darted through the opening. Men screamed and scrambled backward, and Hagano shoved the fallen man through with his foot and slammed the door closed once more.

"They'll be more careful the next time they come calling," he said with satisfaction, and the men began to laugh.

"That was a good joke, Hagano," said Laidrad softly when some time had passed without further action. "But we would not be in this spot if you had not played so roughly with the child. That was an evil deed, and he your own kin."

"Would you rather see Attila's brat in the high seat of the Niflungar?" asked Hagano tiredly. "Queen Ereka told me that is what he intended. While the child lived, Gundohar and his brothers stood in the way, and now or later, our lives were forfeit. Now, if we can pay the weregild, he may find us more valuable as allies."

Gislahar gazed at him in amazement. "By the gods, brother, do you propose that we pay the price for Gudrun's child with Sigfrid's gold?"

"Do you doubt that Attila would accept it?" Now Hagano laughed.

"I do," said Gundohar slowly. "Some insults cannot be compensated, even by gold. He is a king, and must think like one; if he allows us to live, he will lose standing in the eyes of his men. Do not try to cheer us with false hopes, Hagano. I remember what Brunahild told me about this man. He does not allow anyone to tamper with what he has claimed for his own. . . ."

"All this action has given me a thirst," said Wolcgar when the silence had gone on too long. "Would anyone like a sip from my waterskin?"

Once more the men began to talk, and a few finished strapping on their gear. Presently the sounds from the other side of the door told them that their enemies were gathering again.

"My lords, you are surrounded, and we have taken the rest of your men," someone cried in the Gothic tongue. "Open the door and my lord will speak with you."

Gundohar nodded. Once more Hagano opened the door, but no one came through it. A ring of warriors surrounded the house. He moved into the opening and saw Attila, with Gudrun at his side.

"You were my kindred, my allies. Once we fight side by side. I feed you at my own table, make you welcome as honored guests in my land. Now my child is dead, and many good warriors besides. What reward is that for my hospitality?" Attila spoke with chill dignity, but to Gundohar it did not seem that his sorrow reached his eyes.

"The death of the boy was not intended, and as for your warriors, it was you who attacked us, and I fear we have lost as many men as you."

"Come out then, and we will talk," the khan replied.

"I do not think so," said Gundohar. "You have given us this fine house to stay in, and I do not want to insult your hospitality by leaving it. Perhaps things will look different in the morning."

"In the morning you can see how many warriors wait for you. . . ."

"Before I answer I must confer with my men, since the outcome concerns them as much as me," said Gundohar.

"Take counsel if you can. This is the shortest night, and we will not go away." This time, Attila smiled.

As Dancward began to close the door, Gudrun took a quick step forward. Her hair had come down from its pins and her eyes were like a Walkyrja's. "Take counsel, but do not lie to those who have followed you here!" she exclaimed. "If they stand behind you, they are dead men, too. Do you remember how Sigfrid's fire burned beside the river? Do you remember how I cursed you? The time has come, my dear brothers, for those words to be fulfilled. Your enemies surround you—do you miss the strength of Sigfrid's arm? Those you trusted have betrayed you—do you miss

his loyalty? I tell you now that your deaths are near you—
and Sigfrid is not here to delay your doom!"

Gundohar gestured, but they could still hear Gudrun's
wild laughter as Dancward slammed shut the door.

"He can afford to wait," said Hagano when they had
settled themselves around the lamp once more. "My guess
is that he has sent for reinforcements. Our numbers are
unequal now, but they will be more so come the morn."

"But we will be able to *see!*" said Wolcgar the bard. "I
would like to see the sun once more."

From this moment on, thought Gundohar, *the sun, like us, can
only decline.*

"Gudrun has grown terrible in this wild land," said Gislahar sadly. "Even at Sigfrid's pyre she did not curse with
such power. She will never forgive us now."

"She will never forgive *me*," corrected Hagano. "She
blames me chiefly for her sorrows, and she has some reason.
I am thinking that if I were to go out to her, perhaps she
would be satisfied with my blood and let you go."

They all stared at him. After a long moment Gundohar
shook his head.

"You warned us, brother, that we were riding into danger,
and we would not hear. It would be a dishonor to leave
you now to bear the blame. And in any case, I do not think
it would serve. Gudrun hates us both, but Attila's business
is chiefly with me. I can negotiate with him far better if
your sword is guarding my back than if your head is re-
proaching me from the point of a spear!"

"Do you think there is a chance that he will bargain?"
asked Gislahar.

Gundohar sighed. "In truth, brother, I do not. I am sorry
I have led you to this doom—I am sorry for all of you—"
He looked around him. "If I cannot make terms with the
khan, perhaps he will at least let you go."

Dancward stared at him. "Of course! And we will scuttle
homeward to tell the tale of how we left our king, the
gracious ring giver who has fed us so much good meat and

ale, to be butchered by the Huns!" He began to laugh, and in a moment the other men were laughing too.

"My lord, do you think so little of the oaths we swore at the mead-drinking when we boasted of hard strife in your hall?" Wolcgar said finally. "This is no different than the battlefield. We would be dishonored forever if we deserted you, or if we allowed you to be taken while one man of us can still hold a sword!"

"In that case, as it would appear we will be fighting tomorrow," said Hagano grimly, "I suggest that you get what sleep you can. I will keep watch at the door."

"And I—" said Wolcgar, "will sing you to your rest!"

The voice of the bard wove in and out of Gundohar's dreams.

He was walking on the banks of the Rhenus with someone—he realized it was Brunahild and was surprised, because he could not remember ever having walked with her so companionably before. It must be because he was dead, he thought then, though he could not remember dying, only expecting death soon.

"Did you come for me as you did for Sigfrid?" he asked. He had wondered whether the priests of the old religion or the new were right about what came after. He had not thought the afterlife would look like his own country. But he saw now that this was not quite the land he remembered—the fields he had left had not been so golden, or the river so blue.

Her first answer was laughter. *"I bring a promise and a warning,"* she said then. *"You must not trust my uncle's word."*

"And what is the promise?"

"That when you have gained your victory, you shall choose where you shall dwell."

"What is the victory?" he cried, but her form was becoming translucent, and all the bright land around them a mist that darkened until he could see no more.

But he could hear someone singing.

> *"Valiant the heroes for victory are vying,*
> *Boldly the Burgunds bear spears to the fray . . ."*

"Fine words," came Hagano's voice, "it is a pity that no one in the Burgund lands will hear the song."

Gundohar blinked, and realized it was Wolcgar who had been chanting. He sat up and winced, abruptly aware of the mail shirt's deficiencies as a sleeping robe.

"When a bard makes his deathsong, it is himself for whom he is singing, himself and his god," Wolcgar replied. He stifled a yawn.

"My friend, whether you are singing or slaying, you will do it better if you are rested," said Gundohar. "Lie down. I will take your place here, for I do not think that I will be able to sleep again."

It seemed very quiet when the bard had gone to his bed, but though the men lay like the dead, the silence was alive with their breathing, with the whisper of wind in the thatching, the hiss of the fire. Once, Hagano went to the door and listened, then he sat down again.

"How long until sunrise?" asked the king.

Hagano shrugged. "The rings on my mail shirt have grown cold, so I suppose it cannot be far from dawn."

"Do you believe the dead speak to us in dreams?" Gundohar began to tell his brother what he could remember of his own. "That laughter was certainly Brunahild's!"

"Better she should speak to you than to me!" Hagano forced a grin.

"I wish I understood her meaning. She spoke of my death as if it would be a victory. Sigfrid's death had a purpose. What use will my dying be to anyone, so far from my own land? I wish you had not tried to drown Laidrad's chaplain, brother. He might be some use to us now."

"The bishop absolved you at Batava," rumbled Hagano. "Has the holiness worn off so soon?"

"For a little while I felt some sense of blessing, but I have been a poor Christian. Is your god so great a comfort that you can afford to gibe?" he snapped, and saw his brother recoil.

"Ah, Gundohar, Gundohar, he is always with me, whispering. . . ." Hagano shivered. "I fought like a madman at Treveri, but no blade touched me even though I had offered my life for the Burgund victory!" He slapped his hand against the mail below his breastbone. "I bear his mark! Why does he mock me?" He turned away, one hand covering his ruined eye. "He knocks at my head like a raven pecking at a skull."

"You offered your life, not your death," said the king slowly. "And then you would not let him have it. What would happen if you let him in?"

"I did, once," came the harsh whisper. "When Sigfrid died, it was Wodan's hand on the spear." Now he was holding his head with both hands.

"I wish . . ." said Gundohar very softly, "that he or any god would talk to me."

He could barely hear Hagano's whisper. "The men . . . say I have grown grim, and it is true. But I do not deny responsibility for my deeds or the choices I have made. Our mother . . . tried to make me her tool. I have bound myself more tightly than she ever could. You do not know what you ask, when you bid me . . . let go. . . ."

Gundohar thought the lamp had begun to flicker, but it was his brother, trembling. The shudders grew more violent, traveling up Hagano's spine, jerking his head from side to side. The king stared—he had not meant this! He started to speak, but the silence between them had become a wall.

Suddenly Hagano was on his feet, swaying. Gundohar reached out, but before he could touch him, the armored body grew still. Instead, the king found himself stepping backward. Hagano was barrel-chested and stocky, how had he suddenly become so tall? The only way in which this figure resembled Gundohar's brother now was that he lacked an eye.

"Ah . . ." Breath was exhaled in a long sigh. He extended

one arm, flexed it, and looked curiously around the room, his single gaze settling finally on the king. "So. Your need has accomplished what mine was unable to achieve. He lets me in. You asked to speak with Wodan—" He smiled grimly. "What do you wish to know?"

Gundohar gazed at him wide-eyed. He had, in that moment, no sense of disloyalty to Bishop Peregrinus or his church. The Presence that spoke through his brother's lips was as undeniable as wind or water, and as little concerned with human rituals or creeds. And the response it woke in him was poetry.

> *"All names and knowledge, now I would wish for;*
> *A word-hoard to have and the wisdom to wield it;*
> *Tales of times past and the truth of their heroes—"*

He stopped, for the god was laughing.

"And had you the time, I would teach it," came the answer. "It is not the spilled stuff you have drunk, but the true mead. . . ." Slowly his amusement faded. "Now I will answer the question you have not asked.

"Listen, Burgund king! You fear to leave your people unprotected, but their wyrd is their own. Fight for them if you can, but if you fail, know that neither for you nor for them is this the end.

"Do you love your folk? I know how to speak to the dead, in that language that cannot be understood by living men. When you are freed from the flesh, you dwell in the raw stuff of reality, and how you see that realm depends on you. If you fall, you may choose to ride the hidden paths until you come home once more."

Gundohar found himself on his feet, staring. "You are saying I will die?"

The god looked at him and began to laugh. "Of course. Are you not a man? What matters is not when you die, but how. You have sung of Airmanareik. When you understand his wyrd, you will know your own." He paused, and turned a little, listening. "Now you must take up your sword, Burgund king, and wake your men, for your foes are near."

His eye closed and he swayed.

Gundohar's bad leg started to give way as he took his brother's full weight. He lowered Hagano to the floor, trying to hear. Was that Deorberht's snoring, or the sound of something being dragged across the ground? The faintest scent of woodsmoke teased at his nostrils and his grip tightened on his brother's arm.

Hagano sat up, shaking his head as if he were coming out of deep water. "What? What is it?"

"Smoke—" said Gundohar. "I think our sister has lighted a final Midsummer fire!"

Chapter 16 ✲ The Offering

Hagano fought his way to his feet. All around him men were reaching for weapons, swearing. Had he slept on guard? Even as he shrugged his shield onto his arm and reached for his spear he could remember a dream in which he had been talking to Gundohar. But in that dream he had been someone else. Images flickered through his memory, dissolving as he tried to grasp them. There had been something about the Burgunds, a battle—the Burgunds were in danger—he had to tell Gundohar!

At the thought of his brother, Hagano felt a wave of amused affection that staggered him. Where had *that* come from? It was certainly not the painful tangle of duty, pity, and reluctant admiration with which he served Gundohar!

"Are you all right?" The king had his own shield now and had put his helm back on. Warriors were taking up position around them, many still rubbing their eyes, but fully armed.

"Yes. Of course." Hagano shook his head and the last of the memories slipped away, leaving only an echo of the love with which that Other had viewed the men at his side. Whatever had happened, it had washed away the tensions that so often tormented him, leaving a great peace behind it. He smiled, and this time it was his brother who looked away.

297

The smell of smoke was growing stronger. Someone banged on the door.

"Come out, Burgund worms, or you roast in your armor. Throw down swords and take our mercy, or come and fight like men!"

"The mercy of the Huns!" exclaimed Gislahar. "The compassion of wolves! I do not think so!" They all looked at the king.

"Nor do I. But neither need we give our necks to their swords," said Gundohar thoughtfully. "If we can charge through their ring and seize the house of Attila, we can hold it. I do not think they will be so quick to burn their own king's hall!"

The men's laughter changed to coughing as Hagano pulled open the door. Through the smoke that rolled inward he could see dim figures, too close for spear work.

"We will fight," he yelled into the smoke, "and Wodan take you all!"

Snarling, he leaped through the door, his arm drawn back by the weight of the spear. Forward momentum continued as he landed, lifting the weapon from his fingers and bearing it in a singing arc above the heads of the foe.

He heard howls from the Goths, who understood that he had given them to the god, and took the first man's swordstroke on his shield as he wrenched his own blade from its sheath. In the next moment Wolcgar was guarding his right. They pushed forward, striking down everyone before them, and the war cries of the men who followed rose above the screams of the foe.

Pale flame and grey smoke billowed from the dwelling behind him; above, streamers of cloud flared with the fires of dawn. A tall shape rose to block his way, fair hair flying above the rim of a shield; a half turn and lunge, his own shield crashed against it, and as the man spun, his back was for a moment open to Hagano's sword. He braced as it struck, sliced through the leather hauberk, skin and muscle and the bones beneath them; blood splattered as the man's fall released the blade. Wolcgar's shield took the next blow that came at him, he stabbed and shoved a falling body to one side, stepped over the man his companion had killed, and settled into position to meet the blows of a new enemy.

This was not the berserk fury that had carried him through the battle of Treveri, but a joyous ecstasy of balanced power and skill. No one could touch him; he sensed his enemy's movements as he did his own, each attack pushed him to a higher pitch of skill. Wolcgar fell behind, but it no longer mattered. Hagano's blade blurred, clearing the way to Attila's hall.

The wall loomed before him. Belatedly comprehending his purpose, men sprang to guard the door, but he swept them aside. He reached the door and kicked it open. Women screamed and scattered, men grabbed for weapons even as he cut them down.

Hagano stood back as the Burgunds pressed in after him, kicking aside the benches. Gislahar, who had brought up the rear, stayed in the doorway, fending off their pursuers with his spear.

"Get those women out of here—"

Hagano heard Gundohar's voice and turned, willing his pulse to slow. The king, flushed but unhurt, was giving more orders. Men dragged the enemy dead and wounded to the door and stacked the benches to one side. He dropped down on one of them, suddenly drained of energy though he had no wound.

There was a cry of rage from outside as the bodies were thrown through the door. Not all of them were dead; he heard groans from men whose wounds had not been improved by the fall. The female slaves were dragged out after them.

"We thank you, king of Huns, for your hospitality," cried Gislahar. "But the dwelling you gave us has proved too warm for the season, and we have taken the liberty of moving into your own. We know you will not deny us—have not you sworn us oaths of brotherhood, and are not brothers bound to share?"

"As you shared with Sigfrid?" came Gudrun's cry.

Hagano got to his feet and pushed through the men to his brother's side. A half dozen of the Burgunds remained where they had fallen in the cleared space between the houses, but a great many more Huns lay on the ground. Those who survived were gathered in a half circle around the doorway, Attila and Gudrun to one side. It was a pity the khan had not been in the hall, thought Hagano. He would have made a good hostage.

"Lord of Horses," he called, "you and Sigfrid are not so nearly related that you should feel bound to avenge him. It was long before she met you that Gudrun held him in her arms. Why did you invite the Niflungar here with such friendly words if you meant to kill them all?"

His words were interrupted by his sister's screech. "Men of Hunland, can you stand by and hear such words? You have eaten your lord's bread and boasted around the fire, but now you are standing here with quaking knees. If one of you will bring me Hagano's head, I will fill his shield with gold. Hang back, and shame is all you will earn!"

She looked as if her night had been almost as wearing as their own, gaunted and wild-haired as a battle-hag. Hagano felt an unaccustomed pity. More than one of the warriors flushed red at her words, but they stayed where they were, watching the khan.

"Good, he has his men in hand," said Gundohar at his ear.

"He is waiting," answered Hagano, meeting Attila's watchful gaze. "We may have a better chance if we fight now, before reinforcements arrive."

"You know now that it will not be easy to take us," called Gundohar. "Let us make a truce. Enough brave men have died."

"Too many," replied Attila. "Your deaths must pay for them. In the *gers* women weep; my own son is dead as well.

If I let you live, my honor is gone. There is no mercy for you now."

Gundohar sighed. "Then let us come out to face you in single combat, rather than besieging us here until hunger and thirst finish us off."

There was a murmur from the Hun warriors, but no one moved.

Hagano stepped past his brother, glaring. "Gudrun's taunts have not stirred you, but perhaps you will hear those of an enemy!" He gazed around the circle, recognizing a few men he had known when he was a hostage here. "Long ago, when I served among you, I was second only to Wald-hari—" He grinned sourly, knowing how that reference to the man who had gotten away with Attila's gold would sting. "Have the Huns become so weak that no one will test whether I have lost my skill?"

There were a few uneasy glances toward the dead, and Hagano laughed, wondering how many of them he had killed. Then one of the men, too young to have been here in Waldhari's time, received a nod from the khan and stalked forward. Clearly he fancied himself a great warrior. His belt and the hilt of his sword gleamed with gold, his hauberk was armored with overlapping scales cut from the hooves of mares, and black horsehair flowed from the point atop his helm. He moved well, too, his gaze watchful beneath the metal rim.

But as Hagano stalked out to meet him he laughed. He had already fought his way unscathed through Attila's best. Today, he knew, he would fight like a god.

Gudrun squatted in the shade of the old oak tree at the edge of the bluff, watching the door of the hall. The khan himself had gone off to meet the men who were coming in to reinforce what remained of his house-guard, but since early that morning she had not stirred. From time to time she saw movement in the dark doorway—one of the other men was on guard there now, from his bulk, Laidrad. But soon enough Hagano would return.

Midsummer heat pulsed in the air; she was soaked with perspiration even in this thin gown. It would be far worse for men in mail. The Burgunds had killed a dozen more of Attila's warriors since the dawning. The bodies had been dragged away, but blood still soaked the ground, its stink mingling horribly with the reek of burned straw. They had fought by twos or threes or sometimes singly; four of the Burgunds had gone down and been dragged back inside the hall. But more often than any other, the defender of the door had been Hagano. By now, without food or water, even he must be tiring. Soon, surely, he too would fall.

Gudrun frowned, imagining all the ways in which he might be killed. But he must not die too quickly. . . . For a moment, instead of Hagano, she saw Sigfrid lying on his bloody bier, and she shuddered, forcing the image away. But even that was better than remembering the broken body of her son. Sigfrid's death was an old agony, a legitimate grievance. She swayed, nursing her fury at those who had caused it as once she had nursed her child.

There was a stir beyond the houses; horses neighed in greeting and one of the warriors ran off to see. Gudrun got to her feet. With more men, perhaps Attila would order an assault on the building. She licked dry lips, waiting to see. In a few moments more she saw the riders and recognized Rudegar's burly figure in the lead. Her pulse quickened. Suddenly she was aware of her grimed face and wild hair. She would not look like the radiant princess whom Rudegar had escorted from the land of the Burgunds now. She combed her hair with her fingers and drew her veil forward, trying to remember how it felt to stand with regal grace.

Rudegar saw her and slid down from his pony, handing the reins to one of his men.

"Lady!" he exclaimed. "The khan sent a messenger— surely he has garbled his words!" He looked around him, taking in the watchful patience of the Hun warriors, the bloody earth, the glint of mail from the open door of the hall. "This is a dreadful thing!"

"They are terrible men, these Burgunds," said old Kursik. "It is in an evil hour our lord welcomes them to his land. They kill nearly a hundred men."

"It must be stopped! I made them welcome in my hall and saw them on their way with such joy! I did not mean to send them to their doom." His honest face was flushed with heat and emotion.

"We ask, for there are many who weep already for this day," said Kursik, "but the khan does not allow us to cease."

"Easy for you to protest, Rudegar," said one of the other men. "You are not the one these wild men are battering. Our lord gives you cattle and lands—you want to repay him by complaining? These are not the words of a brave man!"

Rudegar rounded on the fellow, his face working. "To say I have a heart is true, but do not question my courage!"

The man shrugged. "We have seen no sign—" he began, but before he could finish, Rudegar's fist shot out and knocked him sprawling. Kursik hurried to his side, shaking his head.

"Has my lord not suffered enough loss that you should add to it?" exclaimed Gudrun.

"Lady, they are your brothers! And I am bound to them by ties of hospitality and kinship! I was their guest in Borbetomagus, and I feasted them in my hall, gave them costly gifts as well. Let the khan take back the gifts he has given me before he asks me to betray my honor this way!"

Gudrun shook her head and began to laugh, a wrenching, terrible sound that made the men around her look away. "These men are not worthy of your loyalty. They were guests here, and look what they have done!"

Rudegar was still shaking his head. "I have sworn them the oaths of a kinsman, given my daughter to young Gislahar as his bride—"

"Why should you honor such oaths?" hissed Gudrun.

"*They* do not! They swore brotherhood with Sigfrid, to whom they gave me when I was young, and they killed him. They swore oaths to Attila, and they have killed our little son!" His face blanched, but Gudrun's gaze held him.

"And before you swore friendship with the Burgund kings," she said slowly, "you took an oath to me! Do you remember what you said when we stood in my brother's hall? You swore troth to me for yourself and all your kin, and you vowed that if I suffered insult, you would be the first to avenge my wrong! *There* stand the nithings who have destroyed my life!" She turned, pointing to the open door. "If you will not fight for me, I brand you traitor and coward before all men!"

Rudegar covered his eyes with his hands, swaying back and forth like a man in pain, but Gudrun would not pity him.

"Oh Diedelinda, oh my poor girl! You were so happy in the husband I found for you! How can I face you if I go against him in arms?"

I was happy with Sigfrid, Gudrun thought, and smothered her pity. "How will you face my husband if you will not help him in his need!"

"I will fight . . ." Rudegar said heavily, "but no good can come of this."

He turned without meeting her eyes, calling to his men. In silence, she watched them march toward Attila's hall.

"Rudegar!" Gislahar came out from the doorway, his smile fading as he saw that the the older man had laced his helm for battle, and that the men who followed him had their shields up and their spears poised.

"Defend yourselves, bold Niflungar! From me you should have profit, but instead I must make you pay. We have been friends, but this blade must cut those ties!" He came to a halt before the doorway, legs braced and shield up, his sword poised above his shoulder.

"More than friends!" exclaimed Gislahar. "We swore the

oaths of kindred! The sword you gave me has saved my life a dozen times today!"

Gudrun came to her feet, heart pounding. Gislahar's only guilt lay in his loyalty to his brothers. She did not want him to die. He turned away, his face working, and Hagano came out to stand beside him.

"Your shield has protected me," he said. "It would shatter if I were to bear it against you."

"Is there no way we can preserve our friendship?" asked Gundohar, coming up on his other side. "Your mail shirt wards my hide, and the oaths I swore to you still bind me!"

You were quick enough to forget the oaths you swore to Sigfrid! thought Gudrun.

"My dear friends, older oaths compel me! One of you must come out to fight. Promise that you will care for my wife and daughter if it is I who fall!"

"With a good will, if we live," said Gundohar gently, "but that is unlikely without your aid. . . ."

Gislahar turned back to face him, weeping openly now. "If one of the Niflungar must fight, then I claim this battle. I am your daughter's pledged husband, Rudegar, can you lift your sword against me? You are Diedelinda's father— can you kill your son?" He stepped forward, opening his guard. The iron rings on the breast of his byrnie glittered in the sun.

Rudegar recoiled. "Not you, lad," he said brokenly. "Any other, but not you!"

"You cannot do it. . . ." said Gislahar. He took another step, the point of his sword trailing in the dust, and smiled.

"May the holy gods forgive me! I must!" Rudegar's cry tore the silence as the tip of his own blade sliced through the heavy air, through the iron rings and leather of Gislahar's hauberk and the flesh beneath it and plunged into the earth below.

An instant too late, the boy responded. His sword was still lifting as his lifeblood spattered the ground. He staggered, his body swung around by the weapon's momentum, sunlight flashing from the blade. Rudegar was still bowed before him. He made no effort to pull his own sword free as Gislahar's turn continued, the weight of the weapon that Rudegar himself had given him bringing it down to strike through mail and bone.

Rudegar's head flopped sideways, blood fountaining, but for a moment longer his body remained leaning on his sword. Then he sagged to his knees, and Gislahar's corpse crashed down to bear him to the earth in a final, bloody embrace.

A wail of mortal anguish shattered the silence.

It was not until she saw men looking up from the sprawled bodies to stare at her that Gudrun realized it was she who had screamed.

The day had passed its nooning, and in the confined space of the hall, heat was an enemy as deadly as the warriors who waited outside. Some of the men had pulled off their mail shirts, saying they would rather take their chances against an enemy blade than stifle in their armor. Gundohar, remembering how Gislahar had helped him into his mail, kept his on, though sweat had long ago soaked through tunic and padding.

His brother's body lay on one of the beds by the wall. His features, still fixed in a look of faint surprise, seemed those of a boy. He would never grow older now. Gundohar licked dry lips and told himself not to waste his tears. It was unlikely that any of them would outlive this day. Despite the heat, Gislahar's flesh was cool; he no longer suffered from thirst or hunger or sick despair.

"What is going on outside?" asked Sindold, wiping his brow. "What are they waiting for?"

"More men have come in," said Hagano, who was once more watching the door. "I see some of Thiudimir's guard."

"I would welcome an attack," said one of the others. "Better to die fighting than to expire of thirst in here."

"This is a poor feast your sister has invited us to," said Laidrad hoarsely.

"Do you think so?" answered Hagano. "Is not the table spread before you? You drink the blood of slain beasts when you go hunting. There lies your mead—in this heat, the blood that flows from the wounds of our companions will be better than wine."

Gundohar stared at his brother in amazement, but Laidrad went to the body of a man who had died from a spear thrust and bent over the wound.

"They have already given us their lives," said Hagano more softly as they watched him drinking. "We have taken their weapons to replace broken swords and shattered shields. Do you think they would grudge us this last offering?"

When Laidrad had finished, several of the others went to the bodies of their friends to do the same. They seemed eased by it, but Gundohar stayed where he was. *It is I who should be shedding my blood for my people*, he thought grimly, *not them for me!*

From outside came the sound of many horses. Hagano stiffened, and Gundohar moved to his side. The sun must be dropping toward the hills across the river, its long rays flamed from spear tips and gilded helms, barring the trampled earth with the lengthening shadow of the oak tree and the shapes of armed men with the wicked recurved Hunnish bows in their hands.

"Attila is back," said Hagano quietly. Gundohar felt the sweat on his body grow cold despite the heated air.

The crowd of warriors parted and he saw the khan, armed in a hauberk covered with plates of steel, with the golden bow of the warleader slung across his shoulder.

"Gundohar, one last time I call to you!" His deep voice carried clearly.

Hagano stepped through the door, holding his shield so that the king would be covered, and Gundohar followed.

"Husband of my sister, I am still here—" Behind him, he

could hear the men who had taken off their armor pulling it back on.

"When you come here, I ask you to give me gold to feed my people. Now I am not asking. You will tell me where you keep Sigfrid's hoard."

Gundohar stared at him, his heart bounding.

"Very well. I am your hostage. Give me your oath to spare the Burgunds and I will write an order to my brother to send you the gold."

Slowly Attila shook his head. "Does a dead man read letters? Before you come my word is given to the Master of Legions and my riders gone. Litorius attacked Borbeto-magus a week ago. Your brother Godomar is dead. The only Burgunds whose lives you buy are those who stand with you here."

If the men behind him shouted, Gundohar could not hear it above the roaring in his ears. With every heartbeat, light and dark pulsed through his vision; only Hagano's strong grip kept him from going down.

My people . . . he shook his head like a lung-shot stag. *Dying, and I not with them!*

"Brother, we all stand behind you—" Hagano's voice seemed to come from a great distance. "Not a man would buy his life, having heard that news. Shall we go out fighting now, and make an end?"

"Now . . . yes . . ." It was hard to form words.

"Take a deep breath, Burgund king," came that calm voice at his ear, the voice he had heard in the dark hours just before dawn. "And my strength will fill your arm. . . ."

His first try was a hoarse gasp; the second came easier, light flared through his limbs as if he had breathed in flame. With the third, vision cleared. His men were taking up position around him; he could feel the rising heat of their rage.

"We will not buy our lives with the blood of our kin!" he said hoarsely, lifting his shield. "And we will make you pay dearly before we die!"

As one, the Burgunds began to move forward. Gundohar saw Attila raise his hand, but the madness of battle was flaring through him and he did not care. He jerked into an awkward run, screaming, as the sky darkened and the arrows came.

It seemed a long time later that Gundohar found himself standing still at last, but the sun had slipped only a little farther toward the hills. He was covered with blood, but he could not tell how much of it might be his own. The hacked remains of his shield dangled from his arm. He shook it off, trying to understand why he was still alive. Dancward lay at his feet, Wolcgar nearby, sprawled across the bodies of Goths. It took all his will to force his head to turn.

The open space between the houses was covered with fallen men. Many of his own had been felled by arrows, but those who survived to reach their foes had taken three times their own numbers with them. He saw Laidrad's head lying near Sindold's body, others in Burgund armor, too covered with blood for him to tell who they were.

Attila had been dragged off to safety, but beneath the oak tree two men in hacked mail shirts were struggling. Their helmets were gone. He blinked, recognizing Hagano and Thiudimir.

The Goth is like me, he thought numbly. *As long as he could, he held back from the battle, but I suppose he had to fight after we killed all his men.*

Gundohar lurched toward them, each step a conscious act, for his bad leg had been wrenched so that he could hardly walk on it, and he was suddenly almost too weary to move. Hagano should have been a match for his opponent, but he had been fighting for a night and a day without food or water, while the Goth had come fresh to the fray. Hagano had lost his helm and was bleeding freely. He groped for a hold, but his wounded arm betrayed him and Thiudimir broke free, swinging wildly; his fist crashed into his opponent's skull and Hagano went down.

Thiudimir straightened, breathing hard, saw Gundohar, and made a grab for his sword.

Gundohar swayed, shaken by voiceless laughter. "Don't be afraid . . . I won't . . . run after you!"

"How should I know what you can do?" said the Goth. "Today you Burgunds fought like gods, not men. Ah, Gundohar, when we rode together behind Aetius I never thought our friendship would end this way."

"I too could wish . . . I had never heard his name . . ." He lifted his sword.

"Give it up, man, and surrender," said Thiudimir. "You can hardly hold your blade."

Gundohar shook his head, gathering the last of his strength to swing. He saw Thiudimir's return blow coming, but could only turn his own blade to guard. The Goth's sword hit his, driving it from his hands, then continued onward, the flat of the blade slamming into his good leg with a force that knocked him to the ground.

"I am sorry. . . ." said Thiudimir softly above him.

Blinded by the pain in his thigh, Gundohar lay waiting for the mercy-stroke. But what he felt was the rasp of ropes as he was bound.

He must have lost consciousness then, for when he was aware once more he was back in Attila's hall. His feet as well as his hands were tied—an unnecessary precaution, he thought grimly. The ache in his bad leg was minor next to the throbbing agony where Thiudimir had hit his good one. He wondered if it was broken. Hagano was lying beside him. But his brother must be alive, thought the king, or he would not still be bound. As he stirred, he heard Hagano sigh.

"To lie trussed like a sheep awaiting the knife is not how I expected to end this journey. . . ."

Gundohar started to laugh, though a dozen other hurts he had not noticed when he got them ached fiercely at every breath. "I do not suppose, when he invited us here, that our sister's husband expected to lose so many men. What I do not understand is why we are still alive."

"If we are," said Hagano gloomily, "it is because the khan has something worse in mind for us. Among the Huns, reputation is the foundation of power, and we have damaged his badly today. To regain his honor, he will have to punish us so terribly that men will sing of it for a thousand years."

"What matters is not when you die, but how . . . " whispered Gundohar, and felt his brother jerk.

"Who said that?"

"You did," answered the king, "or perhaps it was your god. He spoke through you, don't you remember?"

Hagano swore. "He calls me his son. Sigfrid belonged to him as well. If this is how he treats his children, no wonder so few claim kinship!"

Gundohar shook his head. "I do not think we can blame Wodan, or any god, for the sins and confusions of men. We have woven our own wyrd, brother, and all that remains to us is to complete the pattern with as much courage as we can. But I do not mind telling you that I, too, wish I had fallen in the midst of my battle-fury. This waiting in cold blood is a hard thing to do."

Hagano began to laugh, then the door opened and he stilled. "I think we will not wait long, and what follows will be harder still. Brother," he added in a rush, "there was a time when I envied you and fought against the ties that kept me at your side, but my life has been centered on you. Be true to yourself, my king, and it will not matter what they do to me."

"Too many oaths I have broken, but I will be true to your trust, Hagano—" He broke off as Attila came in.

"You wake? That is well," said the khan. "Now you tell me how to find Sigfrid's gold."

Gundohar felt his brother's silence as a physical thing and pressed his own lips closed. All he could see of the khan was his boots, of red-dyed leather appliquéd with scrolls and spirals in black and gold.

"You do not answer? You are wounded already, Niflungar, but not so bad you cannot feel more. If you wish an easy death you will tell me. . . ."

"If I had wished to have things easy, I would never have left the Rhenus, my khan," muttered Hagano. One of Attila's men started to kick him, but the khan stopped him.

"They draw strength from each other. Take this one out; tie him to the tree."

Two men bent to lift Hagano. He tried to kick, but he was too weak to do much damage. Gundohar heard him gasp as they hit him. Then they dragged him through the door.

"Brother," called the king, "we will meet in Wodan's hall!"

When they had gone, Attila knelt beside his captive, gripping his hair so that he could not look away.

"So. He is gone. Now, perhaps, you will say?"

Gundohar fought to sustain that black gaze. Death was the best they could hope for. How could he make sure the khan would allow Hagano to die?

"Not yet," he whispered. "I cannot reveal that secret while any of my followers live to see my shame."

"Is it so? Well, that is easily achieved." Attila rose to his feet, his teeth bared in a smile that did not reach his eyes.

Afraid that he would weep, Gundohar closed his own, but he could feel the earth trembling beneath him as his captor strode to the door.

After so many hours packed into armor, Hagano shivered at the touch of the cool air upon his skin. They had stripped off the mail shirt, the sodden padding, and the soaked tunic beneath it before binding him to the tree. The ropes on his wrists pulled his arms back around the trunk, crossed and went down to hold his ankles; another went around his neck. If he stood straight the pressure on his arms soon became painful, but when he slumped, the rope at his neck cut off his wind. A simple system, but quite effective, he thought as he straightened once more.

The slash on his shoulder had reopened when they stripped him; he could feel the warm blood running down his arm. *They had better hurry,* he thought hazily, *or blood loss will finish me and cheat them of their fun.*

"Hagano, what have you done with Sigfrid's gold?"

He blinked, and saw Gudrun standing there. She had washed her face and put on fresh clothes and all her ornaments. The light of the setting sun glinted from the gold and blazed in her hair.

"Look at her, all got up like a Beltane tree," he muttered. "Is this splendor to cheer me up, Gudrun, or to celebrate your victory?" He heard her hiss and smiled, felt the rope cutting off his wind and raised his head again.

"You always hated me; everything I loved you have destroyed. Do you expect me to weep for your pain?"

He shook his head. "Do you know, sister, how much your anger makes you look like Brunahild?"

Her eyes widened, and he knew that this shaft, at least, had struck home. She started to reply, then stopped. Attila was coming back from the hall.

"He has not told you?" asked the khan. He cocked his head, considering Hagano. "If you know where the hoard is hidden, you should say so now. Your brother says he will not tell while any of his men is left alive. . . ."

For a moment Hagano stared at him, then he began to laugh, understanding now how the king meant to keep the troth he had pledged with his final word.

Attila raised one eyebrow. "You do not believe me? Cut out his heart—" He gestured to Berik.

"Lord—" exclaimed old Kursik. Hagano remembered that his son had been one of the Hun warriors slain. "Then he dies before we have time to make him pay. Take the heart of my thrall Hialli. He is good for nothing else—when the fighting starts he ran."

One of the men in the crowd that had gathered to watch the execution went white and started to edge away. Whooping, the warriors went after him. Hagano could hear their shouts and the thrall's laments as he dashed among the *gers*. But soon enough they dragged him back again, weeping that he was suffering for quarrels that were none of his own, and bemoaning the loss of the pigs he had tended. A wet stain spread on his breeches and the stink of shit filled the air.

"This shrieking is a greater torment than your knife," said Hagano. "Finish what you have begun with me and let the poor sheep go."

"I don't think so. I want you to see." He nodded, and Berik drove his spear into the thrall's chest, just beneath the breastbone, and jerked upward. The man screamed as the sharp edge burst through his rib cage. Berik bent, worked the blade around and reached into the heaving chest. As he pulled out the madly pulsing heart, Hialli's voice was at last mercifully stilled.

"Now, show it to Gundohar."

Hagano swallowed bile. The warriors were eyeing him curiously, murmuring. He had been right. Attila's people would remember this day. Presently Berik came back, wiping his bloody hands.

The khan stood with arms crossed, waiting. "What does the Lord of the Gundwurm say?"

"He says this was a coward's heart, not that of Hagano. If it was quaking so in my hands, it must have trembled still more in the man's breast."

Hagano sighed. He did not know if the thrall's heart had quivered, but Gundohar must have heard the man's screaming and refused to believe that his brother would have cried out even in extremity. It was, he supposed, a compliment. His own gut was cramping unpleasantly. *Wodan*, he thought, *let me die without shame. You owe me at least this much of a victory.*

Attila looked back at him and shrugged slightly. Hagano pressed his back against the oak tree, feeling the rough bark dig into his skin. Nine nights, he thought, Wodan had hung on the Worldtree before the blade went into his breast.

"Look," said someone. "He has a scar upon his belly already. Berik will have no trouble deciding where to aim the spear."

At the words, Hagano felt the crossed lines of the *Gebo* rune began to tingle. He took a quick breath as the sensation spread, filling the space beneath his rib cage with fire. Another breath, and warmth shot up to his throat and down through his belly, a strange sweet pulsing as if he had been drinking strong mead. Hagano's body twitched and they began to laugh, thinking it was fear.

Now that strange energy was jerking his head from side to side. He blinked as for a moment the rush of sensation blanked vision. When he could see again, he did not quite recognize his surroundings, and yet it was not the world that had changed, but his perspective. He felt as if the self he knew had been shifted to the sidelines, while another used his senses to see the world. He had felt this once before . . . he remembered Gundohar's astonished face, and a Voice that said—that was saying now—*"Hagano, my son, let me in . . ."*

Hagano's awareness retreated inward; he sighed, and as he drew breath once more, the god was there.

"You do not reconsider?" asked Attila, eyeing him narrowly. "Then I must take your heart to your brother and see if it will persuade him to tell me where he hid Sigfrid's hoard."

"This is not about the gold." Hagano's lips moved, but it was not his voice that they heard. Gudrun straightened, staring. "This is about power. You seek it, Lord of Horses, and what you seek you will find, but what you find will not be what you thought you were looking for."

"Fine words," said Berik, picking up his spear. "Let us see if he can still babble when he feels my sting!" But Attila, his gaze fixed on the figure bound to the tree, made no move.

"What do I look for?" he said harshly.

"Mastery . . . It is not enough for you to rule the Western

Huns. Soon you will draw the Sword of War and make yourself lord of them all. But you will not be able to rule as you like, for you will always be halted by the walls of Rome. What will you do when your brother Aetius turns against you as he turns you against the Burgunds now?"

"Him too, I master, when it is time!" rasped the khan.

"Sixteen winters you will have, and then your time is done."

"I leave an empire behind me! That is more than these Burgunds do!"

"You will leave what they leave—your name. . . ." The Voice seemed to roll upward through Hagano's body from the roots of the tree. "It is your choice what that name will mean."

Attila recoiled, staring in appalled recognition. "Now I understand. I am right to wish you back in your own land when you worked through Brunahild. You are the one who betrayed her. But I know how to banish you, Rider; you do not deceive *me!*" He snatched Berik's spear and plunged it into Hagano's breast.

Agony flared out along the rays of the rune in waves of white fire, encompassing the world. He was the tree whose leaves moved in the wind, he was the bending grass, in each breath he was one with the men who tormented him.

"You do not stay now, Old Man," Attila hissed, "when your horse is suffering!"

I have suffered many times, I am Lord of the Slain, came the thought from within. "I am the one who offers," his lips moved, "and I am the offering. . . . Let Gudrun set her hand upon the spear."

Attila turned to his wife, who had been watching with a pale face and blazing eyes. "You hear him. He is your kinsman, the one who kills your first man, and your child. All this time you cry about your grief and your vengeance. Do it! Take the spear!" He grabbed her wrist and jerked her forward, slamming her hand down upon the shaft and holding it there with his own.

Force flared from Hagano's breast in a mingled pulse of pain and power and out through his back, another shot up his spine and down to the earth on which he stood. His body arched, transfixed between all realities.

Gudrun stood like one struck by lightning in the moment before he falls, her eyes white-rimmed and staring. His single gaze met hers, and suddenly his vision was doubled, seeing her, seeing himself transfixed upon the tree, twinned in a single, incandescent exchange of power.

Without blinking, she twisted the shaft, reached into his center, and wrenched it free. For a moment longer he saw with doubled vision. Then white darkness whirled around him. His head dropped forward and the rope around his neck released his breath, and Gudrun cried out as that part of her that had been Hagano whirled away.

Chapter 17 ❧ The Gundwurm

It was too quiet.

Gundohar shivered, remembering how the thrall had screamed, and the palpitating heart in Berik's hand. To deny that it could be Hagano's had been a reaction born of revulsion, confirmed a moment later by the flicker of disappointment in the man's eyes. Had that been a mistake? He had hoped they would give his brother a quick death. What were they doing to him now?

There is nothing you can do, he told himself, but he could not keep from wondering. So often he had imagined the feelings of others—heroes like Airmanareik or Aeneas, and now Hagano—it had always been easier than confronting his own. But even Airmanareik had not been captured by his enemies.

Someone spoke outside and his gut twisted. He struggled to sit up, biting his lip as the movement set his broken leg to throbbing. The door opened. Attila stood in stark silhouette against a sky that blazed with banners of gold. Then the khan came in, turning so the light fell full on the bloody mass in his hand.

It was still dripping. Gundohar looked at it and swallowed his nausea.

> *"This heart in your hand belonged to a hero—
> beat steady in breast when Hagano bore it. . . ."*

318

To say it in staves clothed the terror with meaning, but a voice in his head was gibbering.

"You speak truth. Hagano is dead." The khan's voice sounded strange. "You are alone. Now you tell about the gold."

Gundohar looked at him and began to laugh. "What will you do to me if I refuse? You have no more hostages." He shook his head, aware how close he was to hysteria. "The gold is in the Rhenus. Before we left Borbetomagus I told Hagano to hide it there."

Attila's face darkened. "Where?"

Gundohar shrugged and grinned at him. "I did not ask. If you want to know more, you must go where Hagano has gone!"

For a moment he thought the khan would strike him. Then Attila rose to his feet; the dying light from the doorway gilded his features like a mask.

"A small revenge . . . it does not save you."

"Will you cut out my heart, too?" asked Gundohar wildly. "I will try to die as bravely as Hagano."

The khan shook his head. "Do you forget the oaths we swore? You are my woman's brother; I do not raise a hand against you." He turned to the men who had followed him. "You—begin now to dig a pit, and you others, go to the heath and the marshes where the vipers dwell. Capture them—many serpents—bring them here. We see then, Lord of the Gundwurm, if your kin will welcome you. . . ."

Gundohar's face must have shown his revulsion then, for Attila smiled.

Gudrun . . . I am Gudrun. . . . She took one breath, then a second, as her vision cleared. She was clutching the earth where she had fallen. She forced her fingers to open, pushed herself upright and tried to wipe them off on the skirts of her gown. The smell of blood filled the air. She looked up, and the level rays of the sinking sun, blazing now just above the western hills, blinded her with light.

She gasped, overwhelmed once more by simultaneous awareness of dust motes shimmering, the movement of air through the leaves, the rush of blood in her veins and the Pattern to which they all belonged, a pattern that resonated with her Name. Then the sun slipped behind the hill; she blinked, and saw with mortal vision the bloodstained spear on the ground and the empty body that hung on the oak tree. With the ropes around him he looked like the Old Man of the Harvest in his bonds.

Brunahild's spirit must be laughing, she thought hazily. *She only killed a faithless lover. I have slain a god.* But that was not quite true, she corrected, Wodan was not gone—she could still hear him calling her. It was the blood of her brother that stained her hands and soaked the ground.

She got to her feet. None of the men who stood around her would meet her eyes. Did it disturb them that a woman had helped to strike that blow? No use to say that Attila had forced her to do it. She would still have been responsible, as Brunahild had been responsible for the death of Sigfrid, even if she had not touched the spear.

"The choices were mine. . . ."

She was surprised to feel approval from the Presence that haunted her as she whispered those words. Had he *wanted* all these men to die?

The warriors stood to attention with an air of relief as Attila came toward them. Gudrun straightened.

"Well, husband, has Gundohar told you where he hid the hoard?"

"You want it? Seek it in the Rhenus." His flat gaze rested on Gudrun, and she shivered. "It is true. The gold does not matter. Aetius gives me all I need."

"Then why—" She gestured toward the figure bound to the tree.

"My name. . . ." he said reflectively. "Men hear how the king of the Burgunds dies, and learn to fear."

"Kill him yourself!" Her voice shook. "It was Hagano who was *my* enemy."

The khan shook his head. "You think he would act alone? The king commands, or he is not king. But I do not touch Gundohar—his own spirits punish him when the serpents come."

"What do you mean?"

"Ask him—" He smiled mockingly. "Sister to brother— tell him how you dealt with Hagano. . . ."

When Gudrun started toward the hall, four warriors followed her. Did they expect the prisoner to attack her, or did they think she might try to harm Gundohar? With the passing of the sun, all color was fading from the world, and the doorway was an entrance to darkness. She sent one of the men to bring a lamp before she went in.

Gundohar was lying on his side. The silk tunic he had worn to the feast was soiled and torn, and beneath the breeches on his right leg the flesh was swollen and the fair skin already purple and bruised.

"Cut his bonds. His leg is broken. I do not think he is going to run away. And you," she said to one of the others, "bring a fresh tunic from his baggage and water for him to wash in. He is your captive, but he is still a king."

Gundohar opened his eyes. "What about some food and drink?" he asked, massaging his wrists. "Or would that over-stress your hospitality?"

Gudrun nodded to the men. That had been meant to sting, but Hagano's passing had washed all her hatred away.

"Or you could slay me, as you did Hagano."

He looked at her and she realized that there was blood on her gown. *My brother's blood. . . .* She shivered.

"That would be a mercy, don't you think, compared to what your husband has in mind for me?"

She pulled over one of the benches and sat down, frowning. What did she feel? Gundohar looked from her to his guards, sighed, and levered himself to a sitting position with his back against the wall. Clearly the movement pained him, for his color grew worse and there was sweat on his brow, but there seemed little point in trying to splint his leg, even if the swelling had allowed it.

"Well?" he said finally. "Still silent? I thought you came to mock me, Gudrun, now that you have won."

She shook her head. "Is this a victory? You should have let me stay in the forest!"

"Your marriage seemed necessary to secure the Hun alliance—" He started to laugh and caught his breath. He looked like a half-starved bird, sitting there with his thinning hair all on end, and she felt an unexpected pang of pity.

No, that is weakness. I cannot afford pity for him or for myself, now.

"The only winner here is Attila," she answered in a hard voice. "He could not break Hagano. Now he will try with you."

"But why? He has already ended the alliance—"

"To grant you a hero's death would diminish his victory. Everyone has to do his will."

The door opened and men came in with the baggage that had not been burned in the guesthall. Gudrun rummaged through it, setting aside belts and ornaments, a wax tablet and stylus and a small harp, while they stripped off Gundohar's ruined clothing. When she turned with the new garments in her arms and saw how it hurt him to move, she took the cloth and began to bathe him herself, as once she had bathed her child.

Handling the man's unresisting body brought a flickering image of Apsik, whose slack limbs she had washed before they laid him out for burial. She rubbed Gundohar dry with a brisk efficiency that made him wince and thrust the memory back into the dark.

Bathed and dressed, he attacked the stew they brought him as if he expected it to be snatched away, but after he had taken a few bites, he paused.

"This body," he said reflectively, "does not know whether it wants to live or die." He scooped up a little more, and after a moment, got it down. Then he set down the spoon and looked up at her.

"Gudrun . . . you have reason to hate me, but do not turn your back on the Burgunds. I have failed them. You are the last of the Niflungar. They"—he swallowed—"the ones who survive, will need you now."

She shook her head, hearing once more a voice in a dark wood—"*You are the Holy Queen.* . . . "

"Go to them, and they will know that the goddesses have not forgotten them, even if they doubt the gods. Galamvara . . . has been a good queen, but she is not of their blood, and perhaps by now she is a prisoner. Send for Gundiok, our cousin's child."

Gudrun sat silent, curled around her own pain.

"I will not beg for my life, but I plead for our people, Gudrun!"

"You do not understand—" she said bitterly. "I bring only evil on those I love!"

"Do it," he repeated. "And I will find a way to deny Attila his victory."

She raised her head. "How? You cannot even stand up long enough to swing a sword."

Gundohar gave her a twisted grin. "I was never that good with a blade anyhow. But Hagano had no weapon either. How did he do it? How did he defy the khan?"

Gudrun got to her feet, trembling, dizzied once more by that terrible multiplication of vision in which she had been Hagano, feeling his agony, her own fingers wrapped around the spear, and that Other, encompassing them both in a union so profound that it transcended grief and became ecstasy.

"He gave himself to the god."

Gundohar had meant to spend the hours that were left to him in constructing curses for Attila and composing his own soul, but when Gudrun had gone and they took the lamp away exhaustion claimed him. He slept uneasily, dreaming of serpents that dragged him down into darkness, but he could not wake.

The next thing he knew someone was kicking his sore ribs, and it was morning.

Don't think about what is waiting for you! he told himself, *live from moment to moment, or you will babble like a nithing and Attila will win. . . .*

"Here is drink for you. Your sister sends it—" said his guard.

Gundohar took the horn, wondering whether to hope or to fear that it had been poisoned. The first taste told him it was only honey-ale, but it was strong stuff—*"the true mead . . ."* He felt it light a tiny flame in his belly and let out his breath in an appreciative sigh, drank the rest of it down, and regretfully handed back the horn. One of the men gestured toward the door with his spear. Gundohar shook his head.

"My leg is injured, remember? If you want me to go anywhere, you will have to carry me." So long as he did not move, the break was only a dull ache, but he had nearly fainted when he tried to stand the night before. To be carried out unconscious might be preferable, but it lacked dignity.

There was a short conversation in the language of the Huns, then they lifted him onto one of the benches, a man picked up each end and they bore him out into the day. *Like the goddess in the cart when they carry her around the fields—* Gundohar caught his breath on a hiccough of laughter and an aftertaste of mead.

It was already midmorning, the great bowl of the sky filled with a golden light so radiant that even the river seemed to shine from within. The thatched roofs of the houses of Attila's Town glistened; the scattered *gers* beyond them glowed. He gazed around him in wonder. *It is a good day to die. . . .*

But he wished that he could have seen the Rhenus and his own hills once more.

There seemed to be a great many people gathered here. Warriors from different tribes in the Hun hegemony who had come in answer to Attila's call, and now that the fighting was over, women and children emerging from the *gers* in which they had hidden to see the last of the strangers who had killed so many of their menfolk die in turn. Gundohar tried to sit up straighter, stifling a hysterical impulse to smile and wave as he had when they cheered him through the streets at home.

They carried him past the charred ruin of the hall in which the Burgunds had been brought to bay and down the slope past the clustered *gers*. At the edge of the settlement was a meadow, still green despite the season. No doubt the soil was moist there, and easy to dig. Attila was waiting, dressed in crimson silk, with Thiudimir and some of his notable men. The Goth prince had a sour look and would not meet Gundohar's eye. Even Queen Ereka had come, her dark eyes watchful beneath her veil.

He did not see Gudrun, and did not know whether to feel disappointed or glad she did not want to watch him die. But it was hard that no man or woman of his own folk would witness his end.

They brought him to the edge of the pit. Gundohar tried to keep from looking, but his gaze was drawn to the gaping hole, a man's length deep and about the same across, and the sinuous tangle within. There was a horrid fascination in wondering how many snakes they had been able to find. The sun was not quite overhead, and where the ground was still in shadow the reptiles lay unmoving. But where the warm light fell, he could see them writhe. Soon, he thought, he would know.

"Hear, men of the Huns—" said Attila. "Hear, lords of the Gothic clans, Gepids and Sarmati, you who follow the Lord of Horses." His dark gaze moved from one to another, and they became, if possible, even more still. "Burgunds

come to share our feasting. They were bad guests. Instead
of gifts they give us battle, blood for mead, flesh for meat.
Many women weep for butchered warriors; maidens mourn
for their slaughtered men. My own son is slain."

Gundohar gazed at him with appreciation, almost forgetting the purpose of this rhetoric in his admiration for its
style.

"What gift do such guests deserve?" He turned to the
people.

"Death!" came the answer. "Let them die!"

"Death we give them. Their blood feeds our earth." He
smiled grimly. "One only still lives, the Burgund king!"

"Send him after his warriors!" came the cry. "Spill his
blood on the ground!"

"With the Burgund king I took oath as brother," said
Attila. "Let the spirits of this land avenge us. If the Gundwurm is guilty, the serpents claim his life, not me!"

"Hear, ye men of the Huns and subject peoples!" cried
Gundohar. If he could distract himself with words he could
keep the fear at bay. The men he had left behind at home
had died as bravely as those who had been killed at his
side; he must bear himself so that any who had survived
could say the same of him when they heard of this day.

"We Burgunds came at your invitation, trusting ourselves
to your hospitality. The death of the boy was not intended,
but you gave us no chance to offer compensation. When
you attacked, we defended our lives and our honor, and my
warriors proved our innocence by defeating three times our
own numbers before they were brought down. Now I am
in your power. Lord of Horses, I am ready to endure your
ordeal."

There was a murmur of appreciation from the crowd.
There was more sport in a challenge than an execution.
Attila might frown, but it pleased them to hear the Burgund
king's defiance. Gundohar only hoped he would be able to
live up to it. He took a deep breath and lifted his hands to
the skies.

"I salute the radiant day! I hail the gods and goddesses. I greet the holy earth and the spirits of this land and submit myself to their judgment."

"Let them judge, then. . . ." In the khan's dark eyes Gundohar read a grudging respect. Attila nodded to the men who had carried him.

"Shall we tie him?" asked one.

"My legs are hurt and I cannot stand," said Gundohar quickly. "You need not fear I will climb out of there."

He bit his lip to keep from screaming as they lifted him, then he was falling. He landed hard, and for the first few moments the pain from his broken leg and the muscles around his old wound was a white fire that drove all other awareness away.

When the king could think again, he could see snakes all around him. But his sudden arrival appeared to have been as much of a shock to them as it had been to him, for they were recoiling in all directions. In the wild, they would have tried to escape, but in the pit there was not far they could go. Presently, as he made no move, they settled down and began their slow exploration of their prison once more.

Gundohar tensed at the feather touch of a forked tongue on his bare ankle, but the snake, not perceiving it as food, lifted its triangular head and curved away. It was an adder, its body a dull grey with distinctive wavy markings along the sides. Another, lighter in color and smaller, flowed over his foot; he shuddered at the silken coolness of the scales. *Sit still*, he told himself. *Like any creature, they will strike if they are threatened. Make no move and perhaps they will leave you alone.*

He had heard that there was a kind of grass snake whose markings imitated those of a viper. He wondered if the snake catchers had caught any by mistake. Except for the slimmer, red-brown asps, the reptiles all looked much the same, patterned with diamonds and meanders on a dozen shades of brown and grey. He supposed he would not know until one tried to bite him, and so far, none of them had made a hostile move.

As his heartbeat began to slow he could hear the speculative murmur of the crowd. *Are they making wagers on how long it will be?* The shaman Eskam was dancing around the edge of the pit, singing and beating two pieces of iron together; the serpentine ribbons on his tunic jerked and fluttered to the clangor, and the adders twitched unhappily as he passed.

Slowly, trying not to alarm his companions, Gundohar levered himself up so that he was sitting with his back against the side of the pit. One of the adders moved into the space where he had lain, full in the sun. Another coiled against the warmth of his thigh. *Think of something else,* he told himself, striving to keep the voice that was gibbering in his brain from betraying his fear.

Serpents . . . rivers were serpents . . . the Rhenus was a mighty dragon. He closed his eyes, seeing in memory its sinuous silver moving past the warm red walls of the city of the Gundwurm, saw sunlight dancing in the air above the vineyards, the peak of the Donarberg against a sunset sky. *My own land . . .*

There was a stir above him; he looked up and saw Gudrun, her bright hair uncovered, in the grip of two of the warriors. The lap harp that had been in the king's baggage was tucked under her arm.

"Fools!" she snapped. "This is no weapon! My brother fancies himself a bard—will it not be amusing to see if he can sing where he is now!"

Attila started to speak, but the guard had already let her go. Gudrun knelt at the edge of the pit, her long braid swinging forward, and dropped the harp into Gundohar's waiting hands. For a moment he could not speak, and then he knew he must not, but his eyes met hers, and saw her bitter, triumphant smile.

For a few moments it was enough to caress the smooth wood. *This is the only thing I have never betrayed! If I must die, perhaps I can make a deathsong that will live!* But first he must praise those who had gone before.

He struck a chord on the harp, frowned, and twisted the pegs to tune it, plucked again, adjusting until he was satisfied with the harmonies, grinning as the snake by his leg lifted its head and eased away.

"*Slain are the warriors,*" he sang, "*shields are shattered,*

> *Bold heroes boast on bench no more,*
> *Nor to the fray fares the feeder of eagles,*
> *Wound-serpents sleep in the hearts of the slain—*"

That was a good line. "*Wound-serpents sleep. . . .*" he repeated, looking around him, and indeed, the snakes around him seemed to be listening to his song.

> "*Red blood runs to feed the rivers,*
> *Horses of Hun-lords trample the heroes.*"

—As they had the Goths, so long ago. He had never finished his song about Airmanareik. But now he could do so, when like the Goths his people had perished, and like their king, he faced his own end.

Feeling the familiar prickle of excitement that came when the words were flowing, he sang on.

> "*Enslaved the sons of earls, or scattered,*
> *Wound-serpents sleep in the hearts of the slain—*"

He looked up at Attila, grinning. *Do you understand now what I am doing? The harp is a weapon after all.* He struck the chords boldly and the serpents lowered their ugly heads and grew still.

> "*The lord of peoples alone lay waiting,*
> *Finished with fighting the proud folk warden,*

Airmanareik knew his need was upon him.
Wound-serpents sleep in the hearts of the slain—"

Need drives us all, he thought grimly. That Airmanareik had killed himself, all knew, but was it in despair or had another purpose compelled him? *What good can come from the death of a king?*

"Unwished the wyrd for this king woven,
His own life all he now could offer,
Given to the gods to guard his people,
Wound-serpents sleep in the hearts of the slain—"

Above him, the Goths in the crowd were muttering angrily, but Gundohar no longer cared. As the words had come to him, so had come meaning. Like the Goth-king, life was all that he had left to give.

He repeated the chords. *Holy gods, will you receive me? I give myself gladly if you will preserve whatever remnant of my people remains!* It came to him then that this sacrifice had always been inherent in his kingship. Gudrun had taunted him for having destroyed Sigfrid, whose strength might have defended them. But Sigfrid had already saved him, nine years ago, laying down his life in place of the Niflungar to bring health to the Burgund land.

He must not die without honoring that sacrifice.

"Sigfrid also, the son of Sigmund,
Fafnar he fought and fearless, felled him,
Won from the Wurm a wondrous hoard,
Wound-serpents sleep in the hearts of the slain—"

Sigfrid's sword had found the heart of the shape-shifter who had guarded his treasure in the semblance of a wurm. There was a symmetry here that he needed to understand.

> *"Happy the hero when all men hailed him,*
> *Woeful the wolf by Wyrd ensnared;*
> *The Leaf King's life blood fed the leaves,*
> *Wound-serpents sleep in the hearts of the slain—"*

He looked up, and saw that Gudrun was weeping. But he himself had forgotten the fear that had sickened him. Even the ache in his leg was unimportant now. This was truth—the serpent and the spear were the same. But it was Hagano who had speared Sigfrid. What did his death mean?

> *"Upon the Tree the truest traitor,*
> *The spearman speared in sacrifice,*
> *Hagano's heart a holy harvest;*
> *Wound-serpents sleep in the hearts of the slain—"*

The words came faster; he was very close to understanding now. He gazed around him, seeing in the asps and the adders the Wurm on his banner. How many times he had fed that serpent blood in battle. . . . Attila had meant to mock him, but it was true—those that surrounded him now were his kin.

I choose this! he thought, *this death, this victory! Do you hear me, Wodan?* He laughed as the wind lifted his hair.

> *"Beneath the ground the Gundwurm guests,*
> *By serpents circled, I sit and sing,*
> *To win from Wyrd a warrior's meed."*

Gundohar let his voice out fully; it seemed to him he had never sung so well. Attila looked angry; he was giving orders to one of his men. *Bring a spear to finish me since your serpents will not help you!* he thought, but he did not stop singing. *I have won, Lord of Horses! You cannot break me now!*

> *"Wound-serpents sleep in the hearts of the slain—"*

A warrior's meed, and a poet's mead—for him they were the same. There was movement above, but he paid no attention, for it seemed to him that from somewhere within came the laughter he had heard when the god spoke through Hagano. *Wodan, you have given me the gift I asked for after all!*

"*Wodan's will the word-hoard opens—*" he sang.

Something like a pale brown rope came writhing through the air. It landed on Gundohar's belly; he jerked, harp-strings jangling. Muscular coils bunched, for a moment he saw clearly the sand adder's horned snout, and a warrior's instinct brought his hand up to bat it away. Too quick for sight it blurred toward him, missed his fingers and struck his chest, fangs piercing his tunic and the flesh beneath like red-hot wires, back teeth catching in the cloth.

The breath went out of him in a grunt. The adder was chewing at his chest as if it meant to burrow to his heart. Gundohar looked down at it, feeling the burning already beginning to radiate from the wound. He thought, *I should not have moved.*

From above came cries, gasps of horror or satisfaction. Gritting his teeth, Gundohar grasped the adder behind the head, yanked it loose, and hurled it away. A wave of dizziness made him blink. *Was this your gift too?*

He fumbled for the harp, managed to strike the strings once more.

> "*Brew of bards to banquet brings,*
> *Allfather bears me ale from Asgard.*"

Now his whole chest was tingling, but where the snake had struck him was a spreading numbness. A man bit in hand or foot might take days to die, and then it would be from putrefaction of the wound. But over the heart was a different matter, it would seem.

He looked up, saw Gudrun's white face, her eyes huge as she stared back at him. Suddenly he felt very ill. Sight darkened and he blinked, it returned and he tried to smile at her, then turned to his harp again.

Had he sung the refrain to that last stave? He could not remember. He tried to make the next chord, though his fingers did not seem to want to obey him. But he could hear a ringing in his ears, as if from some distant song. He pulled in breath, adding his own harmony.

> *"Idises come, my days are ended;*
> *Fearless, I follow fallen heroes—"*

His vision had gone again; the harp slid from his fingers. Chills racked his body despite the heat of the sun. *Finish it*—he told himself. *You must finish the song!*

> *"Life I will let go . . . with laughter. . . ."*

Gundohar's lips moved, but he could no longer hear what he sang. Agony stabbed down his left arm and he felt himself falling. Someone was calling him; he tried to turn toward the sound.

"*Gundohar . . . will you come to me?*"

Home . . . he thought hazily, *I would go where Galamvara and my people are. . . .*

"*Ride the hidden paths, Burgund King. . . .* " came the call, "*Your sister will show you the way.*"

The only one who heard the last verse was the god.

> *"A wound-serpent sleeps in the heart of the slain—"*

Gudrun watched over her dead.

They had laid out the bodies in Attila's hall, shrouded in linen, with lamps at their head and feet. Hagano's was bloodless as white marble, his flesh already shrinking on the bones so that one could glimpse the shape of the skull beneath the skin. But Gundohar had swollen, his skin black with the poison. Though he had died first, Gislahar was less marred than his brothers; his face still bore that look of faint surprise. There was, as yet, only the faintest scent of corruption, though in this warm weather, that must change soon.

Ah, Brunahild, she thought grimly, *I am the Walkyrja now—see how I Choose the slain!*

But her thinking went no further. When Sigfrid died she had at least been able to hate his murderers; but these deaths were like some catastrophe of nature; they had changed the landscape of her soul, and she was lost. Where now was the god who had pursued her? Was he going to abandon her as well now that she had done his will?

But that was not entirely true—she remembered the moment of insight that had come to her the day before. *He did not force me to watch Hagano suffering, he only made use of me once I had chosen to come.* And it had been her own idea, she thought, to take the harp to Gundohar. He, at least, had died with joy. *We are tools that shape ourselves . . . with which the god must work as best he can. . . .*

The lampflames flared fearfully as the door opened. Attila came in, dressed for traveling in a lapped tunic of leather and high boots with colored stitching, his sword at his side.

"They said I find you here." He hooked his thumbs through his belt, watching her. "I leave at dawn."

Gudrun shrugged. He had never bothered to inform her about his plans before, when there had been, if not love, at least respect between them. Why should she care now?

"I ride west to join Aetius. . . ." he said. She looked up then, and he laughed.

"To finish killing my people?" she asked bitterly.

"The Burgunds—all that matter—are dead. We fight the Visigoths now."

"And what compensation will you give me for these murders?" Gudrun pointed at the three bodies on their biers.

"What price do you pay for the death of my son?" he answered her.

"Apsik was my son, too!" she exclaimed, getting to her

feet to face him. That loss was a deeper pain beneath the others, that she had tried not to feel. To be reminded shattered the insight she had just begun to attain.

"Then why did you put him in danger?"

Gudrun felt the color leave her face. "Hagano killed him because he found out you wanted to make Apsik king over the Burgunds," she cried. It was not her fault; she had not meant harm!

"You send the child to taunt him—"

"Are you angry because my brother spoiled your plot?" Only by attacking him could she deny his words. "You no longer need a son by me—there are no Burgunds left to rule!"

"That is true." Attila bared his teeth in another smile. "You have no people, no kindred, no family to defend you, and no son to bring you power."

"I can have other children—" she began, but he shook his head.

"Not by me. I give no more children to a woman who sacrifices her own brothers for revenge. Brunahild avenged herself on her lover, not her blood-kin. Even Rudegar you taunt to his death. You are alone, with no one but yourself to blame!"

"I can blame *you*—" she said dangerously. "These deaths are at least as much your doing as mine, though you made the serpents do your killing for you and put my hand on the spear. It was you who invited my brothers here!"

"I do what must be done for the sake of my nation." Attila's voice had an edge that made her shiver. "Like Gundohar when he ordered death of Sigfrid. I do not need to explain my deeds to *you!*"

"For the sake of the Huns?" Gudrun caught the note of hysteria in her laughter and caught herself on a gasp. "I think you do it for your own glory!"

He looked at her, and for a moment she found it hard to breathe.

"They are the same. . . . I am Lord of Horses, Master of

the Sword of War. I will be khan of khans. Your god says it. You yourself say it, when the spirits take you. I would have ruled your people through your son, but you killed him. It no longer matters. My warriors take your eastern lands even now. I will rule from the Danuvius to the Liger one day."

Gudrun shook her head. "The Emperor Attila! Does Aetius know?"

"Woman, be silent!" he exclaimed.

The trembling began to shake all her limbs; her teeth chattered, her hearing was filled with the rush of great wings.

"You speak of my prophecies—would you like to hear my cursing? Ask *them*"—she pointed at the bodies—"if you doubt that my curses strike home! As you betrayed those to whom you swore oaths of alliance, may those you call allies now one day betray you! You scorn me as a woman, may you one day die at a woman's hand! And those sons your queen has given you, the ones you prize so highly, may they rend and tear each other as the Niflungar have done until they, too, are destroyed!"

His face darkened. She saw his arm blur; felt the blow, and suddenly she was on the ground. She tried to get up, but the dagger from his belt was suddenly in one hand, the other gripping her hair. The point pricked her throat and she stilled, breathing hard.

"Are you going to kill me?" The knife was very sharp. She could feel blood on her neck already. It would be faster than the serpent's tooth or the spear. She had only to press forward and it would let out her lifeblood. Her brothers would be avenged, and she would follow them. Such a simple solution—why had she not thought of it before?

She took a deep breath, muscles tensing—and in the same instant Attila, too good a horseman not to have interpreted her movement, grabbed her braid and jerked her head away.

"Kill you? That would be a waste—" The knife flashed,

she felt her scalp sting as he began to saw at her hair with the sharp edge of his blade. She screamed as the first pale strand fell.

"What are you doing? I am your wife! You cannot dishonor me this way!"

"Are you?" he snarled. "Our marriage was for the Burgund alliance, but that is over. You care for the child of Sigfrid and protect her, but not for mine—" he added. "Did you think I would not know Sunnilda is gone? What use do I have for you now?"

The khan grunted and his grip twisted; he severed another hank of hair. Gudrun jerked and clawed at his leg, but a knee in the small of her back forced her down again.

"You and your kin cost me many good men. Now you have nothing. You repay by serving Ereka, my queen!"

His weight crushed her to the floor. When she tried to heave him off he shoved her face into the dirt so that she could not breathe. Consciousness came and went in red waves as handfuls of hair were severed and cast aside. Burgund law, she thought dimly, exacted a heavy weregild for the cutting of a free woman's hair. . . .

After what seemed a long time, he released her. She heard his breathing harsh in the silence; despite his taunts, this had not left him unmoved. She gathered enough force to turn her head, sucked in air, and with it, a fragile clarity. Her husband was moving toward the doorway, his shadow lengthening across the floor.

"You have conquered . . . the Burgunds," she whispered, and saw him pause. "But you cannot win against Wyrd, which is shaped by your own will. The Niflungar destroyed . . . themselves. Fight all the world, Attila—you cannot fight Wodan. He will use your own might to bring you down."

"Maybe . . ." Attila said quietly. "But all the world will know I lived!"

For a moment longer he stood between her and the light. Then he turned and she saw him no more.

* * *

Gudrun lay as still as her dead while the day faded into darkness, breathing in the faint sweet scent of their mortality, as if Attila had killed her body as he had tried to destroy her soul. Night had fully fallen when she became aware of torchlight. Someone came in—to her dimmed sight they seemed two shadows—and knelt beside her.

"Khatun . . ." More than the voice, she recognized the scent of old leather and herbs that marked the White Heron. But who was with her? "Get up now. It is time to go."

Gudrun moaned and tried to turn her face away, but the old shamaness held her, sponging her with a damp cloth, scowling when she saw what had been done to her hair. Presently she began to feel sensation returning, and drank from the skin bottle the *kam-kadin* put into her hand. It held some kind of tea, the sharp taste of mint covering other herbs, that cleared the mists away. She sat up, shivering. Her shorn head felt weightless, her body permeable as if she had lost her skin.

"Eat this—" said the second hooded figure in an accent that belonged to the Rhenus. "It will bind you to earth again."

Gudrun turned, staring. The old woman who was holding out the flap of thin Hunnish bread was Huld. She started to speak, but the Walkyriun gestured for silence. Outside she heard men's voices. Quickly the two women draped a Gaulish cloak around her, drawing up the hood to hide her hair.

As they helped her to her feet, Thiudimir came in. "The pyres are ready. We have tried to do them honor. May my men take the bodies now?" He spoke to Gudrun, but he would not meet her eyes. Why so careful? Nothing he could do would hurt her or hers now.

Men came in and took up the bodies. The three women followed them out into the night, like norns come to witness the final knotting of the wyrd they had wound.

They had built the pyres in the meadow near the pit of serpents. The larger, on which they were burning the bodies of the warriors, was aflame already. Gudrun was grateful that the wind was blowing from behind her, carrying the odor of burned meat away. The piled logs of the second pyre waited. Rudegar's body lay there already. She watched dry-eyed as they set the biers of her brothers beside him.

There was a little pause. "Khatun," said Thiudimir, "is there anything that you would say?"

She stared at him. When Sigfrid burned, she had been swift both to curse and to praise. That was another lifetime, when she had been innocent, and young. "Gundohar was the bard," she said harshly, "and he sang the deathsong for them all. Remember his words! For what they have done, good or ill, Wodan must reward them now."

Thiudimir bowed to her and took a torch from one of his men.

"In the dwellings of our people women are weeping because of what these men have done. They were valiant allies and worthy enemies. Even I could not have overcome them if they had not been worn out with war. Curse or bless them, but do not deny them honor. We shall not see such heroes in this land again." He cast the torch onto the pyre.

For a few moments it sputtered, as if reluctant to burn. Then a licking flame found the oil-soaked brush that had been packed between the logs and exploded in a tongue of fire. Swiftly the pyre became a furnace, and the watchers had to stand away.

"Thank you . . ." Gudrun said softly to *kam-kadin*. "I hope the queen will not punish you for helping me."

"The queen says bind you, but Thiudimir wins you this night to honor your dead. But you go by morning or Ereka makes you bondswoman in her hall."

"I will take your place here—" said Huld. "I still have magic enough so that they will not know."

"But what will happen to you after?" exclaimed Gudrun. "Can Heimar protect you?"

"Heimar is gone. After Bertriud died he began to fear. He has taken Asliud away with him to the north, beyond the reach of Attila's arm."

"Then you are in danger. Why are you helping me?"

For a moment Huld was silent. Then she nodded toward the fire. "Sigfrid and Brunahild are avenged. I will not fight the god."

Gudrun shivered. Wodan had used their opposition. What, she wondered, would have happened if they had all, even Sigfrid, known how to work with him? Had the god intended to destroy the Burgunds? What purpose was Wodan working *for*?

"Come back with me to the Rhenus," she said after a little while. "I will find a place for you."

"You will be hard put to find a place to lay your own head, and I could not bear the journey," the old woman replied. "The priests would call me a witch in Christian lands, but here they know how to value a *haliuruna's* wisdom. And I have lived long enough to see Brunahild's daughter grown. It does not much matter what happens to me now."

I might say the same, thought Gudrun. But as she watched flame glowing through the shell of Gundohar's body she remembered the duty he had laid upon her. Perhaps when it was accomplished she would die, but not until she had returned to the Burgund lands.

"Then do one more thing for me," she said to Huld. "Go to my *ger*, and put shoes and clothing for my journey into a bag. In my chest you will find a long pouch of doeskin with a rod and a neck ring inside. Pack them as well. They are the last of Sigfrid's treasure, and I will not leave them for Ereka to defile."

It took a long time for the pyre to burn down. As the sky began to pale, Gudrun saw that though all else was ash, the hearts of Gundohar and Hagano, which Thiudimir had recovered and placed with his body, had not burned. Though the *kam-kadin* was urging her to flee, she wrapped them in a silk veil and placed them in the bag with the rod and the ring.

Then she kissed Huld and the White Heron and began the long journey home.

To those set to guard her, three women seemed to stand there still. If they saw anything other, they thought it a spirit and looked quickly away. But even those who looked longest did not suspect it was Gudrun who was stealing past them, for what they saw was an old woman with two strong warriors striding behind her, who passed swiftly into the mists of dawn.

Chapter 18 ⚲ The Black Goat

Land of the Burgunds
Fall, A.D. 437–Spring, A.D. 438

Gudrun made her way homeward through a land filled with rumors of war. The Romans, it was said, had crushed Tibatto's rebellion at last, and the young emperor, to show his gratitude, had made Aetius consul. The Visigoths, pursued by Litorius, were retreating all the way back to Tolosa. The land between the Moenus and the Nicer was full of Huns, burning farmsteads, killing men, and carrying off women and children for the slave markets of the Empire. Where the Hun warriors passed, their families followed, rolling forward with their wagons and their flocks and gathering up the wandering animals the fleeing Burgunds had left behind.

As Gudrun traveled westward, she found the roads full of refugees seeking their kindred on the other side of the Rhenus. In that confusion, no one took note of one gaunt and crop-haired wanderer.

She had thought of going to her uncle in Batava to rejoin Sunnilda, but as the dangers of the countryside became more apparent, she knew she dared not try to travel with the child. Whether it was Huld's magic or Thiudimir's friendship that had prevented an immediate pursuit, Gudrun did not know. But she was sure that Attila had already sent watchers to Batava who would report her presence if she appeared there. He might not want her himself, but no doubt he still considered her his property. For that reason alone he would pursue her. She was better off alone.

Her own safety was a matter of indifference to her, nor was she lonely. She might seem undefended, but two ghosts went always with her, Hagano on her left and on her right side Gundohar. No one else seemed to be able to see them. Gudrun could not always see them herself. But they talked to her constantly. She had always thought that Hagano hated Sigfrid, but she was discovering now the dreadful intimacy that can exist between a murderer and the spirit he has wronged.

For a time she rode on a trader's wagon, cooking for the man and sharing his bed. It was not a hardship; she scarcely noticed his brief and clumsy caresses. But when he began to speak of taking her back with him to Argentoratum she slipped away one night while he was snoring. She would have had to leave him soon in any case, for her way lay northward. At the next holding, an enameled brooch from the bag she had brought with her bought her a shaggy black mare. After that she made better time.

After that sodden spring, the weather had relented with a summer that was golden, although in the lands between the Moenus and the Nicer there were few to work the fields. Sometimes Gudrun saw Hun war parties, but her ghosts always warned her in time to avoid them. She slept under hedges or in the sheds of burned-out farms, or sometimes at the campfires of other refugees.

Though the fields were fallow, the unsettled times had sprouted a flourishing crop of rumors. Some said that Gundohar had been killed when the Huns attacked Borbetomagus, along with the rest of the royal kin. Others, who had heard of the journey of the Niflungar to Hunland, said that the khan had murdered him there. Some murmured that Gudrun had slain her own son by the khan and fed him to his father in order to avenge her kin. Others said she had killed both Hagano and Gundohar with her own hands, and that she herself had been killed by Attila or one of his men in revulsion against the deed. Sometimes she herself was not certain what was true.

Gudrun rather liked the story about her own death. There were times when she felt as much a ghost as the two shadows who walked with her, a hag-spirit like those who screamed through the treetops when Wodan hunted the skies. But she was not yet free to drown her memories in death or madness. She heard always that whisper, *"Take me back to my people, Gudrun, take me home...."*

As she neared the Rhenus the stories grew wilder and the refugees more numerous. Now she began to encounter folk who had fled eastward from Borbetomagus mingling with the others like conflicting currents when two floods meet. Just before Midsummer, she heard, the Huns had come upon them. At first, seeing the Roman standards, no one had been concerned, but then they began to loot and burn. Godomar had summoned the war-host, but the message reached many late or not at all. Perhaps that was just as well, for all the warriors who had gone out to face the foe had been slain.

Twenty thousand dead.... Twenty thousand Burgunds had been killed, the flower of their fighting men, and Godomar with them. The refugees were too hard-pressed themselves to spare much grief for others, but from time to time she would hear someone mourning for the might of Godomar, or the beauty of Gislahar, and most of all, for the wisdom of Gundohar their king.

At such times the bag she had carried so carefully all the way from Hunland seemed very heavy. *Don't blame Gundohar,* she thought. *His heart is with you!* Only when folk looked at her strangely did she realize she had laughed.

At the end of the moon of Harvest, when any farmers whose fields were still untrampled were getting in the last of the grain, Gudrun and her ghosts came to the city of the Gundwurm. No one was manning the ferry, but she found a small boat and, abandoning the horse, managed to scull herself across the river to the western shore.

The red stone of the Roman walls was scorched where they had burned the gates of the city. Gudrun wept as she made her way through the streets, remembering houses which were now blackened shells decked with flowers and draped with hangings for her wedding. Not many still lived in the town, and those she met, hurrying homeward at day's ending, had little attention to spare for a ragged wanderer. She came to the square and stopped, looking around her. The little church had been spared, but the basilica had burned down. Still, most of the royal hall seemed to be standing; at the gate a Roman legionary stood at attention.

Folk said the royal women had been made prisoner, but no one was sure where. Apparently there was still someone here to guard. "*Go to the queen,*" whispered Gundohar. "*Find Kustubaira,*" murmured Hagano.

Though the main entrance was watched, the gate to the garden, overgrown with vines, was not. It creaked a little as Gudrun pulled it open, but as she had suspected, there were not enough folk left here for anyone to have heard. The air was pungent with the scent of herbs warmed by the sun. She took a deep breath, something that had been tensed for longer than she could remember beginning to ease.

My own earth . . . she thought, coming to a halt. For two moons need had driven her; now the next step seemed impossible. Once, this place had been the center of her world. Memory rose up to engulf her—the scent of soil and the fragrance of growing things, Sigfrid's kisses as he bore her down on the path, the feel of earth on her hands when they brought his body home. She did not know how long she stood there, but when she came to herself again, dusk was falling and her cheeks were wet with tears.

"Ursula told me there was a stranger in the garden," said a cool voice behind her, the words slightly accented in the way of the western Goths. "Who are you? How did you get in here?"

Gudrun turned, saw a stocky woman with brownish hair coppered by the rays of the setting sun, a woman whose eyes widened as that last light fell full on Gudrun's face, then turned upward as she swayed and collapsed to the ground.

Gudrun hurried forward. The other woman was beginning to stir as she reached her, murmuring, "Gundohar . . ." Gudrun did not need a ghost to tell her that this was her brother's queen.

Galamvara reached out, then she blinked, and her arm fell back. "You're not Gundohar."

Gudrun sat back on her heels. Had she grown so thin that they could be mistaken, or was it his wraith that the woman had seen? She cradled her pack with its precious burden against her breast.

"I am Gudrun." She had meant to add, *I have come home*. . . . But Galamvara had called her a stranger, and even in the garden it was true. The queen's eyes glistened, but despite her faint, Gudrun guessed Galamvara was not a woman who lost control easily.

"They said . . ." She swallowed. ". . . That my lord was killed in the land of the Huns. Is it true?" Gudrun nodded, but when she opened her mouth to reply, the queen held up her hand. "Not yet. Kustubaira will want to hear your story as well, and I do not know . . . if I could bear to listen to it a second time."

Gudrun nodded. It would be hard enough to tell it even once.

"And so they burned. . . ." Gudrun finished her bald recital, feeling as if those last words had been dragged up from her gut. "By now Thiudimir will have raised a mound above their bones. . . ." Galamvara poured out more wine, while the other woman, Kustubaira, watched with burning eyes. She wore her gown of coarse brown stuff as if it were patrician silk. A white veil covered her hair.

"That is all?" she asked.

Gudrun swallowed wine. "All that I can tell." She could not explain her own actions, which despite two moons of self-examination, she herself did not understand. And these were Christian women; she could not tell them about the god.

"Attila killed them but he could not defeat them. Hagano died like a hero. Gundohar died like a king. He . . . spoke of his love for you."

"We warned them . . ." said Galamvara dully. "They knew the danger, but the king judged it worth the chance. Could not *you* have warned them? They would have been too late to save our war-host, but if they had escaped they could lead us now!"

Gudrun shook her head. "The khan kept the news of the attack on Borbetomagus even from me. That was the hardest for Gundohar, to know his people in danger and he not there."

"Who rules now?"

At the whisper, Gudrun blinked and looked behind her. *Be still, brother,* she thought, *I have not forgotten you.* Galamvara was eyeing her oddly when she turned back again.

"Who rules here now?" she asked.

"The Romans, or no one—" said the queen bitterly. "There are only enough soldiers to 'protect' us here. Most of the servants have fled. Ursula cooks for us, and the lad Andulf helps as he can. The Roman landholders who were not in the battle try to maintain order, but the land is full of refugees from across the river, and runaway slaves and masterless men prey on them and on each other. There is no man of the old blood to bring them to order again."

"I have heard that your father has made peace with Aetius. Send to him," said Gudrun. "Ask him to send Gundrada's son Gundiok with enough men to support his claim. Even Rome will not see a threat in a boy."

Galamvara nodded. "Gundohar spoke of that. He foresaw all that might happen—he *knew!*" She shook her head in frustration.

"He knew," said Kustubaira quietly, "but he thought there was still a chance to stop it. So thought they all, who followed him." She turned to Gudrun. "Will your people follow Gundiok, if he comes?"

"If I tell them it was the wish of their king."

"You can sleep in my chamber," said the queen, "and we must find you some clothes. Mine would be too small, but Kustubaira is tall—"

Gudrun shook her head. "I cannot move freely with a guard on the door, or in the clothes of a queen. And there is another thing. Word of my return may spread among the people, but the Romans must not know it is more than a rumor, for what comes to their ears will be known by the khan. Can you write? Give me the letter for Theoderid and some money and I will find a messenger."

"I understand," said the queen, but she looked unhappy. "We are watched, but I can let it be known that I support you. Stay here tonight at least, and rest."

When she had gone out to fetch some food Gudrun rested her head in her hands. She had thought she could not sleep in this place of memories, but perhaps exhaustion would claim her after all. Beside her, Kustubaira stared into the candleflame, the light sculpting her face to beauty.

"Now that she is gone," she said in a low voice, "tell me the truth about Hagano."

Gudrun sat up, staring at her. She could well understand why her half brother had loved this woman, but not why Kustubaira had married him.

"You would not believe me."

The Roman woman gave a bitter laugh. "I know that my husband was a very strange man. Did he find peace, at the last?"

Gudrun shivered, remembering. "He found . . . ecstasy. There was a time when I hated him above all men. But he had grown—" She shook her head at a surge of emotion which was not her own. "Perhaps because you taught him how to love."

Kustubaira turned away quickly, weeping. Gudrun wanted to join her, but her eyes remained dry. *I believed I knew love, when I had Sigfrid,* she thought then. *But how quickly I turned to hating. When I shared Hagano's death I felt his joy, but ashes are all that remain.* She knew now how Brunahild had felt, when love and hate alike were spent and all she could do was carry out her own self-condemnation. *I will do this last thing—try to make amends—but when it is done I do not think my own life will be long.*

The letter to King Theoderid was ready the next morning, and Gudrun went out the same way she had come. It took her two days to find a trustworthy messenger, but presently the letter was dispatched, and they had only to wait until Gundiok should come. Gudrun became once more a wanderer, moving through the countryside with a sack of herbs and treating what ills she could with the remedies the White Heron had taught her. Some claimed to see in her a resemblence to the old queen, Grimahild, but only to the elders did she confess that she was Gudrun. Wherever she went, she spoke of the last days of the Burgund kings and of Gundohar's wish that Gundiok should be his heir.

When the little troop of Visigoths came clattering up the road from Argentoratum at the end of the Hunter's Moon they found a populace well disposed to make them welcome. Gudrun watched them ride in, and her breath caught, seeing in Gundiok's face, just beginning to firm and lengthen as childhood slipped away, a reflection of what her brothers had been when they were all young.

That night the newcomers feasted with the queen. When Galamvara returned to her rooms, Gudrun was waiting, in her lap the carved wooden casket in which she had placed her brothers' hearts.

"Call Kustubaira," she said. "There is one thing left for us to do."

"What do you need?" asked the queen. She was dressed in white, for mourning, but the fabrics were silk and damask, with pearls hanging down in the fashion of the Byzantines. "Our sorrow remains, but you have given us hope again."

Gudrun shook her head. "When my brothers' bodies were put on the pyre, their hearts did not burn. Since that time their spirits have walked with me. They must be put to rest. Then I will be free."

Galamvara looked at the casket and her face grew as white as her veil. "I will call Father Vidulf—"

Gudrun shook her head. "And let him and Father Priscus fight over which will have the honor of burying them? Gundohar called on Wodan at the end, and Hagano was never a christened man. Together they died, and together they should lie. Will you dare the night and help me to bury them in Sigfrid's howe?"

It was after midnight, and the new king of the Burgunds was asleep in his bed, when the royal women of the Niflungar set out to perform their last service to the old. The moon was just past the full and the skies clear; they needed no lantern to find their way. Swathed in dark cloaks, they passed through the streets of the city and out along the road to the water meadow. At that hour there were few to see them; those who did thought them the idises of the Niflungar, come to bless the new king.

Sigfrid's howe had been heaped high. The spring floods had eaten away at one corner, but it had been built strongly, braced with timbers. In time, thought Gudrun, the river might take it entirely, but it would last as long as the Burgunds in this land. And as long as they lived here the folk would remember him—the top and sides of his mound were covered with stones that people had laid there to honor his memory. She cut a square of sod just above ground level, from the side that faced toward Borbetomagus, and began to dig into the mound.

Though she had wrapped her brothers' hearts in leeks and herbs, as they dried they had shriveled. The box that held them was pitifully small to hold the organs that had felt such passions; it did not take her long to dig the few feet needed to set it safely in the ground. Galamvara and Kustubaira stood watch while she was working, clutching their cloaks close against the chill and glancing around at every murmur of the river or rustle in the trees. Once, Gudrun might have done the same. It was a measure, she thought, of how far she had walked on her mother's road that now the dangers she feared most were not in the world outside, but within.

She straightened, rubbing her back, and set the spade aside. "It is done. Say your farewells."

Kustubaira, who had been holding the casket, murmured a few words in Latin and made the sign of the Cross above it. *Hagano loved her*, thought Gudrun. *He will not mind a blessing from her god.* She handed the box to Galamvara.

"The church, with its carved stones, belongs to history—" said the queen. "I have heard what Gundohar said when they made this mound. He did his duty with his mind and soul, but his heart was given to the legends. It is fitting that it should lie in a hero's howe."

"Hagano was a creature of the old magic, and though I imperil my soul to say so, I would not change him. He struggled against his own bonds and broke them; he could not set me free. My beloved," murmured Kustubaira, "I give you back to the wind and the river. I will pray that somehow your light and mine may one day be the same."

Gudrun took the casket, feeling it suddenly grown heavy, as if more than those two shriveled bits of meat were held within. Trembling, she thrust it as far as she could into the hole she had made in the mound, then began to fill it up again. The scent of the moist earth was dizzying in its intensity; she drew in deep breaths, wondering if she would faint before she was done. But at last it was finished and she sat back, the grave soil still on her hands. Wind sighed in the leaves of the ash trees and she shivered, though it was not cold.

"Oh my brothers, we did such scathe to one another as the children of one mother should never know. I hated you for killing Sigfrid, but you showed me how Wyrd can weave a web so tightly that the only way a man can win is to accept his doom. Sigfrid did not flee from it; neither did you. Therefore, I give you into his protection, not in revenge, but because he, of all men, can understand why you died. The people come sometimes to make offerings to his spirit, here by the river that gives life to the land. Those gifts shall feed you as well, that you may continue to watch over them."

She waited, listening. She could feel power in the howe, but the voices that had haunted her for three moons were still. After a time she got to her feet and turned to the others. For a moment they held each other, three forms merging into one.

Gudrun remembered how Brunahild had embraced her before she mounted Sigfrid's pyre. The touch of the other woman's cool hands was suddenly as palpable as Galamvara's; she could hear Brunahild's voice at her ear—"*Remember that the Well from which the Lady spoke to you also holds Wodan's hidden Eye....*"

"It grows late. We must go back," said Galamvara.

"You must go," answered Gudrun. "I will watch here until dawn."

"And then you will return to us?" asked Kustubaira.

"Go. The young king will need you. I would only be a liability."

Galamvara sighed. She was a queen, and understood how it must be. "If you have need of anything, you have only to ask...."

Gudrun nodded. But both of them knew that what she needed most was beyond the power of even a queen to supply.

Gudrun stayed by the mound until morning, bidding farewell to her memories. Then she went down to the river, and found a fisherman to row her across to the other side. By evening she had reached her mother's old house in the Charcoal Burners' Forest. For seven years it had been abandoned; thatch had blown away, letting in the rain, and in one corner the mud plastering had melted, but the wooden framework was still sound. With hard work, she could make it snug again before the winter storms arrived.

She had learned long ago that work was a good anodyne for sorrow. If she worked herself to exhaustion, thatching or plastering, gathering wood or nuts from the forest, she would sleep as soon as she lay down, too deeply to remember her dreams. One day a shaggy black she-goat wandered into her yard, bleating mournfully for someone to milk her, and soon Gudrun was making cheese. Sigfrid had taught her some of his skills in the forest. She snared waterfowl and rabbits, dried their meat, and wove strips of furry hide into blankets or stuffed feathers into sacks to make a mattress; sometimes her traps would even net her a deer.

It was harder when the snow began to fall and she had to huddle indoors. She had got some wool, but spinning did not keep you from thinking—quite the opposite. When the body's motions became instinctive, the mind ranged freely though the fields of memory. When she fell ill just after Yule, she almost welcomed the pain. Fever made thinking impossible. Perhaps, she thought hopefully, when it got too bad she would die.

She had just enough strength to feed the fire and to drink from the teats of the goat, who had been brought into the stable at the other end of the house when the snows began to fall, and came to her at morn and eve when her bag grew full.

Gudrun's fever reached its height on a night of storm when gusts of sleet battered the forest. The houseposts quivered with each blast; timbers creaked as the roof flexed to the wind. She tossed on her bed, pushing away her covers as she burned. Then the chills would take her and she would burrow back into the tangle of furs, coughing.

With each breath a spear of pain stabbed her chest; in her confusion she thought she saw Hagano behind it, and begged him to tear out her heart and be done.

The pain became an agony that darkened her vision, but she could still hear the roaring of the wind. It tore at the thatching, an icy gust blasted through the opening; she glimpsed wind-tossed treetops and tattered clouds racing before the moon. Clouds or shadows? Shadows or figures whose darkness glittered where the light caught harness and helms and the tips of spears? Above the scream of the wind wild horns wailed.

The riders came with a rush and a tumult that battered the senses. She strained to see Sigfrid, but it was Hagano who appeared before her, beckoning with his spear.

"I have no mount—" she began, but the black she-goat was suddenly beside her, tossing her curving horns. In that moment it seemed quite natural for Gudrun to sit up and swing her leg across the shaggy back. As she settled herself she felt the goat growing larger. Her coat was so thick Gudrun's legs sank into it, so long it nearly brushed the ground. She felt strong muscles bunch beneath her and buried her fingers in the thick hair, gripping tightly as the she-goat leaped through the tear in the roof, balanced a moment on its thatching, then launched herself into the air.

She had seen this before, these spectral riders, these ghastly hounds, men with their death wounds gaping, and others not quite human, riding skeletal steeds. She had seen, and fled before them. Now it seemed quite natural to let the black goat bear her through the skies. Perhaps it was because she recognized so many of the riders. There went Unald and Deorberht, Rudegar and Wolcgar, and beyond them her brothers Godo and Gislahar, men who had fallen in Hunland and on the Rhenus all galloping together. She named one man after another as her steed sped past them. Tonight the war-host of the Burgunds was riding once more.

Hagano led them, but she did not see Gundohar. *He stays*

with the land, with the living, in the mound . . . she thought, clasping the goat's neck as the wind whipped her hair. Branches thrashed furiously below them; the wind of their passing swirled snow from the fields and whisked the cold waters of the Rhenus to froth. But the doors of the houses were barred, the windows of Borbetomagus shuttered; no living man went abroad when the Wild Hunt rode the skies.

Ahead galloped an advance guard less human in aspect even than those who had gone before. But she recognized Grani and urged the she-goat after him, calling Sigfrid's name. He turned. "Let me ride with you!" she cried.

"Now you understand what it is to be both betrayer and betrayed." Sorrow filled his eyes. "But you do not yet belong here—"

"I will not go back! There is nothing there for me!"

"That is not for you to decide—" Sigfrid gestured, and the great horse that led them slackened its speed, its blur of legs, far too many of them, becoming uncannily visible. The rider turned, single eye burning from beneath the rim of his helm.

Gudrun met that gaze; pain speared through her once more. His black cloak flared outward, blotting out sky and storm and the Hunt itself and swirling her down into the dark.

She woke soaked in sweat and weak as a new lamb. But her skin was cool and the agony in her chest was gone. For a few moments, confused by the silence, she could not understand where she was. She had been riding with the dead. There had been a hole in the roof—that was true, anyway, but through the tear in the thatching shone the pale, featureless light of a winter day.

From that time on Gudrun grew stronger in body, but more sorrowful in soul. The dark days of winter began to lengthen, new buds were swelling on the branches; now the scattered snowfalls melted as soon as they fell. Autumn's melancholy had found its echo in Gudrun's mood, but these

signs of returning life depressed her spirits further, as the
other harpstrings increase the dissonance of the one that is
out of tune. She had told Galamvara that there was nothing
for her in Borbetomagus. But if there was no joy for her in
the forest, whose subtle changes had once comforted her,
then where on Middle Earth could consolation be found?

Bishop Peregrinus will take care of Sunnilda, she told herself,
*and Gundiok will lead the Burgunds with Galamvara behind him. No
one has any need of me. . . .*

One day, searching through her gear for some scraps to
patch her tunic, Gudrun's fingers brushed something hard.
Frowning, she opened the bag and pulled out the rod and
the ring. They glinted dully in the dim light from the doorway. There must be some reason she had taken the trouble
to bring them this far, she thought as she turned them
between her hands. The gold was cool and smooth, the
scratched runes caught on the rough skin of her fingers, but
she felt no magic. Perhaps the fever had burned it all away.
Even if she put the neck ring on, she thought she would
feel nothing. She did not even want to try. It was easier to
be dead. Her spirit was already extinguished; surely from
illness or starvation her body would soon follow.

Yet still the days grew brighter, mocking the shadows
within. Gudrun went through the motions of spring cleaning, shaking out her bedding and setting it to air, sweeping
the floor.

One morning early in Hretha's Moon Gudrun heard a
clamor above and came out to see a line of singing swans
undulating across the sky. She took a quick breath and felt
blood tingling beneath the skin. The sun was warm on her
back; she took off her shawl, then frowned. She had not
noticed how dirty it was before. Suddenly even her skin,
washed only in quick dabs at the spring, felt grimy. She
gathered up all the clothing she could find and rolled it
into a bundle to carry down to the riverside.

The Rhenus flowed strongly, brown with runoff from the
spring rains. Nearby, swans were feeding before they flew

northward once more. A dozen other kinds of birds paddled around them. The sky was skeined with clamoring water-fowl. But where the stream came down from the forest the water was clear.

Gudrun waded in, soaping each garment and beating it against the rocks to loosen the soil, then spreading it out to dry on the tangle of branches brought down by the floods. Behind them living trees walled the forest, their new leaves filtering the sunlight in a haze of green. A rich scent of moist earth and new growth came to her on the warm wind.

She soaped herself as well, shivering at the chill, and grimaced as she saw how thin she had become. She could see her ribs, and her hipbones poked at the skin. Even her breasts had begun to flatten. Her reflection showed her eyes grown huge above high cheekbones. Only her hair, defying Attila's barbering, had grown, falling past her shoulders in lank strands.

My husband . . . Gudrun thought, shivering. Among the Burgunds, the old punishment for a wife who left her husband was drowning, pinned by withies to the mud at the edge of the stream. Her gaze fixed on a fallen tree, its roots twisted like a wicker basket, that had lodged against the riverbank. The water below was shadowed, and very chill. If she were to force her body beneath them, it would be hard to get out again, even harder once she was weakened by the cold. Soon, she thought dully, the struggle would exhaust her, and she would sink down into the dark.

Why not? she wondered. *My brothers worked out their own Wyrd, but I still bear the blood-guilt for my son.* She shuddered, a grief that until this moment she had not accepted wracking her body. *I should have died six moons ago.* The fires of fever had not killed her; she would see what water could do.

Gudrun moved slowly through the eddies, scanning the tangle of tree roots until she found one that curved beneath the surface. Then she took a last breath, and sank down.

As the waters closed over her head, she remembered dark hair swirling in the Sacred Well, and a voice promising that from Water all gifts should come.

Memory showed her the roots arching into the depths. Arms at her sides, she thrust herself into their implacable embrace.

In moments, the pressure of pent breath made her head swim. She felt bubbles swirl past her cheeks as she let it out, clamping her throat shut, resisting the compulsion to breathe in. Instinct brought her arms up; her fingers smashed against wood as she rose, then her head banged hard, propelling her downward. Her mouth opened and she swallowed water, flailing wildly as her body, overriding her intention, fought to survive.

Something brushed her thigh; Gudrun kicked out, but it tightened hard around her legs. Awareness was beginning to flee; her struggles grew feebler. She was being pulled back, falling upward, slammed into a flat surface and pummeled until she convulsed, coughing, and gulped in a lungful of sweet spring air.

Gudrun retched, gasping, until air burned through her body like liquid fire.

"Breathe . . ." said a deep voice above her. "Breath is life. Your body wants to live."

Gudrun's face was pressed against the earth; the rich scent of the damp soil was intoxicating. In amazement she realized that it was making her hungry. Groaning, she pushed herself onto one elbow and looked up at her rescuer.

At first she had an impression of grey—grizzled hair and beard, a ragged cloak, dark now with water, sodden clothing leached of color by hard wear. These days the roads were full of such ragged wanderers, though this one looked hard muscled and healthy, as if he had not been without a home for long. One of his eyes was the blue-grey of a stormy sky. But the other had the opaque sheen of an opal. She stared, recognizing the spirit that had looked out at her from Hagano's eye, and her skin went cold.

"*Why?*" she breathed. "You were swift enough to let Sigfrid die, and Brunahild, and my brothers. Why not me?"

His dry chuckle made the hairs lift on her skin. "What use are their deaths if there is no one to remember? Your garments are dry now," he added. "Put them on."

In silence she obeyed, gathered the rest of the clothes, since he seemed to expect it, and bundled them up once more. As she worked, she eyed her rescuer, wondering if she had been mistaken. But her resurrected vision saw everything sharp-edged and glowing—each light-edged leaf on the oak tree, the force that flowed from its roots to the sky. Points of brightness sparkled in the spear the Wanderer had leaned against its trunk. The body he rode was sheathed in a haze of power, the moisture already rising from his own clothes in curls of steam.

"You are too thin. You need food. I will eat as well."

She flushed at the tone, but perhaps he was justified. Her stomach growled audibly, and he laughed.

It was not until they had returned to the house in the forest, until she had milked the goat and started simmering a gruel of dried berries with the last of her barley that she spoke to the god again.

"Here is a beaker of milk. I regret that I cannot offer you a horn of mead."

He took the wooden cup and smiled. "I have drunk the milk of a black goat before. It has more power than you know. What do you think has kept you alive so long?"

"But why? You never answered me." Gudrun sat back on her heels, staring at him.

"Men have called me faithless. Do you think I was cruel because I did not save Sigfrid from Hagano's spear, or Hagano from yours?"

"—Or yourself?" Her voice cracked as she remembered that moment of unity.

He reached out and drew her toward him. As gently as if he touched some wild thing, he stroked her hair. Gudrun wrenched her gaze away from his, knowing that if she continued to look at him she would be lost.

"Gudrun . . . it is living that is hardest. I am Lord of the Slain. Do you think I do not know?"

"And yet you descend into this body—" She touched his wrist. It was corded with vein and muscle, smooth and warm. She could feel the flow of blood beneath the skin.

"There are things that only the flesh can know. The mind reasons from the evidence of the senses—that is a way of knowledge I would learn." He looked around him, and Gudrun, following his gaze, saw texture and symmetry.

"And what about the one to whom this body belongs? What does he know?" she asked.

"I only borrow it for a day. While I am here, its owner walks in a fair dream."

Gudrun nodded, remembering how it had been when the Frowe wore her flesh on the Donarberg.

"But he himself has only borrowed it for one lifetime," the god continued. "Presently Erda will reclaim it, and his spirit will walk in the other worlds until it is time to return."

"Why should anyone want to come back again?" Gudrun exclaimed.

"Because . . ." He turned his hand beneath hers and captured it, caressing the tender palm until she shivered, tracing along the veins. "This shape you wear *is* Erda, and without Her, you are not whole. . . ."

"But You are—"

"She and I are part of one thing. That is always true, but She awakens and knows Herself in you. And when your spirit opens, she knows Me as well. Do you understand?"

I do not trust this gentleness—Gudrun remembered how Attila had courted her. *When you blasted me away from the Hunt, you wore your Face of Terror. You badgered and challenged Sigfrid and Gundohar and Hagano, forcing them to choices beyond their strength until they fell!*

"That was the only relationship they understood. . . ." he answered, though she had not spoken aloud. "Men have a harder time; most of them want always to be in control."

"What do You want?" She turned her hand in his, gripping it. *I am mad*, she thought, *setting my strength against a god!*

He raised one eyebrow. "What I always want. You. . . ." Gudrun jerked her hand away, and he let go. "You are my Bride. I want you to open yourself to me utterly. . . ."

There was a term for that. Between men, it was used as an insult. Her flesh understood it; she could feel the heavy beat of her pulse, the first throbbing sweetness between her thighs.

"You want to lie with me!" she said baldly.

"That is the language your body understands."

Gudrun twitched with every brush of cloth against her skin. The body he had pulled from the pool was alive and hungry for the feel of flesh against flesh. Attila had possessed it without touching her spirit. Wodan wanted more.

"Gudrun," he said softly. "Look at me."

She had been staring into the fire. She blinked, and found herself gazing at his blind eye. But instead of the ruined orb, she saw darkness, and then, a swirl of stars, dizzying, so beautiful it carried her spirit away. She stood up, and began to undo the fastenings of her gown.

She sensed, rather than saw, the movements of the body Wodan wore. When he bent to kiss her feet, she felt as if they were taking root in the packed earth floor. His lips moved upward, touching the sacred places one by one until power surged up from the earth along her spine and became a flame, exploding in sweetness that ran in waves of sweet fire through every limb. Then his mouth fastened on hers.

"Lady, will you receive me?" Her own spirit echoed the god's words.

Gudrun no longer perceived the ground she stood on or the roof above her head. She was every particle of humus decomposing into soil, every blade of grass. She was the goat that munched it, the sow that rooted for nuts beneath the trees. She was the she-bear suckling her cubs in the thicket. And she was in the Forest, roots linking to roots until they reached the great River, and through the River her awareness flowed outward in ever-widening circles, exulting in its own myriad manifestations.

The Power that pulsed through her body spoke in answer, *"Lord, You are welcome."*

Like a great wind he came to her. The world drew breath and let it out again in a great shout that was all runes, all names, all meaning. The divided Self was once more, in a union beyond time or place or person, self-known.

I am . . . For a time that was sufficient. Then awareness shifted, became *"We,"* consciousness and manifestation, the god who spoke, the goddess who answered. A further transformation—spirit and body, bound together in interpenetrating unity. A female body, a personality, that together were the means by which an eternal soul experienced the world.

I am . . . Gudrun. . . . She opened her eyes.

Late afternoon sunlight slanted through the door. She was standing beside her cooking fire, her body perfectly balanced and at ease, and she was alone. No—that was not quite true, for she could sense, like an echo of her own thinking, the presence of the god. It was only the body he had been riding that had gone. As long as she was conscious and breathing, Wodan was still here, as he was always on the Worldtree, and in the Well.

Gudrun's nostrils flared at the scent of cooking food and she realized that this shape of Earth she wore was hungry. She looked into the kettle and saw that some of the porridge had been eaten. A used bowl sat on the hearth. The god was a careful horseman, she thought, feeding the body he had mounted before taking it away.

She ate, marvelling at the mingled textures, the flavors that burst upon her tongue. She drank the rest of the goat's milk, and tasted its power. Everything around her she saw with new eyes, and seeing, understood that this part of her life had ended as surely as if she had drowned. At least, she thought wryly, her clothes were clean. She moved about the dwelling, putting away things that she could not take with her, packing those she would carry into a neat roll.

Presently she found, beneath a half-cured deerhide, the bag she had brought with her from Borbetomagus. It had been many moons since she had thought of it. She drew out the carefully wrapped treasures inside. The golden rod with the runes of power that Hagano had desired, and the Frowe's shining ring that had caused Brunahild so much pain . . . the last of Sigfrid's hoard. She had borne them all this way, neither understanding them nor willing to use their powers, and now, she realized in wonder, she did not need them. Thoughtfully she put them back into their bag and set it with the other things to take away.

That night Gudrun lay in a waking dream, mind and memory continuing their dialogue. She rose while it was still dark and went out into the pallor that precedes the true dawn. The she-goat, who had been ranging free since winter's end, bleated inquiringly.

"Good-bye, my mother," Gudrun said softly. "You cannot go with me, but I believe that you can take care of yourself very well." She stroked the wiry black hair on the goat's poll and turned away down the path.

When she reached the river, the sun behind the eastern hills was kindling the scattered cloud into pale flame. The dull surface of the Rhenus brightened suddenly, like Frankish enamel, golden ripples separating pools of color. Gudrun took a deep breath of the moist air, interested to find that she had no desire to throw herself in. The god had reconciled her to the world, but what was she supposed to *do?*

From a nearby treetop a raven called. From the far side of the river, another answered it.

"Very well. I am here, and I am listening—" Gudrun frowned up at the bird. It cawed again, and she remembered what Gundohar had told her about Sigfrid's gold. From the waters it had come, and to the waters Hagano had returned it. All except the rod and the ring.

But they were the soul of the hoard. Gudrun unwrapped them, caressing the smooth curves.

"I will give you back to the river," she whispered. "Let you be my offering, for I have been healed."

She held them up, blinking as the growing light sparked from the bird shape on the head of the rod, drew back her arm as if she were casting a spear, and hurled it toward the river's western shore. Behind her, the sun was lifting above the hills. The rune rod, catching its first full rays, left a trail of light where it passed.

"As my people move westward," she cried, "I dedicate all that lies in your path!"

Gudrun lifted the neck ring and light blazed from her hands. "Lady, though your light be hidden, remain in the depths to guard us still."

She cast the ring wheeling across the water. It splashed once, then disappeared.

Epilogue Andvari's Tale

Light in the water!

The light of the rising sun struck deep through the billows; a wheel of light followed, illuminating the depths. For a few moments the bed of the Rhenus blazed, then it settled to a steady glow. Then came I, Andvari, a silver-scaled swirl from the shadows, settling back into the shape of the great, long-jawed pike in which I had so long guarded that treasure. But the rod and the ring were for the moment secure. I rose toward the surface, compelled by curiosity.

Above me a long shadow cut through the water, trailed by the silver swirl of a steering oar. I slid beneath it and arrowed upward, leaped in a high arc to see.

One of the wide barges that ply the Rhenus was coming up with the current from Borbetomagus, laden with people and livestock and gear. The steersman had a familiar look, like someone I had known as Harbard on another river long ago. As I hit the water again I heard a shout from the shore.

Once more I leaped. A woman was standing at the edge of the water, golden hair flying about her shoulders. She waved at the boat, and the steersman leaned on the oar.

"Where are you going?" she called.

I fell back among the ripples, following the barge as it curved toward the landing. As the day brightened, the heavens rang with the calls of migrating waterfowl.

"We go north," replied one of the passengers. "Fleeing war and destruction to find new homes in the broad lands by the sea."

"Take me with you—"

"What can you give us?" the man replied.

"I have no gold. . . ." The woman laughed, and I knew that it was she who had thrown the rod and the ring. And with that, I knew her as Gudrun.

"—But I can spin and weave, I have knowledge of herbs and medicines, and I can tell a tale to make the heart crack of the deaths of kings."

"A story is good enough payment for me." The steersman's laughter echoed across the water. Above him, a flight of swans sketched a wavering arrow across the sky.

A stroke of the oar brought the boat inshore, and Gudrun waded through the shallows. Willing hands hauled her on board. Then the men on the shore side heaved with poles until the barge floated free again, and the current took her once more.

I sank once more beneath the surface, hearing above me the singing of the swans—northward bound, like the barge, like the story. But the gold of the goddess stayed in the Rhenus, with me.

And there I have guarded it, through flood and drought, sudden fire from heaven, and the slow wearing of the centuries. From the heights of the Great Mountains to the marshes that edge the northern sea flows the river that men now call the Rhine. A great deal of blood has flowed with it over the years. The Wolves of War range widely. Men of a hundred kindreds and tribes have fought over these lands. I do not think their motives have changed much since the gold was returned into my keeping. They have become more efficient at killing, that is all.

Wodan still walks the world, though men no longer recognize him, learning, experiencing, testing the new ways of thinking to which they turned when they abandoned their old gods. He is very curious, that one, and will follow the path to its end. When that time comes, perhaps he will seek a new way of knowing, and take up his conversation with Erda once more.

I guard the gold, waiting for the day when men will come once more to make their offerings, giving back to Erda something they value instead of what they despise. The children of Gudrun's children live in a world in which the gods are only names on a printed page. But though they are forgotten, they are not destroyed, for they are all that you are. So long as the children of Ash and Elm walk in Middle Earth, they will be there, and if once more you should call their names, perhaps they will reply.

Holy Earth abides, for She was here before either men or gods. Though humans forget that it is She through which matter and spirit are united, She will remain. The folk who live where the Rhine joins the sea may know nothing of its sources, but the river knows. And so long as the river winds its way across this land, the story of its gold will be remembered; a blaze of brightness in the shadows of your people's beginnings.

The ravens still fly, and to whom do they report, if not to the god? In every word that you speak and thought that you think, in the ecstasy of every new idea he is there, whether or not you know his name. . . .

Afterword

When I began work on this trilogy, one of my hopes was to find a resonance between the situation of my characters, first and second generation migrants into Western Europe, and modern Americans, the children and grandchildren of migrants from across the sea. However today, the parallel exists in Europe as well. The newly united European Community is struggling to assimilate refugees of various ethnic origin in numbers which are beginning to approach those of the tribal groups who streamed into the late Roman Empire, and it is reacting as anxiously as the Romans faced first the Celts, then the Germans, and finally, the Huns.

The pressure of new peoples wanting to settle in the rich Roman lands increased steadily from the first century through the fifth. They came for the same reasons immigrants seek to cross the borders of Western Europe today, fleeing war and destruction to seek their fortunes in a place with a stable political system and a prospering economy. Fortunately for Europe, today they are seeking asylum legally rather than forcing an invitation with the sword.

In the fifth century, as today, some immigrants were more easily assimilated than others. Although the initial reaction of the Romans to the northern peoples was one of shock, after several hundred years, they had gotten used to

Germanic barbarians. It was only in the fifth century that the tide became so overwhelming that the Roman system broke down. The group that created the most difficulties was the Huns.

Their ethnic differences caused no particular problems for the Germanic tribes, who reacted to the Huns as they would have to any other tribal enemy of superior military effectiveness. The Romans, on the other hand, perceived the Huns as alien, inhuman, and monstrous, even though it was not until nearly the end of the period of contact that they directly threatened Rome. Indeed, for much of the fifth century, they were extremely valuable as mercenaries.

When the migrations period was over, Europe had been changed. The tribes were no longer Gothic, Vandal, or Burgund, but the lands in which they now lived were no longer Roman either. Both sides had adapted, and a new culture emerged which was European. The process of assimilation is never easy, but the movement of populations is a recurring fact of human history. An alternation between periods of homogeneity and times of transformation appears to be the norm, and attempts at racial purification and ethnic cleansing are never successful for long. Perhaps today we are seeing the birth of a culture which belongs to the world.

Background:

In addition to the *Volsungasaga* and the *Nibelungenlied*, the primary sources for the episodes covered in this volume are found in the Old Norse "Atlakvida," the "Greenlandish Lay of Atli," "Thidreksaga," the lost German "Epic Diu Not," and we assume, in earlier Lays of the Fall of the Burgund kings, now also lost. In my version, the role played by Dietrich of Bern (apparently based on the historical Theodoric the Great, who was not born until approximately 453) is given to Thiudimir the Amalung, Theodoric's father.

The fall of the Burgundians, to which everything else in the saga was eventually attached, has its origins in history. From the Roman *Chronica Minora*, we learn that in A.D. 437, the Huns attacked the Burgund lands around Wurms and killed King Gundaharius, his whole family, and twenty thousand of his men. From the chronicles we also learn of Aetius's troubles with the Visigoths and the Bacaudae and his eventual triumph, and some historians have speculated that he ordered his faithful Hun allies to attack the Burgundians to keep them from once more attempting to take Trier as they had tried in 436.

The history of the Burgundian survivors immediately following the massacre is unclear. However in 443 they were given feoderate status once more in the territory of Sapaudia, north of Lake Geneva. Their king was Gundioc, whose reign is assumed to have begun in 437, and who continued to rule until 474, when he was succeeded by his son Gundobad, who extended the territory into what is now southeastern France. Name forms suggest a close link to the earlier royal family. Eventually the Franks overwhelmed this second Burgundian kingdom, but it retained sufficient identity to survive as a duchy into the Middle Ages.

The subsequent career of Aetius has been reported more fully. He was unable to prevent the Vandals from taking Carthage and attacking Italy from Africa, and does not appear to have cared about the Anglo-Saxon takeover in Britain, but he remained in power until 454, when he fell to a palace intrigue led by Petronius Maximus, and was murdered by order of the emperor. Valentinian himself was killed by some of Aetius's officers in the following year.

Aetius's most notable achievement was his victory against Attila himself in the Battle of Chalons (the Battle of the Catalaunian Fields). From the 440s on, the Huns had become increasingly aggressive. In 444 or 445, Attila's co-king Bleda (Bladarda) died, firmly believed by the Romans to have been killed by Attila. In 451, the khan, now sole ruler of the Huns, mounted a major campaign into Gallia. Aetius called upon his old enemies the Visigoths, and with their help (and that of the surviving Burgundians), was able to defeat them. However, he held back the Visigoths from pursuit, no doubt wishing to keep a few Huns alive to help out on another day.

The next year Attila invaded Italy, but stopped short of attacking Rome, according to the chronicles, because the Pope came out and vanquished him with his prayers, but more likely because there was disease in his army, and the Romans offered him a great deal of gold. In 453, Attila himself died, to everyone's amazement, in bed. Contemporary gossip tells us that he had taken a new young wife called Ildico (Hild), and died of a nosebleed on his wedding night when he drank till he passed out, and choked on his own blood. Other commentators called it an Act of God. Hungarian folklore holds that Ildico was a native princess who killed him.

The origins of some of the material in individual chapters may also be of interest.

The harvest rhyme in the first chapter comes from a ritual reported from Shaumburg in Germany in the nineteenth century (Grimm, Volume 1, p. 157). Harvest customs varied from district to district, but bear a family resemblance all over Europe. Sometimes the last sheaf was identified as the Old Man, and in some areas the custom of marrying him to a harvest bride survived. Grimm identifies the spirit of the harvest with the figure of "Wish" (Wunsch), and equates him with Wodan, whose functions on the Continent were broader than they later became in Scandinavia.

The song for the Yule father in Chapter Five was inspired by a traditional German song for St. Nicholas, a figure strongly akin to the Weihnachtsman (Man of the Holy Night, or Father Christmas), who comes accompanied by his goblin servant Ruprecht or an old woman.

The strategies for the battle in Chapter Eleven are loosely based on the battle of Argentoratum, A.D. 357, in which thirty-five thousand Germans were beaten by the Emperor Julian with thirteen thousand men. For the etiquette of Hun feasts, and Attila's abstemious nature, I am indebted to the account written by Priscus of Panium of the embassy of Maximinus to Attila's court in 448.

The story of how the Sword of Mars was found is also told in the Roman chronicles. My speculations on its nature are based on a theory proposed by C. Scott Littleton and Ann C. Thomas in "The Sarmation Connection" (*Journal of American Folklore*, #91 [1978]), in which they point out certain resonances between the legends of the Ossetes (the only surviving Sarmatian people) and the Arthurian stories, and suggest a connection through Iazyge auxiliaries stationed on the Wall at Ribchester.

One of the mysteries of the *Nibelungenlied* is Hagen's unprovoked attack on Kriemhild's (Gudrun's) son. *Thidreksaga* provides the answer, in which "Grimhild" tells the child to hit his uncle in the face, knowing this will start a fight. However the most difficult problem in motivation in the final sequence of this story did not involve the human characters, but the adders in Attila's snakepit.

The European Adder is among the most mellow of venomous reptiles. German herpetologists catch them barehanded, and it is rare for anyone to be bitten, much less die. The sand adder is slightly more poisonous, but even so, it would probably require serious provocation to get the snake to strike at the body of a man, and it would have to hit something vital, in which case the poison could produce catastrophic shock and loss of blood pressure.

Traditions of the Wild Hunt are found from Germany to Norway, where the passage of the spectral riders is called the *Oskerei*. The identity of the hunters varies, but in some of the songs, Gudrun is among them.

Sources:

Theodore M. Andersson, *A Preface to the Nibelungenlied*, Stanford: Stanford University Press, 1987.

Phil Barker, *The Armies and Enemies of Imperial Rome*, Wargames Research Group, 1981.

Katherine Fischer Drew, *The Burgundian Code*, Philadelphia: University of Pennsylvania Press, 1972.

C.D. Gordon, *The Age of Attila*, N.Y.: Dorset, 1960.

Jacob Grimm, *Teutonic Mythology*, Dover, 1966.

A. H. M. Jones, *The Later Roman Empire, 284–602*, Baltimore: Johns Hopkins University Press, 1986.

Otto J. Maenchen-Helfen, *The World of the Huns*, Berkeley: University of California Press, 1973.

Lucien Musset, *The Germanic Invasions*, N.Y.: Barnes & Noble, 1993.

The Nibelungenlied, trans. A.T. Hatto, Harmondsworth, Great Britain: Penguin, 1965, especially Hatto's Appendices.

Otto Perrin, *Les Burgondes*, Paris: Bacconière.

Jennifer Russ, *German Festivals and Customs*, London: Oswald Wolf, 1992.

The Saga of the Volsungs, trans. R.G. Finch, London: Thomas Nelson & Sons, 1965.

Herwig Wolfram, *History of the Goths*, trans. Thomas J. Dunlap, University of California Press, 1988.

The Chronicles of
Fionn Mac Cumhal
Prophet, Poet, Warrior, Outlaw

@@ @@ @@

by Diana L. Paxson
& Adrienne Martine-Barnes

MASTER OF EARTH AND WATER
75801-6/$4.99 US/$5.99 Can

Safely hidden from the world of men, an ancient warrior will teach the child called Demne many things—but never speak about the boy's mysterious parentage.

THE SHIELD BETWEEN THE WORLDS
75802-4/$4.99 US/$6.99 Can

Now the time has come for Fionn to assume his tribe's mantle of leadership—to restore his fian to its former greatness.

SWORD OF FIRE AND SHADOW
75803-1/$5.99 US/$7.99 Can

It is the bitter twilight of a noble hero's life as enemies mass on all sides, waiting to strike the killing blow. But from the terrible wreckage, he will arise victorious once more.